The Tragedy of Miss Genera Flowers

The Tragedy of Miss Genera Flowers

Joe Babcock

CARROLL & GRAF PUBLISHERS

NEW YORK

THE TRAGEDY OF MISS GENEVA FLOWERS

Carroll & Graf Publishers
An Imprint of Avalon Publishing Group Inc.
245 West 17th Street
New York, NY 10011

AVALON
publishing group incorporated

Copyright © 2002 by Joe Babcock

First Carroll & Graf edition 2005

Library of Congress Cataloging-in-Publication Data is available.

ISBN: 0-7867-1520-0

Printed in the United States of America
Interior design by Maria Elias
Distributed by Publishers Group West

To my mother

{ acknowledgments }

I would like to thank everyone at Carroll & Graf, my editor Donald Weise, my agent Michael Mancilla, Ron Hanby, *Publishers Weekly, Writer's Digest* Magazine, The Lambda Literary Foundation, and *Lavender* Magazine.

Special thanks to Tori Amos, Stephen King, J.D. Salinger, Oscar Wilde, Madonna, Parker Posey, Diana Ross, "The Mary Tyler Moore Show," and the movie *Clueless.*

Extra special thanks to Oprah Winfrey.

Thanks to all my teachers for putting up with me in class. Also, none of this would have been possible without the support of my friends and family, especially Mom, Dad, Sis, Little Elvis, Josnatch, Ms. Monto, Beth Meth, Dr. X, Sparkles, Sadie White, Rachel, Patricia Rieger, and my Daniel.

In loving memory of my aunt Mary.

Part One

{ one }

I was sitting in class, my junior year of high school, when I finally came out of the closet. Sister Mary Jean was up at the blackboard lecturing about something related to geometry. I suppose it was geometry itself, but I wouldn't know. I was busy doodling a woman's face with pointy features and makeup everywhere.

Suddenly I heard, "Hey, Erick," hissed rudely from behind me. It was Justin Hankshaw, my archenemy since seventh grade. "Are you gay?" he asked, just loud enough for everyone but Sister, who was deaf in one ear from a stroke, to hear.

I just kept drawing, like it was nothing.

"Why do you wear makeup? Aren't you a guy?" he questioned. Then, to a couple of girls: "He's not answering." The girls began to giggle. "Hey, Erick, do you have any powder? My face is all shiny." Now the whole room seemed to be laughing. He was so cool I could puke.

Then his best friend Terrance yelled, "Faggot!" in one short burst. It was an outrage.

"Erick?" Sister Mary Jean asked as soon as she became aware of the situation. "Do you need to leave?"

Me? I couldn't believe it. How was I to blame for any of this? Normally, my policy in one of these situations is to sit there silently, face as red as a tomato, chin up, taking it; but I'd been pushed too far, and I finally snapped. "You bitch!" I screamed at her. Then I turned to Justin and went off: "What the fuck is your problem? Yes, I'm gay! I wear makeup and I'm gay! Are you happy now? It seems like you have more interest in my sexuality than I do. Well, now the big question on your mind has been answered, and you can die happy!"

The room was silent. I had screamed so loud that I was seeing flecks of light, like iridescent soap bubbles, pop around my head. I was standing over him, my fist poised over my shoulder, ready to strike. I was shocked at myself! I had never raised a fist toward anyone. And he was terrified. I felt that if I tipped him out of his chair, he'd shatter on the floor like porcelain.

Then, in front of everyone, Justin Hankshaw began to choke on tears. After all those years of him humiliating me—and me never once giving him the satisfaction of seeing me cry—here Justin was, blubbering like a fool for all the world to see. "You sissy!" I said, suddenly laughing maniacally at the irony of my life. I, Erick Taylor, the token "fag" of St. John's High School, was a no-shit kind of guy. Who would have guessed?

I laughed in bursts of triumph all the way down the hall to my locker. *Finally!* I rejoiced, flinging the contents of my locker into the trash. For once, I had stood up to him. I'd never felt more elated in my life. For I already knew that this, my moment of liberation, would be the last anyone at St. John's Evil Penitentiary would ever hear from me again.

When I got home, I shut the door silently and tiptoed down the hall to my bedroom. I didn't want my mother to cut me off and interrogate me about my truancy. Luckily, she was preoccupied with Tim, my adopted brother. They were in his bedroom doing a jigsaw puzzle. I kind of wanted to steal him from her, just to share the joy of freedom with a six-year-old, but that would have to wait. For now, I had to call my best friend, Chloe, a twenty-six-year-old self-proclaimed "grandiloquist" drag queen, who had promised me that I could move in with him when I finished high school. Hopefully, he wouldn't mind that I found myself done a year and a half early.

"Hellah," he snapped on the first ring.

"Hey, girl," I said, rolling up in bed with my comforter.

Upon instant recognition, Chloe began hurriedly, "Oh my God, girl, you will not believe this shirt I tried on today at the mall. It was black Lycra and had mirrors glued to it like a disco ball! It was so fabulous! It was like two-fifty—" From there he went on to describe a scene in which he ran out of the dressing room and began twirling in circles like a disco ball to see if it actually worked. It didn't. But he received applause from some woman and her daughter, who were shopping for purses. "I was like, 'Thank you, thank you, no autographs please!'" he said, in his best impression of a movie star. Finally, he asked me, "And how are you today, darling? Did you just get home from school?"

"Actually," I tried to sound very nonchalant as I began painting my fingernails with mint green nail polish, "I sort of flipped out during geometry. No one was hurt too badly, but I got to leave early."

"What?! Oh my God, girl! What happened?"

"Justin Fuckshaw was making fun of me again, and I finally stood up to him. I said I was a fag and made him eat every word he'd ever said to me. I wish you could have been there, Chloe. You would've died! He was so humiliated that he'll probably have to transfer to another school or something."

"Well, good for you, girl," Chloe beamed. "It's about time someone put that little prick in his place."

"You wanna get together?" I already wanted desperately to leave my house.

"Sure," he said. "Why don't you come over?"

"Gimme an hour."

"Okay."

"'Bye, baby."

"'Bye, girl."

I got out of bed, letting my pants drop to the floor, thinking how glad I was to have worn that hideous uniform for the last time. I turned on my stereo: Tori Amos, my obsession. Once I heard the opening beat followed by her celestial, hateful voice, I pulled on a pair of pants from the mess on the floor. They were tight maroon cords, flared at the bottoms, and they made my butt look super perky. I pulled a yellow belt through the loops; it was covered with silver stars and glitter. Then I slid into a tiny T-shirt that didn't even come all the way down to the rim of my pants, so I could show off my belly-button ring. It was army camouflage, except the colors were orange, yellow, and brown with the words "Army Girl" printed in silver letters across the chest.

Singing and dancing, I stepped into my six-inch platform shoes and stood 6′3″ before my streaked up, full-length mirror. I ran my hands down my body all the way to my ankles, ironing out the wrinkles. I used black eyeliner to give myself that sexy, strung-out, model look. Next, I messed up my bleached-to-death hair madly, making it stick up like a punk. Then I put a couple of red streaks in my bangs with this dye Chloe had given me. Finally, I touched up my newly polished nails, added a silver ring to each finger, turned off the stereo, and gently shut my bedroom door on the way out.

I gritted my teeth when I realized that despite my best efforts to hurry, I was too late to sneak out of the house without my mom spotting me. She and Tim were now in the living room watching afternoon talk shows. Mom watched talk shows every day, in spite of the fact that she claimed everyone on them would go straight to hell when they died. I quietly stopped off in my parents' room, tiptoeing over the hardwood floor (in platforms!) to my mom's vanity. There was a little wooden jewelry box with a picture of the Virgin Mary and Baby Jesus. I pulled a neatly folded up wad of cash from inside it, selected a ten-dollar bill, then tiptoed back out, exhaling in relief that I wasn't caught.

"Hey, Erick, you wanna play trains?" Tim was waiting for me in the hallway with a red car in one hand and a yellow school bus in the other. To him, anything with wheels was a train.

This never failed to make me laugh. Happily, I scooped him up into my arms and swung him in a circle, stomping on the wood floor with my wood heels like a stampeding elephant. Tim squealed in delight. I plopped him back down to the floor. "Sorry, kid, I gotta go."

"Are you coming home tonight?" he asked, looking straight up at me from the height of my knees.

"Not till after you're in bed."

"Stay here," he begged.

"I can't . . . but give me a good-night kiss now." I lowered my cheek.

He did.

"Thanks, baby."

"Thanks, baby," he repeated, smiling widely.

I shot him a wink and headed to the door.

Just as I had anticipated, the second I entered the living room my mom looked up. *"Erick?"* she said in an accusatory drawl.

I stopped, hanging my head in defeat. "Yeah?"

"Why aren't you in school?"

"We got done early."

"Since when does school get done early?"

"We had a half day." She didn't believe my lie at all. "I swear to God."

"You swear to *whom?*"

"Sorry ... I swear to gosh. Anyway ... I gotta go, Mom, I'm late."

"You just got here."

"I came home to change. Can't you tell I'm not in uniform anymore?" I said very sardonically, gesturing at my wild garb.

"Listen, if you want to dress in those ridiculous costumes, I don't care anymore. I just wonder why you bother to come home at all."

I didn't respond.

"Doesn't your family matter to you anymore?" she asked, as though it pained her to think about it.

I hated her guilt trips. "Of course you matter," I said mechanically.

"Sure. I doubt that, considering that last stunt you pulled with Father Tom."

"Whatever," I said, pulling on my navy-blue coat with the fake-fur trim around the wrists and hood. I let the door slam behind me.

For a moment, I felt like I might storm back in, dash right past her, and promptly hang myself in my bedroom closet. Of course, I couldn't do that. One more family tragedy would kill her. Plus I'd made plans with Chloe. Usually killing myself in a frenzied haste only seems like a good idea for a second or two. It wasn't like I was one of those people that constantly threatened suicide. I wasn't that desperate. Although, if Chloe were to renege on his invitation to move in with him, I'd definitely reconsider. My parents' house strangled me.

The sky was streaked purple and orange. With winter on the horizon, night in Minnesota came so early. I lit a cigarette, smoking and walking so fast, I almost had to run. The sooner I escaped my neighborhood, the better. With every click of my heels, I felt the shocked Christian families ogling me from the bay windows of their factory-produced ramblers. My neighborhood was a classic Midwestern suburb: Golden Valley, where decent citizens survived by polluting the planet as much as they possibly could, and one out of every two kids had an inhaler as a result. I refused to associate with any of these people. Whenever anyone asked me where I lived, I just said 'Minneapolis.'

I threw down my half-smoked cigarette and began to jog. Partly to get to the bus stop sooner, but mostly to stay warm. Winter was coming. All the birds were heading south; the tree branches were bare. Soon the temperature would be thirty below, and the air itself would seem like it was frozen solid. I couldn't stand winter. Everyone was depressed this time of year, especially me.

Winter made me think of my younger brother, Tommy, who died in a car accident five winters ago. He was only six years old, which is five years younger than I was at the time. The night he died, Tommy and my mom had been out shopping for Christmas presents, even though it was sleeting and news reporters had urged people to stay indoors. On their way home, she hit the brakes on a slick sheet of ice and slid into an intersection. A truck plowed into them, flipping their car into a ditch and crushing the entire passenger side, Tommy included. An ambulance rushed them to the hospital, but he didn't have a chance. His death was pretty much secured when the roof of the car crushed his skull.

Meanwhile, my dad and I were waiting for them at home, merrily drinking eggnog and watching *The Neverending Story*. It was my favorite movie, but I was allowed to watch it only when Tommy wasn't around because it scared him too much. When we got the call from the police (Tommy and Mom were already at the hospital), my dad burst into tears, looking at me like he wanted a hug or a time machine, and I was supposed to deliver. But at eleven years old, I'd already stopped hugging him, and I didn't know how to build a time machine. So I just watched, awed by the tears I would never have been able to picture on his face before that night. I was mad at him for crying. I was being selfish. When

I found out Tommy had died, I cried, too. But mostly, from then on, I was mad, because nothing was ever the same in our family.

For my mother, the loss was catastrophic. It was like she stopped living that night. Like she couldn't bear the thought of continuing her life without Tommy. I called that first year her Tommy Trance, because the look in her eyes was always so distant. My dad is a psychiatrist so he started Mom on a regimen of therapy and depression drugs. But none of that really helped. Finally, she got sent to a mental institution, where she was "cured," and three years later we adopted Tim, my new little brother. Although I love Tim, and feel sorry for Mom, I miss her Tommy Trance days. Now she's a crazy Bible-banging Christian, who constantly preaches the Good Word to anyone who will listen. I think she blames herself for Tommy's death and is scared she'll get sent to hell if she doesn't act like a total nun.

When I reached the bus stop, the bus was nowhere in sight. I lit another cigarette. I needed all the nicotine I could get after a day at school. That place *really* pissed me off. All my teachers were pricks, and I hated my classmates too. I was so glad I dropped out. I used to be scared to even ditch a day because I thought my parents would find out and send me off to one of those Christian boot camps that bad kids on talk shows get sent to. Now it made me laugh just to picture them opening my report card and seeing straight Fs.

The bus came to a wheezing stop. I stepped on, plunking a dollar of change into the coin slot and looking down the aisle for an unclaimed seat. There were several, so I took the nearest one. I wanted to sit as close as I could to the driver, just to be on the safe side. I've discovered that troublemakers like to give crap to anyone who dares to dress fabulous.

I hate the bus. On every ride, all the passengers look depressed—always. Especially on a cold night. People who are alone on the bus stare forward or out the window, blinking, their mouths cracked. There's always a noisy group in the back, and a talkative old lady up front bugging the driver. Looking back on my two years of public transportation, everyone seems the same. Hidden in their oversized coats, keeping their hands warm with their breath, and saving half-smoked cigarettes behind their ears. It's a guarantee that if you don't know what time the bus is coming and you light a cigarette, it will show up after the first couple drags; so you have to waste the whole stupid thing, or save it behind your ear. Whenever I'm on the bus, I go through my backpack, organizing things, just to keep busy. I'm always pulling out clothes, poems, notes, toys . . . anything but schoolbooks. On this trip, I took out my leopard-print day-planner and began drawing pictures of clothes I wanted to design when I became a famous fashion designer. Yes, I hated being on the bus, but it was better than math or biology class—at least it took you somewhere.

I was dropped off three blocks from Chloe's apartment—another damn walk. I promptly lit a new cigarette and blew a stream of smoke into the cold wind. The lit-up buildings of downtown Minneapolis gave me a feeling of excitement. I felt like somewhere close by there was fun to be had. On LaSalle Avenue, McDonald's wrappers and newspapers whirled at my feet. I kept my eyes up and my hands in my pockets just to look like I had some real purpose for being there. Chloe's neighborhood was definitely lousy and dangerous. It was located on the outskirts of downtown and filled with an unwanted element: gay prostitutes, crack dealers, and gangs. All the buildings were dilapidated red-brick boxes that looked like they should be evacuated.

Chloe's building was covered in leafless ivy branches and had arched windows with peeling green trim. I rang the bell twice.

"Hey, girl," came his voice through the intercom. The door buzzed. I ran inside and up the spiraling staircase two steps at a time, to apartment 312. Chloe was sitting on the floor of his brown carpeted studio surrounded by fashion magazines and painting his toenails glittery red. He was mostly Native American and extremely attractive. Even though he was a drag queen, he wasn't wearing fake boobs or a wig or anything like he did when he was onstage. Instead Chloe wore denim bell-bottoms and a black tank top with a silver cross on the chest. His dark hair, streaked fire-engine red, was wildly spiked. But it was his face that could kill you. His features were smooth and angular, very androgynous. Even with his five-o'clock shadow, he was a handsome cross-dresser.

"What's up, baby?" he smiled, rolling onto his back in one of his yoga positions. "Wanna paint your nails?" He wiggled his toes for emphasis.

"I just painted them. See?" I said limp-wristed, dropping my coat to the floor. I sat down cross-legged, facing him. I was beaming. We weren't lovers in any way, but nevertheless, every time I saw Chloe, I glowed. "What'cha doin'?"

"Check this out, girl," he jumped the gun, flipping through a magazine. "Doesn't she look fierce?"

"Yeah," I said, eyeing the model in the tight metallic-blue body suit. She had thickly painted blue makeup, glitter, and blond hair blown straight back. It made me think of some futuristic nightclub in an action movie. "Did you go nuts at the magazine rack, hon?"

"Gee, you think?" he grinned, closing the magazine. "I'm going to make a collage for over the futon."

"Cool."

"You want to help?"

"I'd love to."

"Well fan-tabulous! But wait. We can't do any art until we get high." He pulled a joint rolled in rainbow paper from a glass candy dish.

"Oh my God, right on!" I eagerly watched him light it up. He closed his eyes and sucked deeply, his nostrils flaring. He could fill his lungs with more smoke than two of my hits combined. I watched the stream of smoke jet out of his mouth then hang in the air like a cloud. Chloe licked the run that was burning into it and passed the joint to me. I hit it as hard as I could before letting the smoke push itself back out. That made me cough like crazy; I couldn't stop for about two minutes. Chloe sat there and laughed. He had powerful lungs—*nothing* made him cough.

Chloe's apartment was my all-time favorite place to be these days. He had decorated his one room with a gaudy purple lamp that had beads hanging from the bottom, and a small bookshelf that contained all these psychotic little glass figures, candy dishes, and ashtrays. The futon was piled high with furry cheetah-print pillows and the only other seat was a red beanbag chair. Except for a little rickety end table, which held the lamp, an ashtray, and the daily clutter of living, he didn't even have a table. I'd never heard of anyone who didn't have a table until I met Chloe. By far his most ornamental possession was the birdcage. It was antique brass, carved with intricate patterns and symbols. The cage hung delicately from the top of a hoop that circled it like a halo and was balanced on a five-foot-tall post. Inside was a buttercup canary. Her name was Suz, and she chirped and pooped constantly, and sat on our shoulders nibbling our earlobes.

My favorite things to do at Chloe's house were try on clothes and do my makeup while listening to music and dancing. Chloe had taught me about style. He was also the absolute funniest person I'd ever met. Once he told me about a road trip he took with this other drag queen, Miss Babs Arlington, to Chicago for a drag pageant. They were in this big, ancient boat of a car, which they had painted pink. On the roof there was this enormous plastic alligator with red lips, and the circular headlights each had a big set of rubber eyelashes. The seats were covered with fake furry cow print, and hanging from the ceiling was a disco ball the size of a grapefruit that spun in circles and lit up the car like it was a dance floor. Chloe used to do coke (he quit a few years ago), so the two of them were all coked out at the time. The first thing they did when they got to Chicago was crash into a cop car while trying to parallel-park. They got out, both in full drag, right in the middle of rush hour, telling this huge lie about how they drove all the way from Hollywood to go on *Oprah* and tell her a thing or two. They got into some big catfight with each other about whether the topic of the show was going to be being a career girl in the nineties, or leaving that *slob* of a man. I guess the cop was too freaked out to even deal with them because he drove away without giving them a ticket or anything, even though his passenger-side door had a dent in it. Just thinking of it now made me laugh.

"So are ya getting even with Justin Fuckface?" Chloe asked, stubbing out the roach in a glass Harley-Davidson ashtray he'd stolen from a leather bar. He rolled over onto the red beanbag. His apartment was arranged so that he never had to actually stand up to walk anywhere. He'd roll from place to place, or crawl across the floor. He had a lot of kinky feline moves.

"No . . . I mean, what could I do?"

"Well, what do you want to happen, dear?"

"I don't know. I'm just sick of all his shit. I want to give him a taste of his own medicine."

That made Chloe shoot to his feet like a rocket. "I have the perfect herb!"

He was always doing that: saying, "I have the perfect herb." He was already searching his little heart-shaped tin cabinet in the kitchen through vials of potions and remedies before I had the chance to object.

"Here we go." He returned with a little brown bottle. It was corked shut and wrapped with twine, like it was so potent it had to be doubly sealed.

"What is it?"

"The answer to your problems with Justin Fuckrot." He spun in a circle, then crashed back onto the beanbag.

"What does it do?"

"It will shrink his dick into a tiny, shriveled black worm. And he'll never be able to have sex or breed children or anything."

I laughed at his impression of Justin Hankshaw discovering he's lost his manhood. "You're so full of shit, Chloe."

Then Chloe started laughing, too. "I'm just kidding. God! Little Miss Sensitive . . . It'll only give him really bad gas."

"It will?"

"Hell, yeah. He'll be fartin' all day long if you slip this shit into his drink."

"No, thanks."

"Well, if you ever change your mind . . ." he trailed off, dropping the potion into a gold velvet bag filled with other little jars and nail polish.

"Hey, you were around my age when you dropped out'a school, right?"

"Why? Are you thinking about quitting?" Chloe asked.

"I dunno."

"Well, transfer to public high school. A smart girl like you needs her education. Besides, aren't you supposed to be getting into advertising or something?"

"Graphic design," I corrected. I'd once told him that that's what I really wanted to do for my career. Now he always brought it up, like he was going to hold me to it. Even though it was practically just a whim, really. I showed him this stupid sample ad I had created on a desktop publishing program for an imaginary restaurant. He kept it on his end table for a while, saying that it looked "very official." Then someone spilled beer on it, and I never bothered to print another one.

"Don't graphic designers need a degree or something?"

"No, they don't *need* it. And besides, someday I might go to some tech school and get some type of certificate, and then the job offers will be pouring in," I assured him. "Until then though, I am fed up with school!"

"Whatever you want, girl . . . It's your life." He sighed with a bitchy attitude, then lit one of those nasty clove cigarettes and began to wave it around like a maniac, watching the twirls of smoke. "I wonder if I could spell my whole name in smoke!" he declared, but didn't succeed in his attempt. "I guess I'm just not fast enough. Jackie Chan could do it though, I'm sure."

"You are *such* a freak."

"Do you even know how many people tell me that? I don't even notice it anymore, darling." He rolled his eyes, smiling.

"Big surprise," I said, laughing.

"Oh, hey! Before I forget . . ." He jumped up and skipped to the closet, pulling out a tiny red sequined dress, followed by red tights and big red platforms. "For my next show."

"My word, Miss Chloe! 'Psycho Spice,' I should say!"

"That's not all," he said proudly. Then he pulled an enormous blond Dolly Parton–style wig from the top shelf. "How 'bout that?'"

"It's fabulous!" I applauded, then ran over to play with it. Up close it was obviously plastic, but an outstanding piece nonetheless. I could picture Chloe as an amazing woman, up onstage with lights on his face and a dance in his step, lip-synching to Blondie in that sparkling costume. All the men below him handing him cash or stuffing it down his bra. "I was worried you were going to quit doing drag," I said because he never actually did drag anymore.

"I just don't do it very often . . . You want to try it on?" he asked.

"No, I'd look stupid."

"Oh, c'mon. You make a great blond."

I felt my face flush with the compliment. "It's just not me."

"Well, then, you don't know who you are, honey," he said, lifting the wig off the Styrofoam head and placing it on my own.

He stood in front of me, pushing my bangs up under the wig. I stood there, defenseless to his seduction, watching his mouth crack a smile. Then he led me to the bathroom with its clutter of makeup piled high on every surface. Tissue with lipstick prints on it overflowed the little purple wastebasket. I looked at my reflection in the mirror, giggling and stoned. I was amazed by the difference. I hardly recognized my own face. My young, soft skin—which was finally past that acne phase—glowed, and the blond hair wrapped 'round the curve of my face and made me look . . . female. I'd never seen myself as a woman, and I never saw myself as being so beautiful.

"See, it looks great on you." Chloe adjusted the wig, all the while admiring his own reflection.

I started to play with it again, too, brushing and stroking the wig as if it were my own hair. "Will you do my makeup, too?" I asked, getting excited. It was turning me on to look at myself. Not making me horny, but I definitely felt sexier than I had in a long time.

Chloe sat me down on the toilet seat and applied all sorts of powders and paints, until I looked like a total girl. No way would anyone be able to tell the difference. With my youthful features . . . I could be a star!

{ two }

Though my parents would never acknowledge it, I was different from most boys, even at a young age. Whereas boys enjoy shooting each other with plastic guns and throwing balls around, I wanted dolls. In fact, I begged my parents, my preschool teachers, and my four-year-old female peers to include me in the girl games. Everyone set out to put a stop to this unconventional behavior, of course, taking away Barbie and giving me instead a plastic baseball bat. My only option at age four was to steal the smallest of the girl toys—plastic makeup and baby-doll key chains—and hoard them for nighttime play. I was a liar and a thief by the time I started kindergarten.

Every time I made a wish, it was always the same: "I wish I was a girl with long blond curls and a pink dress with flowers on it." Naturally, I kept this fantasy to myself. We learn at a very young age that crossing gender boundaries is unacceptable behavior. The lessons start when girls realize that boys are mean and stupid and ugly, and boys realize that girls are mean and stupid and ugly. The sexes divide and are at war until puberty. Meanwhile, people like me are left standing on the sidelines, displaced and confused. I couldn't play with girls because I would be teased, and I couldn't play with boys because I didn't understand them and wasn't good at their games. Still, I tried to play by the rules.

When I began elementary school I forced myself to play this never-ending football game with other boys during our twenty-minute recess. This was my entire social life outside of the classroom. But because I never really understood the rules—and was quite awkward with any type of ball—I was pretty much ignored by those I suspected were on my team. My strategy was simply to follow my teammates around the schoolyard, keeping a safe distance from all the violent action.

I did have one moment of glory, though, during the winter of fourth grade, the year before Tommy was killed. As usual, I was watching Andy Flynn, the quarterback for the other team and the *cutest* boy in our whole grade. He had pink cheeks all winter long and never stopped smiling. Plus he was a jock. His balls always tore through the air in perfect arches, his throws so strong that they'd surely knock me off my light feet.

I don't know what came over me on that particular day. Perhaps it was just that I was watching him so intently when he was about to throw the ball that, when he did, I jumped forward and intercepted it. It didn't hurt like I had expected, either. My thick winter coat must have saved me. Without a clue what to do and all eyes on me, I decided that I had better run before I got pulverized by whoever I stole the pass from. I bolted toward the end zone and scored a touchdown, the only points I ever scored in a sport. Except they weren't for my team. I ran the wrong way, and everyone laughed.

Dazed, I didn't yet know why they were laughing. Then Andy Flynn yelled, "Slam it!" How I knew what that meant, I can't be sure, but I slammed the football onto the pavement and, like magic, they all began to cheer and clap me on the back. Andy lifted me onto his shoulders and carried me, hands wrapped tight around my thighs. It was the most glory I had ever felt. By fifth grade, I had realized finally what my first and last sports story meant. I was gay, and I had caught that ball not because I was athletic, but because I was in love with Andy Flynn.

Being gay was like having a very hideous birthmark on my wrist. As long as I kept my wristwatch balanced on the exact spot of the offense at all times, no one, including me, would ever have to see it. Of course, I was always twirling my wrists. Then I realized *I* was the wristwatch, my hands spinning around me in a countdown to flames.

Being gay was *such* a distraction, too. First my grades dropped. I went from getting mostly As to mostly Cs, and I started to get in trouble with my teachers for interrupting class. I think my biggest problem in school was not fitting in. No matter what I did or said to try to make everyone laugh, I always got picked on. I was called every girly name imaginable, and I never felt like a normal kid because of it. I don't know how they all guessed my secret. Was it the way I talked? I don't *think* so. Obviously, it wasn't my clothes. You can't be led astray by a uniform. And my hair was pretty standard, too. My laugh was a little girly, but so are most preteen laughs. Maybe it was the way I ran and threw balls. Yes, that must have been it. I was terrible at sports. But it couldn't have been just that. There was something more about me that made me stand out. I felt like I was going through junior high with a "kick me" sign taped to a spot on my back that I couldn't reach, and no one would help me take it off. All that bullshit lasted until I met Chloe, who tore the "kick me" sign off my back, replacing it with another sign that said "fabulous!" in big rainbow letters.

I met Chloe at Shades, the sunglasses boutique in the Uptown Mall, where he worked. The first thing I noticed was his outrageous pair of plastic frames with blue lenses. He looked like such a rock star. Instantly, he was the coolest person I had ever seen in real life. His hair was spiked with fusions of red. He wore a silver tank top with a picture of the Virgin Mary, red pants, and a black leather belt with steel spikes. I was attracted to him, and that scared me. Somehow I knew he was gay, though I hadn't yet seen many adult gay men. I wanted him to rescue me from my misery and take me to the island of gay men, where sex is carefree, no one is straight, and you can do whatever you want.

With the determination of a hungry beggar, I grabbed the nearest pair of sunglasses and laid them on the glass counter. We looked down at the same time. The glasses were hot pink and had fake diamonds glued to the lenses in the shape of hearts. I thought I would die.

"Nice," he said, nodding as if impressed.

My jaw went slack and I thought I could feel the sweat on my back. "I have a sister," I said quickly. But I knew he could see right through me.

"I'm sure she'll love them."

"She's six."

"Oh, then I know she will." He smiled at me.

"How much?"

"Twelve dollars."

I took my wallet from my back pocket and only came up with seven dollars, one of which was torn in half; I had been carrying it around for two years in case of an emergency.

"How much do you have?" he asked with mock impatience.

"Seven dollars."

He smiled. "Well, normally I wouldn't do this, but I wouldn't want to deprive your sister . . . So they're on the house!"

"Really?"

"Yeah, sure. Why not?"

"Will you get in trouble?"

"Naw."

"Well, thanks."

"Don't mention it."

I stood there for a moment too long and when I came to my senses I said, "Have a good day," and rushed away. I needed fresh air, so I went outside for a cigarette. I smoked quickly because I wanted to go back in there and watch Chloe work. I was planning to sit at the Starbucks across the aisle from his boutique, out of view, so he wouldn't think I was a stalker. Although I wanted to talk to him, I couldn't for the life of me think of anything to say. He'd probably think I was a big nerd no matter what I said. He was older than me. I couldn't tell by how many years, but probably too much older for him to want to hang out with me. People in their twenties are always huge snobs to teenagers.

When I returned to the mall, I headed to Starbucks and sat down at a table where I could watch him. I tried to be inconspicuous, so I started reading the entertainment section of a newspaper someone had left on a chair. I couldn't concentrate on the text, though, because I was too busy thinking about the sunglasses he gave me. If he had thought I was a nerd, he wouldn't have done that, would he? I peered over my newspaper and watched him sell sunglasses to rich suburban people, who approached him cautiously. He was far more flamboyant than what they were used to. I wondered if he gave free sunglasses to everyone.

After about fifteen minutes, I couldn't sit still any longer. I was one of those hyperactive teenagers who can't ever sit still. In school I was always practically pulling my hair out waiting for the bell to ring. And anyway, I'd *finally* thought of something to say to him. So I waited until he wasn't busy, then walked over and asked, "Are you guys hiring?"

"Oh, you're back!" He smiled. He had a ring pierced in his eyebrow, so I looked at that because I was too shy to meet his eyes.

"Yeah . . . I really need a job . . . and I *love* sunglasses," I said, sounding really stupid.

"Well . . . I'm not sure if we're hiring." He looked at me with suspicion. "How old are you?"

"Seventeen," I lied. I wouldn't be seventeen for another six months.

"Well, I can give you an application."

"Okay."

He ducked below the counter and began to shuffle through whatever junk was crammed back there. "Here you go," he said, returning to a standing position with a crisp sheet of blank paper. "We're officially out of applications, so you'll just have to write something about yourself and put your address and references and all that stuff on there, too." He handed me the paper with a pen, a professional airiness in his demeanor.

"The manager won't care if I do it this way?" I asked.

"*I'm* the manager."

"Oh, so you'll be—"

"The one who interviews you? Yeah . . . We can do it today. Why don't you just go back to Starbucks and write something real quick."

I thought I would die right there. He knew the whole time that I'd been watching him. Now he was smiling down at me, trying to look sexy.

"I'll be back," I said, hurrying away. He wasn't watching me, so I threw the piece of paper in a trash can, put the pen in my pocket, and ran out of the mall, trying my hardest not to freak out about it right there for everyone to see.

I was still thinking about him when I got home and buried my face in my pillow, listening to Tori Amos sing a song about being a major loser when you're a teenager, feeling depressed and fat and starving. He probably thought that I was the biggest idiot ever to live. I was certain that if he ever saw me again he'd laugh. He'd probably be with some other gay guys and see me in the mall and he'd tell them what a freak I was and then they'd all laugh.

I pulled the pen he gave me out of my pocket and looked at it. A plain Bic with black ink. There were teeth marks at the end.

I wondered if they were his. I put it in my mouth, but it only tasted like plastic. I wanted to know what *he* would taste like. I imagined a scenario where I worked with him at the sunglasses store, and after work we went into some storage room in the mall and had oral sex. It gave me a hard-on just thinking about it. I unzipped my jeans and let my dick pop out. With my eyes closed, still picturing him and imagining his taste, I beat off until I came all over my stomach. Then I wiped it off with a shirt that was on the floor by my bed and went to sleep, feeling like I had done something wrong.

When I woke up, it was 8:00 A.M. the next day. I'd slept for nearly fourteen hours. I must've needed it. My mom always said that if you've slept really hard for a long time, your body must've needed it. I had to wake up at 5:30 every morning to make it to the bus stop by 6:15. School didn't actually start until 7:00, but I had a crappy route. I never went to bed before 11:00 P.M. either. I always stayed up in my room listening to CDs and drawing. Besides doing graphic design, I also made abstract drawings or else little cartoon people and animals. Sometimes I was super Disney. For too long, I drew stained-glass windows with pictures in them. Seriously, Catholicism was branded into me!

I slept in only tighty-whities, so I put on sweatpants and a robe before going to the bathroom. My mom was awake already and frying up omelets and hash browns, her specialty. She made breakfast for us every Saturday. That was supposed to be our morning together. During the school week she was in bed when I got up, and on Sunday she was in church all day. Sometimes she went to two or three masses back to back. She was practically Jesus' stalker. My mom tried to get me to go with her, but I absolutely hated church and refused to go. I had to go to church at school, anyway, so as far as I was concerned, I put in my time all week.

My dad used to eat breakfast with us, too, until a couple of years ago, when he started working Saturdays. Mom always complained. He was gone a lot, really, probably because she drove him nuts. Sometimes he went away for trips with colleagues and stuff, and he'd be gone for days at a time. Usually, when he went away, Mom hung out with her sister Connie, who's divorced. I bet she told Mom to get a divorce, too. That's just the kind of person she is. Mom will never get a divorce. She's too Catholic. Dad won't either since he's all about having a Christmas-card family. I'm such a bad son, though. Sometimes I wished they *would* get a divorce. They fight all the time, mostly about Tim and me. Dr. Herman, our dumb family shrink, used to tell them not to fight when we were around. He even told me that they were bad for fighting around us. He made all four of us sit down together and write out ideas on how to solve our differences without screaming at each other. Some plan we came up with. They agreed to compromise instead of yell at each other or yell at Tim and me when we got in trouble. Instead they were to talk to us rationally, listen to our side for once. Then, if we deserved punishment, our privileges would be taken away. If we did all our chores and behaved well, we would earn our privileges back. It was advice straight from a textbook—a total joke. No matter what Dr. Herman told them, they still fought. Dad always told Mom to raise the kids she has, not dwell on the past. With that she'd accuse him of being insensitive, saying he didn't love Tommy. I think Tommy was her favorite. She loved him way more than the rest of us right from the beginning.

The only thing I felt right from the beginning was jealousy. Tommy got all the attention because he was the baby and so cute. Even when he burped or shit himself, he was still cute. Part of me was glad when Tommy died, because now they'd say I was cute. But I felt really guilty for thinking that and prayed for about five hundred hours for God's forgiveness. Prayer doesn't erase that sort of guilt, though. It's like committing murder on white carpeting. The stain will always be there no matter how much Resolve you use.

I remember one Christmas (our second without Tommy) I wanted to impress my parents, so I bought this scrapbook kit with my own money. It came with all sorts of colored paper and little trinkets and letters. I gathered all the best pictures of Tommy and the rest of the family (all from before his death because we stopped taking family pictures after he was gone), and I made the coolest album ever. I was so darn creative. When my mom opened it on Christmas morning, she cried, then hugged me and gave me kisses. Dad gave me hugs and kisses, too (which was really weird), and we seemed as happy as we once were. It lasted the whole day, then we went back to normal. That album got put in some drawer. After that we never really talked about Tommy anymore. We just tried to move on. Mom redecorated the family room with some super-ostentatious furniture that we couldn't afford.

I took a quick shower, rinsing off the dried cum from the night before and shampooing my chin-length brown hair. After I dried off and brushed my teeth, I put on classic-cut Lee blue jeans and a plain black Hanes T-shirt. That was all I ever wore when I wasn't in my uniform. I remembered that pen the guy from the sunglasses boutique gave me, so I put it in my shoebox, which was covered with assorted beads and shapes cut from construction paper. I made that memorabilia box in sixth grade and saved all my little important trinkets I've collected in it. For instance: I saved my Disneyland tickets, my rosary from First Communion, this napkin with the phone number of a boy I met and never called, and other stuff people had given me (only the ones I wanted to remember, though).

When I got halfway down the hall, I was overcome by the sweet smell of bacon. "Hey Mr. Hibernator," Mom said, standing over the stove in her blue quilted nightgown. She had her curly gray hair pinned up, which meant she hadn't showered yet.

"Hi," I yawned, walking past her and into the family room. Tim was watching cartoons, but he didn't complain when I grabbed the remote and flipped through the TV stations until I hit MTV. I sat down and began to file my nails. A couple of months ago I started filing them and taking care of my cuticles when I realized that my hands are so sexy that I could be a hand model for sure.

"I'm glad you're finally up, sleepyhead." My mom came into the room holding her blue spatula. "I thought I was gonna have to go up there."

"Yeah," I sighed, filing away.

"You know it's silly for you to do that all the time. You'll end up with no nails left."

"Don't worry about my nails, Mom. God!"

"Hey, watch it buddy," she said, pointing the spatula at me, then disappearing into the kitchen. Tim smiled at me knowingly. He was pretty intuitive for a little kid. He knew as well as I that taking God's name in vain was worse than swearing to her. So of course, whenever I got hurt, I always yelled "Goddamn it," just like my dad, to bug her.

I turned up the TV as loud as she'd let me get away with and continued to file my nails, wishing I had black polish. That would drive her to treatment.

"Come and eat up while it's still hot," she said, setting our plates of food on the kitchen table.

I sat down in my usual chair, across from hers. Tim sat next to her, smiling at me. I poured myself a glass of OJ, then started to shove hash browns into my mouth. Tim did the same thing. We raced through the entire meal like that, laughing the whole time.

My mom kind of rolled her eyes at me for being such a bad influence, and uttered a few words of prayer under her breath.

Then she began to eat her omelet carefully. "So what are you doing today?" she asked, once it was clear that I had won this contest.

"Hanging out with some friends."

"Where?"

"Uptown."

"Oh."

Whenever she asked where I was going I always told her "Uptown" and refused to disclose any more information, which really bugged her. It wasn't like I was lying to her or anything though. That is where I usually went, to the mall in Uptown to hang out with my three friends from South High School: Sam, whose name is short for Samantha, Sean, and Alex. We never actually shopped or anything. In fact, we always got kicked out for smoking cigarettes and loitering. Then we simply went a block and a half away to the lake and sat out on the grass or on the benches. Sometimes we passed around a forty-ounce beer wrapped in a paper bag and discreetly puffed on joints. Or we took a bus down to the Mississippi River and stumbled down the steep hill to the river's edge, where we could do the same thing *and* be loud and obnoxious.

"Can I go with you to the Uptown?" Tim asked.

Mom looked at me to see what I would respond. I considered saying, "It's up to Mom," because that would piss her off. But what if she said yes to teach me a lesson? Then I thought, maybe it would be fun to bring Tim along. Sam wouldn't care. She was a baby-sitter and she always had me come to her baby-sitting jobs to smoke joints with her in the backyard or garage once the kids were in bed. So I said, "Sure you can come. If it's okay with Mom."

My mom shot me a horrified glare as Tim turned to her and said excitedly, "Can I?"

"Honey," she began in a soothing voice. "We are going to Target today to buy Daddy an ink cartridge, remember?"

"But I don't wanna go buy Daddy an ink cartwidge," he whined. "I want to go hang up wiff Erwick in Uptown!" I could tell he was upset because he was talking in baby talk. Which, seemingly unbeknownst to my parents, he used as a manipulation tool. Whenever I was alone with him I actually marveled at how fluent he was, considering he was only five years old and had spent the first two and a half years of his life in an orphanage in Argentina.

"Thanks a lot," Mom said to me. I knew she'd never let him go anywhere with me. She didn't trust me at all.

From there, breakfast turned into an all-out family meltdown. Tim threw the biggest, teariest tantrum of his career, screaming, "Quit controlling me!" Mom screamed at him to calm down and at me to grow up, demanding to know why I had to make her life so difficult.

Finally, she shocked me by saying to Tim, "I don't want you hanging out with Erick and his friends because they're up to no good and they're just biding time before serious consequences come their way!" Clearly, this was directed at me, since Tim didn't understand the grown-up language she was using.

"So you hate my friends?"

"Is there anything a decent Christian should like about a bunch of drug addicts and delinquents?"

Her accusation horrified me. "Don't you realize what a hypocrite you are? Why do you choose to hate?" I yelled, running to my room to call Sam. By the time Sam got on the phone, I'd lost control of my emotions and had busted open a feather pillow on my dresser. White feathers were floating down like snowflakes. I asked her if she could meet me at our usual spot (the fountain in the Uptown mall) and to bring a joint because I needed to get high.

I couldn't believe my mom's nerve. Of course my friends were druggies! Like me, they realized how mundane life was without substances to elevate you to an ethereal state of consciousness. I loved my friends. They were my only source of sanity. We all hated school equally and found more fun in smoking pot and listening to angst-ridden heavy metal. Sometimes we hung out at this coffee shop on the West Bank, where people sold dime bags. We usually smoked pot in Sean's basement and played video games all night. Sean and Alex let Sam and me play Mario Brothers or whatever for, like, five minutes, then they put on some gory-ass war game and ignored us. It's all good, though. Sam and I have better things to do. She's like my sister.

Hard to believe, but we dated for almost six months. And I fell in love with her as deeply as any gay boy could ever love a girl. She was cute, kind of chubby, and had red curly hair, and we both *loved* romantic comedies and boy bands. I thought she was the coolest person around. Her stepdad called her "Punky," which describes her dead-on. We always talked about fun stuff, completely on the same level. I felt really guilty the whole time we dated, though, because I was gay and I knew our relationship would never work out. When I told her I thought we should just be friends, she got mega-pissed and wouldn't talk to me for, like, two weeks. Then she said she realized that we had no chemistry anyway, so she would remain my friend. That made me worry over whether or not she had figured out I was gay. I had gotten very personal with her. We even admitted to each other that we masturbated.

As I walked through the glass-door entrance of the mall, I realized that my plans to meet up with Sam were impossible. I hadn't had the presence of mind to change our usual meeting place, and Shades, the sunglasses boutique with the supercute gay guy, was facing the stupid fountain.

I headed toward my destination cautiously, only to find that the same cute guy was working. His back was turned to me, but I could tell it was him. He was wearing a black, glittery shirt that was so tight you could see his lean muscles and bronze skin through the knit and blue vinyl pants that merely looked like metal flesh. Since yesterday, his crazy hair had been dyed black with streaks of electric blue and was slicked up into two spikes, like little horns. I bet everyone stared at him when they walked by.

Suddenly he turned around! He would see me for sure if I just stood there, so I backed around the corner. I felt like such a jerk. If he saw me again after I freaked out on him yesterday, I'd die! God, I was such a loser. I wanted to be dead . . . or at least another person, someone who could actually speak to whomever he wanted without crumbling into a blubbering fool right there on the stupid floor.

I was so ashamed of my own inadequacy that I decided I didn't want to be at the mall anymore. So I left. I knew Sam would flip out at me for ditching her, but I didn't care. I wanted to be alone because the only person I really wanted to see was the funky sunglasses guy, and I didn't even know his name.

When I got outside I lit another cigarette and sat up against the building. I really had nowhere to go, except home. And I knew that if I went there I'd argue with my mom again and only have to leave again. I searched through my backpack, thinking about what I could write for a job application. I had to do something. I couldn't just never talk to him again and always wonder if I'd missed out on something great.

I opened my notebook and took a pen out of my denim-blue pencil case. My letter instantly began to flow from me: *"My name is Erick Taylor, and I would love it if you hired me because I really need a job and I feel I would be a very successful salesman because I'm good with people and I love sunglasses. I'm a high school student at St. John's and this would be a perfect place to work after school and on weekends. I'd like to work somewhere in the mall, too, so this place would be even more perfect because of that. I appreciate the time I've taken from you. Thank you for giving me the opportunity to apply.*" I finished it off with my phone number and address and everything else. I tore the paper from the notebook and folded it in half. Then I stuffed my junk back into my bag and reentered the mall, holding the letter between my fingers. I was nervous, but determined. I wasn't going to get scared and run away this time. I needed to act like a normal person and have a normal conversation with him. *He won't hate me,* I told myself repeatedly. *I'm a perfectly fun person to know. Besides, he's gay. He wouldn't just turn his back on some gay kid . . . would he?*

"Hey, remember me?" I asked, approaching his counter, holding out the letter to him before I even got there.

"Oh, hi. I didn't think you were coming back." He took the letter. Looking it over, he smiled, then set the letter down on the counter—face up!—which made me sweat, because someone could come up from behind me and start reading it. I would be so mortified.

"Yeah . . . well, I was in a hurry to be somewhere," I lied, trying not to let that letter bother me.

"I thought I scared you away."

"Of course not."

"You can be honest . . . I scare away a lot of people." He grinned proudly.

I looked him in the eyes just long enough to say defiantly, "You didn't scare me." Then I looked down to his glittery chest. "So?"

"You want an interview?"

"Yeah," I answered, meeting his eyes.

He didn't say anything. He just held me in his gaze for a few long seconds, smirking. I wondered if he was *trying* to scare me. "Pop quiz: Who sings, 'What's Love Got to Do with It'?"

"Tina Turner."

"Correct . . . What are the names of the two women on the BBC show, *Absolutely Fabulous?*"

"Patsy and Edina."

"Correct . . . Who was the gay lead singer of the musical group Wham?"

"Um, ah," I couldn't even think I was so nervous. "Michael Jackson."

"Michael Jackson!"

"No, not him!" I retracted. How could I have been so stupid? Obviously it wasn't Michael Jackson. I honestly had no idea.

"George Michael!" He eyed me skeptically. "Who sings 'Karma Chameleon'?"

I cringed. I wanted to say "Cher," but didn't dare.

"Boy George!" he bellowed in disbelief. "I'm starting to get worried about your knowledge of music trivia . . . Name at least one Cure song."

I thought for a moment. I'd heard of the Cure. I knew that anyone who was cool would be able to answer that question. Unfortunately, I wasn't cool. "Didn't they have that prayer song? 'Like a Prayer' or 'Give Me a Prayer' or"—I began to sing—*"Livin' on a prayer . . . Take my hand and we'll make it I swear, whoa-oh . . . ?"*

My companion slapped his palm to his forehead in disbelief. "That's Bon Jovi!" he shrieked, overwhelmed by my ignorance. "That's like the difference between planes and trains! How old are you again?"

"Seventeen," I lied again.

"I feel so old!" he wailed. "I bet you know everything about the Spice Girls, right?"

"Well, actually . . . I'm obsessed with Tori Amos."

"Really?" He calmed down a bit. "The angry one?"

"She's *not* angry! She's a genius!"

"Hmm . . . Alright, you're hired . . . So when do you want to start?"

It was all happening so fast. "I don't know . . . whenever."

"You smoke?"

"Yeah."

"Let's go have a cigarette." He put up a sign that said, "Back in five minutes." He came out a little door in the back with a cigarette already between his lips. I was relieved to discover that he was wearing platforms. That he wasn't actually six inches taller than I was.

"So, what's your name?" I asked.

"Chloe . . . Pleased to meet me?" He struck a pose.

I blushed again. He had a girl's name. "Yeah," I said bashfully.

He sprinted ahead of me and I imagined fairy dust trailing behind him like a glitter storm. When I reached the heavy glass doors, he held one of them open for me.

"Thanks." I quickly slipped past him.

He followed me out and grabbed my hand. "This way," he said. Together we ran, hands held, through the parking ramp to the corner farthest from the mall entrance. There we stood leaning against the concrete wall in semidarkness, facing rows of cars.

"Do you want to hit my onie?" Chloe asked, brandishing a gold onie already filled with weed.

"Sure," I said, taking the onie and the lighter he was offering. I watched his grin as I hit it. For once, I was cool and didn't cough like a lunatic as I exhaled the stream of gray smoke. I handed his paraphernalia back to him.

After he took his hit and banged the onie against the wall to clear the remaining ash, he asked me, "So, are you gay?"

Instantly my heart and stomach collided. My brain pumped with so many endorphins I thought I'd float away like a helium balloon. He'd asked me the dreaded question, the one I usually reacted to like a cat being submerged in water. Suddenly my patented "Fuck you" response wasn't appropriate. I knew that I had to tell him the truth if I wanted to be his friend. So I took a deep breath and, as clearly as I could, while my hands spun like pinwheels on my wrists, I said, "Um . . . Yeah . . . Well, um, I guess

. . . Yeah. I'm, you know, like . . . gaaaay." It felt like it took me five minutes to spit it out. Chloe was, after all, the first person I'd ever told. And that was, perhaps, the biggest thing I had ever done.

"I figured," he said casually. "You want to smoke another onie?"

I was instantly in love.

{ three }

So I started selling sunglasses with Chloe on the weekends. It was already the beginning of May, and Chloe said that when I got done with the school year I could add an extra shift during the week, if I wanted to. And I did want to, so long as I could work with him. Only I didn't actually put it like that. I tried not to be presumptuous, even though I had decided that it was fate that I'd met him. My strategy for getting him to fall in love with me was that I would focus on building a friendship before a relationship.

We had a blast working together. He was always telling me the most amazing stories. Like his tale about a plane he had taken to a drag show in Aspen. Supposedly, it nearly crashed when the pilot had a heart attack. The plane took a nosedive, and everyone panicked because it would've been certain doom! But luckily, Chloe's dad was an ex–fighter pilot who had taught him how to fly. So Chloe saved the day and was honored with a parade when he finally reached Aspen. The pilot survived, and the drag show was an absolute smash! I was never sure if Chloe's stories were actually true or not because he was so dramatic about everything. But I didn't care, because it was fun listening to him.

Now that I had a job at the mall, Sam went there every day to hang out with me. She was completely in love with Chloe and only pretended I was her reason for being there. She went mad when Chloe declared himself clairvoyant and read on her palm that she would soon find a boyfriend who would someday have lots of fame and fortune. He predicted that she would be let down by him many times, though, before she dumped him and found her own fortune. No children, long lifeline. I think she was a bit disappointed with the reading. For my reading he said I would find love in the summer, but not to put all my makeup in one caboodle. I would have to face the demons of my past before I could ever be successful and famous. No children, long lifeline. I couldn't believe I was actually getting paid for this! Aside from selling a few expensive pairs of sunglasses to customers, it was like I wasn't even working. I spent my days with my crazy, lying, yet beautiful and cool, new best friend ever.

"It sounds like you're falling in *love* with Chloe," Sam teased. We were lying on the beach at Calhoun Lake. I had never been a big fan of lying out because, prior to coming out, I thought that being too high-maintenance would blow my cover. But Sam had begged, just like the year before, when we went tanning four times in May. It was pretty futile, though, because Sam had such a fair complexion that unless she used SPF 5000, she got as red as a lobster.

"I'm not in love with him," I argued.

"Oh, *please* . . . don't even deny it."

I didn't respond.

"Chloe," she pondered. "Why would a guy call himself that?"

"Because he's cool. Too cool to care about gender identifiers."

"Gender identifiers? Well, you're certainly hip with the gay lingo these days."

"Hell, yeah, girlfriend!" I said as flamboyantly as possible. We both laughed. Then when the giggles subsided we continued our cloud-gazing through our UV-protected sunglasses that were freebies from Shades.

"I like Chloe," Sam began. "He's crazy . . . I think it would be cool if you guys dated."

"Really?"

"Yeah . . . don't you?"

"Honestly? It's all I can think about."

"Would you have sex with him?"

I rolled my eyes. "Don't be so immature, Sam."

"What? You can't talk about sex?"

"I can talk about sex," I insisted.

"So would you?"

"If we were dating? Obviously."

She started giggling uncontrollably.

"I *knew* you were too immature," I said with hurt feelings.

She collected herself quickly. "I'm sorry. I'm just not used to the whole gay thing."

"What whole gay thing?"

"You know . . . Like, is one person the *giver* and one person the *receiver?*" she asked shyly.

"Yeah," I said, like I was a big know-it-all.

"So which would you be?"

I hadn't really thought about that. So far, whenever I fantasized about Chloe, I placed us somewhere private in (or around) the mall, feeling each other up and giving each other blowjobs. At this point in my life, anal sex seemed about as unwanted as brain surgery. But my first inclination was to say, "I think I'd be the giver."

Sam looked relieved. "That's what I figured."

"It is?"

She looked startled. "No . . . I don't know. Why?"

"No reason. Let's change the subject."

"Okay."

I rolled over onto my stomach and began running my fingers through the grass, imagining Chloe fucking me. It felt amazing in my fantasy, which surprised me because I always imagined getting fucked would hurt. Maybe it didn't hurt if it was with someone you loved.

Just as I was getting a hard-on, Sam said, "Erick?"

"Yeah?"

"I was just thinking that if I were you, I'd probably try it, you know, both ways."

I grinned, surprised by her forwardness. "Why don't you try it?"

"Fuck you," she laughed.

"Fuck you too," I laughed back, delighted that for the first time in my life I could talk about sex openly with someone. Maybe life would be bearable after all.

On my second weekend working at Shades, Chloe turned to me and said, "Girl, you need some fierce clothes to show off that bod of yours."

I looked down at my usual black T-shirt and blue jeans, shrugged and said, "I don't know, Chloe."

"What do you mean, you don't know?"

"I just don't think I could dress like you . . . no offense."

"'Course not, dear." He looked at my clothes with a sigh of defeat. "Well, suit yourself. Ha! No pun intended," he added as he began unpacking a box of newly shipped sunglasses. He set aside pairs he would later try on and write off as "damaged" if he fancied them.

My big job of the day was to draw a "buy one, get one half off" sign for the side of the kiosk. Some vandal had written, "FUCK YOU" on the last one. At first I was just going to fill the page with simple block letters, but Chloe's sparkly shirt and funky hair had given me an idea. I drew quickly, sort of hiding the page with my wrists. My picture was a cartoon version of Chloe wearing fierce sunglasses with more pairs of fierce sunglasses filling his hands and pockets. I wrote "Shades" on his T-shirt, using two different colors of ink dots to create sparkle. At the top of the page, I wrote in rainbow letters, "Buy one, get one half off."

"How's this?" I asked excitedly.

"Fabulous!" Chloe applauded. "I love, love, love it!"

I laughed at all his enthusiasm.

"It's so fantastic I just can't even stand it!"

"Thank you."

"Can you make one of me?"

"What do you mean?" I asked, a little disgruntled. "This *is* you."

"That's me? I thought it was *you.*"

I couldn't believe it. "No, silly, it's you."

"Oh, honey. You poor thing. That's you. Just ask Freud if you don't believe me."

"Gimme a break."

"Oh, Erick. My little lost lamb. Just trying to break free from the shackles of oppression," Chloe said, touching his wrists together to mime being handcuffed.

"No I'm not."

"Mmm-hmm," he rolled his eyes and continued unpacking sunglasses.

I looked at the picture, then at Chloe, then at myself in the mirror, then at the picture again. Maybe it *was* me. Or at least the me I wished to be. "You really think I could dress like this?"

Chloe looked up at me as if I had just asked the silliest question ever. Then he smiled. "You want to close the store right now and go shopping?"

"Huh?"

"C'mon, it'll be fun."

"But I don't have any money."

Chloe opened the register and took out one hundred fifty dollars. "Here's your paycheck."

"Cash?"

"We *all* get paid cash, sweetie. The owner of Shades Boutique is quite shady himself. I think it saves him on taxes or something."

I took the money. "Is this for last weekend?"

"Yup. One-fifty a week. Is that okay?"

"Sure."

"Good. Now let's go shopping!" he said, locking up the display case and pulling down the metal gate. Before we left, he took a little bottle out of his bag and with a swig of Coke swallowed one of the vitamins he took religiously. I had noticed the first day I worked with him that he took a variety of pills, including two or three vitamin supplements: echinacea for immunity, ginkgo biloba for memory loss, and who knows what else. When I asked about them, he told me that if I ever met his mother I would understand.

The first thing he said I would need to purchase was a new pair of shoes. We went to a store in Uptown called St. Sabrina's: Parlor in Purgatory. On one side of the brick building was a mural depicting a cartoon woman standing in flames. The interior decor was way Goth, and they specialized scary clothing, paraphernalia, and piercing every body part imaginable. We were there for platforms. Chloe suggested several pairs, but I fell in love immediately with the first pair I tried on and couldn't imagine even looking at any others. They were simple: black leather, square toe, and black wood heels. The salesgirl who assisted us had dreadlocks and wore a perpetual frown, several facial piercings, and what looked more like a black lace nightie than a dress. Chloe told her that she had fantastic sense to know what to wear on this fabulous spring day. She just rolled her eyes.

"I'll never understand the Goths," he said, watching her leave. "Me, I dress in full Technicolor."

"Me, too," I decided, walking around the store six inches taller. "I'll take 'em."

Next we went to Marshall's for cute underwear. "When you're building a pyramid, you have to start at the base," Chloe said, fanning himself with a pair of red Calvin Klein briefs. "And now we shop," he declared, crossing the six-foot aisle to enter the women's section. I felt very apprehensive about going in there. But Chloe pointed out that if I wanted metallic blue flared pants, or red cords, or anything silver and glittery that wasn't as baggy as a damn trash bag, I certainly wasn't going to find it in the men's section.

The trick, Chloe explained gracefully, to finding a good pair of women's pants when you're a man is to get them tight, low cut at the waist, and try on at least a million pairs. The problem with women's pants is that if you're not careful, they give you a hoochie-mama look. So unless you wanna do drag, make sure your ass isn't huge and your package small. Before even trying them on, he advised me to check for belt loops, back pockets, and deep front pockets. You know you've finally found the right ones when you zip up and you look like a diva, not someone who could give birth with them hips. We went to three stores before ending up at Express, where we found a pair of black leather hip-huggers that satisfied Chloe.

"I don't look like a girl?" I asked, standing under an arbor of lightbulbs, staring at myself in my pants and platforms as Chloe admired the results of the makeover. I noticed that the women in Express were all gawking at us and whispering, but by this time I had grown used to the attention and had even begun to revel in it. Being with Chloe made me feel unstoppable.

"You look fabulous!" Chloe declared. "Goddamn, I'm jealous, girl! I can never pull off black leather as good as you can!"

He was talking loud enough for our audience to hear. Meanwhile, I was basking in his compliments like a diva taking curtain calls.

"I'll take 'em!" I declared.

"Divine! They'll be perfect with a big, fat, leather belt. Preferably one with a big, huge, silver belt buckle! I saw one the other day at Urban Outfitters that said 'Acid Bitch.'" He shouted extra loud when he said "Acid Bitch." "Let's go try on that one."

After purchasing the pants, we went and bought the belt. Suddenly I was completely out of money, and I hadn't even bought a shirt. Chloe said I couldn't possibly wait until next week to buy a shirt, so he invited me to his apartment to try on some of his fabulous clothes. I was so excited. I thought I'd die!

When we got to his apartment, shopping bags in tow, Chloe said that we had to get high before we played dress-up anymore. So we sat on the futon, listening to Donna Summer's "Last Dance" and smoking out of Chloe's big, red, plastic, penis bong. Once we were sufficiently high, Chloe took a family-sized package of Chips Ahoy chocolate-chip cookies and a bottle of white zinfandel from his waist-high refrigerator under the counter. We drank and munched while he pulled out piles of clothes. His closet was so big that you could fit a full-sized bed in there if you wanted a separate sleeping space, but he had it filled—five feet high—with clothes—men's and women's. I'd never seen such a wild wardrobe. He could have opened his own thrift store with just his clothes alone.

He flung stuff at me, and soon we were both undressing and redressing into all sorts of different styles. I was a sailor, a seventies disco drag king, an acid diva, a tough leather bandit, not to mention that chick from *I Dream of Jeannie*. Not only did he have clothes, he had hats, belts, makeup, and jewelry galore. I told Chloe I wanted to be a model. Then I told Chloe he *had* to be a model. Chloe just laughed, admiring his own beautiful nude features in the mirror. I ached for him. His dark, lean body was hairless, except for the faint trace of soft black hairs on his legs. He had muscle definition, but without the bulk of a bodybuilder. Perhaps it was the wine, but I wondered what it would feel like to touch that body and to have him touch my body and hold me in bed. I was ready to move into his apartment that night and live with him forever, but unfortunately he didn't seem interested in having sex with me. He just needed someone to dress up with.

Sitting on his floor, listening to Aretha Franklin and dining on buttered egg noodles with Parmesan, he told me that he was so glad we met. "These days," he said, "it's so difficult to make friends with other gay boys because sex always gets in the way. We can't let it get in the way of our friendship."

I grinned jubilantly. Inside, though, I was devastated. I had never wanted anyone so badly. Yet I was so in need of a good friend that I was scared to jeopardize what we had. Out of nowhere I said pathetically, "I want to find a boyfriend."

"Don't we all, baby?"

Duh, I thought. Didn't he realize that his new boyfriend might be sitting right in front of him?

"You'll find one," he said reassuringly. "You're a great catch . . . I bet you'd look great as a blond."

"Really? I've actually thought about dyeing my hair blond before."

"Can I dye it?"

"Blond? Sure."

"Really! You know, I cut and dye my own hair."

"You cut your own hair?"

"Sure. My hair grows really fast, so I have to cut it all the time," he said, taking his last bite of egg noodles. His hair was always spiked perfectly, and he spent a considerable amount of time in the mirror adjusting it. "You finished?" he asked, still chewing. I nodded and handed him my empty plate. He took the dishes to the kitchen and tossed them in the sink. Then he proceeded to rummage through his heart-shaped cabinet. I watched him take a pill out of a bottle and down it with Coke.

"Where can I find a boyfriend?" I asked.

"You never know where you're going to find a boyfriend. It's always in the last place you'd expect, and that's the truth." He rejoined me. "Do you want any more wine?"

"No, thanks." I lit a cigarette.

"So, do you want me to bleach your hair right now?"

"Yeah, sure."

I sat on the toilet seat while he stood in front of me working with his shirt off. All I could see was his six-pack, and it was driving me nuts. I wanted to touch him and practically had to sit on my hands to restrain myself. As he worked the bleach into my hair, he sort of massaged my scalp, which tingled and made me feel like I was melting. I was starting to think that this was the best night of my life.

Once the bleach had done its work long enough for us to smoke a joint and paint our fingernails blue, Chloe had me lean over the bathtub so he could rinse my hair. Before he'd let me see the result, he had to blow-dry it for about twenty minutes, then style it with some Aveda mousse.

"There you go," he said when he was done.

I studied my new reflection with glee. I looked like Madonna in her "Papa Don't Preach" phase. My new blond hair was better than I had hoped! "Thank you so much, Chloe," I said. "It's exactly what I always wanted to do with my hair."

"You look *fierce*, girl."

When we left the bathroom, I noticed that it was dark outside. "Um, Chloe," I began nervously, "I'm not asking this to make a pass at you or anything. I mean, you're right about us being good friends. But, do you think I could crash here tonight? It's getting kind of late, and Golden Valley is super-far."

"Of course! You don't even have to ask."

That night I laid with Chloe on his futon. We wore only our T-shirts and underwear. He fell asleep right away, but I stayed awake for a long time, thinking about him. He was so close that I could feel the warmth of his body, but I never touched him. I was too afraid of upsetting him and ruining everything. So instead I positioned my hand only an inch or so from him on the mattress, hoping that at some point he'd roll over onto me and we could "accidentally" wind up tangled together. He would enjoy that and realize that we were perfect together. But he never budged, and we never touched, the whole night.

{ four }

The day after Tommy died, my school gathered in the gymnasium to light candles and pray for him and our family. Of course, I wasn't there to see it. I missed about a week of class. When I finally did return, it seemed like everything had turned upside down. That scared me at first. Maybe I just didn't expect everything to be so sad. Teachers would look at me and start crying. I felt them doing it whenever I was at my desk working on my assignments or reading some book. One time, it even made me so mad that I knocked over my desk in a rage. I began pounding on it, trying to break my desk into pieces. I was sent home quickly after that. But no one ever punished me. My outburst seemed only to make everyone sadder—and nicer to me. Kids at my school who were normally thoughtless gave me candy, shared their lunches with me, and involved me in their games. Suddenly, I was the first picked on the kickball team. Andy Flynn picked me. In fact, he turned me into his favorite little buddy for the rest of the year.

I was happy to feel loved, or at least thought of. But none of this kindness helped my depression. My mind was filled with demons. I felt myself growing distant from everyone around me. Sometimes when I opened my eyes to take everything in, I would see corpses walking the halls, playing at recess. I became afraid to look at the world. My heart was filled with fear, and I asked God over and over to turn back time, to do *something*. I imagined God was listening to me, and sooner or later Tommy would walk through the front door. He would look just like I remembered him: dressed in his red OshKosh B'Gosh overalls and his blue monster truck T-shirt. And I would run to him and throw him on the couch and tickle him under his chubby chin.

Sometimes, what gets me through the day is remembering special times he and I had together. Like the trip we took to California. He was three and I was eight and we had begged to go to Disneyland. It was the only trip our family ever took together, and we have about three million pictures to prove it. We stayed at the Holiday Inn off of Sunset Boulevard in Los Angeles. My mom wanted to stay in Hollywood because she was obsessed with seeing movie stars and shopping in Beverly Hills—she used to be fun like that. I can recall the color of my mom's enormous sun hat and Chanel sunglasses (both of which she bought at some fancy store) and my dad gathering us for a picture every ten minutes even though we begged him to just let us have fun.

One night our parents went out and left us alone in the hotel room. They hadn't ever left us without a baby-sitter. We were supposed to stay in bed because it was late, but of course we didn't. We sat up and played with the Legos we had purchased at Legoland. We built a space station, then destroyed it with an alien war. We jumped on the beds and ate candy and ran down the hallways, knocking on doors and trying to hide. I really loved my brother that night. I felt as if we were the same age. Like, if I told him my secrets, he'd understand. It's kind of neat having a little brother, because when they stare at you (even though you know otherwise), they think you're the coolest person ever. I think that's what I miss the most about him.

After Tommy died, nothing was the same in my family. For

one, my mom went crazy. My memories of her back in those days are images of her sitting on her bed or standing at the kitchen counter, crying. She was always looking at pictures of Tommy, down on her knees, begging God for another chance. Pleading with him to make her pain and suffering go away. It was awful. She was so depressed that sometimes she couldn't get out of bed until dinnertime and couldn't fall asleep again until breakfast the next day. By spring of that year she had gone so downhill that she stopped showering and began wearing the maternity dress she had worn when she was pregnant. It was red with little white flowers and all the extra fabric for the stomach hung down to her waist.

Finally, my dad couldn't stand it anymore. He arranged for her to go to Ohio on some religious retreat for mothers who had lost a kid. She was gone forever. Weeks, months maybe—I don't remember. Years later, I found out that it wasn't a religious retreat at all. My dad (perhaps because he is a psychiatrist) sent her to a mental institution. I had been snooping through my parents' desk when I stumbled across a letter that said something like: Dear Dr. Taylor, Your wife is adjusting well . . . blah, blah, blah . . . She sees a therapist who helps her through the grieving process and she seems to be opening up at group sessions . . . blah, blah, blah . . . The antidepressants are beneficial . . . blah, blah, blah . . . Sincerely, Dr. Laurie Parnel. Reed Institute.

I imagined her in a little white room with padded walls, wearing a straitjacket. Since I was her son, I was especially scared that I would end up going crazy like her someday. Sometimes I got so depressed that *I* felt completely insane.

Before she left, she went a little manic and began cooking enough to feed all of the Midwest. She made huge pasta meals, a pot roast, pork chops, pies, burgers, goulash, Tater Tot hot dishes, and an array of desserts. She said that it was all for my dad and me, so we wouldn't have to worry about food while she was away. My dad explained to me in private that when people are grieving they sometimes like to occupy themselves with something productive like cooking. In retrospect, I think she was trying to show him that she could still be a caring wife and mother, that she wasn't a zombie. It must have been stressful for Mom to try to have as healthy an attitude toward death as my father expected her to have.

When my mom finally left for the Reed Institute, things settled and my dad and I got over Tommy in *our* way. We rented action movies and chowed on pizza and M & Ms, and didn't bother to clean a thing. Dishes piled up and all. We had what we coined as our "boys' nights out." He took me downhill skiing, bowling, to a hockey game, and to movies. My dad was so cool. He once told me right before we were about to watch some Schwarzenegger flick that if I had any questions about Tommy I should not be afraid to ask. I told him I didn't. Then the movie started and we never talked about it again.

Eventually, though, I couldn't stand to be around my dad. I suppose it began when I started to feel as if I had to hide all my feelings from him. I didn't want him to find out about my attraction toward boys or my fantasies of wearing women's clothes, and wanting to have sex with men almost his age. And there were other things, too. I couldn't ever talk to him about how much I despised my mother because she became a Jesus freak, or how Tommy haunted me daily, or how I thought about suicide. He was a psychiatrist who talked to crazy people every day. Although I was certain that I was the craziest of everyone, he didn't seem to notice. When I went through my three-year phase of never smiling for a photograph, he would say something like: "Don't smile or your face will break." Couldn't he see that I didn't smile all those years because I hated myself? That I hated him for not helping me? Shouldn't a psychiatrist have seen these signs? Why didn't he know that I was in trouble?

I often wonder about his patients, if any of them are gay or have any gay children. 'Course, even if we had talked, he wouldn't have told me anything about them. He took an oath of secrecy, just like a priest. Still, I wonder what he would say to them. Would Dad tell them that being gay was something you were born with, or would he say it was something acquired through abuse and neglect? I once looked up "homosexuality" in one of his books, and it said that being gay was a social—not biological—manifestation. At the time I didn't know what those words meant. "Manifestation" sounded like the title of a horror movie. I wished someone could explain it to me, but there was no one I could ask. My feelings of difference were between God and me. I used to lay awake in bed, begging: "Please, God, don't let me be gay. Please, God, don't let me be gay. Please, God, I'll do anything, just don't let me be gay. Please, God. *Pleeeaase!*"

One time, in eighth grade, my family was in the car on the way to Sunday mass (I was in the backseat with Tim, my dad driving, my mom chattering in the passenger seat) when suddenly, on the sidewalk, I saw two gay men walking together, holding hands. I had never seen that before. It thrilled me, yet made me cringe all at once. Why wasn't anyone kicking their asses? I wondered. My parents noticed, too, and there was an uncomfortable silence that lasted so long I thought I might scream right then: "I'm just like them!" But the moment passed, or maybe it died inside of me. Once it was safe to speak again, my dad chuckled and said, "I bet they weren't on their way to church!" I disintegrated. He was only joking, but his words scarred me. At that moment I realized that my father would never understand me, what I was going through. Yet sometimes all I want from him— just for the sake of comfortably sitting next to him in a movie theater—is one more "boys' night out."

As I had expected, my parents were not thrilled when I came home after having spent the night at Chloe's apartment. My mom freaked when she saw my blond hair. At first she was speechless, staring dumbly at my platinum spikes, opening and closing her mouth like a dying fish. My dad, on the other hand, was upset that I had stayed out all night without permission. He lectured me about responsibility. According to him, as long as I lived under his roof, I would obey my curfew or else. I told him that maybe I didn't need to live under his roof anymore, thinking that maybe I could move in with Chloe. Finally, my Mom caught her breath and started flipping out about my hair and rock and roll and drugs and the devil. In the end I was grounded for a week and told that I had lost their trust. I didn't even care about their stupid trust. Sometimes I thought that maybe I hated them. Luckily, I was allowed to keep my hours at Shades while I was grounded. Had my parents known that Shades was where I had the most fun, surely they would have taken that away too, just to be tyrannical. My ruthless parents wanted to ruin my life!

Still, nothing could get me down so long as I was hanging out with Chloe. At last, I was becoming cool. With my new look, new attitude, and new best friend, it was only a matter of time before I became superpopular. Maybe I would even be a drag queen like Chloe. He explained to me that he wasn't a transvestite. He was merely a vaudeville-type performer. "I guess I just always loved entertaining people," he explained to me one Sunday while we were sitting at Shades fussing with my new hair. "And who doesn't adore women's fashion?" he added, fussing with his own hair in the mirror.

"Did you always know you wanted to be a drag queen?" I asked.

"I always knew I wanted something, but I didn't give it a name until I went to see a drag show for the first time and saw Babs Arlington."

"The drag queen you went to Chicago with?"

"Mmm-hmm."

"She must've been pretty amazing."

"She was. Still is, in fact. Don't worry, you'll meet her."

"So what were you like when you were a kid?"

That made him laugh.

"What's so funny?"

"Nothing. You're just cute, that's all."

"Whatever, I'm serious."

"Actually, it's kind of funny now that you mention it, because when I was really young, I had an obsession with being Wonder Woman . . . You know, Lynda Carter? I used to watch it religiously. I dressed like her and everything."

"Really?"

"Girl, my mom made me the costume and I paraded all around the house in it. I pretended to be some mild-mannered businesswoman, until I spun in a circle. The clothes flew off, and underneath I would be wearing the red, white, and blue Wonder Woman outfit. I even had the Lasso of Truth. I was totally prepared to fight crime. My dad got so pissed. But my mom got a kick out of it. I made her laugh for days."

"When I was, like, four I wore my mom's high-heeled shoes and put T-shirts on my head, pretending I had long flowing hair."

Chloe got all excited. "Did you play with dolls?"

"I used to steal girls' toys at day care," I laughed.

"Well, my Lord, honey. Weren't you the sneaky one!"

"Well, the fun and games didn't last too long," I sighed despairingly. "Catholic school forces you to kick those habits pretty quick."

"Yuck! Catholic school must suck. Do you believe in Jesus?"

"Yeah," I answered without even thinking. "I guess . . . Don't you?"

"Actually, I'm an atheist."

I gasped. No one had ever said that to me before. I couldn't believe it. The first thing that occurred to me was that Chloe was going to hell when he died, and I was instantly sorry for him.

Then I wondered if it was a sin to feel sorry for him, or to even be his friend, for that matter. "You really don't believe in God?" I asked, just to make sure I understood him right.

"Don't be shocked, baby. Not everyone believes in God, contrary to what you may have been raised to believe."

Sam appeared with a bag from Old Navy in one hand and a twenty-ounce Diet Coke in the other. Her red curls were in two braids that touched her shoulders. We had recently been sunbathing, so her freckles were darker than usual. "Hey, boys!" she said, leaning against the counter.

"Do you believe in God?" Chloe immediately turned to her and asked.

"I dunno, maybe." Sam grimaced.

"Maybe?" I repeated in disbelief, even more dismayed by her reply than by Chloe's.

"Well I don't believe in church or anything . . . I know you do, Erick, but I'm sorry, I just think that stuff's a crock of shit."

I'd never heard such insanity before. Not believing in God? It sounded like the most ridiculous notion ever. I could see not believing in Jesus or heaven or the saints, sometimes I didn't believe in those things myself. But the Creator? It was too overwhelming to imagine.

"You know, Erick," Sam said. "If you don't open your eyes to the real world, you're going to kill yourself with all your guilt. All your Christian morality."

Chloe laughed.

I was so mad at both of them that I stormed off. Sam had such a big mouth that sometimes I really hated her. I thought about my mother and how if she had heard them telling me that they didn't believe in God, she would've had to move our family to another state or something so I wouldn't ever see them again. I wondered if Sam and Chloe were talking about me. They probably were. They probably felt sorry for me because I went to Catholic school and I believed in God. I'm sure they thought I was the biggest freak ever for storming away. Suddenly I got so mad I threw my cigarette onto the ground and began jumping on it, my arms thrashing about. Then I was crying and apologizing to God for all my sins. I don't know why I couldn't control my emotions. Sometimes I'm such an explosive wreck. Finally I dried my eyes and went back inside.

When I returned to the kiosk, I gave them benevolent smiles. For the rest of the day, we carefully avoided all mention of Catholicism and God. Instead, we talked about the decline in soulful divas these days. Sam and I both agreed that maybe Chloe could be the next one. He was such a star. He just laughed and got embarrassed and told us that he had far too many skeletons in the closet (no pun intended) to ever be a tabloid queen. I secretly decided that I would try to convince him otherwise. It seemed to me like it was just meant to be.

{ five }

The following Friday we had our end-of-the-year religious retreat at school. This was like a Catholic school's version of a pep rally. Everyone sits in the lunchroom and talks about religion and school pride and all the wonderful things we can do to celebrate Jesus over the summer. We began with a silent prayer led by Father Tom, our school priest. I thought about Chloe and everything he had said about atheism. I didn't know what to think anymore. I was scared for him and scared for myself because part of me wanted to believe him. But how could I believe him? I had relied on my faith too long to throw it all away.

I started thinking about Tommy, how I used to picture him floating on a cloud, looking down at me. In my dreams he was a classic angel with white wings and a halo. Sometimes I talked to him as if I were praying. Like sometimes, when I was getting into someone's car or crossing the street, I would ask him to please not let me get killed. Maybe it was weird of me to do that. I'm probably insane.

I looked around the room, at everyone, wondering if this was really the whole world. I saw Justin Hankshaw and Terrance Welldone behind me. They were clowning around discreetly. I wasn't sure what they were saying. Then I noticed Andy Ripley coming in late. He was the hottest senior. I felt bad because he would probably get detention for being late. The poor guy already had to go to summer school in order to get his diploma. I expected him to join the rest of the seniors, but to my delight he walked toward us sophomores and sat down in front of me.

What a babe! I was instantly in love. I couldn't stop my dick from getting hard. He was too perfect. The muscles of his shoulders flexed under his shirt when he moved, his blond hair hung in his big blue eyes. He was the only guy at our school with a beard. Usually I hate beards, but his facial hair was sexy. It looked as soft as cashmere. And his lips were a natural pink, the kind of pink that girls try to get with lipstick. I completely stopped paying attention to the retreat. All I could think about was my throbbing boner, as I studied every detail of his clothes, his bare blond arms and hands. He was either a god I wanted to sleep with or one I wanted to look like. I wished we were twins. I wondered if he could feel my eyes on him, if he would beat me up if he knew—if he would puke if he thought I had a boner.

After the retreat ended, I headed for my locker with my notebook covering my crotch. When I reached my locker Justin and Terrance were waiting for me. Justin grabbed my notebook, which I tried to take back, but there was no chance.

"Do you have a woody, Erick?"

I blushed. "No."

"Don't deny it, buddy. We saw you staring at Andy Ripley. Everyone saw. I'm sure he's going to kick your ass when he finds out."

My whole face burned. "Lay off, Justin . . . it's not like you think." I seized the opportunity to grab my notebook.

"Did I say you could have that back?" he responded angrily.

I didn't say anything, but wondered if I'd ever have the guts to stand up to him.

"Faggot!" he said with a shudder. "You disgust me." Then he punched me in the gut. Next Terrance punched me and they laughed and ran away.

I sort of collapsed against the locker, then slid down, onto the floor. I could barely breathe. Getting the wind knocked out of you is horrible. I don't have asthma, but I'm pretty sure it's what asthma would feel like.

"Erick! Oh my God, are you okay?" It was Marcy and Beth, these two preppy girls that always got in trouble for talking in history class. "Those assholes! I can't believe they did that."

"I'm fine," I gasped.

"What is their problem? Why the hell would they do that?" Marcy asked Beth, like suddenly I wasn't even there.

"They're just boys, Marcy. Don't even try to understand them."

They eyed me like I was just another boy that they shouldn't try to understand.

"Well, take care of yourself, Erick," Marcy said cheerfully as they walked away. Meanwhile I was still sitting on the floor, watching people pass me by, surprised at myself for being surprised that no one ever bothered to help me to my feet.

Finally I got up, managed to get my notebook into my locker, then got the hell out of school. Once home, I sat on my bed and cried, thinking about how I had just cried a few days ago at work, and how I would probably have something really shitty happen that would make me cry again tomorrow. My life totally sucked every chance it got. I felt like I was the biggest pervert ever. I turned on my stereo and as soon as I heard Tori's ethereal voice sing passionately about rape and hate and the horrors of society, I was relieved. Sometimes her music was the only thing that kept me alive. There was a knock on my door. My dad came in. "I didn't say you could come in." I turned off my stereo.

He looked around my room. "Hello, Erick." I could feel the disappointment. "What are you doing?"

"Nothing." I wanted to know why he was even home.

"Well, I think we need to have a talk." He leaned up against my desk to show me that it was going to take awhile. "Lately you've seemed distant"—he began, not sure how to get to where he was going—"and I was thinking that you might, possibly, have something you'd like to get off your chest."

I couldn't believe it. Right away I figured my mom must have made him come up here. "You don't have to talk to me like I'm one of your cases," I said.

"Sorry, I didn't mean to. How about I talk and you listen?" I looked away. "Basically, son, I understand that you're going through growing pains and don't want to talk to your parents about anything. I can live with that. If you don't want us to know what you do when you're with your *friends,* whoever they are, or wherever you go, that's fine, too. But when you break the rules of this house, such as curfew, I have to interfere. Now, last semester you got all Cs and one D in math. This semester you've been skipping class—we know about that. Also, you've been staying out late, when you bother to come home at all. And, well, your clothes . . . you dress differently now. We don't understand what you're thinking. We just don't want to see you drop out of school and throw away your future."

"You don't understand!" I cried.

He eyed me gravely. "Cut the drama, Erick. I just want to know what you're planning to do this trimester?"

"I'll be fine," I groaned. Cs and one D, in math, again.

"Well, there's three weeks of school left, and you had better go every day, or else you'll stay in your room all summer."

"You can't do that!"

"If you miss even one day, that's exactly what I'll do."

"Since when do you care?"

"I don't want to hear it! You're lucky your mother isn't sending you to CYC."

My eyes bugged out of my head. "What?!" I screamed. CYC stood for Christian Youth Camp. My life was over. "You guys are insane! Get out of my room!"

He slammed the door. I was shocked. He never yelled at me. My mother yelled at me daily, but he was usually passive. I couldn't believe it. I felt like an unwanted fungus on the family tree. I was so going to run away from home. I started thinking about what I should take with me besides my clothes and makeup and Tori CDs. I wondered if Chloe would let me move in with him. I doubted it. His apartment was hardly any bigger than my bedroom. I called him up. "I'm having the worst day ever!" I bellowed.

"Well, cheer up because it's Friday and you are going to your first gay bar ever!"

"Screwdriver?"

"Get used to it, sweetie, it's a one-bar town."

"Oh, I don't know if I can, Chloe. My dad wants to kill me. He said if I don't stop being myself, I'll get kicked out of the house," I paraphrased what Dad said.

"But I have a surprise," Chloe insisted. "Maybe you should go out tonight and just not miss the next three weeks of school."

"But everyone hates me! And besides, it's obvious he wants me out."

Chloe sighed. "Well, I suppose, if you go to school every day for the next three weeks, and no one arrests me for harboring a runaway, you can use my house as a refuge."

"God, you're as strict about school as my dad."

"Honey, that's your sixteen-year-old lifestyle. I'm just scared of what your crazy parents might do to me if I let you live at my house and skip school."

I laughed. "Like they would ever find out! Besides, I already told you they want me out of the house."

"Hmm, poor Erick. So are you coming over?"

"Yeah," I grinned. "I'll be over there in a half hour." We said good-bye, and I hung up the phone. I turned Tori back on and was happy, or at least content, because I loved Tori and loved Chloe and it seemed like that was enough. Laying on my bed, I stared at my ceiling and thought about my family. Not in anger, but in wonder. It had been a long time since my dad had tried to parent me like that. For a minute it felt like we were a real family. It made me wonder if I could tell them I'm gay. Would they send me to CYC if I did?

I emerged from my room cautiously, dressed in platforms, black leather pants, my Acid Bitch belt, and a tiny T-shirt Chloe had given me that said Porn Star in silver sparkles across the chest. It was my favorite shirt ever. From upstairs I could hear my family in the living room. They were playing Monopoly. I couldn't believe it. Tim and my dad were arguing over who got to be the banker while Mom laughed. I was singed by jealousy. No one had ever played Monopoly with me. I went into my parents' room and grabbed ten dollars. When I got downstairs, group awkwardness ensued. "I didn't know you guys played board games when I went out."

"It's always a party around here," Mom joked, sipping her iced tea through a straw just to impress me. "We're even going to have cake!"

"You wanna join us?" Dad asked, trying to be my pal again.

"I can't. I'm meeting friends." I headed for my coat.

"Please play, Erick," Tim begged, which made it hard to say no because he was the only sincere one among us. My parents' enthusiasm, for instance, was completely contrived for Tim's sake.

"Maybe another time," I said. "Come give me a kiss good-bye."

He kissed my cheek and I noticed my parents watching me. I couldn't tell which was worse: that we loved Tim because he held us together, or that we loved Tim because he was the replacement for Tommy.

"Where are you going?" Dad asked casually.

"To Sean's." A friend I hadn't actually talked to in several months. "I'm going to stay the night."

"Stay the night?" Dad said in such a way as to remind me that I was on prepunishment.

"It's Friday," I protested.

I think he thought that if he tried to stop me, it would only start a fight, and the illusion of normalcy would disintegrate. Anyway, I knew the consequences of skipping school. He'd made sure of that.

"Can you roll this for me, sweetie? My nails are drying." Chloe handed me the gold tray piled high with weed.

"Of course you can't roll this, girl. It's filled with stems and beaners." I rolled my eyes at him.

"Well, it's a new bag. Will you clean it for me, baby? Please."

"Fine!" I picked through the sticky green pile.

He returned to the bathroom to do his hair, which presently was dyed red and orange and yellow, like a big flame burning on top of his head. Chloe's surprise for me turned out to be that he was dedicating a drag performance to me. I'd never seen him perform, so I was superexcited. I was also quite nervous because I had never been to a gay bar before and he was planning on sneaking me in. Of course, Chloe assured me that it was a guarantee I could get in if I was with him. But I was still pretty scared. I pictured a black dance floor, strobe light, and half-naked men groping each other, worried that while I was there I might get drugged or raped or something terrible. Or else maybe I'd meet some other gay guy my age who'd also snuck into the bar and we'd fall madly in love and I wouldn't have to worry about the stress of being single anymore. I'd been dressing fabulous for over a month, and I felt like I should've at least gotten laid by now. Chloe said it takes practice if you want to pick up a guy. When I asked him if a guy would pick *me* up, he said I was so young and pretty, I'd scare guys off. Except for the old weirdos who loved young boys. I wasn't feeling very reassured.

It took me about five minutes to roll the perfect joint, as smooth and fat as a cigarette. I was quite impressed with it. How did I become such a pro at rolling joints? I wondered. It reminded me of Sam. She was the first person I'd ever smoked pot with. Back during the summer after eighth grade, when we were dating. She'd only done it a couple of times, but assured me that smoking pot was the coolest thing *ever*. And she was right. I bought the dime bag myself from this supercute Latino boy at her school, South High. He was a senior and a raver and wore phat pants and had wallet chains that hung down to his knee. His name was Jake. Only Sam had introduced him as Jake the Snake, and now I couldn't call him anything else.

We took the pot into her garage, where we smoked out of an empty Coke can. Neither of us knew how much to take, so we just smoked it all, nervously grinning, scared that her mom's boyfriend, Todd, would burst in on us at any moment. After we had smoked the whole bag, we lit a cigarette and shared that, looking at the truck, the lawn tools hanging on the wall, waiting for it to affect us. I still felt normal, though. I was worried that it hadn't worked on me.

As soon as we were out in her sunny backyard, Sam was laughing her ass off and twirling in circles, saying, "I see bubbles in the air!" She said she'd never been so fucked up. I said I'd never been so sober and that she was just seeing bubbles because she was insane. But as soon as I lit a cigarette, the weed hit me. And it was intense! I had never laughed so hard in my life. We ran down her alley, side by side, trying not to laugh but having no control. I felt like I was a robot walking through a swamp. My brain was boiling water, my skin emerged in a steaming bath. Sam and I roamed the city all day long, wishing it would never end. I wondered how I'd lived so long without ever experiencing this kind of thrilling, silly, incomprehensible, close-to-God rush.

I didn't tell anyone at school about it. Instead I began to socialize exclusively with our foursome from South High: Sam, Sean, and Alex. Aside from smoking tons of pot, we did acid and 'shrooms together. We'd trip and go downtown, or to Minnehaha Falls, or down by the Mississippi River. Sometimes we would just trip in Sean's basement, where we could freak ourselves out playing the Ouija board and looking at Sam's books on mysticism. Occasionally we'd take too much acid and just lie on our backs and listen to the Beatles, thrilled beyond imagination, purely in love with one another, yet unable to communicate with each other whatsoever, like a harmonious vegetable garden.

I lit my perfectly rolled joint with Chloe's mermaid lighter and brought it into the bathroom, where he was spiking his hair in front of the mirror. I asked him what song he was doing for his drag performance, but he wouldn't tell me. He said it was part of the surprise. "So you won't even give me a clue?" I begged.

"Nope."

"C'mon."

"Sorry."

"Well where's your costume then?"

"In that bag." He pointed to a plastic Target bag mashed between the sink and toilet.

"Won't it get all wrinkled?"

"Not this costume, baby . . . and don't even think I'm not keeping my eye on you. You best not peek inside."

"When are we leaving?"

"Ten more minutes. Christ, you're impatient as a child. Scram!" He shooed me away.

"Whatever, sweetie." I sulked back to the living room and crashed onto the futon. I just wanted to get the night over with.

"What, are you nervous or something?"

"*No.*"

"I'm sure you'll have a blast. I'm like, the funnest person at the bar. I'll introduce you to all my little darlings, and we'll dance all night."

I didn't say anything, but I was pretty sure I didn't want to meet all his little darlings and dance in front of them.

"You know," he began reminiscently, "I didn't go to my first gay bar until I was eighteen . . . My friend Theresa and I drove to the Smiling Buck in Wisconsin with our brand-new fake IDs we got from her cousin for a hundred dollars. I was as Billy Idol slash Boy George as it gets—all the essential eighties punk accessories. And I was of course even more androgynous then. A big flamer from day one," he declared, giggling at his reflection. I just listened nervously, smoking more pot than I should have. "Did I ever tell you about the time I met Babs Arlington? Believe it or not, it was in the men's bathroom at Screwdriver. I was wearing my best outfit yet, hair teased down to my shoulders. I was with my boyfriend at the time, Jack, my polar opposite. He was peeing while I reapplied eye makeup. Then suddenly Babs runs in, looking like Diana Ross in *Mahogany,* tears and makeup smeared everywhere from laughing. She looked back and forth at us in shock, then gasped and screamed, 'The men's room!' and laughed hysterically. Then she drunkenly stumbled over to me, swung an arm around my neck, and declared: 'Girl, you're gonna make one fierce drag queen!' I didn't know what to say, except 'Me?' and she said, 'Yeah, you. I've seen you tearin' it up on the dance floor and singing along to Annie. You're fabulous! We just need to get you a pink feather boa and some falsies, and you'll be rippin' the hearts out'a all them queens and dykes on my stage, baby!' Babs and I were instantly friends, just like me and you. I can't wait until you meet her! Okay, I'm ready." Chloe walked out of the bathroom. He was now wearing the brightest red lipstick I'd ever seen.

I laughed. "You're gonna pick up a trick at the bus stop looking like that, you know."

"Which is why I already called us a cab, Miss Thing. My hoochie-mama ass is looking out for herself, ah-right."

I could already see Chloe's outrageous personality doubling with every layer of makeup he applied. I wondered how wild he would get when he was actually wearing a dress, when Chloe became a "she." He told me that he used to perform every weekend, but now he only did it once a month or so because it was just too much work. It took a whole day just getting into costume when he played certain characters. And lip-synching is much harder than any one who's never done it might think. You had to look like you were singing at the top of your lungs without totally fucking up and looking like a junkie telling the truth. And the choreography, the organizing, and the costume design were all overwhelming.

The cab honked three times before we got outside. It was a Rainbow cab and the driver looked Middle Eastern. Chloe said that only the foreign drivers ever came into his neighborhood because they didn't know any better and needed the fare.

The ride to Screwdriver seemed to take forever, but we didn't speak the whole time. We were both getting mentally prepared for the evening to come. I was taken aback to see that Chloe was anxious, too. He always seemed so cool and confident, like nothing could dent his ego. And he would never, ever cry. Meanwhile I always bawled my head off for no reason.

When we pulled up to Screwdriver, my jaw dropped at seeing the line of people waiting to get in. They were mostly butch men and black drag queens. Some of the guys wore Gap jeans, T-shirts, and Doc Martens shoes. Some had on fancy slacks and dress shirts. Others were dressed in tight-fitting club outfits, and leather—lots of black leather.

Chloe gave the driver six dollars and told him to keep the

change. I stuck close to Chloe's side as we headed for the door. Instead of stopping at the end of the line, we walked straight up to the front.

"Miss Chloe!" The tall, muscular, gray-haired bouncer greeted him in a surprisingly gentle voice.

"Hey, Bubba." Chloe squeezed against his big belly for a hug.

"You look like a piece of candy, girl, what's up with that? Are *you* performing tonight?" he asked with a wide grin.

"Yes. I *am* the evening's entertainment." Chloe was blinking his long lashes and gripping the bouncer's big ball of a hand flirtatiously. "This is my makeup assistant, Erick," he said, shoving the bag that held his costume into my arms. "You'll treat him nice, won't you, big daddy?"

Bubba looked at me, then my crotch, and chuckled. "He should get along just fine." The man wet his big gray lips.

"So you gonna be watchin' me onstage?" Chloe asked him.

"I wouldn't miss it." He grazed his hand over Chloe's chest.

Chloe giggled and held his hand for a moment. "I'll see you inside, then." He took my hand and led me in.

There was a skinny guy sitting in a booth collecting money and stamping hands. He looked at underage me, then over to Chloe. But he didn't ask for my ID. "Four bucks," was all he said.

"Don't worry, Buzz, baby, he's with me."

"Sorry, Chloe."

"Don't worry about it," I spoke up, pulling crinkled bills out of my pocket. I flattened them out on my thigh and handed Buzz four of them. He stamped my hand "Under 21" in red ink. Then we walked through the entrance and into the bar.

It was like walking into a cave. My eyes had to adjust to the blackness. Then, all at once, the strobe light and pulsating dance beat brought me there. It was finally real—I was in a gay bar! The first thing I noticed was that the dance floor was packed with people jumping around and grinding bodies against each other. I surveyed the room, not sure where to set my eyes. The black walls had neon spray paint all over them and they glowed in the strobe light. Multicolored lights came on and off in synch with the beat of the music. The bass shook the floor. For some reason it reminded me of a funhouse at an amusement park. We circled around the dance floor, squeezing our bodies through the crowd of flexed, sweaty muscles. Chloe was only inches in front of me, and I kept my eyes on his butt, afraid to look at anyone. It was hot in there, so many of the men weren't wearing shirts. Some had pierced nipples and tattoos.

"Do you want to dance for a while?" Chloe asked, turning around to face me.

"I dunno . . . No." There was no way I was going to run out there and make an ass of myself unless I got drunk or something. I think all the pot I had smoked earlier was making me self-conscious, because suddenly I wanted to leave.

Luckily, Chloe didn't force me to dance, as I could easily imagine him doing. Instead he led me to the back staircase, which took us up to the drag lounge. Sade was blasting, and I came to see that a drag queen was on the stage lip-synching and dancing to it. She was wearing a black sequined dress and matching feather boa. With broad shoulders and Adam's apple, it was obvious that she was actually a man, but the audience seemed to love it anyway. Men, wearing mostly jeans and T-shirts, were sitting at tables, drinking cocktails while whooping and hooting at her. Some were putting dollars in her garter and down the front of her dress.

It seemed like everyone knew Chloe. First I met this skinny guy whose zits seemed to multiply under the black light. "Buzz off, Tom," Chloe said. Chloe could be such an amazing bitch when he wanted to be! As the guy sulked off, he explained that it was imperative that we avoid the perverts unless we wanted a reputation. When Chloe saw that this concerned me, he assured me that he knew who all the perverts were and he would warn me, so that in no time I, too, would be able to spot a pervert from across the dance floor.

Next, identical twins ran up to Chloe and, after hugs and introductions, engaged us in a conversation about someone named Todd, who had cheated on Alex after taking Ecstasy and running naked across Hennepin Avenue. Todd was piss-drunk again tonight and now he was making out with some Derrick kid from Wisconsin who drove three and a half hours every weekend to come to Screwdriver. Then Terry joined us and talked about how he was doing the fishbowl contest tonight because he was wearing his new thong. He showed everyone his ass, which was small and tan and jiggled when it popped out of his pants. By the time he pulled his pants back up I was beginning to get turned on. Terry was superhot. I tried to flirt with him, but unfortunately he never made eye contact. Chloe saw that I was being rejected and explained subtly that some guys only flirted with their own reflections. Unfortunately, that made me want Terry even more!

Soon more people joined us, and I was completely lost in the crossfire of conversation. I didn't really care what anyone had to say anyway. Between the loud music and the visuals, I was already feeling sensory overload. I just kept thinking how real it all was and how I was *finally* doing something with my life.

After I had met about a hundred darlings, Chloe led me backstage to the drag queens' dressing room. The salmon-colored room was packed with drag queens getting dolled up in front of vanities with mirrors that were smooched with lipstick.

"Well, look who it is, girls! Miss Chloe!" came a thunderous southern accent. All at once the roomful of drag queens turned to check us out. Then out of the crowd came the drag queen who had announced our arrival. She was black, had gnarly shoulder-length hair, wore a lime green smock, and had pink glasses that covered half her face; they were lined with fake, sparkling diamonds.

"Babs Arlington!" Chloe greeted her with a hug. "It's wonderful to see you." After embracing they stared, almost disbelieving, at each other as though they were displaced sisters uniting after some war—to the shock that each had changed her name and hair color.

Babs turned to me, put her hand on my chest, and said, "It's *Ms.* Babs Arlington, honey, but you, my dear, will call me Madam Arlington."

"Okay," I said.

"Chloe, darling, where ever did you find this dazzling twink?" she asked, sliding her hands all over my body.

"You keep your hands to yourself, girl. Erick's with me." Chloe cocked his head and puckered, then said with attitude, *"Okay?"*

Madam Arlington pinched my cheek like some crazy auntie and said to Chloe, "It's not nice to keep a cute one like this from your friends, dear."

"Whoever said you were my friend?" Chloe asked, obviously not making a serious insult.

"Touchy."

"You're just too strong a woman for me," I said, lifting her hand gently off my stomach.

"Ooooh, he talks cute, too."

Chloe laughed. "C'mon, girl," he said, grabbing my hand and taking me to the mirror. Prince was playing from a big silver boom box covered in glitter, *"I Would Die 4 U . . . Darling if you want me to."* I sat on a little stool next to Chloe. He began to fuss with himself in the mirror, tinting his face with heavy makeup.

I wanted to say something, so even though I already knew the answer, I asked, "When do you go on?"

Chloe told me in half an hour, adding, "Now that you've met the girls, you'll have to go watch the show while I get ready."

"By myself?" I whispered.

"Go downstairs and pick up a guy like you wanted to, silly."

"I can't."

"Good, 'cause I was just kidding. You're with me tonight, alright?"

"Okay."

"Go sit out in the audience and watch the show and wait for me. And if anyone bothers you, tell me and I'll shove a stiletto up his ass."

"Okay," I said, standing up and heading for the door. "Break a leg," I added, then burst into guffaws for no apparent reason. I'm sure I sounded like the biggest airhead ever.

When I got to an empty seat I immediately lit a cigarette, putting my feet on the bar across the bottom of the chair in front of me. I looked at all the men surrounding me, hoping to spot the eyes of my future boyfriend. But no one seemed to notice me, maybe because the show grabbed their attention instead. The drag queen on stage was coming to the end of some show tune and shaking her plastic tits to the big-band finale. She smiled widely, holding a gloved fist full of cash. I wondered how much money a drag queen made in a night—did they perform more than one song?

Once the music cut out and the drag queen had waltzed off-stage, Babs Arlington strutted out with a catlike walk. She shouted into her microphone, "Give it up, everyone, for the fabulous Miss Dueshka! I don't know about you boys, but I can say for myself that I think she is *purrr-ty* amazing. I wouldn't mind joining that one for a Technicolor encounter!" She flung glitter onto the crowd, laughing, and making the audience laugh. I realized she was the comic host, introducing each performer. "You know what I love about Minneapolis?" she asked.

"What?" the audience screamed.

"It's so *fucking* gay! Just the other day I was at my bank, and you know what I saw? They had stuck a pink triangle right on the glass door. I thought to myself, we've come a long way when a conventional institution like Twin Cities Federal comes out of the closet! But then I thought maybe it was just marketing to the people who had the most money. Lately I've been sucking some rich cock, let me tell you. Fags these days sure do have money to spend. Who else would pay two hundred dollars for a wallet, right? All this Gucci and Prada and Dolce & Gabanna. You know it's for the fags! Th'ain't no breeders out there who care about that shit. They squander all their money on groceries and diapers and all that other bullshit. Fags know better though, right? Now, let me ask y'all to raise your hand if you're wearing designer tonight." Everyone raised their hands. "Well, damn!" Babs acted surprised. "Okay, now everyone with their hand up form a line right here and come give me my tip!"

As people laughed, a man in the audience screamed, "I love you, Babs!"

"Well, now what the hell do we have here?" Babs asked. "Why don't you come up here and give me some cash then!"

The man walked up to the stage to applause, his face red from excitement. Clearly he was drunk. He reached in his wallet and handed Babs a bill.

"Oooh, five dollars," she teased. The man whispered something. "Oh, that's all you have? Well, too bad for you, honey"— Babs turned away—"I'm looking for a fifty! I need to get my ass waxed!" She slapped her sequined ass. "Anyone out there got fifty bucks?" No one said a thing. "C'mon now. Just because the gay community is a family doesn't mean we gotta act stingy and bitchy all the time. We need to share the wealth!" Still, no one volunteered. "Cheap bastards!" Babs declared. "What's a girl to do? My callused knees can't take one more night on that men's room floor!" she declared, miming a blowjob to the delight and cheers of the audience. "Damn, I'm a whore . . . And speaking of whores, you know what time it is? It's time for *fishbowl*." Once again the audience lost control. "For anyone new out there who's never seen a fishbowl, it's where members of the audience come onstage and make fools of themselves for tips. And here's a hint: Skin sells! So do I have any volunteers?"

Several men raised their hands immediately, and Babs made selections. Soon men were formed in a line across the stage. I noticed that, as promised, Terry was one of them. He was by far the hottest of them, too, and it was clear that he knew it. Some of the contestants were not very attractive at all, and when Babs had them state their names into the microphone one at a time, the audience made their favorites known with boos and cheers. The music started and before I knew it, everyone on stage was stripping with Babs running around showcasing them. Between hard bodies gyrating, flabby bodies giggling, and Babs Arlington's flamboyancy, it was the biggest spectacle I had ever seen. But the real hoopla began once Terry was down to his G-string. He completely stole the show thrusting his black fabric-encased erection. Soon lines formed to tip him and cop a feel. I began to think that maybe I, too, should be a stripper. If I buffed up just a bit, I could really rake in the cash. Admittedly, the thought of men paying to see my sexy body made me horny.

Then I noticed a man my dad's age eyeing me, nearly drooling. I looked away quickly because I didn't want him to come over and talk to me. He had leathery tan skin and a mustache. Before I could think of what to do next though, his finger tapped my shoulder. I turned around and half-smiled, keeping my lips sealed.

"Hey, how are you?" Like he knew who I was.

"Fine."

"What's your name?"

"Erick."

"Hi, Erick, I'm Paul."

"Hi."

"So, are you here with anyone?"

"Yeah, my friend Chloe's a drag queen. She's about to perform."

"Really? Cool."

"Yeah, she's supercool."

"Have you ever been to Hawaii?"

"No."

"That's where I'm from—Hawaii. I just moved here a couple months ago for business reasons . . . I'm in advertising."

"Wow," I said, just to be nice.

"Yeah, it's pretty cool."

I really didn't care what he did for a living. His breath smelled like booze.

"So do you come here a lot?"

"Not really." I blew cigarette smoke at him.

He pretended not to notice my hint. "So do you like to dance?"

"No."

"How come? Do you need someone to teach you how?"

That made me smile, just because his presumptions were so outrageous. "I'm just not in the mood."

"Well if you change your mind, I'll be sitting right over there." He pointed to his chair.

"Alright."

He stood there for moment, waiting for me to change my mind. When I turned back to the stage, he finally left. What a creep! It was pretty obvious that I wasn't more than nineteen or so, at the very most. I wondered how many other boys my age he had tried to pick up, and what would've happened if I'd left with him. He probably would've taken me to some fancy condo and tried to get me into bed. I was pretty sure that was how it worked. Maybe I'd become a hooker. But I wasn't sure if I could be that slutty. I didn't really want anyone outside of my age bracket, anyway. Only the young ones turned me. That made me a little concerned, though, because what if I turned forty and was single and creepy and had to buy hookers? That would be too depressing.

"Well, folks, there you have it. Tonight's fishbowl winner is Terry!" Babs announced to thunderous applause. Terry, holding his balled-up clothes and wad of cash, smiled wildly. "Smell ya later!" Babs said, firmly smacking one of his slick butt-cheeks and making him wince as he scurried off the stage.

Pleased with herself, Babs turned back to the audience and declared, "Our next performer is a young veteran of our stage, here to perform after almost two months of lapsed time. I wonder what made her take such a long leave? Either a boyfriend or a prison sentence, I'd imagine. With oodles of talent and a body to cream over, here she is, with a rather *unusual* piece tonight. Miss Chloeeeee!"

I recognized the song immediately, and I couldn't believe Chloe was actually going to perform to Michael Jackson's "Billie Jean"! Suddenly Chloe came out onstage—moonwalking! He wore dark makeup, a wig, Michael's trademark red vinyl jacket, and even one silver glove. He had all the perfect dance moves. He looked just like Michael, only cute. *"Billie Jean is not my lover / She's just a girl who claims that I am the one / But the kid is not my son."* It was so cool! Even the other drag queens came out into the audience to cheer for the best performer of the night. Chloe was by far the most stunning dancer of them all!

On the last beat of the song, he grabbed his crotch with his left hand as his right arm shot triumphantly into the air. The audience went ballistic. Then Chloe ran off the stage to where I was sitting, laughing with excitement and shoving dollars into his pockets. "What'd ya think?"

"You were great!" I was mesmerized by my friend's coolness. "I thought drag queens all did women, though."

"Exactly!" Chloe laughed. "You wanna go downstairs and dance?"

"Sure." Nothing scared me when I was with Chloe, and we danced till closing time.

{ six }

All I wanted to be in sixth grade was a female rock star. Whenever I was at the piano, I was Cindy, Madonna, Debbie, or Annie. I wore costumes consisting of pajamas, sheets, my mother's one-inch heels, jewelry she never wore, and enough imagination to turn them into the costumes I saw my favorite singers wear on MTV. When I played ballads, my fingers danced across the keys as I sang, eyes closed, pretending to cry to the emotional songs I was crooning. Then I would turn to fast, angry songs, pounding on chords, riding the bench, and crying out the music as loud as I could. That piano was my only release from sexual, violent, scary thoughts.

At some point, I would get so loud, so out of control, that my mother would awake from her Tommy Trance. "Stop that loud nonsense!" she yelled. "You're playing crazy." Instantly, I would release the keys, my hands shaking, take a breath, and play classical: Bach, Mozart, Beethoven, from my intermediate lesson book—perfectly. That made her happy again. Sometimes she'd say things like "You're getting pretty good, you know, but you need more grace in the left and you need more wrist in your two-note slurs. Let's hear from the first repeat—just the first eight measures." I'd follow her instructions, always improving on my original attempt, which impressed both of us. She told me if I kept it up I might lead the choir. I wished I'd taken her advice.

Dinner was always ready when my dad got home. We would sit at the kitchen table with the empty chair, and pray, sort of, with the rehearsed lines Dad would say. They went something like: "Father, bless this food and this family. Give us the strength and will to survive, Lord, so that we can share in your glory, now and forever, blah, blah, blah. Amen." Then my mother would add a brief Bible quote, and we would eat with the TV in the living room visible from the table. It was always prime-time family sitcoms.

I was in seventh grade when they told me they were adopting Tim. They walked into my bedroom, hand in hand, glowing. I hadn't seen them hold hands since Disneyland. I was sure we had won the lottery or something, but instead they told me that they had a tape of a little boy in Argentina who they were adopting. I couldn't believe it. This was even better than the lottery. I had been begging them to adopt a kid, but I never thought they would. We watched the video together, with Mom leaning on Dad and me leaning on Mom, our arms wrapped around each other. The tape showed us fifteen minutes of the cutest child ever, playing with toys in his foster home in Argentina. He was fourteen months old, had light brown skin, wispy curls, and big black Os for eyes. The women in the video were calling his attention to the camera: "Timotee?" they would say in Spanish. He answered them with drools and giggles and complete gibberish. Every toy they gave him made him smile and laugh like crazy, and after spending only seconds on it, he'd throw it aside and grab the next.

I watched the video five times at least. Our new baby seemed like the answer to everything. I felt like I would never be lonely again, like I would get a second chance. I was determined that when Tim arrived, I would be the best brother ever. I wouldn't be jealous or mean, like I had been to Tommy. I would make sure he grew up happy to be in my family.

When he arrived two months later, everything changed. My mother was no longer distant, so removed from reality. For the first time in years, she began to act like a mom again. Now, with my little brother back from the dead, we were a family again. We stopped watching television during dinnertime and instead had conversations about our day. We talked about what we wanted to do on the weekends, which included trips to the zoo, popcorn video nights and, once, a camping-and-fishing trip. We got eaten alive by mosquitoes and were caught in such a bad storm that we had to sleep in the car. But that wasn't the point. The point was that we were normal again. And for me, having a "normal" family was bliss.

Of course, there were new things about my mom that drove me insane. Suddenly, she became very controlling, insisting that we go to church, that I did my homework, cleaned my room, washed dishes, and went to bed on time. She was also very protective of Tim. She wouldn't let him out of her sight. I wasn't allowed to take him to the park, or even into my bedroom without her there with us. Plus, she got mad at me for everything I did, including stuff that wasn't bad. Like, every time I rode in someone else's car, she'd freak. Mom always got scared that whoever I was with would crash and I'd be killed. Also she accused me constantly of being a bad influence, because I taught Tim lines from Madonna songs, and expressions like "What's up?" "Hey, sexy baby," and "Who's your daddy?" I liked to throw him up in the air and spin him around and tickle him. Once he landed on his head when we were roughhousing, and she grounded me for a week. I felt like I was a burden to her. Like I was such a terrible kid that there was no redemption.

Eventually my mother and I ceased to get along entirely, and it seemed that fights broke out between us daily. Sometimes our fights got so bad that she would grab me by my arm with her pinch-and-twist gesture that made my arm throb for hours. When I tried to push her away, she would slap me. In tears, I would scream that I hated her guts. During these outbursts, my dad and Tim usually left the room, refusing to get involved. I decided that my dad had no backbone if he could just sit back and let her hurt me. I figured he must be the worst psychiatrist ever.

When I started eighth grade, I realized quickly that it would be my year of utter disappointment. Not only had adopting Tim failed to resolve the issues between my parents and me, but also Andy Flynn transferred out of St. John's, and Justin Hankshaw, the most menacing character I had ever met in my life, transferred in. He came to St. John's from public school, so he knew all about rap music and was popular right away. During church he never went to take Communion because he wasn't even Catholic. His parents enrolled him only because he was such an awful brat that they wanted him to be disciplined. He bragged that when he went to public school his teachers were all afraid of him and he called them "bitches" to their faces. That made me afraid of him, too. And he must have known this, because I was his main target of harassment.

He was cruelest to me when we were in art class, the only class I liked. Everyone knew that I was the best artist in our class. I had been praised for my skill, until he came along and decided that drawing was for faggots. Soon everyone agreed that drawing was indeed for faggots, and I started spending class alone in the supply room. Then one day I got kicked out of art class for vandalizing supplies with graffiti since that was the only type of art Justin deemed acceptable for boys. That's when I gave up drawing and started spending my sixth hour in detention with Brother Luke.

The only thing that saved me from killing myself that year was Tori Amos. I had always been a lover of all kinds of music and had spent my allowances on CDs, but when I discovered Tori, it took my appreciation for music to another level. The first time I heard her, I was at a Sam Goody in Mall of America, where I was looking through the singles for the theme song to the movie *Pretty in Pink* In the background I heard her song "Baker Baker." I was instantly mesmerized. Usually, I have to hear a Tori song a few dozen times before I absolutely love it, but this song was pure ecstasy from the start. It told the story of my life, and by the time the song was over, I had forgotten what I was even doing there. I asked the clerk who had just been played. Her eyes lit up. "Isn't she amazing?" she said. "Here." She handed me a CD called *Under the Pink,* and I was like, "Oh my God, I came here to buy *Pretty in Pink,* but I think I'll get this one instead." Turns out it was way darker, and now Tori Amos is the only music I listen to.

"What do you mean you're not coming home?" my mother asked. I had called her from Chloe's bathroom to tell her that I was staying the night at Sean's house for the third night in a row.

"Mom," I groaned. "School's over. It's summer vacation. What's the big deal?"

"The big deal is that you're only sixteen years old. We don't even know what you do when you're gone . . . Besides, what's so terrible about spending an evening or two with your family?"

"Well, for one, you guys are insane, and it's depressing to hang out with crazy people all the time." As soon as I said it, I knew that I had crossed the line.

"*You're* the one who's insane, if you think you can get away with talking to me like this! I've never heard of such a disrespectful son."

"Oh, God, give me a break."

"There you go again! What are you going to say in your defense on your day of judgment?"

"I have to let you go, Mom. Sean and I are going to a movie."

"What's his number?"

"Why do you need his number?"

"In case of an emergency."

"What could possibly happen?" I asked, even though as long as she had a driver's license, that was the dumbest question ever. I didn't wait for her to answer. Instead, I gave her Sam's number, figuring that I'd just have to ask her to cover for me. My mom continued to ramble at me about responsibility for an eternity. Then, finally, after she was satisfied with her demonstration of insanity, our conversation ended.

"That bad?" Chloe said when I returned to the living room.

"You heard?"

"It's a studio," he responded, as if that explained everything. "Are you ready?"

"Yeah." I checked myself in the mirror one last time to make sure I hadn't smeared my eyeliner or smashed down my blond spikes. "It's bar time, baby!"

Once school had finally gotten out for summer vacation, going to the bar became a weekly event. Normally, they were strict about IDing people. But after a while, my face became well known, and everyone just assumed I was of legal age. I could have probably gotten in even without Chloe. The bouncer, Bubba, called me "jailbait" whenever he saw me. We spent most evenings dancing and attending occasional drag performances. Chloe hadn't done any performing since that first night. But even though he wasn't doing himself up like a woman (or Michael Jackson) he still dressed fierce. It was the late '90s, and the '70s styles were everywhere. All the designers were bringing back bell-bottoms; only this time around they were "flared," and everything had a vogue code of techno colors. I always wore my platforms because walking in them made me feel like a supermodel on a runway. Tall, flawless posture and balance, my strut flirting with everyone I passed. With help from Chloe, I redefined my dance moves, learned how to flaunt my package and make my styled hair look undone. I was also improving my cruising technique, meaning I didn't turn red immediately when a hot guy smiled at me. Sometimes I had the fierceness to smile back. I was a kid surfing the rhythms of dance music in a sea of grown men that had careers and cars and apartments. It was only a matter of time before I would be such a diva that with one fiery look, I could make him turn away in shame or fall desperately in love.

Only once, though, did I go home with a guy. I met him at the club one night while dancing by myself, since Chloe was too busy making out with some guy in brown leather cowboy pants to dance with me. I didn't even know where they had disappeared to, which made me superpissed. Sometimes being friends with Chloe was like a slap in the face. Just when I was about to go up to the drag lounge to look for them, a skinny guy with a butterfly-collar shirt and rings on his fingers approached me with a sly grin to say his name was Troy. He told me I was a great dancer. I didn't know how to respond. I had noticed him dancing, too. Of course, I noticed *all* the men dancing. So, with nothing to say, we danced, partners on the floor, staring at only each other and smiling. After a while, we left together.

We hopped into Troy's Saab, and as he drove, Troy made unfunny comments, which he thought were witty, about the radio, then made me laugh at a story about his retarded sister, which wasn't meant to be funny. I didn't even know what he was talking about. I was too excited and nervous and ready—finally, after all this time of waiting for Chloe to come around—to lose my virginity. By the time we got to his apartment, however, I was scared that I couldn't go through with it. He showed me around his place, expecting me to admire his retro furniture, which was bright orange, brown, and gold against white, sterile surroundings.

He took me into his living room, where we sat on his Jetsons' sofa. Then he pulled a tiny baggie out of his pocket. "Do you do coke?" he asked.

I had never done coke in my life. But since I've never been opposed to experimenting with new drugs, I said, "Yeah."

"Good," he replied with a slow drawl and sly grin. He dumped a portion of the bag onto the glass coffee table and proceeded to cut lines with the edge of a Visa gold card. He made two lines (each the size of a joint) then handed me a plastic tube to snort it with.

I tried to keep my cool, but I was so nervous. Those lines looked huge to me. I didn't think I could even get it all in my nose. I wished he would go first so I could watch how it's done. But I couldn't ask because I didn't want him to find out I was a novice. Instead I thanked him and said a little prayer that I wouldn't overdose or that Troy wasn't a serial killer that was tricking me into inhaling rat poison. I leaned forward and snorted the line. Although I didn't make a sound, inside I was screaming. It felt like I had accidentally inhaled a gallon of swimming-pool water.

"Good," Troy said, bending forward to snort his line. Meanwhile, I frantically wiped away tears.

"Can I smoke in here?" I asked, just to be polite.

"Sure," he said, reaching for his own pack of cigarettes. "That's good shit, ain't it?"

"Yeah," I answered, even though I wasn't feeling any sort of high—just snot running down the back of my throat. I couldn't help but sniffle repeatedly. It was like I had a cold, but no tissues to blow my nose.

"You're cute." He put his arm around me. "How old are you?"

"Twenty," I lied. I don't know why I lied. I wasn't feeling sexy. Suddenly I felt really stoned, or maybe just paranoid. The apartment seemed unreal. *He* seemed unreal. I wondered if the rest of his life was as fake as his apartment.

After we finished our cigarettes he took my hand and led me

into his bedroom. We immediately started kissing on his bed—I was kissing my brains out because I didn't know what the hell else to do. All I thought about was, does he know I'm only sixteen? After my face was all wet from his kisses he climbed on top of me, and took off his shirt. It was the first hairy chest I'd ever touched, and it intimidated me. The dark spirals were thick and rough and covered his entire chest and stomach so that only his pale purple nipples were showing. I couldn't get hard when he took off his clothes—or when he took off my clothes—and started sucking my limp dick. I was embarrassed beyond words. It was the exact same thing that had happened to me when I was dating Sam. I completely blamed myself, thinking that there was obviously something wrong with me that made me impotent with real people. Troy was frustrated by it, too. He asked what he should do. I told him that I didn't know. I was so humiliated by my own body that I pulled the blanket between us and told him that I needed to go home. That pissed him off. He said he would have stayed at the bar if he had known this was going to happen. When he asked why I had to leave so soon, I told him reluctantly that I was only sixteen and had a curfew. By his reaction, you would have thought I'd said I had the Ebola virus. He became so paranoid and angry that I thought he might kill me. I apologized again and again while he dressed, but Troy ignored me and stormed out of the room. I found my clothes on his floor and dressed quickly. When I entered the living room, he was on the phone.

"Where do you live?" he asked me.

"Stevens." Which is where Chloe lived. Troy narrowed his eyes but didn't question my lie. He hung up the phone and said my taxi was on its way. I was told to wait outside so I wouldn't miss it. That's when I began to cry.

"Why the fuck are you crying?" he asked.

"I'm not." I wiped back the tears. I felt like such a major loser. Why was I such a crybaby? "I don't have any money," I told him.

"Figures," he said bitterly. He reached into his wallet and handed me a ten-dollar bill.

Waiting outside for my cab, I felt offended and angry and helpless. I lit a cigarette. "Fucking asshole!" I said out loud. I wished now that I had stood up for myself. I really should have said something like "I might have lied and said I was twenty, but at least I don't look like I'm seventy." Troy's body was disgusting. The least he could do was wax his chest or something. Yuck! I would have puked if I had lost my virginity to him.

I had gone over the traumatic event a thousand times by the time I got home. I decided right then that I would never again let a man pick me up at the bar—at least not some supercreep who drove a fucking Saab and saw *Saturday Night Fever* in the movie theater when it premiered in the '70s.

"Where were you?" Chloe asked as soon as I walked in.

"I'm sorry, Chloe." I felt disgraced. "I met a guy and we made out and he took me home. And I don't want to talk about it."

"Well!" Arms crossed sternly. "First you better explain to me why you didn't tell me you were leaving. I *am* pissed." Then light-heartedly: "And you better tell me every detail of that make-out story." With the last comment, I knew he wasn't mad. After I told him a make-believe version of what happened, in which everything was hunky-dory, I found out Chloe had just gotten home after having made out with his brown-leather cowboy until the music stopped. We celebrated both getting our mack on with white zinfandel, facials, and a dress-up session, dancing around in piles of men's and women's clothes.

Finally, it was time for bed. I crawled under the covers, wearing only boxers and my fabulous "Porn Star" T-shirt. Chloe stripped down to his boxers in the dark and crawled in next to me. He always slept on his side, back facing me. I stayed awake, watching his bare back rise and fall with each breath he took. I wondered if he was already asleep. I wanted to tell him I loved him, but I couldn't bring myself to say those words. What if he didn't answer me? I'd have to move out because I'd be too ashamed even to look at him. My boner (finally!) was throbbing so hard that I couldn't lay still. We laid so close together that I could feel the heat from his body. We slept like this every night, and every night I lay awake wanting to put my arm around him. But we never touched, not even by accident. I knew I wasn't what Chloe wanted in a boyfriend, and I couldn't risk losing him by throwing myself at him. If I stopped selling sunglasses and going shopping with him, I wouldn't know what to do with my life.

With Chloe I was the happiest I'd ever been in my life. When we walked around Uptown together, everyone wanted to be us. We were practically famous. We even had our very own group of fans! They were three girls who always hung out at the Starbucks across from our store. Molly, the one that worked there, smoked pot in the back room. So sometimes after the mall closed we would go to Starbucks and smoke with her. She always played Violent Fems or Beastie Boys on the boom box, and she made us Frappuccinos for free. Like every other girl on earth, of course she worshiped Chloe. To everyone else, though, even her friends, she was a total bitch. Molly was one of those people that would trade in all her old friends for all new ones, then complain about having to learn all their names. Chloe didn't like her very much, actually. Of course in her presence he was always his extremely outgoing, funny, courteous self. Usually the people he didn't like still liked him.

More than anything, Molly knew how to throw a party. One of the funnest took place that summer at her high-rise apartment building. Her boyfriend, Bob, spoiled her with lots of luxury. They paid off the security guard to let us use the pool after hours. We blasted techno, got drunk on wine, and smoked pot in the pool room. All the girls from the mall were there with their hot boyfriends. With cocktails and cigarettes, Chloe and I sat by the pool, watching the straight boys go diving off the board. We got totally plowed and, not caring that they were straight, we started cheering along with the girls when the boys dove. They must not have cared either, because they were laughing along with us. They struck sexy poses on the board, flashing us their big dicks just to show off. I was so drunk after taking Jell-O shots that I nearly drowned in the pool. I don't remember exactly what happened after that, but I do know for sure that at some point several of the hottest guys took off their swimsuits and swam naked. I realized that I seriously needed to get properly laid.

I asked Chloe, "Do you think being gay will ever be cooler than being straight? Like straight people will wish they were gay?"

"Huh?" We were at work, and had been for five hours. "Why do you ask that?"

"Because this has been my best summer of my life, and I know it's because suddenly I'm out and I'm so much cooler than ever before. I mean, I certainly *look* cooler than ever before. I used to hate people staring at me, but now I love it because they're finally seeing what I want them to see."

Chloe laughed uncontrollably. I was kind of embarrassed. By the time he stopped, I wished I'd never said anything. "What's so funny?" I asked.

"Nothing! You're just such a *queen,* that's all," he said, shaking his head with a smile.

"What eva', bitch." I snapped my fingers across my face and did my best impression of ghetto fabulousness.

"I can't believe I've only known you for three months!" Chloe laughed. "You've changed so much it's crazy."

I proudly vogued for him.

"You know, I never told you, but I had seen you at the mall once, before you ever noticed me."

"When?" I laughed.

"Right when I started working here, a bazillion years ago.

You were with your friends, hanging out by the fountain. Sam and two other boys. You were laughing like hyenas. I remember thinking you were cute," he teased.

I'd been tripping on acid that day. We were probably laughing about the two little girls that Sean scared by jumping out of a doorway. Sadly, it was so funny to us at the time that we were out of control for the rest of the day, and Sean jumped out from behind every doorway he saw, scaring shoppers until security kicked our group out of the mall for a week. I said to Chloe, "Didn't you think I was a dork?" I figured any cool witnesses would have.

"I just thought you were some tragic cutie pie. You were like a caterpillar in her cocoon . . . and now you're Cinderella. Have fun while it lasts, baby, before midnight comes."

"It doesn't last forever?"

"Youth? Ha! You're so stupid!"

"What about this elated feeling I have from coming out?"

"I don't mean to be the bearer of bad news, but the novelty wears off. One day you'll be so used to your new life that you'll forget what being in the closet was ever like."

"What do you mean?"

"Well, like in my case, I remember my childhood, but my memories are tweaked, you know? It's like I remember what I did, but I forgot who I was. I've forgotten what it was like to look at boys before I actually allowed myself to. I forgot what it was like to control my voice from sounding flamboyant, or to make the conscious effort to sit like a man . . . I see myself in all my memories the way I see myself now—supergay."

I laughed when he said "supergay," but I didn't really know how to respond to everything else he had said. So instead I asked him an even more complicated question: "Do you think that being gay will ever be so normal and mainstream that you won't even have to come out anymore, because it will be something that's accepted from, like, birth?"

Chloe smiled. "Hon, what I think will happen in the future is irrelevant to the present situation."

I changed my question: "Then why do you think it is that people currently hate gays?"

"Not everyone hates us."

"The people at my school do," I managed to confess with a jolt of humiliation. "Justin and Terrance especially."

"Yeah, well, some people are jerks, especially in high school. Don't let them get you down."

"How can I *not* though? I feel like I'm living a lie, and every day kids at school shine the spotlight on me so everyone can see me caught in it . . . And I don't know what to do. Should I come out at school next year? Would that make it stop? I just don't know. I wish it didn't have to be such a big deal. You know? Why does it matter if I'm gay?"

I looked into Chloe's eyes, begging for answers. But, for once, he didn't know what to say.

"I just don't understand why people think it's so unnatural to be gay," I said. "To me it feels like it's the most natural thing in the world. I don't feel like I'm doing anything wrong when I fantasize about a guy. It's a lot more comfortable for me than being with a girl—that's for sure."

"Of course you feel that way. You should feel that way because you are a healthy, sexual person. People are ignorant. They've always been ignorant, and that will never change."

"But why can't people learn to be accepting?"

"Perhaps because people are stuck living with all the traditions that came before them. And because of this ritualistic society, the whole world is turned upside down, not just us."

I observed Chloe's frown, then added reassuringly, "I think it'll change. Someday I bet we'll be viewed as totally normal and natural . . . even cool."

"You're such a visionary."

"Well, women are taking over this country, and gay guys are a girl's best friend."

"We should toast that thought with a cigarette," Chloe said, already hanging up the "back in five minutes" sign.

"Sounds good to me."

On our way outside, Chloe said, "Do you think I'm a bad manager?"

"In my opinion, you're the best manager a gal could ever want!"

"Whatever," he laughed. "You're such a ditz."

We skipped gaily through the parking lot, enjoying the stares from people all around us. Everyone who was anyone knew that we were the sunglass-store fags. We smoked one-hitters out of Chloe's wood dugout on the far end of the parking lot. Then we lit cigarettes. Fifteen minutes later, we were fried. One great thing about working at Shades was that we could always hide our red eyes behind designer sunglasses without anyone thinking anything of it.

It was a gorgeous eighty-degree day, right in the middle of summer. The hot sun made our outfits shine bright. I was wearing an orange, green, yellow, and maroon striped T-shirt and light-weight golf pants from Goodwill that were blue and yellow plaid with flared bottoms. Chloe was wearing red bell-bottoms, a navy blue T-shirt that said "Jam Packed," and a red scarf tied around his neck. At the moment his short hair was bright blue, which clashed with the outfit, so he covered it with an auburn wig, cut in a bob with a navy blue headband.

"Chloe, if you could be a girl, would you?"

"Hell, no! Girl, I'm happy with who I am, and no one could make me want to change for nothing." Smoke curled out of his lips. "Sure I like to dress in women's clothes, but I'm not a tranny. I would never take hormones and try to live as a woman. I'd miss gay sex too much. Anyway, I absolutely love being a fag, and there are just *so* many benefits."

"Like what?"

"Like impeccable style and great dance moves." He kicked into the air for effect. Then he sighed reminiscently. "It is fun, though, to get onstage and be a drag queen. I've always been theatrical. And I love all the girls, especially Babs Arlington."

"Do you think you'll be famous someday?" I asked.

"Probably not. But I *used* to want it. I used to dream about it and work toward it so hard."

"So why don't you work hard anymore? You're such a great drag queen. Everyone says so. You could become famous, like RuPaul!"

Chloe smiled kind of sadly, but I pretended not to notice. "Well *I* want to be famous someday! And I want my name to be Miss Erica Lane!" I declared, throwing my imaginary hair over my shoulder and blinking my biggest Bette Davis eyes.

"Mmm-hmm, girl. Strike a pose!" Chloe said.

{ seven }

When I was a little kid, I had the same fantasy every year when summer vacation was about to end. I dreamed that my next year of school would be the best year ever. Justin Skankshaw's father would be sent to prison for being an asshole and Justin and his mother would be deported to China, where everyone would hate them because they were so ugly. With Justin out of the picture, I would return to school to finally be recognized as an outstanding artist. I would decorate the school halls with beautiful paintings of my peers doing all types of different school activities: playing at recess, working together on art projects, helping one another with math. I would call it my "Yearbook Collection," and everyone would love and envy my talent and school spirit so much that I would be the most popular kid in my whole grade. Of course, reality set in every year on the first day back at school. And by eleventh grade, I had given up altogether on wishful thinking. I dreaded my return to school.

Then one morning, after a night I spent at home because Chloe let some guy named Anthony-with-a-Mustache stay the night, my mom woke me up. "Get dressed, Erick, we're going uniform shopping," she said, snapping the sheet off my body.

"What are you doing?" I sat up, wide awake. *I could've been naked!* was my first thought. "Go away." I pulled the sheet back around my body.

"Don't talk to me in that voice, young man!" She continued, snooping around my room.

"What are you doing? Get out of here!"

"I found this in your school bag!" She jammed a glass marijuana pipe decorated with swirls of iridescent color in my face.

My eyes widened in disbelief. It was the pipe Chloe had given me as a gift for summer solstice. "How dare you!" I said, reaching to snatch it from her unsuccessfully.

"You're not getting this back! And you're never going to bring drugs into this house!"

I felt a wave of panic.

"I haven't told your father, but don't think I won't," she threatened. "Now put your clothes on . . . and not your fancy ones," she added, eyeing my makeup and platforms and T-shirt that said "Porn Star" all over my floor. She slammed my door shut.

I groaned, pretty sure that I'd seen the last of that pipe. I was so pissed at myself for not hiding the stupid thing. What I really needed right now was one of those *Star Trek* transport devices, so I could transport myself over to Chloe's apartment. But there was no escape. I'd have to go *uniform* shopping with her. I slowly put on a pair of baggy jeans and a black T-shirt. When I looked in the mirror, I felt like *such* a dork. It was how I used to dress when I was in the closet, only now my hair was bleached and I had eyeliner smeared on my face. "What the fuck!" I screamed quietly, hitting the mirror as hard as I could with the side of my fist and watching it wobble, glad it didn't break.

There was a knock at my door. "Erick!" Tim yelled through. "Are you still sleeping?"

"No!"

"You wanna do somethin'? Like maybe play with trains or somethin'?"

"I can't right now." I opened the door to find him looking up at me shyly. He was a very shy little kid in general, I suddenly realized. "Mom and I are going uniform shopping. You should ask her if you can come with."

"She already said I couldn't," he said sadly. "But Dad is taking me to the park to play with Jared."

"Oh, that sounds like fun. If I didn't have go uniform shopping, I'd want to do that with you for sure."

"Why?"

"Why! Because you're my little brother, that's why."

"Who's this then?" he asked, running into my parents' bedroom and running back out with a framed picture of Tommy in his first-grade photo. "Is this your little brother, too?"

"Uh-huh."

"Where is he?"

I thought about what my mom would want me to say, God forbid, and explained, "He's in heaven."

"Why?"

"Because at some point everyone goes there." I wanted to change the subject. I should have just said he was dead and left heaven out of it. "Hey, when you're at the park, you should try and think of something me and you can do together, just the two of us. And then we'll do it, okay?"

His eyes lit up. "Promise?"

"Cross my heart and hope to die, stick a needle in my eye." I hugged him.

When we got in the car, my mom had already switched personalities back to the happy, loving mother determined to save her troubled son. Like she could turn me into a straight Christian boy with a single day of back-to-school shopping. "I've decided that you're going to wear all new uniforms this year." She beamed with false pride. "You must've grown a full two inches since last year."

I set my eyes on the radio, wishing I could switch it on but not daring to. I had a mental picture in my head of her bumper stickers: "Jesus Saves" and "Save the Whales." It was like, what the hell? I was so embarrassed to be seen with her, wearing my old straight-boy clothes. I hated having to go back to school. Summer was too short. School was going to suck so much. Everyone there thought I was such a freak. It made me physically ache in a way no one could ever possibly understand.

"I have a present for you," Mom said, as if offering a truce. Out of her purse came a gold chain necklace bearing a gold crucifix. I didn't even wear gold. Only thugs wore gold chains with crucifixes. I swear to God, my mom was living under a damn rock. She seriously knew nothing about me.

"Gee, thanks," I said, wondering its value at a pawnshop. I couldn't figure out why she insisted on driving me insane by pushing Jesus on me. I wondered what she'd say if I told her I didn't believe in Jesus.

"Your life is very precious, sweetheart," she went on. "This gift will be a symbol of change for you. It represents the future because the crucifix represents the forgiveness of sins . . . It's time for you to leave behind your bad past and seek a *bright* future."

You can tell her favorite movie is the goddamn *Sound of Music,* just by listening to her talk. I rolled my eyes, sinking into my seat. She was making me ill.

"One more thing, I called your job and told them that you'd be quitting for school."

"You what? How could you? What did you say?" I was mortified.

"It's not important what I said . . . What's important is that you focus on school. You don't need some silly job when Daddy and I are here to support you."

"My job is *not* silly," I insisted. I wondered if she actually spoke to Chloe. What he must've thought!

She completely ignored my feelings and continued. "I will also require that you will obey your curfew from now on."

"What makes you think that you can go meddling in my life?" I demanded.

"I'm your mother and I know what's best for you."

"It's my life!"

"You're *my* son . . . How dare you disrespect me?" Cruelty was beginning to show through her patronizing front.

I wanted to argue, to scream that I hated her and hated Jesus. But I couldn't find my voice. I was all choked up and I had to stare out the window, watching my life pass me by as I fought back tears. Suddenly she turned off the road, pulling into her church parking lot.

"What are you doing?" I spoke up. "I thought we were going shopping."

"First things first." She killed the engine. "We're going to have a talk with Father Tom."

"You're kidding, right?"

"Not at all. He's expecting us."

I had been in Father Tom's chambers before, and they always reminded me of some old-fashioned smoking room. The furniture and wall-to-wall bookshelves were all done in black wood. Two matching leather chairs were aimed at the desk, and all the lampshades were red, giving the room a sleepy light. I hated being in there. It was the worst punishment I could have imagined. Now every time Father Tom saw me at school, he would know that I smoked pot. It was unbearable.

"So, Erick," he began with a slow smile creeping onto his ancient face. "Your mother tells me you're having a difficult time following rules at home."

"I'm fine," I protested.

"Are you?"

"Yeah."

"Well, I see you're hiding beneath your shell . . . Erick, you can feel free to open up to me. I've taken a holy vow before the church and the Lord Almighty that I will hold all of my parishioners' private comments in complete confidence . . . Erick?" He repeated my name. "Is there anything you wish to tell me?"

I shook my head.

"I wonder if you might tell me why your mom wishes this meeting to take place."

I shrugged my shoulders, avoiding his stare.

"She tells me that she's very concerned with the choices you're making . . . How do you feel about that, Erick?"

"I feel like it's my life and she should just let me live it," I said sarcastically. I meant it and everything, but I knew he wouldn't take me seriously.

"Can you understand why she's concerned about the choices you're making?"

"What do you mean?"

"Well, from what I hear, you're not using your best judgment . . . How do you feel about your sins?"

"I don't believe in sins," I said mysteriously. I could be such a sneaky little brat when I wanted to be.

A confused expression came over Father Tom's face. "Erick," he said my name for the gazillionth time. "Not acknowledging your sins should tell you that you're probably making the wrong choices."

"Maybe I don't *have* any sins."

"Everyone has sins, Erick . . . Even your mother and I have sinned."

"What are my sins?"

"Well, for starters, your mother tells me that she's discovered a marijuana pipe in your possession. I wonder if you wouldn't mind telling me a little more about that." I couldn't believe it: a priest who had read about drugs? Did he think I was going to let him lecture me?

"Erick, is this something you've been doing for a while? That is one of your mom's biggest concerns."

"I only did it once, and I didn't inhale," was my prepared reply.

He ignored me. Instead asking; "Erick, do you understand why this worries her?"

"No."

"You don't?"

"I don't think marijuana is a big deal."

"Well, Erick, as an adult, I can assure you that it is very detrimental to your adolescent years. It numbs your mind and decreases your motivation. Not to mention there are medical complications that can develop from it."

"Like what?"

"It will decrease your chances of procreation and pollute your lungs and lead to brain damage."

What a nerd! I wondered if he'd ever even tried it. He certainly needed pot. "First of all, I'll never procreate. I wouldn't want to bring up a kid in a society as oppressive as ours. And second, there's evidence that marijuana is good for medical reasons. Hello? That's why there's a huge movement to legalize it for medicinal purposes."

Father Tom's face crinkled up. "Erick, it helps those with cancer keep down food and sustain a healthy appetite because chemotherapy makes people sick . . . For them it may be beneficial, but for a healthy young man like yourself, it will only hold you back from your potential."

"What *about* my potential?"

"I know you used to be a fine student, and that you possess artistic talents. In fact, a picture you drew years ago for a church art contest still hangs in the Sunday school classroom to this very day," he smiled.

I remembered that picture: *The Last Supper.* I drew Jesus with brown hair and a beard, a long white robe, and a big orange circle of light around his head. He was holding up a chalice of wine. All twelve apostles sat at the long wood table grinning and eating bread. It was the biggest cliché in Christianity. I should've done *The Scream* instead.

"Yes, you've always been quite gifted," he continued. "However, in the past couple years, you've been slipping academically and you've been exercising poor judgment in who you associate with."

"You have no idea who my friends are," I argued. For some reason, he hurt me when he reminded me of that picture. He was right: In the past couple years, I had lost ambition in art, and that was depressing. But did that happen because of pot, or because of the unbearable circumstances of my life? Maybe it was both. Maybe I was just the biggest loser ever in the history of losers. I couldn't help but plan my suicide right then. Perhaps I would jump off the church roof and impale myself on the cross out front. I'd leave a note: "Catholicism skewered me!"

"Yes, Erick, that's accurate. I've never met your friends. However, I know that whoever they are, they're providing you with drugs and keeping you out of the house for two and three days at a time. Would you be willing to tell me what it is you do when you're away from home? Your mom is concerned that maybe it involves more than just marijuana."

I pictured my new life with Chloe, who had shown me more love and compassion than I'd ever received from the Catholic Church. "She's right," I burst out. "I'm gaaaay. And that means I have *sex* with meeeen," I added, like I was an Academy Award–winning movie star and people were going to remember me for this performance.

His face turned white and he swallowed hard. "Is that so?" He looked away.

"Didn't you know?"

"You may not realize this, Erick, but I pay very close attention to all my students. Since I don't have my own family, I consider all of you young people to be my children . . . If you are having feelings of homosexuality, Erick, maybe I can help you get over them, if only you would be willing to talk."

Get over them? He said the word "homosexuality" as though he was describing a psychological sleeping disorder that you could cure with hypnosis and some chamomile tea. Where did this school of thought come from? Probably some Catholic literature that a bitter, closet-case priest wrote as he cursed the images of hot, naked bondage-boys that he couldn't rid his ravenous mind of. Thank God I wasn't a priest!

Father Tom began to talk about why marriage between a man and a woman was sacred, and I tried to turn my brain off and not listen. However, I couldn't help but notice that with all his bullshit, he failed to mention Jesus. Maybe he thought I was already beyond forgiveness. I started saying in my head, "God, you made me gay." But it didn't seem like God was listening. I thought about Chloe and said to myself, "Thank goodness I have Chloe."

The priest interrupted my thoughts. "Are you even listening to me, Erick?"

"Would you just quit saying my name? And quit trying to save me," I yelled, "because I'm already saved!"

His face flushed scarlet. "What a boy like you needs is the strictest of punishments. Mark my words, young man, if you continue on this path of immorality, you'll find yourself locked up with other delinquents. Furthermore, if you don't repent your sins, you will most certainly be condemned by God."

I was flabbergasted and wanted to scream that judgments are not for mortal men with liver spots to make. Instead, I said very calmly, "You know somethin'? I feel bad for you, because sex and pot are the two best things in this life and you'll never get to feel either of them . . . So kiss this!" I slapped my ass and stormed out of there, hurrying through the maze of halls where portraits of bishops and popes hung on the walls in ornate gold frames.

I stumbled into the chapel. Four strangers were kneeling in pews, their heads bowed toward the altar. My mother was among them. I imagined she was praying for me, asking God to help me change my sinful ways and accept him as my ruler.

"Ready?" I woke her from the hypnotic state.

"Already?" She seemed quite surprised.

"Yup. Father Tom said I need to do three Hail Marys and I'll have a clean slate," I lied.

She eyed me skeptically. "I'm going to go say good-bye to Father Tom," she announced. "Why don't you go light a candle and do your penance." She reached in her pocket and gave me her rosary. The wood beads felt warm and oily on my fingers.

"Can't we just go?" I protested.

"I'll be right back." She hurried away.

I wiped off the remnants of Father Tom's old-man breath, quivering from the drafts that circled the enormous room. I wondered what he'd say to her, whether or not she'd cry right there in front of him.

A craving for a cigarette suddenly overwhelmed me, and I knew I'd start shaking if I didn't indulge myself. So I stuffed her rosary in my pocket, next to the gold necklace she had given me, and headed for the exit that glowed next to a big maroon banner that read "Father, Son, and the Holy Spirit." All I could think was what sort of decorator would put up that tacky sign in side a beautiful stained-glass church?

As soon as I was out the door, I lit a cigarette and was lost in the whirl of smoke the wind wrapped around me. The warm air made me feel free. I skipped down the steps and over to the bus bench, unsure what to do next. I knew I was going to get into trouble for my behavior in Father Tom's chambers, and in even more trouble if I left the church without my mom. But for some reason I really didn't care. These days I didn't care about much of anything, except having fun—and sex.

My fantasies of orgasmic encounters with multiple guys were overwhelming. I kept imagining all the different hot places and positions sex could possibly be done in. There was rarely ever one recurring person in my fantasies, either. Usually I was thinking about someone I'd seen on the bus or at the mall. Sometimes I pulled guys from the old archives, from when I was a kid. I'd think about some cute boy from school like Andy Flynn and imagine running into him now, after we'd both gone through puberty. In that dream we're both surprised to find out the other is gay, and we have terrific sex in some public place (like a department-store dressing room). I swear to God, I'm an exhibitionist.

A bus pulled up to the bench and swung its door open. I reluctantly stepped on, hoping I'd at least get home before my mom. I'd change my outfit and leave without having to listen to her bitch about how I was a disgrace to the family. I wished to avoid that for as long as possible. Maybe if I stayed away for months, all her anger and disappointment in me would dissipate, so that by the time I saw her again she would have forgotten what a shame I was to her.

When I got home, I checked the garage to make sure that she wasn't there. Neither were my dad or Tim. I hurried inside to change. But when I took off my clothes, I immediately got a hard-on. So I cranked my stereo and jacked off to my reflection in the mirror, watching my hand move up and down, my lean muscles flexing. It seemed like I was getting sexier all the time and I now could turn myself on by my own appearance faster than any picture from a magazine. My skinny body had jutting curves. I guess you'd say I had a swimmer's build: flat stomach, strong legs, and a bubbly ass. My skin was really smooth, too, because I always rubbed lotion on it every night. It felt like my cock was growing bigger all the time. I wondered how big it would get. I had heard that five or six inches was average. Lucky me—I was definitely bigger than average! I had my pubic hair styled and trimmed to a perfect V. I wondered whether I could be a model someday if I grew to be six feet tall.

After I came, I turned up Tori even louder and put on a fierce outfit that totally showed off my midriff. I finished off the outfit with my platforms. Satisfied, I dialed Chloe's number. His voicemail picked up after five rings. I waited for the beep and said, "Hey, baby, I'm at home. Give me a call when you get this." I hoped he didn't think I was ignoring him when I failed to call earlier. Who knows what my mom said about me when she may or may not have told him that I had to quit my job?

I called Sam next. Thankfully she was at home, going through her closet to see what new clothes she needed to buy for school. I wished *I* went to South and had the luxury of choosing my clothes. I asked her if she'd spoken to Chloe at all, and she said she hadn't. I told her I really needed some pot right now, but all she offered was the resin in her pipe. She asked what was bothering me, but I told her that I didn't want to talk about it. I knew that she and Chloe would give me shit about having seen a priest. "Let's just meet at the fountain," I told her.

When I got to the mall, Sam was already there, sitting on the bench farthest from where the shoppers passed. I glanced over at my job to see that John, the straight boy, was behind the counter. He saw me and waved hello, so I smiled and waved back. I contemplated going over to him and saying hi, but I'd only met him once for about five minutes and I didn't want him to think I was weird or something.

"Hey, you got any money?" Sam asked, without a hello or small talk.

"Twenty dollars. Why?"

"'Cause Jake said he could get us a bag. I called him after you left."

"Right on. When?"

"Whenever. You want me to call him right now?"

"Twist my wrist," I said sarcastically.

"Then come with me."

We crossed the mall and ended up at the pay phones. She called Jake and told him that we wanted "it" and that we had a twenty. He said he'd come deliver the stuff personally and hung up the phone.

"He's sure being cool today," Sam commented. "He usually bitches if he has to come here."

"Maybe he needs the money."

"Are you kidding? He's doing us a favor."

We smoked cigarettes while we waited for Jake outside. We could hear his car before we even saw it. The sound of his engine turned into an enormous "screeee" as he peeled into the parking lot and skidded to a stop right in front of us. His car was an old junker that had gold hubcaps and a one hundred–disk stereo that played techno. The bass made the car vibrate so hard that your voice became pulsed like a strobe light whenever you rode in it. I sat in the backseat, so I couldn't hear a word they said to each other up front. I didn't care, though. The music put me in a hypermeditative trance.

Within two minutes we were flying down the freeway with a glass pipe jammed full of bud being passed around. I zoned out the window, watching the dashes on the road zip past in a stream of white. Looking up at the sky made me squint. It seemed especially bright blue today, even with my Kenneth Cole sunglasses. I felt the heat of the sun on my face, while the buzz of the pot filled my body. I was so relaxed now and freed from my worries. Neither of my parents' constant nagging got to me because I suddenly felt like my own person—for once. I wanted to hold onto that freedom forever, but I knew it wouldn't last. Soon I'd have to go back to school, back to uniforms, and back to being a joke.

I started to think about what Father Tom had said about helping me get over my homosexuality. It seemed to me like he was the one who had been led astray. I wondered if he was gay and had spent his entire life trying to get over it himself. That would explain why he opted to marry Jesus instead of a woman. He was such an asshole! I should have blown him away with some smart comment about how homosexuality was genetic, but the church was fabricated by pre-science man. Too bad I always thought of my best responses hours after the conversation ended.

At any rate, one thing I got out of that meeting with Father Tom was my realization at last that Catholicism was not for me. It was far too oppressive and had almost nothing to do with love. Maybe Chloe was smart to be an atheist after all. Sometimes it seemed far more realistic to believe that we were all a bunch of incidental atoms, and that the universe (not God) had always existed. Besides, why would God sit up in heaven watching me (along with billions of other people) and judging my every move as right or wrong? Why would He even care what we did? It didn't make any sense that He would create us in his image, then damn us to live in hell if we didn't act all pious like my mother or Father Tom.

Maybe I would be an atheist for a while. I certainly couldn't get in any more trouble with God than I already was in.

Still, I kept calling on God whenever I needed help or luck or to feel less lonely. I did this possibly out of habit, but it seemed much easier than asking for help from one of my fellow humans. And sometimes—though it was surely due to my belief in miracles—I swore I heard Him answer.

{ eight }

After we had killed about twenty minutes and two bowls, Jake turned the music down to a quiet hum. "So where do ya want to be dropped?" he asked me.

Startled out of my trance, I noticed that he was rubbing his right hand around Sam's left inner thigh, almost underneath it, and her hand was on top of his, guiding him.

"The mall, I guess," I decided, since I didn't know where the hell else to go.

"Here's your bag." Sam flicked a sandwich bag of weed into my lap. "It's ten bucks."

"I thought I was buying a twenty."

"He's selling it out of his personal, Erick."

I realized Sam was trying to get rid of me so that she could get laid. What a bitch! I couldn't believe her. "All I have is a twenty," I said in the bitchiest voice I had.

"Do you have change for a twenty?" she asked her new "boyfriend" in a wishy-washy voice.

"Sorry, man, I don't."

"Well?" I asked, impatient with them both.

"Just owe me, man. You're good for it, right?" He almost

crashed us into the guardrail in order to put his hand down Sam's pants.

"I guess," I said bitterly. I couldn't believe Sam was ditching me for Jake the Snake. "Can I at least get some papers from you, though? I don't have any paraphernalia."

"Sure, man. Here." Jake handed me a package of orange Zig-Zags. I took a few out and handed him the rest back. When we pulled back up to the mall entrance, I got out of the car with a benevolent "Thanks," and never looked back to watch them speed off. I lit a cigarette outside the mall, my day totally ruined. I was so pissed. Some friend! I swear to God, no one could possibly understand how pissed I was.

I tried calling Chloe from a pay phone but got his voicemail. I left a message saying that I wanted to come over, but I didn't get my hopes up. He was probably out for the night. I used part of the twenty dollars I still had to get some pizza from the food court. It was so greasy that I had to sop up the pools of oil with my napkin before eating it. That made me feel fat, so I went outside for another cigarette. I was sitting on the sidewalk, leaning up against the wall of the building, when I heard a voice from behind say, "Hey, there?" I turned to see that a boy was smiling at me. He was from Sam's school. I didn't know his name, though he had bought sunglasses from me once. He was supercute and kind of shy. I had wondered at the time if he was gay.

"Hi, how are you?" I ventured.

"Good." He looked down at his own feet. Then, suddenly, he seemed to remember his question: "You got an extra cigarette?"

"Of course, have a seat." I gestured at the space to the left of me. He sat down cross-legged in front of me. I lit a cigarette for him.

"Thanks."

"No problem . . . What's your name again? I'm sure I've heard it but I'm just so terrible with names."

"Mike."

Mike. I repeated the name in my head. It was so straight sounding. I wondered if I could call him Michael or Mikey without making him mad. He was so adorable that he really should have been called Mikey Baby. "So what brings you to the mall?" I asked.

"Just hanging out. My parents gave me money to buy back-to-school clothes." He opened the Gap bag beside him and pulled out a pair of boot-cut jeans and an orange polo shirt from Marshall's. "I couldn't find very much. What do ya think?"

"They're cool."

He smiled and put them back in his bag. "Thanks . . . You know, you and your friend dress *really* cool. Where do you shop?" he said, referring to my tight-ass shirt.

"All the funnest stores," I said, realizing this day might turn out good after all. Mike was absolutely dreamy! Sandy blond, perfect lips, and delicate fingers. His hands were definitely a turn-on. I wanted to hold one and have it gently running along my body, like Sam had gotten Jake to do. I was starting to feel pretty sexy. "You should come shopping with us sometime," I said, "us" meaning Chloe and me.

"That'd be sweet. I want to start dressing more . . . you know."

"Gay?"

He blushed and smiled bashfully.

"Sorry . . . I didn't mean to offend you."

"You didn't . . . So, what grade are you in?" he asked eagerly. "You're in school, right?"

"I'm going into eleventh. How'd you know I didn't already graduate?"

"Sam told me."

"Oh, you talk to Sam?"

"Yeah, well, you know." He changed the subject quickly. "I'm a senior this year. By the way, what school do you go to?"

I didn't want to answer that out of complete mortification over my school's name alone. "St. John's," I said reluctantly.

"*You* go to Catholic school?" He seemed amazed, like it wasn't even possible.

I was suddenly more humiliated then I'd ever been in my life. "Unfortunately."

"Oh, man, that sucks. Do you wear one of those uniforms?"

"Yeah."

"And you got such great style," he groaned. I was in love with him!

"I'm probably going to transfer out of there. To South High."

"Really? That's where I go."

"Yeah, I know . . . Sam's school?"

"Oh, yeah," he said, laughing at himself.

I smiled at him and he smiled back. "So how tall are you without those platforms?" he asked.

"I dunno, five-nine, five-ten."

"I bet we're about the same height. Take 'em off."

I was embarrassed to take off my shoes in public, but I did anyway. So did he. We stood facing each other, wearing only our socks. We were pretty close in height, him being maybe an inch taller. He might have had a more sporty build, too, but I really couldn't tell. Right then I was feeling pretty sporty myself.

I remembered I had all that pot on me. "Do you smoke weed?" I asked.

He looked at me like he was unsure how to answer. Finally he replied, "Yeah."

"You want to smoke a bowl with me?"

"Sure."

"I know the perfect spot." I sat down to put my platforms back on. He watched me the whole time. I was so embarrassed by how cute he was that I couldn't even look at him anymore.

"Where are we goin'?" he asked.

"To this hidden spot by the lake. I go there with my friends and smoke all the time. It's really cool."

"You sold me on it."

"So, did you finish all your shopping?" I asked, just to keep the conversation going.

"No, probably not. It takes me a while to shop because I'm so picky. That's why I usually go by myself. Believe it or not, my mom still tries to come clothes shopping with me. She's crazy, though, no sense of style at all. I can't imagine anyone being dorky enough to go shopping with their mom, right?"

"Yeah, that's, like, the dorkiest," I said, thinking about how I almost had to go uniform shopping with my mother earlier that day. "Parents are always so lame anyways. They never know what's cool. They think tapered jeans are cool or something. And, girl, I hate ankle-biters."

"Girl?"

"Oh, sorry, I call all my friends 'girl.' Hopefully that doesn't bug you." I said it in a way that accidentally sounded like "It better not bug you." For a second I wished I wasn't so gay.

"I dunno, why? Should it?"

"Exactly, why should it?" I said, unsure of whether or not to call him "girl" again. He seemed faggy to me, like he might turn into a big queen if he started hanging around Chloe too much. I wanted him to stay the way he was, though. Bashful and boyish. He had a certain naïvéte to him that I found tremendously attractive.

"So what kind of music do you like?" he asked.

"All kinds." I thought about what was in my five-disk player now: Tori Amos, Tori Amos, Tori Amos, Tori Amos, and the Lemonheads. "Mostly alternative, I guess."

"Do you like Radiohead?" he asked.

"I love them."

We were walking side by side, and his finger accidentally

touched my hand. That split second of contact seemed like it would last forever. I imagined what it would be like to hold his hand, in public, without caring what people thought. I wondered if he'd make a good boyfriend. Like if I dated him, maybe all my other problems would go away. I wondered also what he was thinking about, if he wanted me, if he'd ever been with a guy before. I wanted to know if he was gay like me, meaning, he always thought about men and sex and sometimes wished he'd been born a girl instead of a boy. I bet his life was better than mine. For starters, he didn't go to Catholic school. His parents were probably normal, too. His parents would probably accept him if he were gay.

When we got to the edge of the lake, he stopped and skipped a rock across the water. I watched the way his body arched when he moved. Just like Andy Flynn. I bet he was a good football player—fun to watch, at least. He turned to me, smiling.

"So where's your secret spot?"

"This way." I walked ahead of him. He ran up to my side, just like I'd hoped he would.

I took him into a tunnel where water flowed through. Above our heads was the sound of traffic. "I lost my pipe" (actually it was stolen by my bitchy mom) "so I'll have to roll a joint."

"That's cool." He watched me handle the weed. By the way he was watching me, I realized he probably hadn't smoked very much pot before. Which was to my advantage, because being high was basically second nature to me. I'd smoked enough of it that it didn't really impair me anymore. I could go to school or work stoned and no one would notice. Once we were high, we'd be playing in *my* territory.

As soon as I had a good-sized joint rolled, I lit it and took a few harsh puffs before handing it to him. "Thanks." He put the joint between his lips and sucked harder than necessary, a determined expression on his face. I think he wanted to impress me.

Make me think he knew what he was doing. He *was* a senior, after all, and he had to act like a big shot in front of me.

We passed the joint back and forth. He'd take only little puffs when it was his turn, even though I was taking a couple big hits on each of my turns. After we finished it off, I lit us each a cigarette and we spent a brief moment smoking in silence, sitting next to each other on our butts with our backs against the tunnel wall. The only daylight inside came from the openings at both ends, and so the reflection of the light off the water flickered all over the walls and ceiling like golden dancing butterflies. I wanted to take off my platforms again, but I thought that might be weird. Instead I clicked my wood heels together. I couldn't think of what to say next.

He turned to me and said, "What do you want to do now?"

"I dunno. You feeling it, or what?"

"I'm not sure . . . I can't tell," he said with a puzzled expression. "Do you?"

"Oh, yeah . . . You'll feel it soon . . . You want to get up and walk around the lake or something?"

"Let's just sit here for a minute. It's kinda nice, you know?"

"Yeah, I know," I said bashfully.

I turned to him. Our faces were only inches apart. I thought he was about to kiss me, so I turned away out of nervousness. It was too soon for that to happen. I had just met him fifteen minutes ago. I wanted to savor the feeling of wanting him. I liked to anticipate the kiss for a while first. "So what's it like at your school?"

He seemed momentarily turned off by the question, then said, "What do you want to know? Like, academics, sports?"

"No, not that. What's it like if you're gay?"

"I don't know." He stood, as if to avoid the subject. "But I'm sure *you'd* like it."

"Well, do *you* like it?"

"It's fine . . . Hey, let's go for a walk."

"Alright," I agreed, hoping I hadn't insulted him. He was very touchy about the whole gay thing. Suddenly, it already seemed like he wanted to end the flirtation that we had just started. How stupid of me to smoke weed with him! Now he'll never want to be my boyfriend because when he sobers up he'll disregard me as some stupid stoner. "You feeling okay?" I asked as we walked back out into the daylight.

"I'm fine." He scanned the view of the lake, the beach, and city street. He flinched when he turned a full circle and saw my face. "I think I'm really stoned," he remarked in a daze.

"Yeah, me, too," I exaggerated.

Then he started laughing obnoxiously and took off sprinting down the beach, scaring away three ducks. He did a somersault before running back to me. What a total fool. "You're crazy," I said, laughing at the people who stopped to watch his display.

"Oh my God! It's so intense!"

"Haven't you ever smoked pot before?"

"Yeah, but not that much. I mean, I didn't feel it like this!"

"Well, I get real good shit, that's all," I bragged. "If you need a bag, come to me and I'll hook ya' up."

"Hoop me up?"

"Hook—hook you up, silly." It was obviously a whole new concept to him.

"Cool."

"Yeah, it's *really* cool," I teased. "So what do want to do now? Eat some pizza, start drinking, dress up in our best disco jump-suits?" His laughter was so loud that he got the attention of the ducks that were wading nearby, the same ones he'd just scared the feathers off of.

"Or better yet, we could dress in drag and go egg some houses. Can't you just imagine the news we'd get? 'Two teen she-males go on a vandalizing rampage through South Minneapolis. It'll be hysterical."

"Oh my God!" he declared wide-eyed.

"What?"

"We'd get in so much trouble, though," he whispered, as if there were spies lurking nearby.

"No we wouldn't, because once we took off our costumes no one could finger us. We'd be doing it incognito."

"Do you think it would work?"

"Of course. Why the hell wouldn't it?" He was so gullible. Like I would ever do that!

We headed toward the sidewalk. I was trying to lead him away from the lake. He was so excited, yet completely unaware of how vulnerable he was both to me—and my using pot to seduce him—and to speeding cars. I had to hold him back from running out into the street and getting splattered.

"Mmmm, McDonald's," he said, happily pointing to the golden arches.

"Are you hungry?"

"Yeah," he said laughing. "Starving."

We hurried across the street to the restaurant, where he ordered a Big Mac Value Meal and I ordered my own small Diet Coke. Unlike him, I controlled my pot munchies. I didn't pig out unless I had to. Like after I hadn't eaten for two days because I'd been feeling fat. We sat down at a booth, and without saying a word, he began to devour his extra-large fries, smearing them red with ketchup. I watched him eat, thinking about how cute he was. How geeky and funny and sexy he was. He remembered I was there so he opened his mouth to show me chewed fries and laugh. What a boy! Trying to be funny by being gross. Obviously, pot was too much for him.

"Slow down there," I said when he nearly choked on the pink mush in his mouth. He ignored, gulping down Coke instead. He reminded me of all the boys I went to school with, of boyishness in general. He was probably into sports video games, war movies, and talking about cars. We probably had nothing in common, and that's what I liked about him. I always hung around girls when I was young because I had more in common with them. Boys like Mike were always a curiosity to me. They were the types that turned me on.

After playing with his burger until the bun was mangled and the toppings were spilled onto the table, he said he couldn't eat it because it had once been a living animal. I told him that McDonald's didn't use *real* beef, that they used genetically altered meat pumped with steroids, but he refused to eat it anyway, deciding at that moment to be vegetarian.

"I just think it's so sad the way they torture those poor cows before they kill them," he blubbered into a napkin. So much for him being my tough guy.

"It's true that farm animals have it rough, but it's lab animals that really get abused. The ones they test consumer products and radiation on."

"I think animals should be treated fairly . . . Don't they have rights?" he cried. His emotional outburst had people staring at us.

"Definitely!" I slammed my fist onto the table. "We should do something about it! Maybe get together a sit-in at some grocery-store meat aisle or at Famous Frank's Barbecue."

"That would be way cool!"

"Totally! Let's go make signs!" I helped him throw away his uneaten burger.

Just as we walked out the door, he said, "I'm still hungry."

"Just don't think about it. I have this place I want to show you before we begin working on our campaign against the mistreatment of food."

"What?" he asked, already forgetting about his stomach.

"It's a surprise."

"Where is it?"

"Well, we'll have to take a bus. And that's the only clue I'm allowing you."

I took him to the railroad bridge crossing the Mississippi River. When you entered far enough inland, on the St. Paul side, you could walk out onto the bridge. It was wide enough for trains to cross paths, but still pretty scary. You had to cross wide wooden planks, and there was nothing to hold onto. In between the planks you could see the Mississippi River, like, twenty stories below. Mike was terrified from the second we stepped onto the bridge. At first he tried not to let on, acting macho or something, but soon his legs were wobbling and he was gripping the back of my shirt. And, like, every three steps, one of my large wooden heels slipped through a crack and we stumbled. He nearly screamed every time. I asked if he was okay and he said he was fine, he didn't want to go back. When we were about halfway out, we reached the secret place that I had promised him. It was this spot where you could crawl through a small opening and step down onto a narrow ledge underneath the bridge. I went first, then helped him down. There we sat, our heads inches below the tracks, hanging onto steel beams, our legs dangling over the edge. It felt like gravity could pull us right off.

"You okay?" I asked again, noticing that Mike was shaking.

"Yeah." He was looking at the water. He'd calmed down a bit during the bus ride, and now it seemed like he wasn't going to make a peep unless I prompted him.

"Isn't this place great?" I said, looking at the view. I was watching the tangerine-sized sun setting over the river. "I like being high up, looking down on the world."

"I'm kind of afraid of heights," Mike finally admitted. Then he put his hand around my biceps. I was so overwhelmingly aroused by him that I almost fell right off the ledge. It seemed inevitable that we'd soon kiss. I wanted to make a move on him right then, but I was still too nervous. I worried that if I didn't act soon, I'd lose my chance.

"Do you want to leave?" I asked.

"No. I kinda like it here . . . with you . . . I don't feel too scared."

"There's nothing to be scared of. I won't let you fall."

"So why do you like being up so high all the time? You don't like what we got on the ground?"

"I don't know," I said, embarrassed. "I guess . . . I just always wanted to fly."

"You mean be a pilot?"

"Or a superhero."

"How 'bout an astronaut?"

"Going to space would be a dream come true," I said dramatically.

"Really? God, not me, man. I'm staying right here on the ground—on earth. There's nothing out there that could get me to blast off into space."

"Don't you think there's something adventurous and romantic about it though?"

"I dunno, maybe. I guess I just don't get what there is to see up there."

"The possibility of forever . . . Of something never ending," I drifted off into my imagination's picture of outer space and eternity.

"What?"

"Never mind . . . Hey, do you like roller coasters?" I asked, craving the feeling of falling.

"Yeah, sure."

"Do you want to go to Valley Fair with me before the summer's over?"

"Sure. I haven't been there in years."

"Neither have I . . . But I bet it would be fun."

"We could get stoned again," he said slyly. Obviously that was something he liked. Then: "Oh, it's just about to set!" he declared, pointing at the sun.

We fell into silence. I had a million things that I wanted to say, but I couldn't think of any of them. He moved his grip on my arm down to my hand and we laced our fingers together. That's when I realized I didn't need to say anything. I could just hold his hand, and we could just watch the sunset together, and that would be enough.

After dusk settled, Mike asked me if I wanted to go back to his house. "Will your parents be there?" I asked.

"My mom is. But don't sweat it. I have so many siblings that as long as we're quiet no one will even notice we're home."

When we entered Mike's bedroom he didn't tell me where to sit, so I just laid on his bed, resting my head on my arm so I could see him. He didn't join me right away. Instead, he showed me his fish tank and his baseball trophies and his Nintendo 64. Finally, he sort of crept over to me, and sat on the edge of the bed, looking down on me with a longing expression painted across his face. "I've"—he was all choked up—"never done this before."

I smiled at him just to be reassuring, even though I was the one shaking.

"Have you?" he asked, noticing.

I thought briefly. The most I'd ever done really was make out with Troy. "No . . . not really."

"What do you mean?"

"Well, I've kissed a guy before . . . But it was unromantic . . . there wasn't any type of connection. I've never really, you know, had sex or anything." I was shocked by how casually I told him all of this.

He put his hand on my side, then lowered me onto my back so that he was above me, purposefully, almost lovingly, gazing into my eyes. For some reason, I reached up and touched his braces. I hadn't ever felt braces before; my teeth were naturally straight. Then he took my finger into his mouth and sucked on it. I couldn't even breathe. I imagined, gloriously, that I was the luckiest boy ever, that we both were, and before I could figure what any of it meant, he leaned down to my mouth and kissed me. Instantly, our slow, careful affair turned into wrestling. We were wild, rushed, pulling each other's clothes off like we couldn't waste a second. We kissed each other everywhere. Trying like mad to do everything all at once. I reached down and wrapped my hand around his cock. He let out a quiet moan. His dick was slightly smaller than mine and felt light and solid. Its soft skin slid up and down as I stroked his shaft. I pinched the bulbous pink head like I was testing fruit for ripeness. With my thumb and finger, I pried open the slit to make an O. When I let go, a single drop of cum squeezed its way out like a tear. I licked it off, and he shuddered. Then I rolled on top of him and stared down at his dick, studying it, wondering what it would taste like. I felt apprehensive, though. Putting it in my mouth seemed like some imaginary line that, once crossed, marked the end of my innocence. But I wanted Mike so badly. I looked into his eyes. They seemed so pure and sweet that I felt like I wanted to swallow him whole. Finally, I slid my tongue along the length of his dick. Then, without humiliation, I took the whole thing into my mouth at once. He gasped and clutched my hair as I slid him in and out of my mouth. "Let's sixty-nine," he said. And with that we gave each other head at the same time, rubbing our bodies together, producing wonderful friction that tingled every inch of me. We came on my stomach together, then collapsed into each other's arms. We laid there naked, our cum sandwiched between our tightly pressed bodies. I didn't want to move, ever. I was afraid that once I moved, it would end. I couldn't bear to let that happen. Maybe he was fearful of this, too, because neither of us let go. We fell asleep with our cum holding us together like glue.

When I awoke, we had changed positions, but were still tangled together. His room was dark. A streetlight cast shadows across the blue wallpaper. I looked at his face, calm, asleep. His complexion was so pure. Like he'd never in his life had a zit. Then he opened his eyes, saw me, frowned, then quickly smiled.

"You okay?" I asked.

"I thought maybe it was a dream."

"A good dream?"

"Yeah, a wonderful one . . . I was in trouble for a while, then I was saved."

I didn't know what he meant, but I knew it was good. "What do you want to do now?" I asked.

He sat up in bed, reaching for his shirt on the floor. I watched his body, sadly, disappear into his shirt. Then his legs disappeared into his pants. I got up and dressed, too. We sort of looked at each other awkwardly, unsure of what to do next. "I should probably get home," I said.

"Do you want to hang out again sometime?" he asked quickly.

"Definitely." I grabbed a pen from his desk and wrote my phone number on some paper. "Call me . . . tonight if you want to," I said. He smiled. We didn't hug or anything. I just smiled back, and left.

When I got home, both my parents were having cows. Tim was in bed, so there was no one to save me from them. My mom immediately started yelling about my behavior in church, saying that I was horribly disrespectful, that she didn't know what to do with me, and that she was at her wit's end. She cried the whole time she yelled. I gathered that Father Tom had said that I was rude, obnoxious, starved for attention, and that I said everything I could think of to try and shock him. Luckily, it seemed he hadn't told her I was gay. Maybe it was his vow of secrecy, or maybe he was embarrassed. Either way, I was relieved. If Mom found out I was gay from a priest, she would probably commit suicide—or at least homicide—over the news. When she asked me how I had dared to disappear on her like that after she had gone to go speak with Father Tom, I looked to my dad for empathy. But he was a stone. My mom noticed it, too, and demanded that he tell her why the hell he was just sitting on his hands while she was the one doing all the parenting. I wasn't the center of attention anymore. Suddenly, everything she directed at me turned into a fight between the two of them. It was the same old fight where they blame each other for everything that is wrong with our family. It was both their faults and, deciding that nothing would be resolved, I ran upstairs to be alone in my room.

In the dark I saw the red light on my answering machine blinking. The first message was from Chloe, saying he was having Babs Arlington and a couple other girls over for cocktails and that I should come. The second was from Sam, apologizing for ditching me earlier, then talking about how wonderful and sweet Jake was. I didn't even finish listening to her message before I hit the delete button. The last one was from Mike: "Hi, Erick, it's Mike. I was just, um, calling to say I'm going to bed now and have a good night . . . I hope you had a good day and, um, I'll call you tomorrow." (Beep.) I was so excited that before I went to bed I played it back twice more, rejoicing and falling in love.

{ nine }

𝒯he next day Mike called and asked if I still wanted to go to Valley Fair. I couldn't believe how sweet he was. He told me he'd pick me up in his mom's car in about a half hour. I was so excited, I didn't think I could wait that long. The first thing I did when I hung up was call Chloe to gloat.

"You did what?"

"We had sex! Well, not booty sex. But, oh, my God, it was so fun. I can't even believe it. It was like, the greatest experience ever. I think it was probably the greatest sex in history actually."

"Well, brag about it, why don't you?" Chloe laughed.

"Don't worry, Chloe. Someday it will happen to you, too," I mocked.

"Whatever, you little twerp," he joked. "So is this Mike guy your boyfriend now?"

"I don't know. Probably."

"Oh, how cute!" Chloe cheered. "Your first boyfriend. You'll remember this forever!"

"You're such a sap."

"I know. I'm just like my mother. I'll be forever a romantic."

"I'm sure you will, Chloe. But, hey, listen, I should let you go. I have to get ready for Valley Fair."

"Alright, well, have fun . . . Watch out for breeders."

"I will. 'Bye, girl."

"'Bye, baby."

I hung up the phone. Then I called Chloe right back. "What should I wear?"

"Well, it's almost ninety degrees. Probably shorts and sandals."

"But I have no tan and my sandals are from Wal-Mart."

"Trust me; Fashion doesn't even matter at Valley Fair, hon."

"But it matters to me. Mike likes me because I dress cool."

"Then it will never work because you only dress cool sometimes."

"Whatever. I'm serious."

"You're both boys. Wear something boyish. Wear a tank top and khaki shorts and work your Wal-Mart sandals like it's the runway . . . And for God's sake, wash off your eyeliner now in case you go on water rides."

"Alright," I sighed and got off the phone. I spent the rest of the half hour in front of my mirror, trying on my two pairs of khaki shorts, my three tank tops, and my four little button-down shirts with fun beach pictures. Finally, I made a decision and began messing with my hair. I started getting nervous when he was five minutes late, then upset when he was ten, then certain that he had died in a car accident at fifteen minutes. By the time he arrived, twenty-five minutes late, I had proclaimed my love for the late Mike Whatever-His-Last-Name-Was and had vowed to never love another man again as long as I lived. But when I saw his car pull into my driveway, I forgot it all and began jumping and clapping with excitement. Then I had to run frantically around my house and find my keys, my money, my bag of weed, and put on my sandals that had about fifty bazillion hideous buckles and were a huge pain in the ass.

"Hi," I said, climbing into the big black family car with a car seat and toys in the back.

"Hey," he greeted me. I was relieved to see that he had dressed similarly. "Sorry I'm late."

"No problem. Was the house hard to find?"

"Naw. Piece of cake."

"Great . . . I'm so excited."

"Me, too."

Valley Fair was a half hour away, so we had plenty of time to talk. At first he was really shy. Everything I asked made him blush. But finally, after a million random questions, he began to spill his guts. I found out that his dad was a realtor whose picture was on bus stops, and his mom was a stay-at-home, which was a tough job because he had four younger siblings. They lived in a nice house, naturally, but it was always messy because of the kids. Mike was planning on going to the U of M when he graduated. He wanted to play basketball there, but didn't know if he could because he was second string on the high-school varsity team. Above all, it seemed that he passionately loved video games, comic books, and science-fiction/fantasy novels. It was sort of sad for me to hear it all. It turned out that the only thing that we had in common was a shared hatred for math. Maybe that was part of the reason I liked him, though: His life seemed straight out of an old TV show—*Picture Perfect*.

When we got to Valley Fair, we immediately went on Wild Thing, the biggest coaster there. The lines for the roller coasters were superlong, and it was so hot that people had to stand where The Wave constantly splashed water everywhere. Still, it was a lot of fun. I felt like I was in junior high again, except this time with a date. Mike was afraid of heights, and every time a roller coaster got to the top of the hill, he'd hold his breath and clutch my arm. He was so cute. Throughout the day, I was sort of pondering the two of us, trying to figure out what we were. Boyfriends perhaps? If so, I couldn't figure out the dynamics of the relationship. I wasn't sure if I was supposed to be the "boy" or the "girl," or if either of us were. Or if we were just like brothers and shouldn't even be messing around. I watched the way he talked to people, or ate his lunch, and he seemed so straight. To me, a person like Mike being gay seemed too good to be true.

By the end of the day, we were completely soaked from water rides and broke from grubbing on too much pizza and Coke. Mike spent his last two dollars on a picture that a Valley Fair employee took of us. In it, our arms are wrapped around each other's shoulders with me staring at him while he's looking at the camera. We're both smiling, despite drenched clothing and dripping hair. It was a great picture, actually.

On the way back to his house, I told him about how nuts my family was. I said that they drove me insane and that I just had to move out or I'd kill myself. He said that he thought I was too hard on them. When I told him about my mom taking me to a priest, he remarked that I should respect her beliefs because I'd be nowhere without her. It sort of bugged me when he said stuff like that. No one understood my angst, even though it was as plain as day to me. But I wasn't going to complain about that to him. I didn't even care, really. I just loved talking to him.

When we got back to his house, we smoked a joint in his garage, then played Mario Racing on his Nintendo 64. I had never been interested in video games, so I never got the hang of it. It was fun anyway, just because I was doing it with Mike. It eventually led to wrestling, which turned into sex. And our second round was just as passionate as the first. Only this time we weren't in such a hurry. It was kind of weird, too, because I never knew you could talk during sex. Afterwards, he fell right to sleep once again in my arms. Meanwhile I laid awake, thinking to myself that I finally had everything I wanted.

"So what do you want to do now?" I asked, stubbing out the joint we'd just finished smoking.

Mike and I were in the same tunnel I had taken him to the first time we had gotten stoned together. It was "our spot." That's what I called it, anyway. I watched our feet, pointed toward the water, his left foot crossed over my right foot. I had stopped wearing my platforms around Mike because I liked him taller than me. Instead, I wore a pair of blue Adidas, which he was jealous of. He was always complimenting me on the way I dressed and how my hair always looked cool and everything. This was one of my favorite things about him.

"Let's go shopping at the mall," he suggested.

"Do you have any money?"

"A few dollars."

"Alright," I sighed, even though I hated the mall.

Mike walked ahead of me toward the mall. He was smiling merrily, oblivious to how big of a dork he was when he was stoned. He was still sunburned from Valley Fair, and I watched his bare legs stride back and forth. I had rubbed aloe on his legs and back for days, yet he still peeled. He told me once he was Irish, which may explain it. In the sun his hair was strawberry blond. He had a few freckles on his face too, but not as many as Sam had. I wondered if she was Irish, too.

When we got to the mall, Mike wanted to go to Spencer Gifts. He led me up and down the isles, and we picked up all sorts of gizmos to laugh at and ponder over. Mike stuck fake vomit to my forehead, and I was so mad. But my anger made him laugh even harder. He ended up buying a *South Park* key chain and a Superman refrigerator magnet. He gave me the magnet when we left. I couldn't believe how lucky I was to have such a perfect boyfriend!

I didn't really want to be at the mall anymore, so I decided to call Chloe instead. I wanted to bring Mike over to his apartment and introduce them properly, since I'd already told both of them everything about each other. Well, not everything. Some things I kept from Mike. But Chloe knew the whole dish. He practically knew what Mike was like in bed. I tell Chloe *every*thing. I discovered that he was at home with his friend Tammy, waiting on a bag. When I told him that I had a little bit of pot left, he begged us to visit him. I'd be that eager, too. Waiting for your bag sober bites a big one.

"Hey, girrrrrl," Tammy said, applauding as we walked in.

"Hey, gorgeous," I returned. "This is Mike."

"Oooh, he's cute," she continued, waving her bottle of Corona. She had brought over a case.

"Oh my God!" I exclaimed, noticing the birdcage. "When did you get that?" It was a gold cage held from the top by an ornate gold arm that was connected to a post. Inside was a buttercup canary. It began to chirp as if on cue.

"Don't you love it?" Chloe asked, getting up to hug the cage. "It's an antique!"

"Did the bird come with it?"

"Of course, darling!"

"Where on earth did you get it?"

"You remember Anthony? That wonderful man I'm dating?"

"The one with the mustache?"

"The very same."

"Chloe . . . I think a couple of them have mustaches."

"You know, the one with the car!"

"Oh, okay, yeah."

"God!" He rolled his eyes. "Well? Do you like it?"

"It's awesome. I think it's the nicest thing you own."

"Hey, don't be dissin' my shit," he snapped. Then he looked at the cage proudly. "I bet it's worth a ton. They don't have stuff this nice at even Marshall's."

"You're right about that." Tammy took a swig off her beer. "Come sit down, babe." She was patting the spot Chloe had been sitting in.

"Hey!" Chloe argued.

I stuck my tongue out at him as I sat down. "You snooze you lose . . . Wanna smoke?" I said, reaching into my backpack for my stash.

"You read my mind." He crashed onto the beanbag. "Oh, my man is so sweet!" He was still talking about Anthony. "I think maybe I'll marry him!"

"He sounds like a real catch."

"So this is your man, huh?" Chloe asked, noticing Mike for the first time.

"Yeah, this here's my bitch," I joked.

Mike obviously did not think that me calling him a bitch was very funny, but he sat down on the floor in front of me anyway. He was too shy to get mad at me in front of everyone. I knew that Chloe intimidated him. Just like Chloe scared me when I first met him. I suspected Mike already had a curious crush on my friend.

"So, Mike, what do you know?" Chloe questioned.

"I don't know?"

"You don't know what you know?"

"Well, no."

Tammy started giggling, being that she was the same type of girl who would laugh when Justin Snatchface was making fun of someone for being gay at St. John's High School.

"Just ignore Chloe's little remarks." I put my hand on Mike's shoulder.

"Oh, Erick, he knows I'm just teasing him. Right?"

"Sure." Mike grinned at Chloe.

"I love my birdcage so much!" Chloe said again, stroking the post like he was jacking it off. "It's *so* big!"

"Will you hand me that, dear?" I asked Mike, pointing to the red penis bong that was standing in the corner. We all watched him stretch to reach it. His T-shirt slid up past his shorts, and you could see his lower back. I wondered what Chloe was thinking.

Did he want Mike? Did Mike want him? After he handed me the bong, I jammed the bowl full, took a hit, and handed it back to Mike. The cloud of smoke I exhaled made me cough, "Whew, that's rough."

"Rough's the way to do it," Chloe declared.

"So how'd you meet this weirdo?" Tammy asked Mike after his hit.

"I bought sunglasses from him."

"I remember that," Chloe said.

"You do?" Mike was feeling special.

"How could anyone forget you?" I jumped in.

"I remember you, too," Mike said to Chloe. I couldn't *believe* they were flirting. I should have known it was a mistake to introduce them.

"What's your bird's name?" I asked, if only to distract them from each other.

"Suz. Isn't she the cutest?"

"How do you know it's a she?"

"Honey, that's what people always say about me . . . I think you should treat my pet with a little more respect than that."

"Whatever, you're crazy . . . I don't think canaries have to deal with the whole drag-queen thing."

"Lucky them!"

"Yeah, really," Mike agreed. I could never get Mike to say anything about being gay, and now Chloe has him ready to be a drag queen. It was so unfair. Chloe was *such* a bitch.

Suddenly the most unexpected thing happened. When Chloe took his bong hit, he began coughing like a maniac. It was the first time I'd ever seen him cough like that. In fact, it was probably the first time I ever saw him cough at all. And he totally could not stop. He hurried to the bathroom, where he hacked up junk from his lungs. Although he had the faucet turned all the way up and the door closed, you could still hear him easily. "What the hell?" Tammy said, confused. Obviously, Chloe's cough was new to her, too. Before long, the hacking turned into gasping for breath mixed with a choking cough. I could picture him on the other side of the door, knelt down in front of the toilet.

"Is he okay?" Mike asked worriedly.

"I'm sure he's fine. He's just a huge freak, that's all," was what I said to try to calm all of us. "I wouldn't be surprised if that fool has lung cancer." No way was I going to let Chloe woo Mike away from me.

"More pot for us." Tammy took a big hit from the bowl.

"Right on, sister." I packed the last of my weed into the bong and took a monster hit. On my exhale, I said politely to Mike, "Do you want to sit here?"

"I'm fine."

"Are you sure? 'Cause I don't mind sitting on the floor."

"Yeah, I'm cool." Then he leaned up against my leg. It made me think he was finally starting to get comfortable, touching me in front of other people. I put my hand on his shoulder, and he put his arm around my leg. He was a very affectionate person, once he warmed up.

When Chloe came out of the bathroom, he acted like nothing had happened. Rather he just seemed upset that we were smoking without him. He loved to pout. After that we listened to Madonna and played a drinking game with Tammy's case of Corona. Pretty soon we were all so drunk that nothing made sense anymore. Then the bag Chloe and Tammy were splitting arrived, so we passed around about fifty joints. Chloe coughed and cleared his throat about every five minutes and kept saying in a joking voice, "I can't believe my poor lungs." For the rest of the evening, Mike and I kept our arms around each other, but he was watching Chloe and laughing at everything he said the entire evening. I could tell he wanted Chloe to think he was cool. Chloe impressed me, though. He remained true to our friendship and didn't flirt back for the rest of the night. Maybe he realized how important Mike was to me. Or maybe I had it backwards and it was me who was important to Chloe. Was I the one he was showing off for? I was truly sure about only one thing: Watching Mike stare at Chloe's antics, completely star-struck, I realized that if Chloe wanted to, he could recruit tons of straight boys into a life of homosexuality. Everyone wanted to be Chloe's friend.

Once the case of beer was gone, Mike and I left. Completely trashed off our asses, we stumbled through the ghetto. I can't even remember what we sang, but it was something really silly. I'm sure anyone walking the streets would have thought we were escaped mental patients. When we got back to Mike's house, everyone was asleep, and we wasted no time having sloppy sex. After a while, Mike was too drunk to participate, so I ended up doing all the work. While he just laid there, moaning with his eyes closed and occasionally remembering to push his hand down my back, I got us both off. Soon after, we fell asleep. But before I did, I told him that I loved him. Although I'm quite sure he was still awake, he acted like he was sleeping, not saying a word.

{ ten }

The night before my first day of school, I had stayed up till 2:00 A.M. watching television and therefore got only four hours of sleep. I crawled out of bed and put ice in some coffee and slammed it. Although it tasted disgusting, I felt much better once the caffeine kicked in. At least I was revived enough to leave the house. I felt pretty ridiculous by the time I got to school. Running out on Father Tom had cost me my new uniforms. I had grown at least an inch since last spring, so my faded pants stopped above my ankles. Normally, making fashion faux pas led to the kind of embarrassment worth faking mono over. However, this year I really didn't care what I was wearing. I figured all anyone would notice anyway was my eyeliner, green nail polish, and platinum spiked hairdo.

They did. Most people stared like they'd never seen a movie star before. I couldn't believe what losers they were. At lunch I sat with a fat girl I'd never met. I tried to be nice to her because she was fat, but we didn't really talk much. Justin and Terrance walked by and laughed. Justin asked if we were "together." What a dork! I couldn't believe that was the best he could come up with. As the day wore on, my attitude toward school got worse and worse. I felt like I hated everyone. Finally, I just gave up trying to stay awake and put my head down on my crossed arms. When the last bell of the day rang, I woke up with the imprint of the spiral wire on my notebook carved into my face.

I crashed on my bed once I got home, sleeping until Mike called an hour later. "How was your first day of school?" he asked.

"Lame. I can't stand my school."

"That sucks. Too bad you can't go to mine. It's really cool."

That's when I realized that if I went to school with him, I'd probably hate him, too, just because he had such a preppy attitude about everything. I felt so depressed that I almost told him I hated him and hung up on him right then. But of course, I didn't. "Do you want to hang out?" I asked.

"I can't. I'm about to go play basketball up at the park."

"You are?" That sounded like a punishment to me. But just to be a good sport, I said, "Maybe I'll come watch you play."

"That's not the best idea," was his immediate response.

"Why not?"

"Because . . . you hate basketball."

"Where'd you get that idea?"

"Well, I can't imagine you'd like it."

"Why not?"

"Well for one, it doesn't involve makeup," he said, only half-jokingly.

"You're right." I wanted to kill him for that remark. "Are you just too embarrassed for your friends to see me?" I asked finally.

He laughed. "I wouldn't want them to think I was a drag queen."

"They probably already do."

"Whatever," he blew me off. "I'll call you later."

"Fine." I hung up the phone after he had hung up on me. That closet-case bastard, I thought as I went back to sleep.

The next day I slept through my alarm and my mother came pounding on my door ten minutes before I had to leave. Putting on my uniform, I realized that I probably did have mono. I hadn't even showered in two days, and I was so miserable I could have screamed. When I got to school, I slept through all my classes, including art class, which was my favorite. None of my teachers bothered to wake me up. By eleventh grade, it was apparently all up to me to pass their classes. In that case, I figured I should just drop out.

When I got home, I called Mike right away but his mom answered and said that he was busy auditioning for a school play. I was really irritated with him. It was only the second day of school, and already he was too busy to hang out. I hadn't seen him in four days. It was the longest break since we began dating, and I was starting to wonder if there was something wrong.

Later that night I took a bus over to Chloe's to smoke bowls and talk about my relationship problems. But when I got there, I saw that pills had been scattered all over the floor and his end table had been knocked over. When I asked him what was going on, he snapped, saying he didn't want to talk about it. He was in the worst mood I'd ever seen him in. I figured he was just cranky because he'd been sick nonstop since he got that sudden cough. Some people can be the biggest whiners over the littlest colds. Then, when I tried to help clean up all the pills on the floor, he snapped at me again. He told me not to go near his vitamins, which he scooped up into a white plastic bottle with no label. I didn't even bother to recommend dumping the stupid vitamins he took every day and try using cold medicine instead. We hung out for a little while, but I never brought up Mike's name the whole time. I just made Chloe some ramen noodles and lent him my ear while he complained about how miserable his life was and how diarrhea was the worst possible thing imaginable. I was sort of repulsed that he would talk so casually about his shit, but I didn't say anything. Eventually I went home, feeling more miserable than ever.

When I got to school on Friday, my homeroom teacher, Mr. Jefferson, announced at the beginning of the day that from now on we would gather together at lunch every Friday for an expression of prayer and school spirit. Sometimes we'd have an inspirational reading, or a sing-along, or perhaps even student skits, he said. Whereas most of the kids in my class got excited—even giddy— about the possibility of community fun, I came to the conclusion that St. John's had finally reached the highest possible level of offensiveness. Why couldn't they just let us eat in peace?

By last period, I was so sick of school that I seriously thought about committing suicide. The only bright spot was that the school week was finally over. I decided that I had to celebrate surviving my first week of classes. I figured Mike and I could go camping, or to a hotel (or anywhere where we could make booty love for the first time). I was imagining we'd drink wine and do it on a blanket in the wilderness.

Unfortunately, he was busy when I called. After only one week, he had a huge science project he had to work on all weekend with his lab partner, who remained nameless. Clearly, it was the biggest lie I'd ever heard in my life. Then, just to make matters worse, he told me that he didn't want me calling his house anymore because his parents might start to suspect something was going on, especially since I acted like a girl. I'd never felt so insulted about my sexuality. But I said nothing, and he ended the conversation by telling me that from now on *he* would call *me*.

So for the entire weekend I waited by the phone. Chloe called me to apologize for his temper on Tuesday night and to tell me that he was feeling much better—he invited me to Screwdriver, but I said no. Sam called to see if I wanted to go over to Jake's house to trip on 'shrooms, but I said no. Molly called to invite me to her Halloween party, which I said I'd go to because that date was a long way away. Even Tammy called me from Chloe's house to see if I had changed my mind about Screwdriver. I didn't budge for anyone. I was sure Mike would call to take back all the mean things he'd said and to tell me that he loved me. Why wouldn't he? Even though we'd had a fight, clearly love always prevailed. Love was something you couldn't avoid, or turn off, or ever forget about. Love lasted forever, I thought. But, alas, Mike never called. Finally, on Sunday night, just to be sure he wasn't dead, I gave in and called him.

"Hello?" he answered.

"Mike?"

"Oh, hi, Erick." He didn't sound very excited to hear my voice.

"What's up?" I asked.

"Nothing . . . Hey, not to be rude or anything, but I thought I told you not to call me here."

All my hope sank. I knew I'd made a mistake. "Sorry, it's just that I haven't talked to you in a few days, and I was wondering what's going on with you."

"Nothing."

"Well, what have you been doing? Have you been busy with school?"

"'Course I've been busy at school. I wanna graduate . . . But what about you? Are you still sleeping in class?"

"Whatever," I said with hurt feelings. What happened to the boy I'd met at the mall? He was so insensitive and could never understand my suffering.

"Listen, I have to go, alright?"

"Fine . . . Are you going to call me sometime, or are we just never going to speak again?" I asked dramatically.

"I'll call . . . when I'm not so busy. Maybe I'll come over to Chloe's again sometime. That was kinda fun."

"Yeah, it was." I hated him for that comment.

"Hey, guess what?"

"What?"

"I met this girl named Courtney. She's really cool. You'd like her. She's fucking hot, too."

"Are you kidding me? You like her? Where does that leave me?"

"Nowhere."

"Nowhere? What about us?"

"Hold on a minute now. There isn't an 'us' . . . That was just something we did. It didn't mean anything. Look, maybe we just shouldn't see each other for a while."

"I can't believe you're dating a *girl*," I said it as an insult. "How *can* you?"

"Easy, because I'm not even fucking *gay*."

"Yeah, right! You're the biggest fucking faggot I ever met!" I screamed, hanging up first. That asshole! I was so furious that I didn't know what to do. I felt like all my emotions were trapped inside of me, raging out of control, and I had no way to vent them. I was actually shaking. Finally, in blind madness, I dropped to my floor and began tearing apart my clothes, ripping T-shirts into rags, throwing them against my wall. There had never been such an attack on fashion! Once that outburst ended, I sat in a daze in my pile of insanity, until, at last, I turned on Tori. I had spent the entire weekend wanting desperately to leave my house, but unable to because of Mike. Now, because of Mike, I didn't want to leave my house ever again. I felt numb and wanted to sit and sing, barely, to Tori. How could he be so mean when he was so sweet only a few days ago? I was angry with myself for believing in love, for wasting an entire weekend to loneliness, frustration, and despair, only to find out that love hadn't turned out to be what I had imagined at all. Finally, after four hours and five Tori albums, I felt halfway over him (the other half of my heart, I was certain, would never quite mend). I called Chloe to tell him what had happened.

"You mean he's dating a girl? Like, a *real* girl?" For Chloe, the word "girl" described someone with fashion sense. You had to clarify yourself if you meant "biologically female."

"Yes, a girl. Her name is Courtney," I said despairingly.

"Isn't he a little too gay for that?"

"Duh."

"Oh, poor Erick, my little lamb. I'm sorry. That really sucks ... I can't believe it. He seemed so normal to me ... But don't they always seem normal until you find out they're screwed up as hell?"

"What do you mean? He *is* normal," I said bitterly. "He's straight, isn't he? How much more normal can you get than that?"

"He's not straight. He's a lesbian! Mike the Dyke. Who would have thought?"

I started laughing in spite of myself. Leave it to Chloe to lighten my heartache. "Chloe, it's not funny." I wasn't ready to blow it off. "Now I'll never have a boyfriend."

"So what? Neither will he."

"Ha-ha. That doesn't help."

"Well, look at it this way, kid. Now you're single again, and tomorrow we can go shopping all day and dancing all night. It'll be just like old times ... Anyway, if it makes you feel any better, Anthony and I are through, too."

"Really?" Somehow it *did* make me feel better. "Why?"

"He said I'm too dramatic and that he can't handle me. That I'm the kind of person who would turn his life upside down and leave him with nothing. And it all started because I didn't want to wear my seat belt in his car. Can you believe that?"

I was laughing again. "That totally sucks ... Do you get to keep the birdcage?"

"Of course. He gave it to me ... I'm looking at Suz right now. I think all that I need in this life is my bird. I'm through with men. Maybe I'll do what Mike the Dyke did and become a lesbian. I bet Tammy would date me ... What are you doing at your house? Why don't you come over, and I'll have a big fat joint waiting for you when you get here?"

"I have school tomorrow."

"Oh, that's right. How is school going anyway?"

"Duh. It sucks. I hate school. I don't think I can make it through the year. It's so pointless for me to be there when I should be out in the real world making money and supporting myself. I don't even care if I'm poor. I'll wait tables or something." Chloe didn't say anything, which meant he didn't approve. But what could he say? He had dropped out of school when he was my age.

Laying in bed that night, I thought about how badly I wanted a boyfriend. And not one like Mike at all. I wanted to find my soulmate. Someone who would appreciate me and who wouldn't be embarrassed to introduce me to his friends. What I really wanted—but couldn't have—was Chloe. I had wanted him since the first day I met him at the mall, five months ago.

I was so taken by my fantasy of Chloe that I had to get out of bed. I went outside for a cigarette on my front step, where I imagined Chloe as my boyfriend. We'd be like Thelma and Louise if Susan Sarandon and Geena Davis had been lesbians. We'd be so fabulous.

Of course, I couldn't forget the fact that Chloe had told me the first time I ever went over to his house that we could never date. Why would he say that? I realize that I'm only sixteen—but couldn't he wait a couple years? I ached for him in every inch of my body. He just had to feel the same way about me. Love like this couldn't work in only one direction. Maybe I needed to do something differently, or become someone different. I thought about that night I brought Mike over to Chloe's apartment. Chloe was such a bitch that night. And then when I told him that Mike dumped me, he was elated. Was he jealous of Mike? Maybe that was the trick. I had to find a new boyfriend ASAP to make Chloe jealous. Then I would make the big switcheroo, and Chloe and I would live happily ever after!

{ eleven }

y new goal was to find a boyfriend and make Chloe jealous. And since I knew that I wouldn't find anyone at school, I started skipping class regularly. By October, I had pretty much stopped going altogether. Instead, I hung out in Uptown at a gay coffee shop called Plato. Chloe had introduced me to it once, but he never really hung out there. He said that it was a trashy dive where old men went to pick up young boys. And this was true, in some instances, but mostly the people there seemed harmless. Plus, I liked the atmosphere. It was kind of small and intimate. They had tables to sit at and sofas to lounge on, with tall plants and cheesy artwork on the walls. Almost everyone was a regular, so I made new friends right away. Luckily, my new friends were my age, and we simply sneered at the old men who stared at us. It was perfect for me because I fit right in. I think that's why they call the gay community a family. Everyone knows each other, and everyone's a gossip.

The first time I went to Plato without Chloe, I dragged Sam along for company. We sat in the smoking section and sipped strawberry Italian sodas. She talked about Jake this and Jake that—how he was so sweet, despite being a hard-ass. I wasn't paying very close attention to her, though. My eyes and ears wandered the room, eavesdropping in and out of conversations, as I searched for a replacement for Mike. I don't know how Sam could have been oblivious to my lack of interest her gushing Jake stories. Perhaps it was because I was disinterested that she gloated. We used to date and Sam was always trying to make me jealous of Jake.

After an entire afternoon spent there, we left. I was saddened to be with her rather than the man of my dreams. Of course, I felt guilty for thinking that. In truth, I loved Sam, and I didn't want to treat her as my consolation prize. But when finding love is the only thing on your mind, you tend to neglect those people who love you already.

Friendships are resilient, though, and for some reason, maybe from her lack of having anywhere else to go, Sam decided that she *loved* Plato. She, too, began skipping school to hang out there regularly. Other days, when Jake wasn't busy with his multitude of drug buddies, we'd go cruising around in his car, which was a party in and of itself, until I inevitably got dropped off somewhere alone. It only happened once a week, which led me to wonder if *I* was actually *Sam's* consolation prize. All she ever did was complain about Jake's lack of commitment. She swore all the time that she would dump him. Mostly, I think she couldn't trust him. Who could blame her? Jake's reputation for being a snake wasn't acquired due to his honesty. Everyone knows that snakes are sneaky. Sam was vulnerable, and it worried me to see her involved with him. Of course, whenever I brought any of this up she got defensive, or attacked me for being a hypocrite. Like one time I casually asked her, "So what *is* the deal with you two anyway? Are you exclusive?"

She snapped back: "We're together and that's all I want to say about it . . . And anyway, you shouldn't talk, baby, because I don't see Mike beating down your door for some hot Erick lovin'."

She had me with that one. I certainly couldn't play high-and-mighty with her when I had my own disastrous love life to contend with. I think that was what I liked best about Sam. We gave each other shit till doomsday, but we still loved each other in the end. Chloe was my best friend because it was just the two of us against the world. Sam and I were something different. Sometimes I felt like we had a love bigger than either of us realized—more personal than we'd ever admit. Of all the friendships I had ever had, Sam's was the only one that lasted post–coming out. Although all of that drama affected her more than anyone else, we had to stay friends: she was like my sister.

We went from being a couple to being the perfect fag/fag-hag team. Sam took my cue quickly and began dressing more fierce, buying herself platforms, something leopard print, and every kind of glitter. We were so the coolest people at Plato. Everyone wanted to sit with us, and before we knew it, we had a new circle of friends. Two of them were Zack and Jerome. They were eighteen-year-old boyfriends, and I so wanted to be eighteen. They lived together in an apartment not far from Chloe. Jerome was black and Zack was white. Once, when I called them Salt and Pepper as a joke, they got superpissed for about thirty seconds. But before we knew it, the name stuck. Suddenly they were greeted by their new names whenever they entered Plato.

Another time, Sam and I were at their apartment, and we all did crystal meth. Neither Sam nor I had done it before, even though Jake was always raving about it. I was slightly skeptical at first because of the bad sensation snorting coke with Troy gave me. But when I told Jerome what had happened, he said that drugs were weird like that because the effect they have on you has a lot to do with your environment. Besides, I was probably just creeped out about Troy. Zack put a clear plastic bag the size of a postage stamp full of meth onto the coffee table. Seeing it, Sam and I both wanted some immediately. Zack crushed it into white powder, and we each did a line. Jerome was right. It didn't hurt at all. I told him that it just tasted sort of sugary and fizzy, like Pop Rocks for your nose. He grinned and said, "Hence the name 'nose-candy,' baby!"

When it finally hit me, the effect was like caffeine. I wasn't feeling high from it, just really wired. From there the four of us stayed up snorting lines in their apartment the whole weekend. Outside the weather was beginning to turn cold, and every time we left the building for even a few seconds, the wind felt like it was blowing right through us. I swear to God, I never shut up once all weekend. I was completely spun out of my mind, telling them everything about myself—my parents, school, Mike, how I wanted to perform in drag and be a graphic designer. And, of course, I went on and on about how much I loved Chloe with absolute abandon. I managed to convince them—and myself—that I would die if I couldn't be with him.

The drugs affected Sam the same way, too. All she talked about was her mom—how she was too controlling, even though she had no control over her own life. We found out a lot about Zack and Jerome as well. Zack was an artist (a painter), and he was sick of all the posers out there who pretended to be cool but who were actually huge geeks that never even *heard* of techno music. Jerome was sick of the pressures his dad put on him to go to college. No one in their family had ever gotten a college degree, and Jerome was supposed to be the first because he had a high GPA and was accepted into Macalester. He had dropped out his senior year of high school, however, due to the pressure of coming out. I, of course, totally understood where he was coming from. Our conversation lasted approximately a million hours, during which time I felt more connected to these three people than anyone else in the world. Ultimately, we got very serious and cried together about how sad everything was. We agreed that none of us had ever felt so close to anyone in our lives.

Afterwards, when I told Chloe about the weekend, I omitted the part about doing speed. I knew he would lecture about the dangers of drugs, and I didn't want to hear that crap. I figured a little experimentation was harmless, especially since I knew I wouldn't become an addict. In the end, I really didn't even like crystal that much. Although it felt really good at the time, I wasn't able to sleep until the following night—and I woke up the morning after sick as hell and starving. Coming down from a crystal binge is much worse than an alcohol hangover. Still, I was glad I had at least tried it because now I wouldn't have to wonder all the time what it would be like. The mystery of hard-core drugs was solved.

"Hey, baby," I said as I approached Chloe at Shades.

"How's it going, stranger?"

"Good . . . How are you?"

"Bored without you here. I swear, I could kill your mom for calling corporate offices and getting you fired."

"You and me both," I said despairingly. Suddenly I didn't know what to say next. My agenda for this visit was to tell Chloe that I loved him, but suddenly I felt silly telling him that while he was at work. Besides, he was wearing red plastic pants and a purple T-shirt that just killed me to look at because he looked so gorgeous in them. I was terribly afraid of ruining our friendship by saying the wrong thing. I lost all composure and began with a stutter, "Wh-What are you doing tonight?"

"Nothing, why?" He could tell something was up.

I had to think of something fast. "Because I was hoping I could make us dinner."

"Dinner? What are you making?"

"It's a surprise."

"Really? I love surprises!"

"I know you do . . . so come home after work."

"Alright . . . I'll buy some white zinfandel."

• • •

I took a bus back to Chloe's neighborhood. Before going to his apartment, I stopped off at GJ's SuperValu and bought some groceries. When I got to his place I put them away, turned on Tori, and began cleaning the apartment. Chloe lived like such a slob; I couldn't believe it. I started by sorting through his closet and hanging shirts on the rod. I'd barely made a dent in the heap when I ran out of hangers and just gave up. I shoved the clothing that was strewn about the apartment into the closet and squeezed the door shut. Next, I washed all the dishes in the sink and stacked them in the cupboard. I used dish soap to wash the counters, cabinet doors, refrigerator, stove, end table, windowsill, and every surface of the bathroom. Chloe didn't have a vacuum, so I had to use a broom and dustpan to clean the carpeting, which was the most frustrating chore I had ever encountered. At last I finished cleaning and quickly showered. I was finishing getting dressed when Chloe burst through the door with a bottle of wine and a handful of flowers.

"Holy shit! You cleaned," he said in shock.

I looked around the room with pride. The apartment had never sparkled before. "Isn't it nice?"

"It's wonderful," he said, enjoying the lovely aromatic candles. He greeted Suz by smooching at her from outside the cage. "It's like we're a family!" He turned to me and added, "You're not allowed to leave."

"Okay." I was relieved that Chloe was happy with me despite not having a job or paying a penny of rent. "So are you hungry?"

"Starving. What are we having?"

"Huevos rancheros."

"Yuck."

"Oh, whatever! You haven't even given the poor meal a chance. And that's 'cause you don't realize that I make the best huevos rancheros ever."

"Ever? Well what's in them?"

"It's beans and cheese and scrambled eggs on a grilled tortilla topped with Ortega Hot Taco Sauce."

"Yuck."

"It's good!" I insisted.

"What about sour cream?"

"No sour cream."

"No sour cream? How come?"

"'Cause I don't have any. God!"

"Oh!" He flopped down on the futon and flipped through TV stations. That's when I realized that Chloe desperately needed me as his boyfriend. He was completely helpless, and he didn't even realize it. Without me, the place would have remained a total pigsty forever, and the only thing he'd ever eat would be greasy fast food at the mall. All he ever had at his apartment were cookies and candy and an occasional box of Eggo waffles.

"So, how was work, dear?" I laughed at how much I sounded like my mother. Then I added sarcastically, "Did you sell a lot of sunglasses?"

"Fuck you!" he laughed. "I'm the only breadwinner of this house." With that he whipped his bag of weed from his pocket and loaded a bowl.

"Don't worry, I'll get a job," I said.

"Sure."

"I will."

"I know."

I smiled for him to show my sincerity then returned to the kitchen. Cooking was one thing I had always loved to do. My mom taught me how when I was a kid by starting with baking—chocolate-chip cookies, cakes, brownies. Later, she taught me pastas and salads. It was one of our few bonding rituals before our big falling-out. I opened Chloe's two cupboards and brought out all the necessary ingredients. Soon I had a twelve-inch flour tortilla frying in an oiled skillet while I cracked an egg into a bowl. I sang "Happy Phantom" by Tori Amos, which was today's theme song. Next, I spread the refried beans across the tortilla and gave it a lip around the perimeter so the egg wouldn't ooze out. I spilled the egg into it, along with some chopped onion and shredded Kraft taco cheese, then folded the tortilla in half so that it was a clean half-moon, golden brown and crispy. I served our meal on the floor in front of the TV along with white zinfandel in glass tumblers with ice cubes.

"Remind me to get some TV trays," I commented.

"Miss Erick! Is my humble abode not up to par? Let me know if there is anything I can do to accommodate you, because I truly believe that all teenagers need to be spoiled out of their minds!" He took a bite of his food. "Mmm, this is good," he said, chewing.

"I told you you'd like it."

"Dahling, we must learn to cook and clean like this every day!" Only if you'll have sex with me every night, I said in my head.

"Yum, yum, yum," he chirped, eating like Suz.

"So what are you dressing up as for Halloween?" I asked.

"I was thinking about going as Frankentrannie."

"Oh my God!" I cried, as I tried to picture what that would look like. Frankenstein with fake boobs and a wig, I supposed. "Maybe I'll do drag, too," I said, blushing.

"Fantabulous!" he clapped.

"I take it you think I should?"

"Girl, I will help you find the fiercest costume and wig. We are going to look so cool at Molly's *partieee.*" We high-fived.

Suddenly my smile turned upside down, "I don't know if I can do it, Chloe. I mean, I really want to and everything, but I know I'll just look stupid. I'd be way too embarrassed."

"Why?"

"I'd just feel like such a big fag."

"Oh, poor baby," Chloe teased.

I crossed my arms stubbornly, while Chloe urged me with his eyes until I couldn't help but giggle. "Okay, fine, I'll do it," I said. "But what if I'm humiliated?"

"You won't be . . . Girl, I knew that when I put that wig on top of your head, you'd instantly be transformed."

"You could just tell that?"

"Honey, you aren't exactly the most macho man I've ever met."

"I'm kinda butch, aren't I?"

"No, not in the least."

"Oh, well. It's a good thing I don't have any interest in joining the army or going to any monster truck shows or anything like that."

"That's what your life would have been like had you stayed with Mike the Dyke."

"I guess," I shrugged, swirling my last piece of tortilla around in my yolk, contemplating my next sentence. "Chloe, what do you think about me?" I asked nervously.

"What do you mean? I think you're great."

"I just mean, well . . . I thought that when I came out I'd, you know, find a boyfriend and live happily ever after. But it hasn't worked like that. I mean, look what happened with Mike; I turned him straight."

"You mean you turned him into a lesbian!"

"Well, whatever. I'm sick of being single and—" I stopped. Chloe patted my hand. "Don't worry, babe, you'll find someone—Oops, that reminds me, I have to take my Echinacea." He stood up to get his herbal dietary supplement. His cough hadn't gone away, and now he took melatonin and Tylenol before bed. He grabbed the vial from his heart-shaped cabinet and washed a pill down with wine. I picked our plates off the floor and lathered them up in the sink.

"I bet," Chloe said, "that you'll find a boyfriend when you least expect it . . . The trick, I think, is to not look so hard. Just have fun and eventually it will happen. Just think, you have your whole life ahead of you," he declared, lighting a cigarette. He brought the cigarette to me and held it between my lips because my hands were in the dishwater. I could feel his body gently touching my back, and it gave me chills. But I said nothing that night about my true feelings. And as usual, when we went to bed, I laid awake in the dark, watching his body rise and fall, while he dreamed whatever.

{ twelve }

$\mathcal{T}$aking a deep breath, I slouch into a child-size Pepto-Bismol–colored chair and try to relax. I notice my hot pink fingernails. What have I done?! I've chewed off the tips of my brand-new manicure! The frayed outline of my nails is absolutely grotesque! And, of course, this the worst possible time for this to happen. I'm about to go onstage.

I scan my surroundings nervously: the salmon-colored walls, the cluttered vanities with mirrors smooched with kisses. The room is in complete chaos, with drag queens fixing their wigs, caking on makeup, squeezing into girdles. Prince is playing on the boom box.

And here I am, in the middle of it all, wearing a little pink dress, big huge tennis-shoe platforms, and a wig with big blond pigtails. I swear to God, I look like Baby Spice. What's even worse is that I don't know what song I'm supposed to perform when I get onstage. I certainly don't think I'd be wacky enough to lip-synch a Tori song dressed like a Spice Girl!

Suddenly, I'm being pushed toward the stage by all these beefy queens with their talons wrapped round my shoulders and waist. They bring me over to the stage entrance. I'm out of the audience's view but I can see onto the stage. Chloe is performing. I recognize him right away because of his eyes, but other than that, he looks like an entirely different person—a beautiful woman in a dress. Chloe is the only drag queen I've ever seen who can pull it off *that* well.

When his song ends, he walks gracefully off the stage and sort of loosely embraces me. But neither of us says a word. Then I walk onto the stage, looking out at the audience. They sit quietly and motionless for approximately one hundred hours. Then a cough from the audience breaks the silence, and music begins.

I can't believe it. The song is "Somewhere Over the Rainbow" to a dance beat! I can't think of where I've heard *that* before. Somehow I'm miraculously able to ad-lib the whole performance flawlessly. I can't believe I actually know all the words to this song. But I totally do. And I dance and dance and dance, and everyone cheers, and I feel like a million dollars!

I woke up, not at all surprised to have had that crazy dream. For one thing, it was a dream I'd had before. But also, it was 11:30 on Halloween morning, and tonight I was going to make my drag debut! I was as giddy as a dozen puppies. Chloe was already gone for the day, so I had all the time in the world to prepare. To start with, I made myself a cup of highly caffeinated Earl Grey tea, which Chloe got me hooked on, and enjoyed my first cigarette of the day.

Before doing my ten minutes of the Cindy Crawford aerobicize video, I opened Suz's cage to give her a chance to fly around the room and exercise, too. "I'm going to be a girl tonight," I sang to Suz as she delightedly pecked at the windowpane. In the shower, I stood under the hot water and shaved my legs, arms, and underarm hair for the first time ever. Next I shaved my face up and down and all around so it was as smooth as it could possibly be. My body tingled all over from going under the razor. What a gal had to go through in the mornin'! I rubbed Aveda Essentials all over myself to soothe away the rawness and already I was starting to feel superchick-ish. How weird. "My skin is now soft, yet firm," I said aloud in the mirror, laughing. I swear, I'm a nut like that. I couldn't help but be excited though; tonight I'd be making my first-ever transformation into a total diva.

I had the perfect costume planned. Chloe lent me a red sequined dress, which he bought but hadn't performed in, a pair of red heels, and that big blond wig he'd set on top of my head that night I dropped out of high school. I had to spend hardly any money. Except for a red sequined purse I bought from a thrift store, a pair of pantyhose, and some red nail polish and red lipstick.

Chloe was going as a stupid sailor, despite my wish that he'd do drag with me. I told him that even his Frankentrannie idea was better than some dumb sailor. But he just teased me and said it was my debut and he didn't want to take the spotlight off me. This, of course, led to an argument in which I accused him of selling out because he wouldn't do drag anymore, even for his best friend. In the six months I'd known him, I still hadn't ever seen him in drag. I'd seen only the few pictures and heard about his glory days from him and other queens at the bar. When I asked him about all this, he told me that he just hadn't been in the mood lately and left it at that.

The party we were attending was a masquerade ball over at Molly's apartment building. She'd gotten on the waiting list for the party room in time to nab it on one of the biggest party nights of the year. Her invitation insisted that everyone must come in a costume to be admitted, so I was expecting to see quite an outrageous crowd, hoping that some of the heat would be taken off me. I was supernervous.

In the meantime, I had a million errands to run, including picking up a sack of weed from Jake, going downtown to turn in a job application at a coffee shop, buying myself a bus pass, and calling my mom (which I dreaded more than anything). I had been away from home for two weeks, and we had never gone this long without speaking. Surely, my parents had reported me as a runaway and had all sorts of private detectives and FBI agents tracking me down. Or else, my parents were trying to block me out of their memories just like Tommy. That seemed far more likely. I was such an awful brat and so terribly offensive toward everything they valued. They didn't really need me anyway with Tim around. Unfortunately, I still needed them, or at least their money. If I asked Chloe for another cent, I'd feel too guilty to live with myself. He barely made enough to support himself, much less some poor little rich boy that he'd already saved from a life of utter depression. Not that I didn't have my reservations about hitting my parents up for cash. It would be yet another sign that I was unable to support myself.

After brushing my teeth, I threw on a pair of baggy blue jeans and an old, pilly sweater. I wanted to hide my shaved body until I actually had the dress on. Once I felt ready to face the day, I lit my second cigarette and called Jake.

"Talk to me," was his line when he answered the phone.

"Hey, Jake, it's Erick."

"Yeah?"

"What's up?"

"Nuthin'."

"Hey I was wondering if you could still hook me up . . . I talked to Sam and she said she'd talk to you about it. . . Did she?" I felt stupid already.

"You talked to Sam?"

"Yeah."

"Well, she never said nuthin' about it to me. I haven't even talked to her."

"What do you mean?"

"She's been avoiding me."

"Are you sure? 'Cause she didn't say anything about it to me, and she usually tells me everything."

"I think I would know when I was being avoided."

"Oh, sorry."

"Whatever for her . . . I mean, fuck her for dickin' me around, right? She just doesn't know a good thing when she sees it."

I didn't know what to say. I couldn't tell him that lately Sam had been bitching about how he wasn't very sensitive to her feelings. Or that she'd leave him for good if he didn't start treating her the way she deserved to be treated. That basically Jake was as bad at making a relationship work as Mike had been. Mike the Dyke, who wouldn't know a good thing if it slapped him upside his stupid head.

"So how much you want?" Jake asked.

"Pot? Oh, an eighth."

"You partying tonight or something?"

"Of course . . . it's Halloween."

"I hear ya. Well, come on over. But get here before one o'clock 'cause I got shit to do."

"Alright. Thanks, Jake."

Without a good-bye, he hung up the phone. I called Sam immediately to find out what was going on with them.

"Hey, baby," was how I greeted her when she answered in a sleepy voice. "Did I wake you?"

"Not really . . . I was just laying awake in my bed, too lazy to get up I guess." I pictured her in her bed with her red curly hair splashed across the pillow, the phone somewhere between her cheek and the bedsheets.

"This is your Happy Halloween wake-up call," I said.

"Happy Halloween to you, too," she replied with a yawn.

"I just got off the phone with Jake—he's gonna hook me up with a bag."

"That's cool . . . So do you want to get together or what?"

"Maybe later. I have a million things to do before Chloe gets home. So are you coming to the party tonight?"

"Of course. I have my costume thrown over the back of my desk chair as we speak."

"What are you going to be?"

"Promise you won't laugh?"

"Yeah, maybe."

"Pippi Longstocking."

"How darling of you, darling. I'm doing drag."

"Shut up! Oh my God, I can't believe an ex-boyfriend of *mine* wants to be a woman."

"I guess that makes you kind of an honorary lesbian."

"Fuck you!" she said sarcastically.

"Whatever! You like my sexy bod. Better than Jake's at least?"

"God, are you just conceited, or are you trying to imply something by that?"

"No, I was just teasing you."

"Ha-ha. What'd Jake the Snake tell you?"

"Just that you've been avoiding him, that he can't figure out why. Men can be so naïve, can't they?"

"Tell me about it," she agreed.

"Well, I should let you go. But I'll probably see you tonight, right? . . . Also, invite Zack and Jerome if you get a chance."

"They already have plans, darling. Apparently, they're too good for us."

"Well more fun for the rest of us! I'll call you later, babe."

"All right, 'bye."

After I got off the phone, I hauled ass over to Jake's house, taking a bus, then walking several blocks. Jake's neighborhood is far too rich to have a bus pass through it. I was pissed that he was so stubborn that he wouldn't just drive over and drop off the stupid bag. He could be such a prick. By the time I finally got there, it was 12:55. His place was a mansion. All brick with big windows and a manicured landscape. Before ringing the bell, I checked for Jake's car in the driveway. His car was a total junker in comparison to the rest of the cars you'd find in that neighborhood.

I'd been over to the place with Sam several times before. Although Jake bugged me, she'd con me into accompanying her there with the enticing lure of pot. She insisted that she knew my buttons better than I did, that she still had me whipped even though we weren't a couple anymore. If it had been anyone else, I would have said that I'm far too complex to be understood. But I let Sam get away with murder.

Jake answered the door wearing nothing but red sweatpants. That completely caught me off guard. But what eye candy! He was totally buff, with pierced nipples and tattoos and everything. He smoked more pot than just about anyone I knew, right in his own bedroom, too. The rumor was that his parents are both huge alcoholics; they even snorted coke. No wonder they didn't care if Jake smoked pot. He was one of those guys that always had to show you his ever-increasing collection of drug paraphernalia every time you saw him. From glass pipes that change color, to bongs, hookahs, and joint rollers.

"I thought you were in some big hurry," I said, walking into the living room. It was like entering a palace: two-story ceilings, marble floors, and white pillars. "You look to me like you're ready for bed."

"It only takes five minutes to get ready when you don't have to put on makeup, buddy-boy."

I sat down on the leather sofa right in front of the semi-truck-sized fireplace. The first time I ever went there, Sam took me on a guided tour like she owned the place. It had about fifty million bedrooms. Jake's dad was a doctor or lawyer or something impressive. He married Jake's mother, who was a singer in some

South American country, and brought her to the U.S. Jake had one brother, who was an overachieving lawyer with a drinking problem, and two goody-two-shoes sisters who both married alcoholics and had babies. It was a weird family for sure—completely upper-class dysfunctional. And Jake was the blackest sheep of all of them! You'd think that this would have been the red flag that tipped off Sam. But he was cute and he made her laugh, which, in her own words, is all she really wants from a fling. Personally, I thought Sam could do a little better. Dating a guy who sells drugs for shits and giggles was kind of tacky. Not that I wouldn't do it myself.

"You want to smoke?" Jake asked.

"Sure."

"Come on."

We took the nearest staircase (this house had two) down to his gigantic basement bedroom, which was crammed with a double bed, a couch, a fireplace, a TV, a desk, a keyboard, two turntables, and big speakers. Two of his walls were painted black, and he had rave fliers taped to them. The room looked like he hadn't cleaned it since he first unloaded his shit into the place. It was cluttered with records, CDs, piles of clothes, and crusty dishes everywhere. Since you couldn't even find the couch, he flattened the twisted blanket on his bed and gestured me to sit. I kicked my shoes into the pile and hopped on cross-legged. Jake was standing over me, looking down at my face. I couldn't take my eyes off his bare chest, and I'm sure he knew it, too. I began to feel funny about being there without Sam. Jake was totally hot—too hot for me to handle. Especially with his black hair all messed up and those bedroom eyes.

"So what're you going as for Halloween?" he asked, sitting down right up next to me, so close I could feel his body heat.

"Uh, I dunno." I was embarrassed to tell him that I was going to do *drag*. I was suddenly embarrassed to be there. I felt really guilty for thinking he was hot. Why wasn't he dressed? And why was he sitting so close? It seemed very unusual for a straight boy. God, if he were gay, Sam would just die. Two in a row *is* a little much.

"What do you *mean* you don't know? It's a little late to be trying to figure it out."

"Well, I'm probably going to be a sailor," I suddenly remembered Chloe's sorry-ass costume.

"Cool . . . I'm going to be a skeleton."

I instantly had a mental picture of the bullies in *Karate Kid* who dressed like skeletons the night they beat the shit out of Daniel-san. "That's cool," I said, trying to hide a smile.

"Here." He handed me a glass pipe loaded with weed and a red lighter out of nowhere.

I took a big hit, suppressed a cough, then exhaled a long stream of smoke. The stuff tasted good, better than the usual schwag. I handed him his pipe back, then pulled out my wallet. "Is twenty good?" I produced the single bill.

"Whatever's good for you." He exhaled a hit. "It's five bucks a gram."

"Well, then, four grams, please," I said, purposely lisping my voice.

"You're such a fag!" He handed me the pipe.

Takes one to know one, was what I wanted to say. I took another hit, already feeling the dizzying effects of the first. "So, are you coming to the party tonight?"

"I got other plans," he replied.

Good, now I didn't have to dress like sailor, although it would've been funny if Chloe and I had matched. "So what's your big plan?" I passed back the pipe.

"I'm going to a rave."

"What rave?"

"Frightmare . . . you know, like nightmare. They got awesome DJs spinning hard-core. Best costume winner gets flown down to a rave in LA."

"You better be doing a killer skeleton."

He looked at me like I'd insulted him. "I didn't say I was entering the contest."

"Oh, sorry." I was always doing that. Making people mad at me over some stupid wisecrack. I just couldn't help it. All I had was my wit!

"I'll be making myself a pretty penny while I'm there though."

"How's that?"

"Check it out," he said, opening a manila envelope. Out of it came a sheet wrapped in tinfoil.

"Is that acid?" I asked knowingly.

"Hell, yeah, it's acid!"

Already I was thinking that I wanted some. What a great Halloween it would be if Chloe and I tripped. I wondered if Chloe would even take acid. Come to think of it, I wasn't sure if he'd ever even *done* acid.

"You wanna buy some?"

I thought about the money in my wallet. Fifty-five dollars. Twenty was for the weed, and thirty-five went toward a one-month bus pass. "Is it any good?"

"Of course it's good. I wouldn't have bought'n it if it wasn't any good."

"How much is it?"

"Five a hit."

"Five bucks a gram, five bucks a hit. You're a regular capitalist with those prices."

"Those are good prices!"

"I know . . . I'm just givin' you shit."

"Well, do you want it?"

"Give me a second to think about it." I took another hit off the pipe. I was starting to feel pretty baked. I leaned up against the wall, letting my socked feet hang over the edge of the bed. I noticed that Jake had little white dots all over his ceiling. "What are those?" I pointed with one hand and passed the pipe with the other.

"Those are my stars." He got up and closed the shades of his small basement windows that lined the top of one wall. He turned on a black light that sat on his desk, then switched off the overhead light. The room now looked dark purple and the stars above glowed green; the rave fliers taped to his wall glowed, too. It was the perfect room to take acid in. He sat down right up next to me again, with his bare feet hanging over the edge next to mine. "I put them up while I was on a glass binge a while back. It was a bitch on account of the fact that they're kinda in order . . . See, there's the Big Dipper, Cassiopeia, Orion the Hunter . . ."

He caught my attention when he said "glass," which is another word for crystal meth. "They're awesome." I meant it, too; they were really cool. "I didn't know you were into astronomy."

"That's 'cause I never told you."

"Oh."

"See, I can be a wiseguy, too."

"I never said—"

"Just kidding, Taylor. Don't bust a gasket over it or nuthin'."

It sounded funny when he called me by my last name, like we were on a sports team together or something. Boys are weird like that. I've never heard a girl call another girl by her last name, but boys do that all the time. I hate my last name, anyway. It's probably part of the reason why I wanted to be a girl, just so no one will call me "Taylor" ever again. "Sorry," I said shyly. Being in this room, stoned, and up close to Jake was starting to overwhelm me. Usually, I don't get very anxious when I smoke up, but now I felt paranoid. Like I was trapped in an awkward situation. The reason I couldn't tell him I was doing drag was because he was such a straight boy, and I felt like I had to hide from him. Yet now it seemed almost like he was hitting on me. And he was Sam's boyfriend!

"You okay?"

"Yeah, why?"

" 'Cause you suddenly got real pale."

"Oh, sorry."

"You already said 'sorry,' man. What's the matter?" He put his hand around my shoulder. I felt his fingers in my hair.

"Whoa!" I declared, jumping out of the bed.

"What? What'd I do?"

"Nothing, it's just—."

"Hey, sorry about that."

"You didn't—I mean—don't worry about it," I said, too flustered to make any sense out of what I was saying.

Jake became defensive. "I was just putting my hand on your shoulder to be friendly or whatever. I wasn't trying to scare you or nothing."

"I wasn't scared. I was just surprised, that's all."

"What'd you think? I was hitting on you or something? 'Cause I wasn't."

"No, of course not."

"I'm not even gay. I'm with Sam, for Christ's sake!"

"I know, I'm sorry," I apologized. "I'm just in a weird place right now." And that was the truth. I wanted to get the hell out of there.

"Well, you don't have to freak out on me, man."

"I'm not . . . I'm sorry." I sat back down to prove that I was okay. Now we were a good two feet apart. I was so humiliated by my error. It's the most embarrassing thing ever when you think a straight boy is hitting on you when he's really not. I couldn't believe how stupid I was. He would probably turn homophobic about it now. People always turned homophobic whenever they thought a gay guy was hitting on them. And I was so *not* trying to hit on him. The whole situation had me panicked. I was practically ready to commit suicide over it.

"So you want your bag?" he asked.

"Yeah sure." I wished I could turn back time.

Without getting up, he reached over to his dresser and grabbed his pencil box. Setting it in his lap, he opened the box to reveal dozens of bags neatly rolled and stacked. He took some weed out of one, bringing its weight down to four grams; then I exchanged my twenty dollars for it. "Thanks," I said, putting the pot in the pocket inside my backpack.

"No problem." He lit a cigarette.

"I didn't mean to imply that you were—."

"Hey, don't mention it, man." He blew it off in smoke. "You don't have to be uncomfortable around me 'cause you're gay."

"I'm not uncomfortable."

"I know . . . I'm just trying to say that I don't care if you're gay. I have lots of gay friends, I really do," he said in a charming voice. "We're cool, Erick . . . You're Sam's best friend, and I would never try to embarrass you or anything . . . I really wouldn't even care if you were one of those people who likes to have sex with farm animals, as long as I don't have to see it."

"Don't worry, I haven't been fucking any goats or anything."

"Well, that's good, 'cause you'd be a freak if you were."

I started laughing. "You're weird, Jake . . . But I'm weird, too, so whatever," I said, trying to sound like a guy even though I sounded like a girl. "By the way, can I buy two hits of that acid, too?"

"Right on." He blew smoke rings and looked at his stars.

{ thirteen }

*A*fter spending my bus-pass money on drugs, I decided not to call my parents. I also skipped turning in my coffee-shop application, reasoning that I was too stoned to act professional, anyway. Besides, that whole experience with Jake had me shaken up. Men were so hard to figure out. I could relate to females like I was one of the girls myself, but guys scared the hell out of me. I could never figure out what it was they wanted. The straight boys that were nice to me always seemed like they were flirting. But why was that my fault? What was I supposed to think when Jake put his hand in my friggin' hair? Who does that?

When I got back to Chloe's, I picked up the phone to call Sam and tell her what had happened, just to see what she thought I should've done about it. But I hung up the phone, reluctant to stir up trouble. If Sam thought her new boyfriend was flirting with her newly queer ex-boyfriend, she'd think that she turned men gay and would probably have to kill herself. It seemed curious to me that the whole time I was at Jake's house, he never once mentioned Sam. I wondered what they were fighting about. Maybe he wasn't fulfilling her needs as a woman. Poor Sam! Relationships are *so* sordid.

• • •

When Chloe came prancing through the door that evening, shouting "Happy Halloween, baby," I told him about the acid right away.

"Acid?" he questioned, as if he'd never even heard of it. He set his bags on the floor and continued to stare at me puzzled.

"Hell, yeah, I got acid . . . Come on, Chloe, trip with me. It'll be so much fun!"

"Get out'a town, I'm not gonna trip."

"Oh, c'mon, it's Halloween, baby. We'll have a ball."

"Let's see it," he said, sitting down next to me on the futon.

I pulled the small folded piece of aluminum foil out from in between the cardboard and the cellophane of my cigarette pack. Keeping it with my cigarettes was a wise precaution because I'd never lose a pack of cigarettes; they were like my life support. I opened the foil to show Chloe the two small squares of pink paper. Acid fascinated me because absorbed in that little square, was a liquid powerful enough to take your mind to another dimension. Tripping made you see the world in a different light. It was certainly the most intense high I knew of, no exaggeration.

"Do you think we should?"

"Fuck yeah! It's Halloween night, girl . . . Biggest party of the year!"

"I'm just worried I'll freak out."

"No, you won't." For a change, I played the part of the adult. "I'll tell you what; We'll take it now, peak here together, and by the time we leave, the trip will have mellowed and we'll be ready to party."

"Where'd you get it?"

"Jake the Snake."

"Where'd you get the money? You still bought my bag, right?"

"Yeah, yeah, I got the sack . . . I spent my bus money."

"Erick! Don't you think that was a little stupid? What about the job? Did you get it?"

I winced at the question. "I don't know yet," I lied timidly. He eyed me skeptically. "Did you call your parents?"

"Whatever, Chloe, you know I can't stand my parents. Now, please, just be a good girl and eat your acid."

With a smile he said, "You are too spoiled for my own good." Then, leaning over the foil on my lap, like he was about to give me head, he picked up one of the hits with the tip of his tongue. Then he held it out in front of my face, waving it at me before putting it in his mouth.

"Right fucking on, Chloe, baby," I said, dropping my own hit. "Let's smoke a bowl, girl! Woo-hoo!" I screamed, giving my friend a high-five.

Chloe turned on the stereo while I packed the bowl. He told me that it'd been years since he last tripped, adding with a smile that I was *such* a manipulative little bitch. We passed the bowl a few times, but got bored and instead lit cigarettes before it was even cashed. Smoking pot is pretty futile when you're about to trip, anyway. It's like in math, how the bigger numbers cancel out the smaller ones. At least I *think* I learned that in math. I'd already forgotten most of that crap!

We decided to get dressed while we waited for the shit to kick in. After you take a hit of acid, it's best to keep yourself occupied or you'll go crazy anticipating it, almost fearing it. When ten minutes pass, you're already looking at everything differently, trying to decide if you feel it yet. From my experience, it usually takes about forty-five minutes, then another hour before you're really tripping hard; it sinks in so slowly.

Chloe took a shower, then got into his costume. It seems like everything Chloe does is perfect, including dressing like a sailor. He wore a pair of navy-blue crushed-velvet bell-bottoms, a white sailor shirt with blue striped collar, and one of those Boy Scout neckerchiefs that sailors wear, also blue. He even had a blue hat with one of those gold U.S. Navy symbols on the front. His hair was short and dyed black. He looked so cute. Perfect body, perfect face—perfect in every way.

After posing for me, he said it was my turn. Then he gave me a piece of masking tape and told me to hide my package, that it was all part of being a drag queen. I reluctantly went into the bathroom to put on the tape, knowing that it was gonna hurt like hell to take off later. I pulled my dick back into my butt crack and taped it there carefully. I couldn't believe I was actually going through with it. Next, I put on my sexy red dress with the interruption of giggles the entire time. I wasn't sure if the acid was kicking in or what, but I could not stop laughing at myself in front of the mirror. Chloe balled up socks for me with the expertise of a pro and put them in the cups of my bra. He exaggerated a natural boob size so much that I thought I looked stupid, but he insisted that that was what drag queens did, so I went along with it. It wasn't until I pulled on those pantyhose that I really felt *sexy*. With my legs in the air and my toes pointed out like a movie star, I rolled them on seductively, exactly how I pictured Madonna would do it.

Chloe sat on the futon laughing, as I danced around the apartment, singing to Tori, no-holds-barred. I twirled in circles, making huge gestures with my arms and sliding my hands all around my female body like I turned myself on. Soon Chloe was in hysterics, and he got up to dance around drunkenly with me.

"Hey, sailor? Your seamen are welcome aboard these shores any day," I teased in a lispy voice. I started dancing like I was in a jungle, and all the wrist action gave me trails. My whole body felt tingly and intensely hot. My passion for dancing was burning me up! Now both of us laughed hysterically. When Chloe bumped into the arm of the futon and fell over the back of it, I could hardly control myself. I saw stars spinning around his head like they do in a cartoon when someone gets clunked on the noggin with a frying pan.

Chloe pointed at me, laughing uncontrollably, making me laugh myself dizzy. "You need your wig!" he declared. He took that big blond thing from the closet and placed it on my head carefully, just like he did that first time I wore it. I watched his eyes as he tucked my real hair up under the wig. I wanted to reach out and put my hand on his chest. I wondered if he was going as a sailor just to torture me.

He laid his hands on my shoulders and stepped back to inspect his work. "Girl, you make one fierce drag queen! Come see yourself." And he led me into the bathroom.

I stood in front of the mirror, looking at the reflection of a woman. I ran my fingers through the blond hair, observing the way the dress clung to my slim figure as I moved around. It was so . . . real. The trip was beginning to take over the whole apartment. Compelled by God, I touched my finger to the surface of the mirror. It rippled like the silver water of a lake. I was definitely starting to trip! Chloe stood right behind me and I watched his reflection, his permanent smile admiring me. Our faces were glowing. "You're amazing," he said with one hand still on my shoulder, the other lost in my wig.

"Thank you."

"You want to do your makeup?"

"Of course . . . But let's have a cig first," I decided, realizing how much I craved a smoke.

"Mmmm," Chloe agreed, backing into the living room and laughing again.

I followed him to the futon, sitting down close next to him, like Jake had sat next to me. I crossed my legs and leaned back into my seat. Soon I felt like I was sinking into the cushion as if it were quicksand. I closed my eyes until I just couldn't stand it and had to make sure it wasn't quicksand. Either way, it felt so unbelievably sexy that I wasn't scared. Chloe lit us each a cigarette then leaned back into my arm. He told me he felt good when we were together. I flicked the sailor hat off his head and began to run my fingers through his black hair.

"That feels cool," he said, rolling his head around beneath my hand. "We look so fucking hot, girl."

"Yeah, we do. The hottest."

"We are gonna work that party tonight!"

"Hell, yeah!" I imaged that my big hair and boobs made me look like Dolly Parton. All I needed was cowboy boots and a leather jacket with fringe to complete the picture. The music was still playing, only the disk had switched to Deee-Lite, which couldn't be a more perfect selection. I looked around the room, seeing trails off of everything by simply moving my head back and forth. There were images on the floor, too. At first I saw patterns of faces, like demons or something, all intertwined and spinning around each other like a kaleidoscope. They were two-dimensional and seemed to have been burned into the carpet—or even stuck underneath it, trying to push through. Then the faces turned into monkeys, and I felt as if I were looking into a pot of boiling water. "Girl, are you seein' what I'm seein'?"

"You wouldn't be talking about the patterns in the floor, would you?"

"Yeah!"

We gave each other eerie looks, not knowing what to make of the situation, but giggling nonetheless. I climbed off the couch. It felt like the floor was breathing as I crawled in circles on my hands and knees.

"You're going to crush them!" Chloe was laughing hysterically again.

"No I'm not . . . they like it. They survive off my life force . . . Can't you hear them calling you? They want you to come down here, too."

"Shut up, they do not!" He was still laughing.

"Come with me, baby. Please," I begged holding out my hand to him. "Let's take a little trip."

He took my hand and came down to my side. We crawled in circles together around the room, laughing until it hurt. "I think they're aliens." He was trying to be serious for once.

"No, they're not. They're the life force," I explained. I wasn't sure if I sounded intellectual or just stupid. I felt supersmart, though. Like I understood nature. Like I was somehow more in tune with it than any other person.

Chloe rubbed his cheek against the carpeting. "You're right," he half-teased. "I can feel the life force going inside my brain!"

"That's not how it works," I declared, putting my cheek against the floor to prove it. However, I discovered Chloe was right. I could feel it, too. The life force was going inside my brain. It tasted like bananas, and I wondered if that had something to do with the monkeys.

"Oh my God!" Chloe shouted. I jerked my head up to see his cheek was now against the linoleum of the kitchen floor. "You got to feel this, Erick! The life force is even stronger in the kitchen!"

I crawled over to Chloe and put my head down next to his. It was stronger there! At first the sensation felt cold, like rubbing aloe on a sunburn. Then it got warm, almost wet. In fact, my whole body felt warm and wet. I wondered if I was clammy or just hallucinating. Exhausted, I collapsed onto my side. "This is deep."

"Yeah it is," Chloe said. "I feel myself growing stronger, healthier." He rolled onto his side to face me. We stared into each other's eyes fearlessly. Like in the entire world there was nothing to be afraid of because right now all that mattered was us, discovering the secrets of the universe in this apartment. I felt as if we were the only two souls that existed.

Suddenly, we communicated to each other telepathically that we were bored and felt silly for laying on the kitchen floor. We rose simultaneously from the life force. For just a second we were quiet, serene. I heard music playing, as if the trip was coming to an end.

"That was motherfucking intense!" Chloe shouted, wrapping both of his arms around his body, hugging himself.

"Let's have a cigarette," I proposed, realizing how badly I craved one.

We sat back down on the futon. This time I lit them for us. But as soon as I took my first drag, the trip came back to me. It was like electricity swimming through my veins. Now I saw those patterns of monkeys on every surface I looked at—the floor, the walls, the ceiling, the furniture. I started laughing again.

"This is so crazy." Chloe took rapid drags. "I can't even believe how intense this is."

"You don't have to remind me, okay. Trust me on this one, I'm there, too."

"I'm glad we did this together, Erick . . . I feel really close to you right now."

"Me too."

Chloe rolled onto the beanbag giggling.

"Suz!" I remembered, jumping to my feet and running to the birdcage. I started making kissing noises at the little yellow bird and she stared back at me like I was on crack.

"Let her out! Let her out!" Chloe cheered, applauding.

I opened the cage door and stuck my finger inside. She hopped right on. Such a good little bird. Once freed from her prison she went flying around the room. How cool life was! Complex and delicate and wonderful! Suz was the smartest bird ever, I was sure of it. She knew what was up; she knew what was down. All because she knew how to fly.

This acid was speeding through me, so I couldn't sit still. Instead I paced the room and smoked. Chloe lit another cigarette and relaxed deeper into the beanbag. I looked out the window, noticing for the first time it was night. "Oh my God, it's already ten o'clock," I said, reading the time off the clock fixed to one of the banks downtown.

"Wow, time really flies when you're tripping, doesn't it?" Chloe said, stretching and standing up. "We should go soon."

"Do you still feel it?" I asked, knowing the answer.

"Fuck, yeah . . . I can't tell up from down."

"Me either." I crushed the cherry of my cigarette butt in the ashtray. "Ready to help me with my makeup?"

"Sure." He carried his cigarette and ashtray into the bathroom.

Wearing makeup was nothing new to me. By the time I was five years old, I was already secretly obsessed with it. I used to go through my mom's stuff when she wasn't around and decorate myself, pretending I was an actress preparing for my big kissing scene with Michael J. Fox. If either of my parents had caught me, they would've flipped. Luckily, my mom never touched her makeup. She lost all interest in her appearance after Tommy died.

Chloe rummaged through his makeup case while I sat on the toilet seat. He told me he was going to start with some foundation. Since I wasn't performing at a nightclub, I wouldn't need stage makeup or anything. He was going to make me look natural. Almost immediately after he began moving the wet pad across my cheeks, he stopped abruptly, realizing that I didn't need any because I already looked so androgynous. "Girl, I think all's you need is some eye makeup and a little lipstick and you'll be set!" he declared. "Just a touch of pizzazz!" He slathered on blue eye shadow until I felt like my eyes were going to fall out of my head. When Chloe said "just a touch," he meant just barely enough so that it wouldn't peel off from its own weight. "Now some of this shit," he continued, brush-painting black eyeliner onto the rims of my lids. He followed that with mascara on my lashes and brows. Then he pulled out some red lipstick and had me pucker up, while he smeared that on.

"Okay, check yourself out," he said, capping the lipstick tube and standing back to let me up.

I turned to face the mirror for the big unveiling. "It looks perfect!" I squealed. The colors were vibrant and metallic, and I was unable to decipher where the makeup ended and my bare skin began. But that was just the acid. All I knew for sure was that I no longer recognized myself, which was exactly what I wanted. "Thank you," I said to Chloe as I posed for him.

"Don't mention it, darling."

Just then I realized that if I was going to do drag, I would need a drag name. "So what do you think my drag name should be?" I asked.

"I thought it was going to be Erica Lane," Chloe said.

"No, that's boring . . . I hate my name. I need something *fabulous!*" I said dramatically. "Ghetto fabulous! I need a name that everyone will hear and recognize as my own for all time."

"How about Geneva?" Chloe asked.

"I love it!" I declared happily. "Miss Geneva!"

"I don't know though, it needs something more. Some little twist to make it sing."

"I know!" I announced. "Geneva Flowers!"

"Yeah, definitely!" he exclaimed. "Geneva Flowers is the most fabulous name I've ever heard in my entire life!"

Now I was so excited I couldn't even contain myself. I gave Chloe a huge hug. "I love you!" I declared.

"I love you too, girl."

Suddenly I was crying and I didn't know why. I pulled away from Chloe and looked back at the mirror, crying and laughing.

"You okay, girl?" he asked.

"I'm fabulous." I wiped away the tears while trying to keep my makeup intact.

"I'm so jealous of you."

"Why on earth would *you* be jealous of *me?*"

"I remember my first time doing drag, how beautiful I felt . . . how right it felt."

"Why don't you do it anymore?"

"I'm too old!"

"No you're not," I argued, because he wasn't. He didn't look much older than me—except in the morning, when he had his beard and bags under his eyes. Chloe had to shave and hide himself under eye makeup every day. Meanwhile, I still couldn't even grow sideburns.

"Well, I guess I'm not too old. Maybe I'll do it again . . . I just wasn't in the mood tonight."

"Tell it to the judge, girl . . . Let's paint our nails!"

We returned the living room. I painted mine red, of course, and Chloe painted his navy blue. We were so tightly coordinated, it was practically tacky! When we were finally finished getting ready, we checked ourselves out in the bathroom mirror one last time, our arms wrapped around each other's waists. With me in drag and him as an androgynous sailor, we looked like the funkiest straight couple I'd ever seen. We decided to take a cab to the party. No point getting our asses kicked while tripping our brains out!

Walking through the dark hallway of his building, I saw monkeys again on the walls. It made me feel as if we were walking through the tunnel of an Egyptian tomb, and the monkeys were ancient hieroglyphics. We were on our way to the chamber of the mummified pharaoh, where we'd find gold and jewels. But of course the mummified pharaoh who was guarding them would awake after three thousand years and have to chase us out of there. No big deal, because I simply *had* to make my appearance at the party, darling!

We sat in the backseat of the cab, giggling and slapping each other's thighs. The driver kept glaring at us in his rearview mirror, obviously disapproving of our behavior. He was an older man with gray hair and a rough unshaven face. Cigarettes were nearly spilling out of his ashtray. I bet he lived like a pig, bet he wasn't married. I wondered if he'd ever had a drag queen and a gay sailor in his cab. Probably not! He should know to expect anything on Halloween night, though, the night when freaks get even freakier.

It was almost eleven o'clock, long past the trick-or-treaters' bedtimes. Midnight would be the witching hour, and we were going to be drinking cocktails and dancing till dawn. I waved my hand in front of my face, happily watching the cartoon trails, mesmerized by their hypnotic effect. I felt Chloe's eyes burning into me, imagined him ravishing me in this cab, but when I turned to face him, I found him looking out the window. I stared at the back of his head, at his sailor's hat. I wanted to know what he was thinking at that very moment. Was it about me? I was afraid to ask him, however, afraid he would tell me he was thinking about some older man, someone more his type. Just imagining that answer made my heart sink.

The cab pulled up to the entrance of Molly's building at eleven o'clock on the nose. Chloe paid the driver all in one's. "Thanks, Pops." The cabdriver replied with a grunt and sped away like a bomb was about to explode.

We faced the glass doors of the building side by side. Butterflies flapped around in my stomach. Everyone I knew was going to be there, seeing me in drag for the first time. I pulled out my compact to check my makeup and hair. Thank God I did because I had lipstick on my front teeth. I hastily wiped it off with my finger. Great, now I'd be too paranoid to smile all night!

Chloe typed in the security code on the panel at the entrance. The door buzzed open, and we entered the building. The lobby had marble floors and towering green plants on each side next to the door. The security guard smirked as we walked past.

"God, this place makes our humble apartment look like a total dive," Chloe commented.

It struck me how Chloe referred to his place as "our" apartment. "Yeah, no kidding," I agreed.

As soon as we entered the party room, Molly came running over to us. "Oh my God, Erick! You look great . . . You both look so great!" she screamed, grabbing my hands and jumping up and down with excitement. She was dressed as an eighties punk rocker. Her outfit was covered in patches.

"The name is Miss Geneva Flowers."

That sent her giggling like mad. "It's perfect!" she screamed.

"Thank you, darling," I grinned.

I scanned the room. I was tripping so hard that I felt like I was in *The Rocky Horror Picture Show*. I saw a devil, a Statue of Liberty, an angel; someone was even wearing a can of Coke costume. However, I didn't see Sam in her Pippi Longstocking costume. More than anything I wanted her to see me in my dress—just because I was her ex-boyfriend and all.

"Come in." Molly grabbed our hands and led us to the center of the room, where all eyes fell on me. Out of all the guests, I was the only drag queen. I spotted Molly's boyfriend, Bob, at the bar. He was dressed as Frankenstein. "Look, it's Frankentrannie," I whispered to Chloe.

"*Whoa!*" Chloe screamed, because he had no tact.

"Shhh!" I whispered, dragging Chloe to the other side of the room.

When we were at a safe distance from Bob, Chloe asked, "Are you still tripping?"

"Yeah . . . aren't you?"

"I think so. My God, it's bright in here . . . gross, I feel like I'm chewing on my words." Chloe stuck out his tongue.

Meanwhile, I zoned out on monkeys imprinted on the floor. What a relief to see them there! I loved those monkeys as much as I loved my big boobs. I began shaking my tits and whipping my wig around. Chloe caught me and we danced dirty.

"Hey, you guys!" Tammy shouted. She was dressed as a slutty nun, with a low-cut mini-habit and a whip. Tammy was a large girl, and when she said, "I'm a scandalous nun!" Chloe and I almost died laughing.

"What is wrong with you two? Oh my God! Are you guys tripping?" she asked.

We looked at each other, both surprised by her intuitive guess. "How did you know?" Chloe asked.

"I can just tell. Both y'alls pupils are the size of pins, and you just have that look of shock on your faces."

"We do?"

"Oh, yeah . . . So do you feel like you're sinking into the floor? Are you boxed in? Feeling trapped? Do you see trails?" she asked, flipping her whip around.

"Quit trying to fuck with us, girl. 'Cause we are already *fucked* up!" Chloe said.

"Do you have any more?"

"No."

"God, Chloe, you didn't get me any?"

"Miss Flowers here bought it."

"Miss Flowers?"

"My drag name is Geneva Flowers."

She rolled her eyes. "Well, *Geneva,* where's my hit?"

"Sorry, Tammy." I waved her away from us. I was *such* a bitch in drag.

"You guys! I wanna trip, too," she whined. "By the way, Chloe, I thought *you* were never going to do acid again."

"I wasn't . . . but I just couldn't resist this cutie." Chloe put his arm around my shoulder and made me smile.

"You two suck!" she pouted, stomping away.

"Obviously someone has a crab up her ass," Chloe whispered into my ear.

"Oh, my God, I know!" I said.

We decided to give Tammy the silent treatment for the rest of the night. So we totally ignored her when she approached us later, begging for the dealer's phone number. At last she realized that we were serious—we weren't going to give it to her. With that, she stormed off to the bar and swallowed about ten Jell-O shots. Chloe worried about her hurt feelings even though I wanted to ignore her for the rest of the night.

Everyone loved my dress and the sassy attitude it brought out in me. Chloe stole the show when he danced to "Macho Man." Everyone cheered him on just like when he performed his Michael Jackson dance at Screwdriver. I wished, I too, could be a showstopper someday.

Sam never showed up. I'd been waiting eagerly for her all night, but apparently she and Jake decided to make up or something. They probably decided to blow off Halloween and just eat acid and have sex under the stars in Jake's bedroom. For the first time, I felt jealous of Sam. Although I always called Jake a loser, he really was a sweetheart in his own way, and those stars were *so* romantic. They gave me a whole new appreciation for "the Snake."

By four in the morning, everyone was too tired and drunk to party. Chloe and I were the last two on the dance floor, still wide awake from the acid and hours of slow dancing. Once I'd taken off my heels and wig, and he'd gotten out of his platforms, we were exactly the same height. All I could think about was how perfect Chloe was and how imperfect Mike had been. In a million years he never would have danced with me at a party. He was just a stupid boy, a stupid fling. Chloe was my soulmate for sure. How could he not have at least thought about us before?

If I was ever going to kiss him, it had to be now, while slow-dancing. I slid my hands softly from his waist up to his shoulders. But then, just as I was about to pull away to kiss him, the music stopped and bright fluorescent lights flooded the dance floor. Our perfect seal broke, and he let go of me instantly. For a second he looked into my eyes, and I knew at that moment that he knew I was about to kiss him. I looked around the room for the first time in hours, noticing that it was empty except for Molly and Bob, who were cleaning up the mess that was left behind.

"You guys, I'm really drunk," Molly said. "I need to go to bed. Do you want me to have Bob call you a cab?"

"I can call a cab." Chloe walked over to the phone. "Sorry we kept you up so long."

"Think nothing of it," Molly said. "Thanks for coming."

Bob watched me from across the room, staring at my dress as he worked. Suddenly I felt self-conscious and wanted to crawl into a hole wearing boy's clothes. I sick of being gawked at. Geneva Flowers was finished for tonight.

We waited on the curb for our cab. I carried my wig in one hand and my heels and purse in the other. I looked over at Chloe, wishing he'd say something—anything—but he just stared across the street. I wanted him to put his arm around me, but he didn't.

What was wrong with me? I didn't get it. Why wouldn't he love me back? I was sure glad that I didn't kiss him. I could tell now that he hadn't wanted me to. I knew it the moment he gave me that look on the dance floor, when Molly turned off the music and switched on the lights.

When we got home, we undressed in silence. I had to spend about ten hours in the bathroom washing the makeup off my face, not to mention ripping off that damn tape, which made my dick all red and sore. I thought, there has to be better way to do this. Chloe was probably playing a prank on me. When I came out, Chloe was in his sweatpants and T-shirt.

"I suppose you're wondering what's going on, right? Why I didn't kiss you?" he asked as he began to pack a bowl.

"I don't know," I answered shyly.

"I can't date you . . . because . . . because—"

"Because why?"

"Can you keep a secret?" I'd never seen him so grave.

"Of course I can. What is it? You can tell me."

"I have AIDS."

{ fourteen }

IDS?" I repeated. It was like time had stopped. For a second, it was as if the room had disappeared, and there I stood, face to face, with a ghost. It couldn't be true, I told myself. Chloe couldn't have AIDS.

"Yes," he said with a matter-of-factness that scared me even more. "AIDS . . . I don't like to tell people because they look at me funny . . . and it wasn't such a big deal when I was only HIV positive . . . but now I have full-blown AIDS. If you were wondering about that cough of mine, it's just a cold that won't go away—I think it's finally going away now—but that's because I'm taking more drugs. All those herbal supplements you see me taking? They're my meds. The AIDS cocktail," he explained nervously.

Not even HIV—full-blown AIDS. I heard it in my mind over and over again. Not even HIV—full-blown AIDS. AIDS. AIDS. It seemed impossible. He was only twenty-six years old. "Why? How?"

"It just happened."

"Just happened? Oh my God, Chloe!" Tears streamed from my eyes, but I refused to wipe them away. I let them blur my vision until all I saw was the light from the kitchen.

Chloe pulled me into his arms and held me. "It'll be okay, girl. Please don't cry. Christ, *I* don't even cry about it."

"How can you *not* cry?" I asked, pulling myself out of his arms to look at his face.

"I guess I cried all the tears that were ever gonna come out of my head years ago, before I even found out I had HIV, when I was some scared little boy in a dress."

"Are you scared now?"

"Yeah."

"How long do you have?"

"There's no way to know. Some people get HIV but don't develop full-blown AIDS for years. Besides, I'm going to make a comeback. With these new meds, I'll be just fine."

"Oh, my God!" I wailed as the words AIDS AIDS AIDS AIDS flashed into my mind. Oh, God, please save him! Please, God . . . Please!

"Erick! Get ahold of yourself, girl! If I'd have known it was going to turn into a big meltdown, I wouldn't have told you."

"But we're on acid!" I reminded him.

"That was ten hours ago. I don't know—maybe I should have waited to tell you."

"No—I'm sorry, I'm sorry," I repeated, wiping away tears. "I'm glad you told me."

"I knew it was going to be hard telling you no matter what. But it's been eating me up, and tonight at the party, I realized that I couldn't lie to you anymore." He lit the bowl and exhaled a long stream of smoke. Now that he'd revealed his secret, he seemed to want to move on to the next subject. "Anyway, could you believe Tammy freaking out about that acid tonight? Girl, we must have looked like such freaks at the party."

I laughed. Laughed and cried a little. "I love you, Chloe. I've always loved you."

"I've always loved you, too." He passed me the bowl. I waved it away, but he took another hit. "It's weird. Even though there are a million reasons we can't be together, sometimes I feel like we're soulmates. Maybe because we're sisters."

Oh, God! Sister soulmates? What a bomb to drop on me! Now I was crying like a maniac all over again.

"Girlfriend? Do you need a pill or something?" Chloe asked.

I blubbered tears and laughter hysterically.

"Good golly Miss Molly, you're such a drama queen. That's probably what I love about you, though. Oh, Erick, my little darling! You know, I used to not love anyone. And no one loved me, either. What a way to live! All I had was the friends who I partied with, and Babs Arlington." Suddenly Chloe got sentimental. "I came to this city at eighteen years old and became Miss Chloe, diva drag queen. Sure, I was poor and trashy, but I didn't care because I was fierce! I was sure that someday I'd be discovered. And all those people who disrespected me over the years would see me, see what I had become and . . . I wanted them to love me. I really was good, too . . . I guess that was my art. Whatever that means . . . It wasn't until I met you six months ago that I finally fell in love with someone, for more than a wardrobe and a foot in the door . . . Shit, all I wish for is to have something I could give . . . to you. But I was too late or you were too late and . . . I don't know. Sometimes in this world things just get all fucked up . . . You always ask why I quit doing drag. Well, I'll tell you why. I quit doing it for you, Erick. I quit because I didn't want you to see me as Chloe the drag queen. I wanted you to see me as me . . . a man. That's why I never put on a dress around you." He paused to hit the bowl again.

I watched him, saying nothing.

"I'm sure you guessed that my real name isn't Chloe. It's David. David Brown. Whew," he sighed. "I haven't said that name out loud in years . . . You must think that I'm such a nerd. David Brown. I've always hated that name. I think Chloe fits me much better, don't you?"

I nodded in agreement, even though it didn't matter to me. I would have loved him no matter what the hell his name was, even if his name was Boris Shitkingbower, it would sounded like poetry on my lips!

"You wanna know what's crazy?" He shook his head ruefully. "The guy I got HIV from was fifty years old. Fifty! Can you believe that? . . . I met him at Screwdriver. This was back when I was real fucked up on drugs . . . Anyway, he paid me a hundred dollars for sex. That's how much my life was worth to me, I guess. One hundred dollars." He looked down at his hands, shaking his head sadly. "I was so stupid . . . Never fuck bareback," he added with authority. There was a long pause: then, finally, "You must hate me."

"Never!"

"God, I really fucked things up."

I decided to take a hit off the pipe after all. Meanwhile, Chloe spilled his guts to me about everything. He said that the reason we met is because I was his chance to do something right. For whatever it was worth, he was going to share with me what he had learned in life, so that I wouldn't make all the same stupid choices he had. Although I felt proud and grateful that he cared about me so much, I was terrified. My mind couldn't help wandering into dark corners. I asked God what our fate was, and the future came to me like this: Chloe would save me from committing teenage suicide, and I would be the one there for him when he died.

That night I couldn't fall asleep. It was probably the acid or something. Every time I closed my eyes, I saw the word "AIDS" printed hundreds of times in demonic red, spiraling around like a screen saver.

I thought about Tommy, too. If he hadn't died, he would be twelve years old. I often wondered what it would have been like to have had him still around. He would be twice Tim's age, so we'd probably spend a lot more time together than Tim and I do. I'd like to think that we'd get along fantastically. I'd help him with his homework and go see his school plays. He was the screw that held our family together, and when God took him away, our family fell apart.

Fucking Tommy. Mr. Ruin Everyone's Fucking Life By Getting Killed . . . By his own crazy mother. Life is just so fucking tragic. Was life this hard for everyone? Did the rest of the world get so depressed sometimes that they felt like they were being swallowed by something evil? That was how I felt, like I was becoming something evil. Like I was a bad person and just wasn't meant to live. *I* was the one that should've died, or gotten AIDS, or something.

If I killed myself, I know exactly how I'd do it. I'd go to the railroad bridge, walk out to the center, and jump right off. The fall probably wouldn't kill me, though. I'd land in the dark, icy water and immediately be pulled under by the current. It would hurt like hell, but I didn't care. I wanted it to hurt. Just to feel pain. That was what I deserved.

Sleeping next to Chloe that night, I had the strangest dream. A dream that scared me so much, in fact, that it woke me up for the rest of the night. I was at my parents' house, only we didn't live in the city. Our house was way out in some field in the middle of nowhere. Tommy was there, the same age as when he died. However, I was my current age, wearing my red sequined dress and blond wig. I stood outside looking into the house through the window, watching my family sitting at the table laughing and visiting. Visiting and laughing. I wanted to be there with them, but when I banged on the window, they couldn't hear me. Suddenly there was a loud thundering noise behind me. I turned around to see a missile flying toward our house. Before I could warn my family, the missile crashed into the house, killing everyone but me in the explosion. I woke up in a cornfield. The sky had turned pitch-black with stars. Jake's stars. A fiery portal opened in the sky. And in that circle of light I saw a vagina. It opened up like a ferocious mouth with fangs. I wanted to scream but was too stunned as I stared entranced at this grotesque vagina. That's when I felt blood running down my legs, and I realized it was my vagina.

Then I woke up.

Part Two

{ fifteen }

Shortly after our Halloween acid trip, Chloe and I decided we needed more space. So on December first we moved into an absolutely fantastic apartment, three blocks away. It was a one-bedroom divided in half by French doors with glass panes, and it had gorgeous (albeit slightly damaged in spots) hardwood floors. Chloe bought a full-sized bed, so I had the futon in the living room all to myself and slept next to the birdcage. There was only one closet, in the bedroom, which forced us to stack our impossible amount of clothes in laundry baskets and garbage bags around the perimeter of the bedroom. We set a rule: No clothes were allowed in the living room, and no guests were allowed in the bedroom.

For the first month living there, all we did was play house. We went grocery shopping and cooked and cleaned and organized. We bought rainbow Christmas lights for the living room and purple ones for the bedroom. Chloe brought home some fabric called East Indian Print from a fabric store and made curtains for the French doors and window over the futon. Something was missing, though, so we got a houseplant, which tied together perfectly the leopard-print futon and curtains. I was so inspired by the decor that I purchased a plain wooden planter and some paint from an art-supply store, decorating the box to match everything. This led to the discovery that plants thrived in our new apartment! So we decided to get tons of them. We wanted the apartment to have lots of life in it. We probably would've gotten a cat, too, but you can't have a cat and a bird. So we decided that someday, when we had enough money, we would get a supercute dog that we could walk around the ghetto.

Just when we thought the place was perfect, Chloe struck gold when he stole a chair from the scary basement laundry room. The night he came in with it, out of breath from heaving the monstrosity up two flights of stairs, I begged him to get rid of it before the place got infested with fleas or something. It was black from years of neglect. I swore I would never sit in it, but Chloe insisted it was perfect and began washing the chair with soap and water. I was shocked to see immaculate lime-green leather preserved under all that grime. I reneged my oath to never sit in that chair while Chloe gloated with lots of "I told you so's." Plopped down in that seat, I felt for the first time truly confident with the way my life was going. I couldn't imagine anyone ever coming over to our apartment and not wishing they could live there.

My parents didn't even care that I was gone, or at least they were so in denial over the whole drag-queen thing that they preferred to think of me as eighteen and old enough to move out. Besides, ever since that thing with Father Tom, it had been like I was Tommy to my mom. Dead. I bet even my dad hated me. When I finally called them, after weeks of being away, to tell them about my plans, Mom was the one who answered. I said that I had quit school and was moving into an apartment in the ghetto with a guy named Chloe. At first she totally freaked out and said that I was forbidden to do any of this.

Then my dad got on the phone. "What is going on with you? Where are you living?" I explained in my most adult voice that I was growing up (I had turned seventeen a week after Halloween) and I was ready to get a job and live on my own. Of course he didn't think my plans were very smart. He asked how I could be growing up when I was making so many foolish choices with my life. I told him that I didn't care what he thought, that it was my decision. Then he said: "If you want to be on your own, then you have to do it alone. Don't come crawling back for money. Let's see how long that lasts."

I screamed: "It'll last forever and you'll never have to see me again!" and hung up.

I was still upset about that conversation when we moved in. Yet, outwardly, I pretended everything was swell between my parents and me. I told Chloe that they had accepted my decision, and now I just was taking a break from them. It never occurred to me that I might not see them again for years. I composed a letter once, sitting in our green leather chair, notepad on my knees: *"Dear Mom and Dad, The reason I've always been so secretive and rebellious is because I'm gay."* That's how the letter began. Then I went on to explain that being gay was normal, that the Catholic Church just messed everyone up by saying it was a sin, and that I didn't care what they thought of me because I was proud of myself. So unless they accepted me completely, I told them, I would never come home. Of course I never posted the letter. Instead I turned my frustration and anger into determination, and I willed myself to succeed in my new adult life.

For starters, I got myself a job as an official Customer Service Representative (cashier) at Silver Screen Video. The job sucked. Pretty much all I did was check in movies and reshelve them. My manager, Joy, was such a bitch. She seemed to think that her position gave her the right to work everyone like slaves while she walked around barking orders. And she hated me more than anyone there. Apparently, I had a "bad attitude" because I didn't greet customers within five seconds of their entrance. It was so not worth it. At Shades I made one-fifty per week cash, and at Silver Screen Video I was lucky if I got four-fifty a month. I basically started the job with the agenda to quit as soon as I found something better. Perhaps that was part of the reason for my "bad attitude."

I wasn't too worried about my success, though. Chloe and I were practically living like heiresses. Not only did I have a job, he had been given a promotion at Shades. Now he was manager of three different locations: the Uptown Mall, Southdale Mall, and Ridgedale Mall. As if that weren't enough, he began doing massages in our apartment at night for sixty dollars a pop. He said he was doing it all to save money in case his health bottomed out. I also think work made him feel productive and took his mind off his worries. Despite having AIDS, he was usually a cheery and optimistic person.

Of course, I was all doom and gloom about everything. I worried all the time. A cough or a zit or a hair falling out of his head was enough to send me into despair. I couldn't help but wonder how much longer he had, if I would have to take care of him when he got sick. I kept asking God why the best friend I ever had had to have AIDS. Besides, I wasn't sure if I had enough compassion in me to face death all over again. I knew I couldn't run away, though. I wouldn't be able to live with myself if I did.

Letting out his AIDS secret was a tremendous relief to Chloe. Suddenly, he didn't care if Sam and Tammy knew about it, and I was introduced to a world that had been as vague to me as a murder mystery. Along with telling me his usual day-to-day activities, Chloe would tell me about Dr. G——, whom he saw quite regularly. The last time Chloe went in, his T-cell count was 188. With a healthy immune system, the range is between 1000 and 1500. Below 200, you become at risk for opportunistic infections. Luckily, Dr. G—— had hooked Chloe up with some really great experimental drugs. His new regimen consisted of a total of nine pills. They were protease inhibitors, which prevented the HIV virus from copying itself, and nucleoside reverse transcriptase inhibitors (nukes), which protected healthy T-cells from the virus. After his last illness, though, they had to up his dosage, and now he suffered all sorts of side effects, including diarrhea. His entire day was scheduled around his drugs because he had to take them on an empty stomach, which meant he couldn't eat for approximately fifteen hours of every day. How could I have been so blind to Chloe's rigid lifestyle until now? He told me he had wanted to protect me from worrying and was meticulous in keeping his secret. Apparently, even when we had spent entire days together, I had only seen him take 10 percent of his drugs. I asked him how he could so convincingly sustain such a lie for so long when AIDS was on his mind 24/7. He said that gay men are the best liars in the world. Which, of course, made sense to me.

Although I was glad Chloe had told me the truth and everything, I had to admit it was really hard to listen to him suddenly talk about his health all the time. Thinking about AIDS made me feel like I was walking a tightrope, and as long as I kept God happy by thinking pure thoughts, I wouldn't lose balance and fall. Chloe said I was such a Catholic, and I had to constantly keep my fingernails freshly painted so I wouldn't go back to biting them. I hated thinking about diseases. I just wanted things to be the way they used to be last summer, when I was innocent and carefree. It seemed everything had changed. Now Chloe didn't want to go to bars anymore, saying that he had retired from the scene, that he'd outgrown Minneapolis. Meanwhile, I wanted to get into drag and partying.

I thought about all the things I still wanted out of life. Like I wanted to hang out with my friends and find a boyfriend and, most of all, I wanted to be a drag queen. The thought of being on stage exhilarated me. Halloween at Molly's changed my life. In that one night, I overcame so many insecurities about the whole "gender" thing. It was as if Miss Geneva Flowers finally broke free, and I was even more of a nutcase!

Especially when I went to Plato. That place was becoming my second home, and Zack and Jerome now felt like my brothers. We hung out with Sam almost every day. I had finally found a group that I fit in with, found people who respected me for who I was and supported me in my quest for stardom. Occasionally, though, I worried that they were bad influences. We did things that weren't exactly safe or reputable. And, like Chloe and every other homosexual, I, too, was an expert at keeping secrets.

For example: I started doing crystal meth. Well, glass, actually, which is the most powerful type of meth. It comes in clear shards, and when you crush it up and chop it into lines, it gets powdery, like cocaine. Unlike crank (which is just disgusting), glass is brilliant and very addictive. In fact, it was an addiction for me before it ever had a chance to be recreational. When it was nearby, I craved it more than ever. And then—all of sudden—it was everywhere I turned. Not that I had become a serious junkie, though. I only did it on my extended weekends, and my number-one goal was to quit. Its power over me was scary. Plus, I knew Chloe would lose so much respect for me if he found out that I had been doing powders. He always said that bad things happened to good people who used powders.

I felt really guilty about the extreme measures I took to hide it from him, too. It was hard to come up with excuses for staying gone entire weekends. I knew I sounded like a complete jerk when I would tell him that I was going to go party with my friends, but wouldn't tell him where we were hanging out or what we were doing. I always had to go on an eating craze before I could let Chloe see me after a glass binge since whenever I'd been on one, my cheeks would sink in, and bags appeared under my eyes. Also, I got so sketched out after I'd been up for days that I wasn't capable of articulating my thoughts properly. I would get really paranoid around Chloe because I knew he could see right through me. Chloe was very perceptive, and glass was one of those drugs that are impossible to hide. It isn't like pot, which you come down from in a few hours and feel fine. Glass puts your body through a cheese grater.

After snorting your first line, you get really excited and fidgety. You feel like everything in life is as perfect and simple as it could possibly be. You feel happy, like how you remember happiness feeling when you were a kid. You lose all your insecurities; you don't get embarrassed when you're high in public and you make an ass out of yourself because you feel superior to everyone else. The friends you're with are all that matters to you, and you know they feel the same about you. Anyway, everyone you've left behind in reality seems gross to you.

Next, you go into the euphoria stage. This is like being drunk, except you're not sloppy and slurring your speech. You just feel silly and sort of trashed, and you don't care what happens to you because you've lost all your inhibitions and could easily have sex with a stranger or get in a car with a drunk driver. It's like you think you're bulletproof or something. You haven't eaten all weekend, only drank water, so you've become so tight and skinny and horny that you think you look better now than you ever looked in your life. You think you're a supermodel, when you're actually a super-*wreck*. Soon your energy begins to wear (even though your mind is still reeling) and you get cranky. So you do more lines because you couldn't eat or fall asleep even if you tried and you're scared to come down.

The next phase is the craziest of all. It's the point where your body goes into sleep-deprivation mode. You're scared to go sleep since it feels like the world would end if you did. So you do more lines and you begin to hallucinate, chain-smoke, and cry over spilt milk. You feel like you're not even real, like you're a character in a movie watching the scenes of your life acted out for you. You become paranoid; you suspect that everyone who looks at you means you harm, and your eyes nervously dart across the faces that surround you, never daring to make eye contact. That's when you and your friends go hide from society in an apartment, where you smoke pot until you reach total dementia.

By now the room is spinning, and if you stood up you'd most likely fall back down. You see dots in the air, and inanimate objects seem to be breathing. You think you need more crystal—like your life depends on it. But by now you've run out of drugs, run out of brain cells. So finally you fall asleep. Only it's not real sleep. It's called a disco nap, because your brain can't relax, like it's dancing to the beat of your own heart. Your body can't get into the deep stages of sleep, which means you're still basically conscious but you just don't realize it. So when you wake up twelve hours later, not quite sober and sick as all hell, it's because you still haven't really slept. You're so sick, you tell yourself and your friends that you're never doing it again. But three or four days later, after you've slept, you feel better, and you crave glass again. It's like a piece of you that's missing, and only another line can bring it back.

I woke up Saturday morning (at 4 P.M.) wishing I'd taken a couple cigarettes from Chloe's pack the night before. Smoking a leftover butt is nasty as hell after eleven hours of sleep. Unfortunately, Chloe was at work, and I couldn't buy a new pack because I wasn't eighteen yet. Addictions are so irritating. I dragged myself into the bathroom and looked at my reflection in the mirror. My hair was an orangy-red color, with pink, blond, and blue streaks. It looked so retarded. I'd gotten a little carried away with the Punky Colors—just kept adding different streaks of dye with no plan. My muscles were stiff, and sleep goop glued my eyes half-shut. My stomach felt empty and my throat was raw—I imagine red. It wasn't until the hot water of the shower came down on me that I felt half-alive again.

After drying off, I got dressed listening to *The Best of Blondie,* then followed that with Madonna's *Immaculate Collection.* It turned into an event of trying on several different outfits with various accessories. Chloe and I were the most fabulously dressed in our ghetto. No one could match our style. I couldn't figure out why that alone wasn't enough to get Chloe out to the bar.

By the time I had finally settled on an outfit, the phone rang. It was Jerome, inviting me to go to his house and hang out. I was sort of reluctant to go because glass was the first thing that came to mind (and I truly wanted to quit), but I didn't have any cigarettes and he promised to have one waiting for me when I got there. So after downing my tea and toast, I walked over to his place.

Although Jerome and Zack lived only a few blocks away, my trip there was horrible. I had to walk through snow because (I sang out loud in an operatic voice), *"People don't bother to shovel their stupid sidewalks in the ghetto!"* Then a big truck sped around a corner and splashed slush all over my platforms. I was so pissed. The water froze the bottoms of my pants stiff like cardboard. The only thing that kept me moving was the anticipation of that cigarette. I wondered if I'd have gone through all this crap if I'd had my own pack. I might have just stayed home and made dinner for Chloe.

Zack and Jerome's apartment was a one-bedroom, the same size as Chloe's and mine, only a different layout. It was on the corner of the building, so they had more windows and a nicer kitchen. Zack had all his trippy oil paintings on the walls. They were all frameless canvases, dark in color. The largest of them pictured distorted faces within this weird pattern. For some reason it always made me think of the monkeys I saw when Chloe and I tripped on Halloween. I guess because the faces look trapped within the pattern.

As promised, a cigarette was waiting for me, and the smoke I inhaled from it seemed to fill the void in my stomach. I sat in their living room on the big brown raggedy armchair. Jerome sat across from me on the raggedy couch, also smoking. Sam and Zack were in the kitchen, trying (unsuccessfully) to make fresh-squeezed orange juice with the box of oranges Zack's mom sent him from Florida.

"So what're you guys up to today?" I asked Jerome.

"I dunno . . . I think we're trying to get hooked up."

"With glass?"

"Yeah. You wanna go in on some?"

Of course I wanted to. It was all I could think about. "Well, I don't know if I can afford it. I have to save up for rent and everything."

"Yeah, I know how it goes. We've been trying to scrape money together here, too. So if you think of any ways to get some quick cash, don't hold back."

"You could always sell plasma."

"Yeah, right . . . They don't want my blood."

"What about Sam?" I yelled loud enough for her to hear. "She's the one who lives with her parents!"

"You think that means I got money comin' in somewhere?" She entered the living room, wiping orange juice off her hands with a dish towel. She smiled at me. "Hey, sexy, long time no see."

I happily returned the smile. "Come sit with me," I said. And she skipped over and squished up next to me on the armchair.

"Guess who's selling glass now?" she asked with a big grin.

"Who?"

"Jake the Motherfucking Snake!"

"Get out!"

"Seriously. I talked to him the other day, and oh my God, girl, he is such a tweak. Total sketch case and skinny as hell. Zack was with me, he'll tell ya'."

"He's a total Skeletor," Zack said, joining us in the living room with a glass containing one inch of orange juice. "Anyone thirsty?" He held it up. We all grimaced and laughed.

"So are you guys hooking up with the Snake?" I asked.

"Hell, yeah." Sam told me that she could probably get a good deal, too, because he still liked her, seemed to like her even more in fact. They had stopped talking for a while. After she dumped him, he apparently turned into an even bigger freak. It was definitely the drugs that got him. He started staying in his house 24/7, tripping with his hookups, his customers, and even by himself. The only thing he ever left the house for was to dance at raves and take drugs with other people. "Talk about not knowing how to maintain," she said. "He totally overdoes it!"

"Don't his parents care?"

"Fuck, no . . . I'd give up on that freak, too, if I were them."

"God, Sam, have you no compassion?"

"Only with him am I coldhearted, Miss Geneva. Miss Moral Crusader."

"Well, anyways, does he have good glass?"

"He says he does. Says it's clear."

"How much?"

"Duh! Fifty dollars a quarter, like always."

"Well, excuse me for living!" I rolled my eyes.

I loved Sam to death, but ever since we started doing powders together, our relationship had changed. In some ways I felt closer to her, like more open with her. But life wasn't all innocence and bliss like it used to be. We both changed a lot, and now, in many ways, we were much more artificial with each other. It seemed like when we were together now, we cared more about getting ourselves high than just being together.

She seemed like a whole new person. When I dated her, she was chubby, now she was as thin as a post—totally anorexic. She dressed differently, too. Baggy clothes were all she used to wear, but those were a thing of the past. Now she wore a lot of tight jeans with tears in the butt and knees and little tank tops. She certainly wasn't shy anymore. Every time I saw her, I was surprised.

Speed does that to you fast. When meth first came out, it was used as a diet pill. It was called "mother's little helper" because housewives would take it and clean up a storm. But I'm sure whatever they were taking back then was nothing compared to the junk we were doing! We did stuff that crackheads and chemistry dropouts made in their bathtubs. I tried to not even think about it, though, because it really was pretty nasty.

We finally decided that we all needed to get spun for sure, so we began pooling as much money as we could spare onto the coffee table. Unfortunately, it only added up to thirty-five dollars. We refused to call our parents and ask for money, all of us hating to go through that bullshit. We were desperate, though. And sitting around talking about how badly we wanted glass only made the craving worse. Although each of us acted cool, like we were stronger than our cravings, I knew that I wasn't the only one who was obsessed. We were all getting irritated with each other. If we didn't find some soon, I knew we'd all get cranky and snap at every remark anyone made.

But these were my speed buddies. Drugs were the tie that bound our friendship. Sure, we'd have fun together and we liked each other, even felt loyalty to one another, for the most part. However the friendship was all about drugs. When you have fun with someone only because you're both high, you realize that you don't like them when you're sober because you know you shouldn't be doing speed, so you blame them for being such a bad influence. Even though I was aware of all of this, I still wanted glass. And I still wanted to be with them when I did it.

After discussing our options for a year and a day, we finally decided that Zack would raise money by pawning a couple of the CDs he didn't listen to anymore. He was reluctant at first to lose his Luscious Jackson and two Pink Floyd albums, but we convinced him that it was for a greater cause: to get his friends spun. Then we promised he could hold the bag (which meant he would ration our lines at his discretion and do all the chopping). He was such a sucker, too. Zack *loved* to play with the powder, making us watch and wait eagerly until he was ready. Doing speed is kind of like a game. Like when Mario gets his 1-up on Nintendo. The object: to stay awake as long as you can.

{ sixteen }

*C*lick, click, click . . . Click, click, click. That was the sound the razor made tapping the surface of the mirror as Zack cut the lines.

After pawning CDs in Uptown, we had called Jake from the free phone at Lund's grocery store. We waited outside, and Sam made us promise not to let her hook up with Jake again. He arrived with our quarter of glass and a single red rose for Sam. And he looked hot! Thin, but not awful thin. Jake wasn't at all the wreck that Sam had described. Suddenly she changed her tune too and smiled like a madwoman as she accepted her rose. I swear, you could feel the sparks just standing there. He told her that she was looking goddamn fine, which she totally ate up. I would've done the same. Even though Sam had told us not to let her hook up with him, we knew trying get between them now would have been like trying to put out a forest fire with a squirt gun.

Jake gave us a ride home and conveniently joined our group at the apartment. Sam sat on his lap in the easy chair, her legs dangling off the arm. They couldn't keep their hands off each other. *Such* a cute couple. I couldn't help but feel envious of Sam.

The glass came in a quarter-sized Ziploc baggie. It was clear and chunky like margarita salt. Zack used a pen cap to remove a few of the chunks and dumped them onto CD case. He pressed down on the chunks with his driver's license, using the top side of the razor blade to crush it. Then he started tap, tap, tapping on the pile with the sharp edge until it turned into a fine white powder. Next he slid the razor across the mirror, using the corner to draw out four fat lines: rails. You take your first few hits fat so that you get really spun right away. After that, you can reduce the rails to small bumps in order to make the bag last. Our hopes were always that between the four of us, we could make one bag last until the next day. Zack had whispered in my ear on the way back that he hoped Jake would stay with us all night and keep bumping us up when we ran out. I told him I expected it.

"Here, Erick, you take the first one." Zack slid the mirror toward me and held out a Bic pen that had been hollowed out and cut in half.

I thanked him with a grin and took the straw. I put one end into my right nostril, plugged my other nostril with my finger, and inhaled one of the rails. It shot up into my sinuses, burning the inside of my nose like hot water on icy hands. It felt good—the actual snorting was my favorite part. When I looked up, everyone in the room was watching me.

I smiled. "Here you go." I slid the mirror across the coffee table to Zack.

"Sam?" He held up the straw.

"Coming," she squealed, sliding off Jake's lap and walking on her knees over to the coffee table. In a similar fashion, she snorted the next line, then looked back at me, one eyebrow raised. We shared a sneaky giggle.

Zack held the straw up to Jerome, laughed, and popped it right up his nostril. With the straw hanging from his nose, Jerome declared, "Bastard!" and squeezed an explosive laugh out of Zack's sides, then continued to tickle him until he apologized about a hundred times. I just rolled my eyes at them. Another cute couple. I couldn't believe my misfortune of being the only single person present. I wanted a hug!

Finally, I just sat back and lit a cigarette, waiting for the glass to kick in. Zack and Jerome snorted lines, and soon we were all laughing. I was starting to feel superwired, taking fast-paced drags off my Camel Full Flavor. "So what should we do tonight?" I asked.

"To start with, let's listen to DJ Shadow," Zack said, using his remote control to put on the extremely high-energy techno CD. Even without the glass, the music was fast enough that it would have gotten us a little hopped up.

"Are you guys spun?" Jake asked.

"I'm getting there," Zack replied.

"It's good glass, huh?" he continued, impressed by his own stuff. I got lost in his eyes for a second.

"Yeah, it seems alright," Zack said.

"Alright? Man, this shit is the bomb!" Jake declared.

"Are you spun?" I asked him.

"Hell, yeah, man! I just woke up this morning with a big rail after fourteen hours of sleep. I'm good to go!"

Sam started laughing. "You are so weird, Jake."

"What? Why?"

"You just are . . . But you're cute."

"You can't deny that," he gloated.

I thought they both looked pretty cute together—such a match. Jake was wearing black, wide-bottom Jenko jeans, black Skecher sneakers, and a tight white T-shirt that said ATARI in navy blue letters. His black hair was slicked back. He looked like a classic raver—and raver boys are so cute.

Zack decided we needed to do another rail right away because we just weren't spun enough. Jake threw a little of his own glass into the pile, too, so Zack cut five rails, bigger than the last. This time, he and Jerome went first, practically at the same time. It reminded me of *Lady and the Tramp*, when the two dogs shared a spaghetti noodle. Oh, how it was torture to watch such marital bliss.

As soon as Zack finished his rail, he shouted: "God, I really wanna fuckin' party tonight! Don't you guys?"

Of course we all wanted to party! After we each snorted a second rail, we danced to the music in our seats, chatting frantically about the party we went to last time we all got spun together. There was plenty of gossip to spread about that night. A lot of "Oh my God, I was so fucked up, blah, blah, blah. He is so cute, blah, blah blah. Did you see what that weird girl was wearing?"

When five people are all spun, everyone's talking at once, volleying twenty different conversations back and forth. Sam and Jake went into the kitchen for their big "let's get back together" conversation and came back with big glasses of slightly cold water for us all to share. Jerome turned up the thermostat so we all wouldn't freeze to death.

Then Jerome told me about the poetry he wrote. How his poems were both depressing yet uplifting, reflections of his life and the people around him. Many of them were love poems about his sweet baby Zack.

Zack totally grinned at that, and they kissed.

The poems he wrote, he said, would make terrific songs, too. Jerome wanted to sing R & B but was scared to try.

I suggested that we could be an R & B band! I'd of course be the *fierce* drag queen at the piano and he'd be my man—my pimp!

"Ooh, we'll do smooth dance numbers!"

"I'll smoke cigarettes in a red dress."

"I'd be happy to mix the beats," Jake said.

"We're gonna be in a band!" we cheered.

Jerome will sing his poetry, I'll play the piano, and Sam and I will both sing backup—and she'll play a tambourine (and bass if she can learn how). Zack will play lead guitar (if he can learn how). But how could either of them not figure out on speed. All you had time to do on speed was play guitar, anyway.

"Our band name will *Glass* Heads!" Jerome cried. *"Glass* will be italicized, so that people will say the word with extra enthusiasm."

I was like, "Whatever, girl!"

"I'm gonna wear a black suit with hot pink pinstripes," Jerome said dreamily.

"And a pink feather!" I said.

"What will Jake wear?" Sam asked.

"A thong," I said.

Everyone laughed. "That'll work," Zack said. "In fact, Jake, why don't you take off your shirt now so that by the time we get onstage you won't be embarrassed."

"In your dreams, drag queens."

"If you only *knew* the dreams of drag queens," I said.

"What are your dreams?" Sam asked.

"To be a drag queen astronaut in a band!"

"Why would they want a drag queen in space?" Jake asked.

"Duh," I said, "to entertain the space boys."

"I suppose they need it up there all alone in a capsule," Jerome laughed.

Sam joined in, "Oooh baby, with the lights on or off?"

"With a strobe light, techno, and no gravity!" Zack added.

"This guy," Sam giggled, "has his bedroom decorated like outer space."

"I thought you said my stars were romantic?" Jake countered.

"They are." She kissed him.

I was so jealous! Why was I always the one without a boyfriend? I wondered what Mike the Dyke was up to. Could he possibly be happy with that Courtney girl? Blah! Who would want a girlfriend named Courtney, anyway? That's so not sexy!

Zack asked me how I was doing—with work and everything.

I told him that my job at Silver Screen Video sucked, that my manager was such a bitch. "She's always getting on my case about stupid shit. Like, it's the end of the world if the videos aren't lined up perfectly on the shelf. Also, she never lets me smoke, unless I'm on my break. Meanwhile, she's going out for a cigarette every half-hour. I swear to God, I'm going to quit soon. I don't need to take that crap! This city is full of jobs . . . And another thing that really bugs me is when customers get mad at me because I haven't seen the stupid movie they're asking about. Like I sit around and watch movies all day! Like I don't have anything better to do with my life than that!"

"So what are you going to do after you quit?" Zack asked.

"Maybe I'll sell drugs like Jake—or be a hooker."

"I always knew you were a common criminal," Sam said.

"I may be a criminal, but I am *not* common."

"You go, girl!" Jake said.

That made us all laugh. Jake can be such a dork!

After talking about a bazillion different queer-as-hell topics, we decided that we needed to go to Plato, just for a change in scenery. Even though Jake had once been there to pick up Sam, he was reluctant to go because the people there were "gay," and he thought everyone would think he was gay and hit on him. I told him that it sounded to me like he was more concerned that he *wouldn't* get hit on.

"Whatever, Geneva. Everywhere I go, people come on to me . . . They all just want to see my snake."

We all screamed, "Ah, you're disgusting!"

Finally, Sam convinced him that as long as he stayed by her side, he wouldn't have anything to worry about. So we all bundled up in winter clothes and piled into Jake's jalopy. Sam, of course, rode shotgun, and the gay boys got crammed together in the back. Once we arrived, we sat in the parking lot, where Zack cut us each another bump on his compact mirror. He had a little plastic case that held all the "tools"—razors, straws, the mirror, and the drugs; it had a holographic green alien sticker on the lid.

By the time we sat down at a table, I was so spun that I was thinking of a million things a minute—brain overload!

There was quite a big crowd to gawk at, too. Mostly groups of older guys, hanging out and cruising. When Zack and I went to the counter to purchase bottles of water, a whole table of creeps sitting near the bar tried to get us to go sit with them by claiming that they had saved us a couple of seats. Of course we totally snubbed them. Plato is the kind of place where everyone watches your every move, and just one visit to the old-man table will get you shunned for life by the gossips. You'll get maybe one chance to redeem yourself if you can prove you didn't know any better. And that's only if you dress really smart.

"So is this what you fags do?" Jake asked. "Sit around in dim lighting and check each other out?"

"Don't use the word 'fag,'" Sam chided him. "Only gays can call each other fag," she explained.

"It's just like how only brothas can call each other 'nigga.'" Jerome grinned.

"God, Jerome, you get to use all the controversial slang, don't you?" Jake replied.

"Well, *you* can call yourself a honky-straight-boy if you want to," Jerome said.

"Thanks, but I'll pass."

"Can't we just all get along?" Sam rolled her eyes.

"Right on, girl." I winked at Jake.

Time totally flies when you're spun. It seemed like we were at Plato for only a short time, but in reality we must have stayed there a few hours because by the time we left, the sky was pitch-black and the air was freezing. Even with my little red coat and hat, I still shivered.

When we got into Jake's car, Zack cut us each another bump. This time I snorted it up my left nostril just to give my right one a break. Normally, I hated doing it with my left nostril because it burned so much more, but Zack had told me that meth can eat away at the cartilage in your nose, and it doesn't grow back. I figured that if I was damaging the right side of my face more than my left, I wouldn't be symmetrical anymore, and that would totally suck.

We drove around the city repeating: "What do you guys want to do?" over and over again, until at last we decided to go back to Zack and Jerome's place, get all vamped up, and then go dancing at Screwdriver. It was an eighteen-and-up night, so I figured that if Bubba was working he would let Sam and me (the only two under-agers in our group) in without a hassle. Usually the bouncers at Screwdriver were superstrict about that shit.

On the ride to the club, the stereo blaring, I watched Jerome bounce his knee up and down unconsciously, faster than the music. I realized that he had lost control. The exact same thing was happening to me, too, with my sudden inability to stop grinding my teeth. It was so weird. I never ground my teeth, and now it was like trying to control hiccups when you're drunk. Finally, I got a piece of gum from Zack to distract my poor mouth. I noticed Sam up front with the visor down, looking at the mirror. She was applying powder from her L'Oréal compact onto her entire face and whining about how she looked like "absolute shit." Of course, Jake reassured her that she looked fine, his hand on her thigh the whole time.

I caught sight of my own reflection in the visor mirror. My short, multicolored hair was pointed in all directions, my cheeks were flushed, and I was already looking skinnier. I looked and felt like a hot rock star. Thank God I was going to the club spun. Maybe I'd finally get properly laid. I started thinking about how I seriously needed a tattoo. I was so thrilled by my new appearance that I wanted to get something to make it permanent. I was sort of thinking about doing a G.F. with, like, a really cool border that I could design myself.

"Hey, you guys, I'm going to get a tattoo," I announced.

"Me, too!" Sam exclaimed, whipping around to smile at me from up front.

"Oh my God, you wanna go together!"

"Yes!"

We gave each other a high-five.

"Do we need parental permission though?" Sam asked.

"I can hook you up," Jake said as he pulled into the parking lot of Screwdriver. He found a parking spot between two big trucks, and we all did another rail, just so we'd be good to go for a few hours. This time I went back to using my right nostril. I said to myself, "Fuck it. If I get disfigured, oh well." Doing it up my left nostril hurt like hell!

We had to stand in line forever. Eighteen-and-up nights were always crowded. Jake held tight to Sam's hand and whispered about how hot she was, just so that no one in line would think he was gay, I'm sure. When we finally made it to the front of the line, Bubba greeted me with a grin. "Hey jailbait, long time no see."

"Hey, how are you?"

"Not bad . . . Chloe here?"

"No . . . he has to work tomorrow morning," I replied, even though I really had no idea what Chloe was doing tomorrow. "These are my friends."

"Cool," he said, not bothering to take his gaze off me to notice them. "You guys have fun."

"We always have fun, baby." And I led my friends inside.

The bar was packed, music was blasting, and there was a strobe light and red lasers spinning on the dance floor. The first thing we saw was two men in tight jeans making out, their hands in each other's back pockets. I looked back at Jake just in time to see his jaw drop. He held Sam up close in front of him, not sure where to look.

"What do you want to do now?" I heard Zack yell almost inaudibly over the music.

"Let's go check out the drag queens," I yelled back.

"I wanna dance though."

"Then why did you ask me what *I* wanted to do?"

"I was hoping you'd say you wanted to dance."

"Well, I wanna dance, too . . . but first I want to see the show."

"Well, let's split up for a while . . . You and Sam and Jake go watch the show and come find us later," he said, taking Jerome by the arm.

"Do you guys want to watch it?" I asked Sam and Jake.

"Fuck, yeah!" Sam said, dancing around wildly, eyes closed, her raised arms swaying to the beat, while Jake clung to her for dear life.

We made it to the drag lounge just in time to see Babs Arlington introduce the next performer. It was too dark and crowded to go looking for three seats, so we just stood by the bathrooms behind the audience, where we had a semiclear view.

"Our next saucy queen is one of the greatest performers in the local scene of all time! She's been a devoted drag mother to all of us and we *love* her for it," Babs said with crazy theatrical gestures. She was wearing a short plastic sleeveless yellow dress with a big pink necktie, pink platforms, and a brown Marge Simpson wig. As she dished out campy remarks, her eyes roamed the audience and sometimes she would pause to wave at someone she knew. I wondered if she'd recognize me. How exciting would that be!

"So without further ado . . . Mama Jezebel!" she called the name out, flinging her arms into the air.

The music started, and a thunderous black drag queen in a tight gold-lamé gown that flared dramatically at the calves walked onto the stage crooning "It's Raining Men." Everything about her was gargantuan: her weight, her boobs, her wig. Her basketball-sized mouth quivered as she lip-synched the words as if she was actually producing sound. The audience went ballistic. Gay men shouted, "Work it, girl!" "Rock that stage, woman!" and even "Spank me, Mama Jezebel!" The audience stood up from their seats to dance to the beat, waving their arms and shaking their asses. I began to get into it, too, until Jake (being too cool to dance at a drag-queen show) began mocking the audience for its apparent lack of rhythm.

"Ooh, look at me!" He hopped around like Suzanne Somers on Ecstasy.

"Cut it out, Jake!" Sam elbowed him in the gut. "C'mon, Erick, let's go tip her." She grabbed my hand and moved us to the line of tippers that had formed in the front and center of the stage.

When we got to the front of the line, Mama Jezebel leaned her bosom forward, never breaking character. We each dropped a one-dollar bill into her brassiere. The fierce drag queen grinned at us personally, then swung her body up and back into the rhythm. Sam and I shared a giggle and ran back to Jake, who had his arms defiantly crossed across his chest.

"Oh, lighten up," Sam demanded, taking his hands and leading him forcefully into a dance, until finally he just gave up and began enjoying himself.

The next song, "I Will Always Love You," was performed by a skinny drag queen who had Whitney Houston's X factor. I was glad that Jake and Sam were enjoying the show. Jake said he thought that it was one of the funniest things he'd ever seen. Sam found his comments rude, but I could see what he meant. Part of being a drag performer was making the audience laugh. When people watched men dressed as women lip-synch to disco, they expected a spectacle, something to amuse them as they got drunk.

For me it was a lot more than that. I was like an amateur skater watching *Champions on Ice,* learning different styles and moves from the pros, planning the moves I'd make when it was my turn to be onstage. If I ever amounted to anything, I hoped it would be a first-class drag queen. I'd decided already that I'd do my thang to Tori. It would have to be a danceable Tori song, and I would have to have a hundred wigs to choose from. Maybe Chloe would take me shopping when I got my paycheck.

I nearly burst into tears remembering the first time Chloe took me to the bar and performed "Billie Jean." Screwdriver just wasn't the same without him. In many ways I resented Chloe for having AIDS and suddenly not wanting to go out. I wanted us to be showbiz partners. We were supposed to go to Hollywood—getting out of this god-awful city once and for all. But that would never happen now.

I wondered if Chloe would die an atheist. Or would he freak out at the last minute and start praying, just in case? I'd never ask him, of course, just because the question would probably offend him. But I couldn't help but wonder how he could be so sure there wasn't a God that he would bet eternity on it. I know that if I was going to die, I'd at least want to pray on a rosary and possibly even have my sins absolved by a priest, just to be safe. I wouldn't have it done by Father Tom, obviously. I'd almost rather go to hell than talk to him ever again.

"Come *on*, Erick! Let's go find Zack and Jerome and dance!" Sam urged.

We had to squeeze our way through the crowd to get to them, but once we were in the middle of the floor, we formed our circle and pushed our way outward until we had space to dance. When you're spun, dancing is the greatest thing ever. You *never* get tired. The music takes you into another dimension where nothing matters but the sound of the beat. At first I followed the rhythm exactly, doing all the moves I practiced in front of the mirror every morning as I got dressed. But after a while I just closed my eyes and let my body do whatever it wanted. You get to a point where you're so into the moment that it's almost like what you hear is not necessarily what everyone else is hearing. You're dancing to your own rhythm, and everything makes perfect sense.

I opened my eyes and looked at all the faces and outfits dancing around me, recognizing a lot of them, especially the outfits. This town sucked. The boys were so bitchy. Every time I tried to make eye contact with anyone, they were snotty. It was so discouraging. I couldn't figure out why no one ever hit on me when I was such a hottie. The way I looked and dressed, I should have been the fucking belle of the ball. I wondered if it was my age, or whether they just weren't digging my personality. Maybe they could tell I was on drugs. There had to be a reason.

Then, just when I had given up, I saw Troy, the guy who had taken me to his Mary Tyler Moore apartment, dancing toward me. "How'd *you* get in?" he demanded menacingly. "Don't you have to be eighteen?"

"Whatever," I said casually, turning away from him. He gave me the total creeps. I didn't even want to be reminded of the mistake I had made with him.

"Bitch," he said in my ear, close enough that I could feel his breath. "How'd you like my big cock up your ass?"

"Is there a problem?" Jake asked. By now my group had sensed trouble and stopped dancing to stand up for me. There they were: Jake, Sam, Jerome, and Zack, their arms crossed across their chests, giving Troy fierce attitude. "Why don't you prance back on over to where you came from?" Jake continued.

I felt so much pride in my friends that I said, "That's right, you ugly troll doll, get the fuck out of here unless you want your ass kicked." Out of my peripheral vision, I saw Jake put up his fists.

Troy's face went pale as he realized he'd messed with the wrong diva. With one last cowardly sneer, he turned and walked away. We laughed seeing him go. "Way to go!" Zack declared. "He'll think twice before he messes with anyone again."

We merrily resumed our dancing. This time I didn't even bother to look for a boyfriend. It suddenly seemed enough to just have friends like mine. It was the first time anyone had stood up for me before, and I wished I had known that type of camaraderie in high school. Maybe then I wouldn't have dropped out.

Next, the worst imaginable thing happened: Troy told security that I was under eighteen, and a big black bouncer grabbed me by the arm and pointed a flashlight in my face. "ID?" he demanded. I didn't know what to do. Everyone stared at me. Sam grabbed my hand. "What's the problem?" I said to him, as if that was as good as producing an ID. "Come with me," the bouncer said, dragging me toward the door by my arm. On the way out, I saw Troy grinning profusely at his victory. From out of nowhere, Sam slapped him across the face. *"You're* the bitch with the cock up his ass!" she fumed. The bouncer grabbed her with his free hand and shoved us both into the street. "Don't ever come back!" The door slammed behind us. Standing in the street, Sam and I looked at each other and laughed.

Soon the rest of our group had joined us. "You guys should have seen his face when Sam slapped him!" Jake said.

"It was the greatest!" Zack said.

With that, we walked arm in arm down Hennepin Avenue, all of us still as wide awake and buzzed as a bunch of Energizer bunnies. It seemed to me like everything that had happened since we first started speeding had passed by in the snap of a finger. It was weird, though, because all that had taken place before I did my first line of the night felt like another day entirely. To remember getting dressed, talking to Jerome on the phone, and getting splashed by that damn truck while walking to their apartment was like recalling a dream from weeks ago. I was a whole different person when I was sober, and I was reminded that I was leading two different lives: the high life and the low.

In spite of how dangerous crystal was, I must admit that I did it to enjoy the high life. Once I was high enough, I didn't have to worry about my fucked-up life. I had no self-esteem, so I would sit in front of the mirror for hours, searching for any flaw, pinching the slight bit of fat at my waist, imagining that my ass was out-of-control gigantic. My nose looked too big and my lips looked too small. I had zits on my forehead that wouldn't go away no matter how many facials I did. Everyone always told me that I was being insane, that I was *too* skinny, but it didn't matter what they said, because I still hated what I saw in the mirror when I was sober.

On the other hand, when I was spun, I didn't have to look in the mirror, unless it was to admire myself. Glass made me feel flawless. It was like I finally felt normal, and I wasn't scared'a nothin'. People could think whatever the hell they wanted to. Even Chloe and my parents. Glass made me feel that good about myself. My body was all tight.

Still, it was never tight enough.

{ seventeen }

On the way home, Sam said that she needed to talk. So when we got to the apartment, we headed directly for the bathroom. "Secrets don't make friends," Jake called out at us.

"Erick is the only friend I trust with my secrets," Sam replied.

"Fine," Jake said, "We'll be in here having the party without you."

Sam closed the door and quickly turned on the faucet. I sat on the toilet with my legs crossed, lighting a cigarette. She adjusted her red locks in front of the mirror.

"You spun?" she asked.

"Fuck, yeah . . . The night has only begun."

"I know, girl . . . I'm so glad we're doing this together, you know? 'Cause we really get a chance to talk about things. We kind of lost that confidence in each other when we broke up. But now that we're just good friends, I want us to be completely honest with each other again."

"I know what you mean," I said. "I've totally been wanting to open up to you."

"Totally . . . See, the thing is, I know I never really told you this before, but I felt superrejected when you broke up with me

. . . 'Cause if I remember right, you used to try so hard to get me to like you, chasing me around, calling me all the time . . . I thought you were so cute, like a lost puppy . . . And then suddenly I fall in love with you, and you tell me you're gay!"

I knew this would come up sooner or later. It's not like I didn't feel terrible about it, too. "I'm sorry about that," was all I could say.

"You don't have to be sorry. It's not you're fault you're gay."

"I know."

"I'm just saying that after we broke up, I felt really rejected. In fact the first thing I did after you dumped me was have sex with this boy from my school named Christian . . . But I want you to know that the only reason I slept with him was because I needed to feel good about myself again. I mean, God, I was in love with you. I was ready to lose my virginity to you . . . But instead I ended up losing it to some boy I don't even talk to anymore."

"But was it worth it?"

"What?"

"The sex? Was it good?" I asked.

"Well . . . I dunno. It wasn't how I thought it would be." She smiled. "But at least he could get it up for me."

"Oh, low blow."

"Sorry," she laughed. "Anyway, it wasn't that good. It hurt . . . and I just wanted it to be with you."

"Shut up, you're embarrassing me . . . Anyway, I think we're much better off as friends."

"Yeah, but that's partly because you're not such a dork now that you're gay."

"Aren't all straight boys dorks, though?"

"Tell me about it. Men are pigs."

"They're big pork chops, is what they are."

There was a tap on the door. "Are you guys coming out soon?" Jake called through the keyhole.

"Get out'a here, you big pork chop!" Sam yelled back.

"What'cha talkin' about in there?"

"You. Just kidding!"

"Ha-ha . . . Hurry up, okay, 'cause I miss you."

"Alright," she said, as he left the door.

"How sweet," I teased in a corny voice. "Poor Jake the Snake misses you."

"Whatever. He's such a freakazoid."

"Do you like him?"

"I don't know . . . I feel weird dating a glass dealer. I don't want to be one of *those* girls."

"What girls?"

"All cracked out all the time."

"I know. I don't want to do this drug very often. It fucks you up big time," I said. "It really could make me lose my mind once and for all."

"Yeah . . . but if we do it only on special occasions, it probably won't be so bad."

"Exactly."

"Plus it's good for dieting."

"You have gotten really skinny."

"I know . . . Well, kinda. I still have big hips. Only now I have no boobs." She looked at her body in the mirror scornfully. She was wearing a tiny black tank top with skinny straps. "You've gotten thinner, too."

"You think?" I joined her in our reflections. We started playing with our hair. Mine was a multicolored mess. I'd have given anything to be able to go to a real stylist instead of trying to dye my own hair. One time I let Chloe trim it for me, and he cut my bangs at such a weird slant that I had to use extra gel to hide it. I was so pissed.

"I have makeup." Sam opened her bag. "Anyway, isn't Jake a total asshole?"

"Yeah," I said. "He's sweet to you, though, and a killer

dancer. I just worry about the drugs. I don't want to see you turn into one of *those* girls, either."

"That's what I'm saying. I don't know what to do, though. Sometimes, like right now, I feel as if like it might be true love," she said, applying eye shadow.

"As long as he makes you happy, isn't that all that matters?"

"I suppose. It's just that, well, I just hope that someday I can have a family . . . I know it sounds cheesy, but it's true . . . God, I don't think I've ever told anyone that."

"Really?"

"Yeah. I guess I just don't like to come off as being soft."

"I know what you mean," I agreed, finding some mascara and running it through my lashes.

"So . . . how's Chloe?" she asked, her voice sounding a bit reluctant. Sam knew that he had AIDS, but we hadn't really talked about it much.

"He's fine . . . I guess . . . He seems to be doing well. And he likes his job."

"How are you?" She posed the real question.

"Going crazy."

"Honey, we're all crazy these days. Anyway, Chloe will be fine."

"Yeah, I know. He's an experienced survivor."

"Well, isn't gaining experience what life is all about?"

"Beautifully said," I told her solemnly.

"So you wanna go back out there?"

"Might as well."

With that, we refilled her makeup bag and rejoined the group in the living room. Zack and Jake were sitting on the floor playing some boxing game on the Sony PlayStation. Jerome was lying on his back on the couch with a sly grin, eagerly writing in his notebook.

"What'cha writing about?" Sam asked him.

"Nothing really, just the happenings of the day. When I'm spun I can write for hours, nonstop."

"Is it like poetry or journal writing?"

"It's a mixture, I suppose, although most of it, hopefully, is poetry . . . I think poetry is one of the highest arts."

"Mmmm, me, too," Sam agreed.

"Sometimes I write songs, too."

"Really?" Sam asked. "Like what kind of songs?"

"Well, actually, I'd sort of like to be an R and B singer."

"Really?" I said. "I could play the piano for you if you want to give your lyrics a shot."

"That would be so cool!" Jerome said. "We could be in a band!"

"Oh my God. We so could . . . I'm a terrific piano player. And I can sing, too!"

Jake's jaw dropped when he heard us talking. "You guys are nuts!"

"What? Why?"

"High-asses! Don't you remember having this exact conversation already?"

Suddenly we each remembered: *Glass* Heads. And we all stared at each other in silent disbelief for about ten seconds, then all at once busted out laughing. We couldn't believe we had forgotten and decided that we were way too cracked out for our own good.

Just then Sam looked out the window and declared, "Oh, no! The sun is coming up! I'm melting!"

We all looked out the window. It was morning, the most irritating part of the day when you haven't slept and it still feels like yesterday. It reminded me of being a vampire and fearing the sun.

"We'd better do another bump A-S-A-P," Zack said, pausing the video game. He crawled over to the coffee table and opened his little plastic case with the alien sticker on it. All that was left of our fifty-dollar bag was a small amount of white crumbs lining the bottom. Using his pen cap he removed half of what was remaining and dropped it onto the mirror. "We'll do these lines now, then we'll each have one left for when we start coming down."

"Here, add this." Jake dropped a small shard of glass onto the pile.

Zack crushed it with his ID and drew out the lines in his usual careful way.

After doing my line, I felt more spun than I had been all night. More awake than I ever remember feeling. It was hard to believe that we'd already done so much. We'd talked about everything under the sun, gone dancing, watched the drag show, got kicked out of the bar, and it seemed like all that shit was just blurred together. As if we'd only just begun our day.

I lit a cigarette and sat back in my chair, counting the remainder of my pack. I had six left. Since getting the pack, I'd already smoked fourteen. That seemed like a lot. My throat should've been raw and sore. I should've been sick of smoking, but I wasn't. In fact, as soon as I lit a cigarette, it felt long overdue.

Sometimes, when you start coming down off speed, you get really, really, really depressed. I don't know if that's because you stay up for so long, or because it makes you dwell on all the sad things in life. Or maybe it causes a chemical imbalance in your brain. Whatever, it makes you feel super down on yourself.

When we came down that morning, time began to move very slowly. I found myself wondering whether I was in real time and everything seemed slow only because I had been spun, or if time had actually retarded itself, like maybe the Earth had somehow slowed down. I knew that was a ridiculous notion, but when you're strung out, you just can't help thinking things like that. We sat in the apartment together, none of us wanting to go outside and face the cold sun, with Jake passing around a bowl of pot, which seriously obliterated me beyond comprehension. I felt high and low all at once. With sleep deprivation and the rest piled into me, I felt like I was tripping on acid again. And if I stared at any surface long enough, I could even bring back the monkeys. It was like all the creepy things about acid. It didn't make me laugh or try to find the life force or anything like fun acid did. It just made me paranoid. When I held my hand up to my heart, feeling the pounding in my chest, I felt as if I was having a heart attack, like I was going to die. I was quite scared of my friends now, too. I kept thinking that they probably thought I was a loser. That I was freaky because I wanted to be a drag queen and my roommate had AIDS.

At some point that morning (I was oblivious to the time of day), Zack spilled a glass of OJ on the area rug. We all freaked out, scrubbing the stain muddy with sponges. We poured bleach and Dawn dish soap and hot water onto the floor, creating a much larger mess than the one we set out to clean. That's the type of weird thing speed makes you do. When we had finished scrubbing, we all sat back and looked at each other, dismayed by what we had done. There was soapsuds and water everywhere. Both the rug and the hardwood floor underneath it were damaged by the water. Zack said that now they'd have to get the whole goddamn place carpeted!

Even though I probably didn't need any more, I did my last line along with everyone else. It wasn't because I was going along with all my friends that I did it, though. I couldn't have cared less if they thought I was a wussy. I did it because I couldn't let that last line get away from me. It could've been the one line that would take me to that place I always strove to reach and usually did. Complete fucked-up bliss. At least, that's how it was when I first started druggin' a few years back. Being high used to take away all my problems, or at least my depression. Now it seemed like whenever I got high, I had to do more and more every time because no matter how many drugs I did, I couldn't ever get as fucked up as I used to.

The longer we stayed up, the more we began to get on each other's nerves. Zack was extremely pissed about his ruined floor and took it out on all of us. Even though he was the one who spilled his drink in the first place. Jerome insisted that Zack take responsibility for his own actions, which somehow led to a lovers' quarrel about their sex life. Without any regard for decency, they accused each other of everything from cheating to impotence. It was so obscene.

Finally, none of us could stand each other's company any longer. It was already five o'clock in the afternoon by the time Jake and Sam and I left the apartment. Jake dropped me off at my place, and he and Sam went off together to do God knows what.

When I got there, Chloe was gone, which I was completely relieved about because I was not in the mood to contend with him—or anyone, for that matter. I was finally alone to dwell on my thoughts. Although I usually hate to be alone, solitude was actually a relief right then.

Thinking I was finally tired enough to sleep, I laid down and closed my eyes. But the speed had tricked me. Trying to go to bed made me feel even more wired, so I got up. I dragged myself into the bathroom and looked at my thin, pale face staring back at me in the mirror. The makeup I had so carefully put around my eyes earlier was now gray and smeared. My raccoon eyes made me look like a crazy old man. To make matters worse, my multicolored hair was looking slimy. Seeing myself like that made me feel sick. I decided to take a long, hot shower, rinsing away my filth by lathering my entire body with Olay moisturizing body wash. It felt good to get clean, at last, to rid myself of scandal with scalding water. After drying off and putting on baggy sweats, I felt somewhat renewed, but still not tired in the least.

I looked through the refrigerator and kitchen cupboards, trying to find something edible. I had to put some food in my body. Anything, really. I'd gotten so thin from just that one night that I could literally see my bones. I was a skeleton wrapped in pale skin. I even thought I could see my heart beating through my chest. Yet I wasn't hungry at all. Food smelled like mold to me, and my mouth hurt too much to chew. Even bread and water were too much to handle. I had speed bumps on my tongue; these were painful little white sores. But those were the repercussions I had to live with. Who would care if I died of anorexia anyway?

Somehow, looking through the kitchen led me to open Chloe's heart-shaped medicine cabinet. I ran my fingers across all the plastic pill bottles with their labels removed. I knew what they were, though: the AIDS cocktail!

I closed the cabinet and walked back over to the futon. Curling up in my blanket, I lay on my side and switched on the TV. All that was on was news and game shows, but I didn't care what came on. The only reason I had turned on the TV anyway was so I wouldn't have to think.

First thing Chloe asked me when he came home was where had I been all night. I told him that I went over to Jerome's house to smoke bowls and that it got late so I crashed on their couch. I said I didn't call because I figured he'd be asleep. Even as the words came out of my mouth, I could tell he knew I was lying.

"You're on speed, aren't you?" he charged, heavy disapproval in his tone.

"What? No, of course not."

"You can't lie to me, Erick."

"I'm not lying . . . God, why would you even think that about me?"

"Oh, please! You look like a skeleton . . . I can tell when someone is strung out."

I pictured myself from his perspective, lying on the futon, looking all fudged up. Could I explain to him that it was just a silly little case of spring anorexia happening in January? I wanted to deny his accusation again, to try to make him believe me, but I knew I was far too sketched out to fool anyone. "Are you mad at me?" I asked.

He hung up his jacket and sat down on the lime-green chair,

where he began unlacing his platforms. "No, I'm not mad at you. I'm just worried about you, that's all. I know what speed does to a person, and I just can't bear to watch you go through that. Besides, I have enough problems of my own."

"Sorry I'm such a problem in your life."

"The only person you should apologize to is yourself."

"What do you mean?"

"I mean, your choice to do speed is hurting you, not me," he said coldly. Which was typical of Chloe. He always acted like he was bulletproof, like nothing affected his emotions. I knew that he was upset, though. I knew he cared deeply about me.

I couldn't look him in the eyes without feeling guilty, so I rolled over and stared at the back of the futon. "I just—" I couldn't think of what to say. "I can't help it, Chloe. I've only done it a few times, but I think I'm already hooked."

"You get addicted to that junk the first time you do it."

"I'll quit . . . I promise you, I'll never do it again."

"Yeah, you will."

"You don't think I can quit?" It upset me that he had no faith in me.

"You can't quit until you face the repercussions of doing it. And believe me, that drug has some serious consequences."

"I really *can* quit," I insisted. And I honestly believed that I could. I just wouldn't do it anymore. It was as simple as that. "I don't even like doing it. Glass makes me depressed."

"You're coming down right now, aren't you?"

"Yeah, I haven't done any for a few hours."

"Well, of course you're depressed, then . . . That's one of the many side effects."

"You have to believe me, Chloe. I can quit."

"In three days or so, you'll be craving it. Mark my words."

"God, why are you being so mean?" I got up and went into the kitchen. I grabbed the bread I'd bought a week ago with my

Silver Screen paycheck and buttered a slice. I was hungry for the first time in days and I took big bites, which I barely chewed before swallowing. I watched Chloe turn off the TV and turn on the stereo. He put in his *Best of Queen* CD and turned it to "Bohemian Rhapsody." Then he proceeded to roll a joint.

I stayed in the kitchen, and he sat in the chair with his back facing me. We listened to the sad song in silence. Freddie Mercury's voice made me tremble with chills. The song was about facing death, and his voice seemed like it spoke from the grave.

"You know how you said I never cry?" Chloe reminded me, taking sips from his joint. I realized at that moment that there was more on his mind than my well-being.

"Yeah?"

"Well, when I found out I was HIV positive, I came home and put this song on repeat and bawled my eyes out . . . I must'a listened to it twenty times that day." He gave a little laugh. "Singing at the top of my lungs, dancing around the apartment naked, and crying."

I went back over to sit with him on the futon. His eyes were red and damp, but I didn't see tears. He smiled at me almost benevolently. "Was it scary?" I asked.

"Yeah. Well, sort'a . . . It just felt so . . . real, you know?"

I knew that feeling. The feeling that something bad had happened and it was too late to fix it. Like when I realized Tommy was gone. That was a moment of total clarity. I could practically feel mortality, and I understood for the first time how near death was. Death makes you step back from yourself and look at who you are from the outside. You see your body as being simply this thing that is imperfect and vulnerable. That was the most out-of-body experience I had ever had. That's how it feels to be real.

"Do you want to hit this?" Chloe extended the joint to me.

I waved it away. "That's the last thing I need right now."

"I can imagine." He took another hit. "I just didn't want you to think I wasn't sharing." He winked at me.

"Chloe, I really am sorry."

"Don't be so sorry, Erick. Even though I hate to see you do drugs, I can't say that I haven't done them myself . . . I wish I could *make* you quit. I wish I could help you see your potential as an artist. But I know that when I was your age, no one could'a made me do nothing."

"Don't say it's okay, Chloe . . . I need you there to stop me. If it wasn't for you, I'd be way worse off than I am now. I probably would'a killed myself or something."

"Gee, thanks. Put the pressure on me, why don't you?"

"Sorry." I thought about the stupid irony of what I just said. Two minutes ago, I thought I didn't need anyone, and now all I needed was for Chloe to take me in his arms and carry me away from all my madness.

"It wasn't me that made you the cool, smart, terrific guy that sits before me now. You did that yourself, Erick. You just can't see that because you blame yourself for everything. You need to realize what a great person you are before you can make real changes in your life. You need to believe in yourself and love yourself."

I felt truly grateful to hear those words. "Thank you, Chloe."

"For what?"

"For making me feel good about myself."

"Well, thank you for making me feel good about myself, too, then." He extinguished the joint in his Harley-Davidson ashtray. He turned off the music and turned the TV back on. I finally fell asleep while he flipped through channels.

{ eighteen }

I was a zombie when I got to work the next day. I wore my platforms and Chloe's Kellogg's Cornflakes T-shirt, and my nails were painted blue. Joy and this other guy that I worked with thought I was such a freak. Whenever they thought I was out of earshot, they made jokes about the way I dressed and how I "must have partied all weekend." Just because I thought I was dying didn't give them the right to assume to type of life I led. Whatever for them! As far as I was concerned, they were just a couple of movie geeks with no lives.

At the time of my interview, I wasn't wearing any nail polish or makeup. I had on a nicely ironed pair of khakis that Chloe kept for job interviews and a long-sleeved black button-down-collar shirt. I knew how to look normal when I needed to. Much to Joy's dismay and to the shock of the customers, by my second day working there, I had begun dressing fierce. It wasn't like the rest of the staff dressed more professional than me, anyway. Joy had a pierced tongue and wore sloppy clothes—and *she* was the manager. She was a lesbian, and she got in a huge fight one time with her girlfriend on the phone. Afterwards she had to freak out and tell Steven and me about how Casey can be such a demanding bitch. I was just thinking, "Too much information." But I asked instead, "Can I have a cigarette now?"

"No," she grumbled.

You'd think that since I was gay and she was a lesbian, we could at least try to get along. But no, she insisted on being a bitch. Sometimes I wanted to say to her, "I thought people named Joy were supposed to be nice." But of course I didn't. Lesbians are so weird sometimes. Not as nuts as gay boys, though.

"Excuse me, have you seen this video?" a customer asked.

"No," I snapped, thinking what a complete freak circus. It was impossible to tell which ones were the junkies and which were just naturally schizophrenic. They all looked paranoid, like they thought they were being watched as they selected their videos. Or else they'd come in and just walk up and down the aisles, staring at the movies aimlessly, then leave without renting anything. Most of them probably didn't even own a VCR. We also had some trashy drag queens. This one transvestite, who looked archaic and nothing at all like a woman, wandered the store in a trance. She was ghastly thin, her hairline had receded all the way to the very top of her head, and she had long scraggly white hair going down her back. She always wore the same awful stonewashed jeans and a sweater that looked like it was once white but was now stained yellow by nicotine.

I don't know why, but whenever she came in, I was compelled to watch her. She looked so tragic. I felt bad. Sometimes she'd stare out the window, kind of picking at her face the whole time. Then, like twenty minutes or so after she started picking at her face, fucking Joy would go ask her if she needed help finding anything. The tranny would get nervous, like she suddenly remembered she was in a video store, and hurry out. I'm sure drugs had already gotten her. She looked like she was a heroin addict or something, and I decided that I'd kill myself before I ever got to that point.

My new plan was to quit my job on the next payday. At least I'd have enough money to cover next month's rent. Besides, anywhere Joy didn't work had to be an improvement over this place. I wasn't sure if Joy gave me all the crap jobs because I was new, but I got them anyway. I was always the one who had to stay after closing to mop the floors, stock the candy, and rewind the tapes. All the while she offered me suggestions on how to improve my customer-service skills: "You're supposed to smile politely at them no matter what, even if they talk to you like you're an idiot because of the way you look."

Whatever!

It was 1:00 A.M. by the time I got home from work, and my whole body ached. I crawled out of my clothes and fell into bed, jacking off quickly to a blur of pornographic images rolling through my head. I came and passed out immediately. Needless to say, I had a lot of sleeping to catch up on.

I woke up at 4:00 P.M. the next day, hungry again. But I ignored my stomach, staying in bed to smoke cigarettes and watch TV. I'd already pigged out the day before on pizza and fettuccine with seasoned fried chicken strips and pesto that I made in the blender. Luckily, we were completely out of food, so there was no temptation to gorge myself again.

Being seventeen made me so depressed. I didn't want to become a man, but all my parts were growing gigantic! Pretty soon I wouldn't even be able to fit into girl's clothes. I'd grow up to become some big pansy with a gut and receding hairline in no time, and I was *not* feeling very gorgeous about it! If you act like a big fag when you're young and cute, it's funny; if you do it when you're older, everyone thinks you're a big dork. My only hope was that I had a few decent years left of my youth.

I wished Chloe were with me so we could go window-shopping, but, of course, he was at work. I was sick to death of being alone. I hated being by myself. I flipped through TV stations, stopping at a VH1 special on Madonna. It made me realize that I needed to get out into the world while I still was young.

I made a mental list of everyone I could or should call: Sam, Zack and Jerome, Jake, Molly, Mike . . . but I didn't feel up to talking to any of them. Maybe I just needed to meet some new people—a group of perfect friends who led perfect lives. Then my life would be perfect, too, just like the high-school kids on TV shows. Like that could ever happen to me.

I threw my blanket onto the floor, then rose out of bed like the old man I felt I'd become. I pretended I was a hunchback with a bum leg, limping slowly all the way to the bathroom. I acted frantic because I couldn't move fast enough, and I had to rescue Madonna, whom Frankentrannie had tied to train tracks. Madonna would fix my broken parts using the world's best surgeons, and we'd throw a huge party.

I rubbed my eyes awake before opening them in the mirror, smiling already. Supposedly, if you're smiling already when you see your reflection, you look and feel beautiful. And that must be true, because when I saw myself, I remembered that at seventeen, I was still hot shit. Besides, finally getting a good night's sleep had me feel at least as normal as I ever felt—and I had no desire to do speed whatsoever.

Obviously, Chloe didn't know what he was talking about when he said that I couldn't stop doing speed until I faced the consequences. I already felt like shit: Wasn't that consequence enough? Did he expect me to have to go through being a junkie and hitting rock bottom before I could stop? Maybe that was what *he* had to do, but I knew that for me, quitting a drug was all about having strong willpower. If I really wanted to accomplish something, I knew I could do it.

What I really needed to do was to get up off my ass and go for a walk. Stepping outside into the sun was exhilarating. Like I hadn't seen light in days. The sunshine was melting the snow, so everywhere there were little rivulets draining into the sewers and between the cracks of the sidewalk. Soon spring would arrive! No more freezing at bus stops and having to run everywhere. Spring would be a certain cure to my cabin fever.

In the dead of winter, picturing leaves on the trees and grass on the lawns seemed unimaginable to me. Maybe that was why lately I'd been so depressed. All that grayness and gloom and television watching had somehow affected my brain chemistry. I needed summer to come and jump-start my life again.

I decided to go to Uptown and check out what was new in spring fashion at the mall. Maybe Chloe and I could go out by the parking ramp like the old days and smoke onies. That was what I really needed right now. Pot and money. I had no food and only four cigarettes left. If that didn't change, pretty soon I'd be robbing gas stations and all that other crap just to make ends meet.

Life was strange. It seemed like everything I believed in when I was a kid was different now. It used to be that all the rules of the game were spelled out for me and I felt safe because I was protected by my parents and school. Even though I hated school and was an outcast because I was gay, I still knew my place in the world. I never worried about money, or a place to live, or AIDS. My ambitions were easily defined. I figured I'd graduate high school, go to college, and after that I would become an artist. Ultimately, I would be a piano-playing diva slash painter and drawer.

However, everything already seemed out of order, and I wondered if any of those plans would ever really happen. I suppose this is what's called "growing up." I didn't just automatically believe what my parents and teachers told me anymore, and I broke laws but didn't feel guilty about doing so. Between drugs and dropping out of school and everything else, it was a miracle my parents didn't send me off to Christian Youth Camp. According to Father Tom, what I needed was a severe punishment. He was probably right, too. I was a real maniac. I didn't know what I wanted to be anymore or how I would support myself. I wished I had a million dollars.

When I got to the mall, the first thing I did was look for Chloe. He wasn't at work, so I walked around for a while, checking out clothes and the gift shops. But with no money in my pocket, shopping irritated the hell out of me. I was in one of those moods where the only thing that was going to cheer me up was buying myself something new. But when you don't have any money, it just makes you even more depressed to be in one of those moods. I almost had to steal something just to make myself feel better. It was a fake silver ring with a blue stone in it. I would've taken it, too, but the girl working there stared at me the whole time, probably because I'm just too sexy for her to handle.

Finally I decided to call Sam. She picked up after the first couple rings.

"Hello?"

"Hey, it's me."

"What's up, girl?"

"Nothin', I'm at the stupid Uptown Mall."

"With who?"

"Just me, myself, and this little sadist in my pants. The three of us were at home earlier abusing ourselves with television, but we got superbored and decided to go for a walk."

"You are so weird . . . Where's Chloe?"

"At work."

"Aren't you at the mall?"

"He's at a different mall today. Remember, he goes from mall to mall now?"

"Oh, yeah."

"So what are you up to?" I was thinking that maybe she was with Jake.

"Nothing . . . just being bored, too."

"Who's all there?"

"Just me."

"You hangin' out with Jake today?"

"I don't know . . . Why, you need a fix?"

"No, I don't do that shit anymore," I said sarcastically. "Anyway, do you want to hang out?"

"Sure."

"Okay, I'll come over."

"'Kay, 'bye."

"'Bye, baby."

When I got to Sam's house, she was standing over her kitchen counter reading *Rolling Stone* magazine. She wore an enormous pair of jeans. At first I thought they were new, but then I remembered that she'd had those while we were dating. Back then they were tight on her.

She turned to me. "Are you hungry?"

"Actually, I'm famished."

"Right on. I was just about to have lunch."

"What are we having?"

"Salads with fat-free ranch dressing, Village Hearth light wheat bread that has only forty calories per slice, Brummel and Brown spread, and sides of grapefruit."

"Damn, you're a total dieter!"

"I just want to eat healthy. I'm going to keep the weight off if it kills me."

"Tell me about it . . . I was so skinny last time we did speed, and now I feel like a big heifer . . . Look at this roll!" I lifted my shirt to show her how my stomach inched over my waist when I was seated.

"Oh, give me a break! You're a twig!"

"Tell it to the judge." I sat down at the kitchen table and turned on the fan that was mounted into the window next to me.

Sam's mom had it there for when she smoked cigarettes. It sucked all the smoke out the window. I lit a cigarette and watched Sam prepare our lunch, making a mental note that I now only had two cigarettes left.

I don't know why I even bothered to light it, anyway. The cigarette tasted like shit. I'd been smoking way too much lately. "You want some of this?" I offered her the cigarette.

"Sure." She took a couple quick drags and handed it back.

She brought our salads over to the table, along with two grapefruit halves and the fat-free ranch dressing. "Do you want some skim milk?" She poured a glass for herself.

"Sure."

She filled a second glass, then sat down next to me. From where I sat, I could see her Mark McGrath poster hanging up in her doorless bedroom. It brought back the memory of when we were dating and I used to try to turn myself on by focusing on his shirtless torso. God, that was so long ago. Good thing I was over that whole "straight" phase.

Except for my compliments to the chef, we ate our lunch in silence. Remarkably, we finished eating at the exact same time. I wasn't trying to keep pace with her or anything. We just coincidentally took our last bites together. When we were dating, if something like that had happened I would have said that it was a sign that we were made for each other. At this point in our relationship, however, that would be a little silly. She didn't seem to notice, anyway. She started rinsing off our dishes right away. There was a little woven basket on the table filled with floral-print paper napkins and decks of cards and junk. I started digging through it and found her mom's pack of Benson and Hedges Ultra Light Menthols. "Can I have one of these?" I asked, already pulling it out of the pack.

"Sure."

I lit it up. It was kind of refreshing on my throat to smoke such a light cigarette. It practically tasted like I was smoking air or something. I took my time with it, watching Sam. She had absolutely nothing to talk about. I know it sounds horrible, but it seemed like now whenever I was with Sam sober, we were strangers.

"So what do you feel like doing?" she asked me impatiently.

"I don't know," I shrugged. "What do you feel like doing?"

"I don't know . . . We could go to the mall."

"I was just there. It was way boring."

"We could go to Plato."

"We could," I said, even though I didn't really want to.

"Is it cold out?"

"No, the snow is melting . . . I walked all the way to Uptown, and I was fine."

"Going for a walk sounds kind of fun. We could walk to Uptown, and if there's no one at Plato, we could just walk by the lake or something."

"Have you talked to Zack and Jerome?" I just wanted to change the whole stupid walking subject.

"Not since last weekend. How 'bout you?"

"Nope."

"Do you want to call them?"

"I don't know, maybe."

"Do you have any weed?" Like she'd been waiting to ask ever since I got there.

"I wish."

"We could call Jake."

"Okay." And that was what I was waiting for her to say ever since I got there.

Jake said that he definitely wanted to hang out, but that it would be a couple of hours because he had some things to do first. As soon as she got off the phone, I had a sinking feeling in my stomach. What if he brought glass with him and wanted to do lines? I'd practically sworn to Chloe that I would quit, and I wanted to prove myself to him, but I knew I'd fall off the wagon if I even saw glass.

When Jake finally arrived, he smoked a bowl with us, which was perfect because getting stoned made me not even crave speed at all. It was like choosing the lesser of two evils. Jake told us that he didn't have any glass right now, anyway, but that he would be getting some this weekend. Sam said she'd probably want some. I just said, "maybe."

Maybe Chloe would be free this weekend, and I could avoid doing speed by hanging out with him. I really didn't want to get started again, but if there wasn't anything else to do, I'd probably just have to out of boredom. I swear to God, trying to escape boredom is the leading force that drives my life.

After a while, I got a sneaking suspicion that Sam and Jake wanted to be alone together, so I only stayed a short while. Since I had no money, I had to walk all the way back home. Being broke sucked. My life would just be so much easier if I had my very own fortune, no strings attached.

Walking home, I started thinking about my crazy mother. I hadn't talked to her since I had told her and Dad I was moving out. I thought about calling her and at least saying that I was okay, but I wasn't in the mood. Calling your mom when you're not in the mood is like committing suicide on one of your *good* days. You have to save that shit for a rotten day. Plus, I was still mad at her over that last fight. I tried to not even think about it, but sometimes I just couldn't help but wonder what the hell she thought was going on with me. Ever since she found that pipe, she probably decided that I was ruining my life. Surely, she thought of marijuana as a vehicle of Satan or something wacko like that. Like Satan cares if we have a good time or not.

I wondered if she told my dad about the pipe. She probably

did, after I ran away and all. They probably got into a big fight about it and blamed each other for what a loser I had become. They'll probably get a divorce or something over it. My dad will likely decide that my mom and I are both major losers, and he'll take his money and run. He'll go live with some pretty, sane woman, and they'll drive around together in a little sports car. Meanwhile my mom will be one of those preachy, homeless bag ladies that nag normal citizens with those "I love Jesus" propaganda pamphlets, and poor Tim will go into foster care. Everything will fall apart and it will be my fault because I made crappy choices.

I started thinking about something Mrs. Wonderly, my seventh-grade history teacher, said during one of her lectures. She was talking about how after the Civil War, when the African slaves were freed, many of them continued to work on the plantations. Technically, they were free, but they had no other options—and you're not free to make choices unless you have options. Not that I would have the gall to classify my white-bread life as slavery, but I could understand the feeling of being stuck without choices.

I wondered how I'd ever get out of my lame predicament. I completely blamed Tommy. He's definitely the one who made me suicidal. I'd love to be dead if I could be a saint like my brother, unless there really isn't a heaven, in which case, thank God I'm here.

That night Chloe stormed into the apartment and slammed the door. He picked up his plastic juice pitcher from the sink, then threw it back down. "Goddamn it!" he shouted. "This stupid fucking juice pitcher is always dirty when I want to make Kool-Aid. All these damn dishes are always fucking dirty!" He filled a glass with water and angrily swallowed one of his pills with it.

I just ignored him. Like I was going to jump up and run to

clean his dishes for him. "Do you have a cigarette?" I asked. I'd smoked my last two.

"Don't you ever bother to get your own pack?" But he yanked his pack out of his pocket.

"Duh, I'm not even eighteen yet."

He flung a cigarette at me and went into the bedroom.

"What's your problem?" I yelled through the door.

"Nothing," he said curtly. I could hear him tearing through all our clothes. He was constantly getting sick of everything we had.

"Obviously, someone's on the rag," I teased. "Surfing the crimson tide."

"Shut up, Erick!"

"Sorry," I replied in the snottiest tone I could muster. He was *so* sensitive. I decided I didn't even want to talk to him if he was going to be in one of *those* moods, so I just sat quietly on the futon and smoked. I was always bugging someone. I should leave and never come back, and then no one would have to worry about me bugging them anymore.

Chloe came back into the living room and sat on the chair. He'd changed into a pair of baggy jeans and a sweatshirt. "Sorry I was being such a bitch."

"That's okay."

"I just feel like crap today, that's all. I didn't mean to take it out on you."

"What's the matter?"

"I feel sick . . . and I'm so sick of feeling sick that it just makes me want to cut my own head off . . . and I have not been able to get rid of this cough." He followed those words with a loud hack.

"I'm sure you'll be over it soon," I said hopefully, even though I had no idea what I was talking about or why I'd even said that. All I knew about AIDS was that you mostly got it from sex, that it destroyed your immune system, and eventually you got some opportunistic disease and died. It made hearing Chloe's cough scary, too, because I didn't know if he would actually get over it. Maybe this cough was a symptom of whatever it was that was going to kill him.

I think he saw fear in my eyes because right away he assured me that he was fine. "My T cells are up." he reported. "I went to see Dr. G—— a couple of days ago, and he said that I'm doing well. I guess the drugs I'm taking must be working . . . They sure as hell make me feel like crap, though. I've had diarrhea for days and a rash on my inner thigh."

That sort of grossed me out, but I didn't let on. "I'm glad the drugs work," I said.

"Oh, get this. The doc asked if I wanted THC pills to help me eat."

"Really?" I was shocked by that. I'd heard they were trying to legalize marijuana for medicinal purposes in California, but I didn't know you could actually get pills. "Did he give you some?"

"Not yet, but I'm getting them."

"What do they do?"

"I dunno, make you hungry, I guess."

"Have you been having trouble eating?"

"Not really . . . but maybe that's because I already smoke pot, anyway. Doc doesn't *know* I'm a total stoner."

"Do they get you high?"

"Probably. It's the THC in pot that gets you high. Do you want to try some with me when I get the pills?"

"Sure."

"Speaking of pot"—he had to pause to cough in his fist for about ten hours—"let's smoke a bowl." He made his bag appear out of nowhere. Chloe was some magician.

We smoked a bowl together, but it only seemed to make his cough worse. I wondered if he was ruining his health by smoking. Maybe he would quit when he got his THC pills. Hopefully, then his stupid cough would finally go away.

• • •

Over the next few days, Chloe did in fact lose his cough and his complexion brightened, so that when I saw him, it was like I was picking up a friend at the airport who was returning from a tropical vacation. At last he was ready to have fun again, he declared, dropping a bottle of THC pills and a fistful of cash in front of me. He said that we had lived in our place for far too long without having art on our walls, and we absolutely had to go shopping that very instant for some pictures. I was so happy to see that he was back to his old self, that he finally had the energy to resume one of his favorite activities.

We went to Mall of America, where we pretended to be tourists from LA for the day. Of course the outfits we chose were super West Coast ghetto fabulous. We turned in circles around the mall, snapping pictures with Chloe's camera while mockingly oohing and aahing over the fantastic architecture. Then we ran around, forcing the Midwestern shoppers to snap our dramatic intertwined poses in front of Planet Hollywood, Camp Snoopy, and Victoria's Secret. As for art to hang in our apartment, we picked out the most hickish "I Love Minnesota" postcards we could find. The ones that featured corn, outhouses, and an enormous spoon with a cherry on its tip. We bought three strings of chili pepper–shaped Christmas lights and a snow globe with a shivering hula dancer. We went to the Nordstrom makeup counter and asked a hundred–year-old woman what makeup would make us look the most like real women because we were cruising the mall's fourth-floor straight bars tonight. By the time we were back home, we called this the best shopping trip ever. We would always be best friends no matter what.

Lying alone in bed that night, I was overwhelmed by speed cravings. Just thinking of snorting a fat juicy line made me so emotionally spun that I couldn't sleep, so I sat up and smoked. Finally I couldn't handle it anymore and called Zack and Jerome. They said that they had a tiny bit, but not enough to share. So I begged and begged until finally they said I could have one line. So at 2:00 A.M. I walked over to their apartment and sat up all night with them. Luckily for me, they just shared all of what they had, and we had a ball chatting and playing video games.

Of course I felt guilty for sneaking out of the apartment. But at the same time I was angry that I had to sneak out of my own apartment, like I was a child and Chloe was my parent. Wasn't this why I'd left home? I felt like I should be able to do whatever I wanted without him getting in my way. Besides, this truly was the last time I would do speed, I told myself. I was just weaning myself off of it slowly with this last experience. I shared these thoughts with Zack and Jerome, who said they felt the same way. By the time we had run out of speed, we had made a personal pact to never do it again. We would be there for each other for support, we agreed. I was still determined to make it on my own, against all odds, and be a success in life. And I figured that as long as I held on to this belief in myself, it was all I would ever need.

{ nineteen }

Since I'd snuck out to do the one thing that I had promised Chloe I would never do again, I had to sneak back into the apartment while he was still sleeping and pretend I'd never left. For two horrendously boring hours, I faked that I was asleep, while Chloe up, got ready, and left for work. When he was finally gone, I stretched, showered, and flipped on Tori so that I could dance away the excess energy. I thought about eating some buttered bread, but as soon as I looked at the loaf, I felt sick to my stomach. I had eaten so much junk at the mall with Chloe yesterday that I wasn't too worried about eating now. I looked at my slim, nude body in the bathroom mirror, excited about how sexy I was. The only sign of fat on my body was in my butt, which I felt was ridiculously large. I also felt that my head was too big. Actually, it was obscene! The more I dwelt on the size of my head and ass, the more I hated myself. It was all my parents' fault! How inconsiderate for two people with large heads to have a child. By the time I was done obsessing about my head, it was noon. I had to work 6:00 P.M. until midnight, so I wondered if I should try to sleep—or eat, for that matter. I didn't feel like I could handle either. I decided it would be best to just stay up and go to work, holding off on sleep until I got home. I didn't want to hang out at my apartment all day, though, so I decided to go to Plato and get some coffee. Normally, I was anti-coffee, but I needed as much caffeine as possible if I was going to survive my six hours at Silver "Scream" Video.

I chose to dress fabulous that afternoon and searched through piles of clothes. It was all the same old crap that I had tried on hundreds of times before, and I was so sick of Chloe's wardrobe by now that I could have puked. Finally I settled on my black leather pants (which made me feel cozy and sentimental since they were my first cool pants) and a supercute white stretchy shirt that was strategically torn in twenty or so different places to show off my skinny body. I used a grotesque amount of gel to make my multi-colored hair—long overdue for a cut—spiky. Then I penciled in my eyes, streaked my cheeks, and rouged my lips. I took a couple hits off Chloe's pipe—that was probably a mistake because it made me paranoid and apt to hallucinate whenever I let my mind wander. But whatever! Feeling drugged out was becoming my natural state of consciousness.

I ran around the apartment, scraping up change. Once I arrived at Plato, I used the change to buy a cup of coffee. I added tons of cream and sugar and took my coffee to a couch, crossed my legs, and flipped open the latest issue of *Fags* magazine. Gagging, I almost spilled coffee on my face, when my ex-boyfriend, Mike the Dyke, entered the café. He was with two other guys, both of them pretty jocks wearing what looked like expensive sweaters and corduroys from Abercrombie & Fitch. Mike noticed me immediately, and there was intense eye contact between us. Then he pointed me out to his two buddies, and they all laughed. I wondered if he was telling them I was gay. What was he doing in a queer coffee shop, anyway?

The straight-acting and -appearing boys purchased their drinks and sat down in the opposite end of the café, not even bothering to say hi to me. How insulting. I couldn't believe Mike had the audacity to snub me on my own turf. I stewed in my anger for a bit, pretending to read the magazine. I felt like I was back in junior high school: they were sitting at the "cool table" while I was alone at the "geek table." It wasn't fair. I dressed like a rock star and I deserved to be treated as such. I lit a cigarette—my last one—and strutted over to their table. The words that would come out of my mouth, I imagined, would blow their brains out the back of their heads.

"Fancy seeing you here." One hand rested on my hip, the other held my cigarette up high.

Mike rolled his eyes and his friends quietly guffawed. "I should have known I'd run into you," he said coldly.

"Nice of you to stop by my table and say hi."

"I'm sorry. But do you think I give a shit that *you're* here?"

Why was he being so mean? I had only meant to give him some attitude. I didn't think he would get nasty. "What's your problem anyway? I never did anything to you."

"Whatever, Erick. You're just too weird for me, okay?"

"I'm weird?"

With that, all three of them went into hysterics. "Just look at yourself. I mean, what the hell are you anyway? Fuckin' transvestite."

"Oh my God. You are such an ass! I can't even believe it!" I shouted. "How dare you call me that? You fuckin' know damn well who I am!" I was on the verge of imploding. I took a deep breath and said, "Of course, how could you, when you don't even know what you are? Straight boy."

"Hey, I know who I am. I'm gay. And I don't have to wear women's clothes and get fucked up on drugs every day to prove it."

"Oh, so you're gay now? That's the first time you've told me that . . . And what business is it of yours how I dress? And who says I'm on drugs?"

"Oh, please! You look like a fuckin' crackhead with that makeup. How much do you weigh anyway? A hundred pounds? You look like you have AIDS."

"Fuck you."

"Is that all you can say? Fuck you? That's very original, Erick*a*. Gold star for you! Now would you leave so I can chat to my boyfriend and our friend?" He put his arm around (to my slight satisfaction) the uglier of the two.

His ugly boyfriend, who I hated, said, "Nice to meet you, honey. But this table is 'No girls allowed.'" They all laughed. Then Mike made a gruesome face at me, and I turned around and left Plato.

As soon as I was outside I burst into tears. I hated myself for crying. Mike was right. I was a girl, a fucking baby. I was so disgusted with myself. I looked like a freak. Like a small, ugly freak— a small, ugly, and insignificant freak. *How dare he?* I kept saying to myself, *How dare he have a new boyfriend! I thought you were dating Courtney, you ugly queer boy.*

As I walked along the sidewalk, my head felt like it was full of thunder. I was depressed and fat and starving and so tired that I wanted to drop dead right in the middle of Hennepin Avenue. That's when I realized how naïve I was way back when I first met Chloe and believed with all my heart that, like Cinderella, I would become beautiful and fabulous and everyone would want to be my friend. That would never happen. No matter what transformation I made, I would always be left out and by straight people and gay people alike. I was a (wo)man with no people.

By the time I went into work at 6:00 P.M., I still hadn't slept or eaten since the day before. I was so flustered by my encounter with Mike that I had simply roamed around town on foot, oblivious to anything but my own woes. Luckily, I'd gotten a reality check when I noticed the Target clock said 5:45. Somehow, I had managed to come to the conclusion that Mike was an idiot and that my clothes (which he used to adore!) were fabulous and he was just jealous. Of course, upon seeing me, Joy immediately pointed out that Silver Screen Video was not a Bon Jovi concert. But she was an idiot, too! It was the nineties. Like I would actually go to a Bon Jovi concert! No one understood me at all.

Within ten minutes, I was miserable already because I was out of cigarettes and desperately needed one. The only thing that got me through life was cigarettes. So even though I would have rather done anything else, I was forced to beg Joy for one of hers. She was such a bitch about it. She made me dust off all the dirty shelves before she gave me one. Like I wasn't already her slave to begin with. When she wasn't looking, I took three dollars from the register and got Justin to buy me my own pack. He was eighteen years old and, luckily, hated Joy as much as I did, so he was relieved to have an excuse to leave work. While he was gone, I had to work twice as hard to cover for him. Like there was just that much that needed to get done in fifteen minutes. We didn't even have that many customers. At least I got my cigarettes, though. When I couldn't smoke, it was the only thing I cared about. I didn't even feel guilty about ripping off the store, either. Joy would just think someone miscounted the change. Three-dollar shortages happened all the time.

After the store closed, Justin left for the night and I was stuck with vacuuming. Figures *I'd* be the one doing all the cleaning. Joy cursed with frustration as she counted the money and I began to worry that she was going to have a cow over the three dollars. When I left, she was still furiously punching in numbers on her adding machine. I told her "good-bye" very nonchalantly, but she didn't even bother to look up. She was *such* a bitch.

When I got home, Chloe was already asleep and snoring like a maniac. He had never snored until that cough of his came along. I found his pipe and scraped myself a couple of hits. As soon as it kicked in, I was hallucinating. Everywhere I looked I saw the monkeys, which were actually quite comforting. When I undressed and laid down on the futon, slight hunger pains murmuring deep within, I thought that I would never fall asleep. But in less than two minutes, I was out cold.

The next day was the worst day of my whole life . . . I got fired!

Even before I went into the store, I could tell just from seeing Joy through the window that she was pissy as hell. I figured it was probably about her girlfriend again, but soon found out that it was over the missing money. She took me into the break room to tell me the news. It was so scary. As soon as I realized that I was in trouble, my heart was pounding. All I could think about was that I hadn't eaten in two days and I could have a heart attack at any moment. She told me fifty-three dollars was missing from the till the night before. She must've known I was surprised, too, because my jaw literally dropped. At first I couldn't figure out what the hell it had to do with me. Then she said she watched the surveillance tape and saw me take cash out of the drawer and put it in my pocket. I couldn't believe it! I'd taken only three dollars! I knew right away that it had to be a conspiracy to get me fired. But how could I argue when I was, in fact, guilty of stealing? She gave me my last paycheck, including the two days I'd already worked in the next pay period. I left without thanking her or anything. The truth is that I knew that if I tried to say anything—even to defend myself—I'd just start crying out of humiliation. I didn't want to give her the satisfaction. Getting fired is the most embarrassing thing ever.

By the time I got to the bank to cash my check, I was kind of relieved, in a way. I hated that job, and I would've probably quit that same day, anyway. I just wished I had been the one to steal fifty bucks. In a way, I deserved the stolen money more than whoever got it because I was the one being fired for it. Oh, well, whoever did steal that money still worked there, and my only hope was that they stole a lot more, just so Joy would know that it wasn't me.

When I got home, I called Sam to tell her about my outrageous ordeal. I also told her that I wanted to get spun this weekend. I figured, fuck it, I wanted to party. My bills were paid up for the whole month and I had money to spend. Naturally, she got excited about it and called Jake on three-way so we could be on the line together. When he answered, she asked him if he was "breaking a window" this weekend. And with that, the next chapter in our tragic drug lives had officially begun.

{ twenty }

Waiting for Sam and Jake, I stood in front of the mirror, saying, "I don't even think so, okay?" to Joy in all different variations of bitchiness, snapping my fingers and rocking my head with attitude. When they finally arrived, I became so excited that as they walked up the stairs I started jumping around my apartment clapping my hands.

"What the hell's going on in here?" Jake said with a grin as I opened the door.

"Oh, I was just doing my jumping jacks for the day," I replied, pretending to flip my imaginary long hair. "I gotta keep in shape, you know."

"Cool place," Jake said. "It's so you . . . Is your roommate here?"

"No," Sam answered for me. "And he's not supposed to know Erick does speed, so hush."

"Is he your boyfriend?" Jake said in a teasing voice.

"No, they're just roommates," Sam answered for me again. "Chloe's a drag queen, and Erick thinks he's so cool that now he wants to be a drag queen, too."

"Oh whatever, Sam. Quit speaking for me because you don't even know what's up." I laughed. "Besides, you don't even want to get into it because I have *stories* that could *easily* slip out about you, sister."

"*What* stories?" Jake was all excited.

Sam just stared at me sternly. "Never mind *my* stories. We're not going *there*." We both knew that I held the Christian sex-story trump card: She had told Jake that she was a virgin when they met.

"Exactly." I winked at her and licked my lips, like I was all sexy.

We all sat on the futon, Sam in the middle. Right away, Jake produced a couple of baggies of glass, and I quickly handed over fifty dollars for one of them. Then I went into the bedroom and brought back Chloe's mirror from off the wall. I polished it off with a dish towel, thinking to myself from some distant place in my brain, *Don't do it*. Of course, when I rejoined the group on the futon, we immediately started cutting and snorting rails. I told them everything that happened with Joy, and when I looked at the clock, I cried, "Oh my God, we have to get out of here before Chloe comes home!" I swiftly tidied up the place while Sam called Zack and Jerome, and we bolted. At Zack and Jerome's place, we snorted more lines and decided we just had to go to Plato.

I'd forgotten all about Mike the Dyke and his boyfriend, until we entered Plato, and there they were. I made a disgusted face at Mike and started laughing hysterically, telling Sam to join me. I had so many more friends than he did. Sam informed me that they all went to South High. Again, I cursed my parents for sending me to Catholic school when there was apparently a big gay orgy going on at the public ones. Sam added that if it got around at school that they were gay, it would be so completely scandalous. I did my best impression of cool and tried to ignore them (we sat on opposite ends of the café), but it was nearly impossible. For one, every time I heard laughter from Mike's table, I looked to see if I was the object of their jokes. I felt like either Mike was doing everything he possibly could to embarrass me or, worse, he wasn't even acknowledging my existence. It was so high-school cliquish that I wanted to puke. I couldn't even concentrate on the conversation at hand—something about Enter the Galaxy, the rave everyone wanted to go to. "Look who's coming this way," Sam whispered. Mike and his boy toys had gotten up from their table and walked past my group with their fingers on their noses, making snorting sounds in mockery of our drug use. I wondered how they even knew we were on drugs. Maybe even they had caught on to our reputation.

"What the hell?" Jake declared incredulously.

"Ignore them," I said. "It's just my asshole ex."

"To hell with that!" Jake followed the offenders into the parking lot. The rest of us joined Jake outside. I wondered if it was going to be a repeat of the scene with Troy. Jake was always ready, willing, and able to kick some ass during a crisis.

"Hey!" Jake yelled at their backs.

I watched Mike turn around with a look of surprise that they'd been followed. The other two guys also turned around. Mike's boyfriend put his elbow on Mike's shoulder.

"Yeah?" Mike drawled.

"What was all that about back there?"

"What?"

"This." Jake snorted an imaginary line.

"It was nothing. Obviously you're paranoid."

"No, it was something, all right. You better apologize."

"Hey, I don't want to get into it with a drug addict, okay?" Mike said condescendingly.

"Screw you, pussy-boy!" Jake said. Then he turned to us. "This place is wack!"

We all stood there, quite unsure of what to say next. Zack and Jerome were holding hands. If there was going to be a fight, it would obviously be the queerest rumble ever. Stonewall versus Stonewall.

"C'mon, Jake," Sam finally said. "Let's just go back inside.

Those guys are losers. Mike is just jealous because he's a big nerd and he can't deal with his sexuality. Do you really want to fight with some big closet case?"

It appeared that her point was making sense to Jake. Surely he had no desire to fight with someone over their dumb sexuality issues. He took her hand in straight-boy fashion, flicked Mike off with the other hand, and said, "We're out'a here." Zack and Jerome followed silently. For some reason, though, I couldn't move. Suddenly I had an even bigger desire to see Mike's ass kicked once Sam brought up the whole sexuality thing. Because of Mike's inability to cope with himself, *I* was being punished.

"What's your problem?" Mike asked me.

"You."

"Whatever."

"Whatever to you. What the hell is the matter with you that you feel the need to harass me? I didn't do anything to you."

"Yeah, but you're a freak. And you're on drugs."

"That's none of your business, is it? And for the record, I am *not* a freak . . . In fact, if it wasn't for me, you'd still be that poor sheltered little boy in the closet on his way to his senior year. I think you should thank me."

"Thank you? You didn't make me gay."

"No, but I made you realize your deep-down desires."

When I said that, Mike's boyfriend, who had no sense of style at all, made a pouty face.

"You wish!" Mike bellowed.

"You know it! And don't act like you don't. And don't tell me I dress like a freak because you're just jealous that you can't pull off fabulousness! And one more thing: Plato is *my* hangout, and if you're going to disrespect me, I'll ruin you! I'll out you at South, and then I swear to God, I'll turn you into the biggest joke in all the gay world! You'll have to leave the state if you ever want respect again!" I threatened. And even though I was unknown in the gay world and there was absolutely no way I could back up this threat, Mike seemed to take it seriously. He choked out an apology and then got into his car with his friends and drove off. Once they were gone, I laughed hysterically. What a drama queen I was! Finally, I was victorious.

Enter the Galaxy was being thrown at some abandoned industrial warehouse in a very desolate area of St. Paul. The interior of the concrete building was practically one big room. Hollowed out, it made for the perfect underground party space. The music was insanely loud, and the voices of hundreds of people inside were hardly distinguishable over the vibrations. A bunch of green lasers dancing to the beat of the music were projected over our heads. Sometimes the lasers spelled stuff in midair, like "Enter the Galaxy" or "Eat Acid." There were tons of drugs going around. Whenever we felt like it, we just huddled on the floor in a circle and cut lines. No one cared. Or if anyone did care, it was because they wanted to buy some from Jake. If they were some stupid suburban kids who didn't know what he was doing, Jake sold them pinched bags at the full price. Drug dealing was always very shady like that. Jake made a lot of money whenever he went to raves. He knew everyone.

Neither Sam nor I had ever been to a rave, and we knew hardly anyone. Every once in a while, we'd see a few people that we'd recognized from Uptown or elsewhere, but that was it. But we still had a blast anyway. Usually, I'm not the biggest fan of techno, but once I was dancing to it, all spun out with a million other kids, I completely fell in love with the sounds.

When I wasn't dancing, I spent my time people-watching. It was really all you could do, because the music was far too loud for conversations. It was pretty interesting to observe the buffet of fashions. As I had expected, most of the people there were wore phat pants, much the style that Jake wore: pastel-colored, slim and low-riding at the hips, then ballooning out into shoe-eating tents. It was cool the way people danced in them. The motions were very tribal, like dancing and chanting (waving neon green glow sticks) around a bonfire built for the gods. It made me feel like I didn't really fit in because I was wearing tight, shiny pants and platforms, naturally. I decided that my lack of uniform wasn't going to get me down, though. Who cared if I dressed different from everyone else? Who cared that I was gay and loud about it? No one, apparently.

Another thing that seemed almost universal that night was the super-skinny look, especially among the girls, who all wore phat pants and skimpy tank tops that revealed their twenty-inch midriffs. Seeing all those pretty, happy raver girls made me a bit jealous, actually. I wanted to be super-duper skinny and popular, with glitter on my face and a tattoo of a butterfly on my boob. Sometimes I hated being a boy because it meant having big feet, big shoulders, and big hands—big everything! But I can't change what I have. I just need to start working with what I got.

Dancing at the rave was new to me, and I didn't know where to begin. At first I just followed the steps of my peers, awkwardly swinging my legs wide, my hands constantly making a military salute. But I felt like an outsider trying to learn how to line dance in a swinging county joint. So instead I danced my own way, like a fag on a runway. Once I got into the rhythm, I didn't even care if I looked different from everyone else. When you're dancing fabulously, you *want* people to look at you.

For a while I was sort of dancing with this girl I'd never seen before. She liked my moves and started keeping in time. She was super-fun in a girly way. Her phat pants had rainbows on them, and her tank top had a close-up of some tropical fish. She had platinum pixie-cut hair and was wearing those tennis shoes that have red lights that turn on with every step you take.

After awhile, we finally introduced ourselves. Her name was

Genie, and she told me that I danced cute. I told her that she did, too. Then she sort of started flirting with me by putting her hands on my hips. Before it got heavy, I told her I was gay. She said right away that she was on Ecstasy, then apologized about fifty times. I told her repeatedly that it was *so* not a big deal, until finally she stopped talking about it. I took her over to Sam and Jake, and we all did lines together.

Genie and Jake discovered that they both bought glass from the same dealer, a guy named Risk. Genie was good friends with him, so she brought him over to us. I hadn't really considered where Jake got the drugs we bought from him, but now I had a name and a face. Risk was a tall, skinny, extremely hot blond. He and Genie actually looked and dressed very much alike. It was pretty sexy to find out that we were getting our drugs from him.

Jake was in the middle of telling a joke when the wretched screech of a needle sliding across a record forced everyone's hands to their ears. The music stopped and fluorescent overhead lights flooded the dance floor. "Cops!" the crowd screamed all at once. Everyone wanted out, as if we were in a *Jaws* movie and someone had screamed "Shark!" Once outside, we escaped into the night. It was complete chaos, with police cars surrounding the building. Risk and Jake, both drug dealers, were particularly stressed. They quickly formed a game plan. To my surprise, Risk pulled me aside to give me quick directions to his house. He handed me his car keys, telling me to follow Jake and him in Jake's car. Sam, Genie, and I looked at each other in disbelief. Meanwhile, the cops had their nightsticks drawn and were shoving people against the building. When we found Zack and Jerome in the mix of confusion, they said that they already had a ride to Risk's house and would meet us there. Apparently, whenever a rave got busted, all the city kids flocked to Risk's house for a last-resort two-day house party. We agreed to meet them there and offered Genie a ride.

"Erick? You don't even have a driver's license," Sam mentioned once were seated in Risk's Honda Accord.

"Neither do you," I said.

"Do you have your driver's license, Genie?" she asked.

"No," Genie murmured.

We grinned at each other. A new adventure. We buckled our seat belts and I started the ignition. I had driven less than five times, always with my dad and never on the freeway. My first mistake was putting the car in drive when I should have reversed. I smacked the bumper of the car parked in front of me. "Oops!" I blushed. Sam just pursed her lips and tried to hide her fear. I switched gears, backed out of the spot, then put the car in drive. Thank God it was an automatic and I wouldn't have to worry about that anymore! Once on the road, we had to pass several on-scene police cars.

"You have to go faster than ten!" Sam panicked. "They'll be suspicious."

I pressed on the gas, unexpectedly forcing the car to leap into high gear, whizzing past the cops like a bullet. "Shit!" I screamed, slamming on the brakes at the intersection.

"Don't stop! There's no sign! Go, go, go!"

I floored it through the intersection, heading toward 94. Sam watched the mayhem disappear behind us through the rear window. "Yeah, baby!" she cheered.

"Go, Erick!" Genie followed.

"Woo-hoo!"

Sam cranked Risk's stereo to the max. Luckily traffic on the freeway was sparse, although once I had to swerve out of the way of another driver in order not to merge right into his car. I felt like I was in a racing video game as I raised the speedometer to sixty miles per hour and followed my lane over the dips and turns. It was so liberating, an unstoppable feeling. It felt like we weren't even touching the ground, like we were trapped in a video game.

I tried to stay focused, but I was so dazed that I worried I'd forget what I was doing and drive off into oblivion. I was almost sad when I had to exit the freeway. I wanted to keep going, to see where the road took us. My head was filled with sweet vibrations of freedom.

"Thank God we're still alive!" Sam cried out when I pulled up to Risk's house.

"Whatever!" I said "That was brilliant driving."

"You almost got us killed . . . But whatever. Instant death wouldn't have been so bad."

I ignored her dark comment as we walked up the front steps. The big house was white but looked like it hadn't been painted in decades. The paint was peeling, and the siding was broken in places. The front deck was sagging so much that it looked like it might break off the house at any time. It made me wonder if Risk's place was a crack house. I'd never been to a real crack house before.

Without even bothering to knock, we entered a large, yellow-lit room filled with people. The interior of the house was in shambles, too. The plaster walls and ceiling were cracked and water-stained and had random chunks missing, like someone had gone crazy with a sledgehammer. There was one sofa but no other chairs, so everyone was either standing or sitting on the floor. Several of the guys, including Jake, were DJs and they argued over whose turn it was to spin records. They had one of those aluminum tables with folding legs, and on it were two turntables along with piles of records. The boy who was spinning was a little guy wearing an enormous set of headphones and dancing behind the table while spinning the records. He seemed like he was fairly talented, really.

Genie led us over to Risk. I handed back his keys and told him that he had a smooth ride. He thanked me for my trouble and told Sam and me that we were his guests and to make ourselves comfortable. Our heads buzzing with delight, we mingled about until we ran into Zack and Jerome. We found seats on the floor, where everyone passed around joints and enormous balloons filled with nitrous oxide. I was starting to feel so fucked up I couldn't even talk. Pretty soon the room began darkening until all I saw was a haze of colorful movement. I heard Sam asking where Jake was, saying she wanted to leave, that she felt really sick. I was starting to feel really dizzy and sick, and I wanted to leave, too. I hadn't done any speed in what seemed like hours, and I was crashing hard. Sam looked as hellish as I did. All I wanted was to go to sleep in my own bed and never wake up again. In fact, I hardly wanted to live.

"Are you guys okay?" Jerome asked Sam and me. "You both look like shit."

"I don't—I can't—I—I—breathe—" Suddenly I couldn't hear what anyone was saying. I could hear only my heart pounding and I had a very large picture in my brain of my heart exploding, rocketing through my chest and smacking the wall.

"Erick!" Jerome shouted at me. "What's the matter with you? Are you okay?"

I didn't answer him. I was too tired to answer. I just turned to look at Sam. She was sitting cross-legged and kind of swaying back and forth and humming. All of a sudden she collapsed onto her back and laid there, perfectly still. Then she started to twitch.

"Oh my God! Sam!" Zack screamed, rushing to her side. He started nudging her, but she wouldn't move. Now *he* was freaking out and crying and checking her pulse.

I didn't understand what was happening. I think my brain was mush or something. People kept talking to me right up in my face, like they were yelling at me. But they sounded like they were speaking in a different language. I might have been crying, but I was too numb to tell. By now everyone in the room was watching us and panicking. The only thing I remembered clearly hearing was someone scream, "Get them the fuck out of here before they die!"

After I heard that I thought I was going to die for sure. It was weird. There have been so many times I've wanted to die that I thought I wouldn't be scared of it. But I was scared of it now. For some reason, I was so terrified that I couldn't stand it anymore. I almost wanted to die sooner rather than later, just so I'd stop being so scared.

Jake ran into the room and picked up Sam in his arms. Then Zack and Jerome dragged me out of the house. My whole body was limp and uncoordinated so I couldn't help them at all. They had to drag me by the heels of my platforms. I watched everyone watching me. Their jaws were dropped, and I even saw that that Genie girl was crying. Probably because she thought we were going to die. I was assuming she'd never seen a person die before. I know I've never seen anyone die.

Once we were outside I began to breathe a little easier. I sort of began to figure that if I wasn't dead yet, I wasn't going to die. I wondered if Sam was dead, though. How would any of us ever live with ourselves if she died? That would be so tragic. "How's Sam doing?" I heard myself ask.

"She's in the car now. That's where we're going, too," one of them said.

Sam was curled up in the backseat, shivering like she was cold. She was awake now and looking at me with a stunned expression on her face. I crawled in and put my arm around her. Zack sat next to me, and Jerome in the front seat with Jake. None of us said a word during the whole ride home.

{ twenty-one }

When I woke up, I wasn't sure where I was or what had happened. The last thing I remembered was dancing at the rave with some girl named Genie. I looked around and realized that I was in Zack and Jerome's apartment, lying on their couch. Jerome was sitting in the chair across from me, writing in his notebook.

"Where is everyone?" I asked in a hoarse voice.

"Oh, you're awake." He closed his notebook.

"How long have I been asleep?"

"Only for an hour or so, and you were tossing and turning the whole time."

Suddenly I felt my stomach clench up. I stumbled to the bathroom, thinking I was going to puke, but nothing came up. I just knelt in front of the toilet, looking down into the clear water. I started crying. I don't know why. I guess because my whole body ached so badly.

Jerome and Zack helped me to my feet and led me back to the couch. I looked out the window. It was still dark out. What day was this? I realized for the first time that I was in only my underwear and had a hard-on. How embarrassing.

"Where are my clothes?" I asked.

"Right here." Zack handed me a pile of clothes.

I was too fucked up to put them on, though, so instead I just crawled back under the blanket.

"How are you feeling?" Jerome put his hand on my forehead to see if I had a fever or anything.

"Better," I answered, even though I'd never felt worse.

"Are you hungry?" Zack entered the room with a bowl of soup and some crackers.

"No."

He set them down on the coffee table in front of me, anyway. "Well, you have to eat."

"I can't."

"You have to, Erick. If you don't eat, you'll be hospitalized. You're sick. Just eat a little."

"Did you call my mom?" I asked.

"No, do you want me to?"

"No."

"Then eat."

I reached for a cracker and ate it slowly. It tasted terrible, and I could hardly swallow. After I finished a couple, I felt really full.

"Have the soup, too," Zack ordered.

"I can't. I'm full."

"How the hell can you be full on a few crackers?"

"I don't know, I just am . . . If you make me eat it, I'll just puke it up," I threatened.

"When was the last time you ate?"

I thought about the question. At first I couldn't remember, and it made me depressed not to be able to remember. Usually, I didn't forget stuff like that. I tried to think back over the past few days. I knew it was before I bought that speed. Finally I remembered that the last time I had eaten was when I had some fries with Chloe at the Mall of America. "It was either Tuesday or Wednesday. "I can't remember which."

"Tuesday or Wednesday?!" Zack shrieked. "Erick, it's Sunday morning! Are you fucking crazy? No wonder."

"No wonder what?"

"Don't you remember anything?"

"No."

He looked at me in disbelief. "You passed out tonight at the party. We thought you were going to fucking die on us! Don't you remember that?"

"Oh, sorry." I was not really registering what he was telling me.

"Sorry! What do you mean, 'sorry'? Don't you know what you're doing to yourself?" he screamed. "I mean, shit! You're seventeen! You're not even done growing yet! You need food!"

I started crying all over again. I didn't want to hear what he was saying, not right then. I just wanted him to go away. I didn't want to be there. I didn't want to be anywhere. I wanted to disappear.

"Erick," Jerome began. "We're not trying to be mean. We just care about you—a lot. And we don't want to see you get hurt."

"You guys don't have to worry about me. I can handle myself."

"Can you?" Zack asked.

I ignored him. "Where's Sam?" I asked.

"Over at Jake's . . . Has she been starving herself since Tuesday, too?"

"I don't know. Why? Is she okay?"

"She's at least as bad off as you are. We thought you were both going to die. You two passed out at the party, and everyone panicked. We were all fucked up . . . but you guys were so gone. Your eyes rolled back into your head, and we thought you were going to die," he said in the gravest voice I'd ever heard. "Don't you even care about that?"

"Goddamn it, of course I care! You think I don't care? I just don't even want to talk about it right now . . . I need to talk to Sam. Can I please have the phone?"

"Why don't you call her tomorrow? She's asleep right now."

"Well, can I at least have a cigarette?"

"You can have one if you finish your entire meal," he said.

"Why are you being such a bastard? I just want a cigarette. What's the big deal?"

"Oh my God! I give up. I can't even look at you right now. You look like hell!" He stormed back into the bedroom and slammed the door.

Jerome stayed in his chair and watched me struggle to get comfortable. I could tell that he was shocked by what a bitch I had turned into. I probably disgusted him. To be honest, I disgusted myself.

"I'm sorry, Jerome," I said. "Please don't be mad at me. I'm so, so sorry. So sorry that I hate myself. I really do. I don't know why I am the way I am. All I know is that I'm sorry . . . Say something, please."

"You'll be fine," he said. "You just need to learn to take better care of yourself, that's all."

"Are you mad at me?"

"Of course not."

"Zack is mad at me."

"No he's not. He's just frustrated. He just wants to see you eat and get well because he cares about you, that's all."

"I don't know why anyone would care about me," I said, only because I was feeling sorry for myself.

He got up from the chair, then knelt down next to me and rubbed my shoulders. It felt really good. "We care about you because you're a wonderful person. You shouldn't get so down on yourself all the time. I don't understand what it is that makes you want to harm yourself . . . You're a bright and talented and funny person. You should care about yourself as much as your friends care about you."

I liked listening to what he was saying to me. I could fall in love with a guy who talked to me like that.

"What is it that makes you so sad on the inside all the time, Erick?"

"I don't know. Everything."

"Like what?"

"Well, for starters, my parents hate me. They love my dead brother like you wouldn't believe. But they hate me."

"Are you sure about that?"

"Positive."

"I think you'd be surprised to find out that you're probably wrong."

"You've never met them."

"Well, they *are* your parents, aren't they?"

"What do you know? You haven't lived my life . . . I don't mean to sound like a bitch or anything, but for real, you don't *know* what it's like."

"I know how it is, believe me. My parents wouldn't even speak to me when I first came out just because they couldn't deal with it. But eventually they realized I wasn't changing and accepted me, more or less."

"But do they love you like they did when you were straight?"

"I don't know. No."

"See? My point exactly. No one loves you as much when they know you're gay. Everyone thinks you're a freak . . . You *are* a freak when you're gay."

"Well, even if that's true, that doesn't mean you can't love yourself. And your friends love you. Maybe that's why the gay community calls each other 'family,' because everyone needs a family, and you don't have to be genetically related or married to someone to be part of a family. A family is just a group of people who love and support each other."

"You should write the goddamn Gay Bible, Jerome. You really have a lot of good bullshit to say. Besides, if you and Zack are so smart, then why do you do speed?"

"I don't know . . . I can't speak for Zack. For myself, I guess it's just something I started to use as a poet—to take my mind into the realms of fantasy—and it just got out of hand."

"Is that an excuse?"

"I don't know," he said. "I mean, I battle that very demon constantly in my poetry."

"I guess it did give you something to write about, then."

"I guess . . . but is it worth it if it kills me?"

"Don't ask me, because I'll say yes."

Jerome snickered, then asked solemnly, "Why'd you start drugs?"

"I don't know. I was bored. I wanted an escape . . . And because it makes me feel glamorous to be strung out. I feel like I can use it to control my insanity . . . I don't know, I can't explain it."

"It makes perfect sense to me."

"I think about quitting all the time. I really do. Even right, now I think I want to quit, but I don't know if I can . . . Could you?"

"I don't know. I've never tried."

"Do think you'd be happier?"

"Hell, yeah. I think feeling sane would make me a lot happier."

We sat in silence for a while after that, deep in our own thoughts. "Jerome?"

"Yeah?"

"I think I'm ready to try some of that soup now."

"Well, good." He cleared a place at the table.

I sat up and stretched out and gave Jerome a reassuring smile, just to let him know that I would be okay, just in case he was worried about me. I ate every last bite of that meal and earned the cigarette Zack had promised me.

Then I went to sleep.

When I woke up, the sun was rising. I couldn't have been asleep for more than a couple of hours, yet I felt wide awake. Like I'd been asleep for days. I got up from the couch and slipped into my pants, then went to check the bedroom to see if Zack and Jerome were asleep. Their door was closed, and I could hear Zack moaning quietly. They were probably having sex or something. I doubted they'd gotten much sleep since the rave. Recalling the conversation Jerome and I had had earlier, I thought, What a hypocrite! He and Zack did all the same drugs I did—and they didn't eat when they were on glass, either.

I finished getting dressed in the living room. On the table was a pack of Camel Lights with two cigarettes, which I pocketed. I pulled my backpack over my shoulders and left quietly, so I wouldn't be heard. The morning air was freezing, sending chills through my body. I just bit my lip and tried to ignore it. I figured at this point if I was going to get pneumonia or something I might as well accept my fate. There was no way I was going back into that apartment. It was the last place I wanted to be.

Most of the snow had melted over the preceding days. However, the temperature had dropped below freezing overnight, so the streets and sidewalks were all glazed over with a pristine sheet of ice. Birds chirped in the leafless trees, though, which was a sure sign of spring. At this point, all I wanted was to survive long enough to see spring.

I walked aimlessly for about a mile or so until I reached a little breakfast café on Lyndale Avenue. The place was completely empty except for one waitress who was putting plastic daffodils on the tables. Her graying brown hair was up in an old-fashioned bun, which for some reason reminded me of an old picture my mom had of my grandma, Arlene. The waitress wore a bluish-gray pinstripe uniform dress with pockets in the front for notepads and pens and stuff. She leaned over the counter to get more table settings. "Mornin'!" she said over her shoulder. I was told to sit wherever I wanted, so I took a corner booth, where I could gaze out the window at the morning traffic. By the time I had my cigarette lit, she was standing over me, smiling down with a pair of librarian glasses hanging at the tip of her nose.

She set a menu in front of me and said, "You're up early . . . Usually you kids aren't up until at least noon on a Sunday. I should know—I've got a son around your age."

"Yeah, well, I couldn't sleep."

"Rough night?"

"Sort'a."

"You look just like my son's friend Todd. He comes in here sometimes. You know him?"

"Look, honey, the name's Geneva Flowers," I said.

She didn't even look very surprised. I'd expected her to laugh or something, but she maintained a straight face. "What's *your* name?" I asked.

"Elizabeth Ann Swanson-Johnson." The name rolled off her tongue so smoothly that it practically sounded like one word. I was suspicious immediately. That name sounded even more fake than Geneva Flowers. 'Course I wasn't going to ask her about it. I realized neither of us was ever going to know the other's real name now, which was fine with me. It's not important to know people's real names. It's just important to know who they are.

"So how old are you?" She watched me intently, like I was death warmed over.

"Twenty," I lied.

"Oh, well, I guess you're a bit older than my son. He's sixteen, going on twenty-five." She waited for me to ask more about her son, but I didn't say anything, so finally she asked, "You need coffee or anything?"

"I don't drink coffee. It stains your teeth." I concentrated more on my cigarette than on her. "Can I get some orange juice, though?"

"Sure thing." She walked through a swinging door and disappeared into the kitchen.

I opened the menu and looked at the pictures of eggs and bacon and pancakes. I wasn't very hungry, but I thought it would be smart of me to at least try to eat something. I didn't want to be hospitalized or anything. So when she came back with my orange juice, I ordered whole-wheat toast. I figured that would be enough for now.

"You look like you could use a bigger breakfast than that," she said.

"I'm just not very hungry." I handed her the menu.

"Not hungry? Hmmm—if I was your mother, I'd certainly fatten *you* up a bit."

I thought about telling her that I had cancer or AIDS or something and that's why I was so skinny, just to make her feel horrible about insulting me. But I didn't say a thing, and she returned to the kitchen to get my toast. I took a sip of my orange juice, and it burned the hell out of my mouth. I realized it was because I had speed bumps all over my tongue. I hadn't noticed they were there before, but now that I knew about them, they hurt like hell.

When she came back, I told her that the orange juice was bad and that I just wanted water. She seemed perturbed, but didn't say anything. Instead she took back the orange juice and brought me a tiny glass of ice water. I slammed the whole thing like it was a shot; it tasted wonderful. I took a few bites of the toast she brought me, but it was overbuttered, and I thought I was going to have a heart attack from all the cholesterol, so I didn't eat it all. I know butter was the least of my problems, but I'm just sort'a irrationally compulsive about stuff like that. When she wasn't looking, I dropped a five-dollar bill on the table and snuck out. I was sort of pissed that I had gone in there only to pay five dollars for a sip of rotten orange juice and a couple of bites of toast.

The sun was finally all the way up, and the air was already beginning to feel much warmer. The frost on the ground was now water and was quickly evaporating. I threw on my Kenneth Cole sunglasses and started walking sort of towards my apartment, even though I didn't want to go there. Chloe was the last person I wanted to see. I was so sketched out that I'd probably start stuttering when I talked to him, and he would know right away that I was jacked. He'd probably be able to tell just by looking at me. Even that waitress could tell I was too skinny, and she'd never even seen me before.

The thing is, I knew that I was too skinny, I could feel it, but it didn't really matter to me. I *liked* being too skinny. I *liked* starving myself. Everyone always says I'm too skinny, as if they're informing me of something I didn't already know. They go so far as to tell me I need to eat more or else I'll die, as if I didn't know that either. What they don't realize is that I starve myself because I know they'll tell me all that stuff, and I know that when I walked into a room, everyone looks at me because I'm such a freaky drag queen.

I don't know why being who I am makes me such a bad person, but it does. Society says that teenage, drug-addicted, anorexic drag queens are bad. And it's like that old expression: "If you tell a lie a hundred times, it becomes the truth." At least, I *think* that was an old expression. Perhaps it was actually a new one I invented to validate myself. With a creative head like mine, I could probably write for fortune cookies.

Just thinking about the person who had that fortune-cookie job made me feel depressed. Which in turn made me feel totally lousy about myself because I was *always* depressed. Even Jerome noticed that I was always getting down on myself, and I'd never really told him anything very personal before. People must just look at me and be able to tell that I'm depressed, just like how you can tell when someone is gay. Apparently everyone can take one look at me and know everything there is to know about who I am. Obviously I'm just not very good at hiding it. I need to learn to do that better. Maybe then everyone will just leave me alone.

I walked all the way to my apartment, took one look at the building, then kept walking. I didn't even want to deal with that bullshit. I couldn't think of where the hell to go, though. What I really wanted to do was get out of this city and start a new life in a bigger and better city. Like LA or New York or someplace. What I needed was a ticket and a place to go: anywhere but here. As long as I was in Minneapolis, my life would be hell.

I was starting to remember a little more from last night. I remembered Genie and Risk and the crack house we went to after the rave. I remembered smoking tons of weed and crystal and huffing nitrous out of balloons, but I couldn't remember anything after that. I had a strong feeling that I likely did something to humiliate myself in front of a bunch of people. Zack had said I had almost died. I probably freaked out in front of everyone. I pictured myself running through the crowd, gripping my neck like a choking victim and being all-around embarrassing.

I wanted to talk to Sam. She'd been there, too, and might remember what had happened. And she wouldn't be a bitch about it, like Zack had been. I thought about finding a pay phone and calling her over at Jake's, but decided that I wasn't quite in the mood. I was far too cranky to talk to anyone. I'd probably pick a fight with anybody I talked to anyway.

Since I had nowhere else to go, I walked toward my parents' house. I wasn't actually going to show up at their door, but I was thinking that maybe I would go to the little neighborhood playground that I used to play in when I was a kid. Maybe sit on the swings or something. For some reason, I was sort of in the mood to swing.

I hadn't noticed before, but I was beginning to hallucinate again. Watching my feet tread the pavement, I saw that water was beginning to bubble up through the cracks. It was coming out so quickly that within seconds water covered the entire sidewalk and was threatening to continue rising until the whole city was submerged. As soon as I realized that that would be impossible, I rubbed my eyes furiously and looked down again to see that the sidewalk was dry. What a relief! For a second, I thought that God was flooding the world from the bottom up. Sometimes I crack myself up when I think stuff like that. I'd have to remember to tell Chloe about that one, even though I hadn't really planned on telling Chloe anything about speed or hallucinations that occurred because of speed. What I planned to do was lie through my teeth about the whole weekend.

I watched the ground intensely as I made my way to the playground, waiting for it to flood again. Practically *hoping* it would flood again. All that happened, though, was I began to see my monkeys—the life force that tasted like bananas. It's weird—no matter where I went or what I did, the monkeys stayed with me. Maybe they were proof that there *is* a God who is with me wherever I go, and He reveals himself through those monkeys. You never know. That could be true.

The street I was walking along was fairly busy with traffic. Enough traffic that there was a stoplight at practically every intersection. With each passing car, I saw lines of trails follow behind. If the car were blue, I saw blue trails. If it were red, I saw red trails. They looked like smooth streams of light.

Even though it was kind of interesting to see trails and all, it had me a bit worried about my mental state. A person should not be alone walking along a busy street at eight in the morning hallucinating their brains out. It just isn't very safe. I knew, too, that it was crazy for me to keep walking, because the further I went from home, the longer it would take for me to get back. Plus, I was starting to get tired again. That's part of the reason I kept walking. I felt like if I stopped to rest I'd probably fall into a coma or something. Hopefully, the monkeys would fall into a coma with me.

When I entered my old neighborhood, I started getting a little nervous, just because I was scared that someone I knew would see me. My parents lived in one of those ideal neighborhoods where families all pull together to do stuff for the sake of the "community." Everyone knows everyone, and practically all the kids go to the same Catholic school that I went to for nine years. God, if anyone I went to Catholic school with saw me like this, I'd have to kill myself. Given my crappy luck, I'd run into one of the gossips. Then everyone I've been trying to forget about would know I was gay *and* hooked on drugs, and I'd become the laughingstock of the entire goddamn neighborhood. I knew that I shouldn't care since I didn't live there anymore, but I *did* care. That was my problem. I cared too much about what other people thought of me.

I was determined to face my demons though, so I kept walking. To comfort myself, I watched the monkeys on the ground. They really were quite friendly. One of them even winked at me, so I winked back. No matter what happens, at least I'll always have them on my side.

My parents' house came into view, and I started to feel really nervous. It looked the same as I remembered it—I don't know why I thought it wouldn't. I don't know what I expected, really. When I was directly in front of the house, I stopped to have a look from the opposite side of the street. I could see the TV on through the family-room window. They were home. I imagined that Tim was alone in the living room, laying on his belly and watching cartoons. My parents were probably in their room, my mom solemnly dressing for church and my dad snoring into his pillow, occasionally farting in his sleep and making her bite her lip in disgust. I could just see it. She would be wearing her blue-and-purple floral-print dress and her fake-pearl necklace. She would ask him to come with her, and he would say no. To hide her disappointment she would peel Tim away from the television (despite his pleas to stay home), and they would go to church without Dad. My family was so predictable that thinking about them merely sent another tremendous wave of depression curling down my body. I hated them. I really did. But for some reason, I couldn't make myself move from the spot where I stood. I'd heard someplace before that mothers have a sixth sense when it comes to their kids. I wondered if mine could feel how close to her I stood. If she saw me, she'd probably make me breakfast, then drive me straight to Catholic drug treatment. Who could blame her? I probably needed to go to drug treatment but figured I'd wait until it was court-ordered or something.

I lit my last cigarette and began taking hard drags. Suddenly I was so angry, I thought I might tear my own hair out. It was a mistake to come here. It just brought back all my hateful memories. Finally, I started walking toward the park nearby, just because I figured if I looked at my house any longer, I'd probably go ring the bell. I certainly couldn't do *that*. I had enough to deal with in the present without sad memories from the past interfering.

No one was at the park when I got there, so I sat on the swing and started pumping myself as high as I could go, kicking my platforms into the air. Ever since I was a kid, my goal on the swing was to go all the way around the bar, just so I could say I did it. One of these days, I'd probably break my neck trying. Bored with swinging, I walked over to a tree and sat in its shade. I was so exhausted, I laid down, using my backpack as a pillow, and let myself drift off to sleep.

In my dream, I was at the railroad bridge, sitting high up on the ledge, looking down at the river far below. The current was thrashing, foaming . . . then calm and tranquil. Suddenly I was falling. Only I was looking up, so the bridge just kept getting further and further away. And then there was only sky. As cotton-ball clouds shrank against endless blue, I anticipated slamming into the water and swallowing gallon after gallon, until I was more water than me. But I couldn't turn around to see when it was going to happen, so I made guesses, private countdowns, and braced myself for impact. But I never crashed down. I just kept falling.

When I opened my eyes, I didn't know where I was, but the eerie orange glow of twilight could be seen through the branches above me. For a microsecond I thought maybe I had actually died in my dream and this was the afterlife. Then I rolled onto my side, and saw the playground, tennis courts, and houses of my childhood. Alas, I was still in Kansas. My entire body ached, sweating and suffering what must have been the most dangerous degree of star-vation. Now I really did wish I would die sooner rather than later.

Once my internal senses had taken stock of the situation, my extended ones registered. I realized that it was freezing out and I had fallen asleep in the frosty grass. Suddenly I was shivering uncontrollably. If I didn't find shelter, I would be in serious trouble. So I stood up with rusty, robotic motions, attempted to brush dirt and twigs off my clothes, but only succeeded in making myself muddy. I'd ruined Chloe's clothes! How could I ever explain this? A picture of Chloe flashed across my mind but was ripped away by the earthquake inside my head. This migraine was the worst torture I had ever suffered! Like my brain was raw ground beef, and ten thousand fingers were digging into it. I wanted to vomit, but there was nothing inside me.

I opened my eyes and saw monkeys everywhere. They were mean now, with razor-sharp fangs and devils' eyes. I rubbed my eyes furiously to make them go away, but nothing could stop them. It was my most terrifying experience ever. I thought I was screaming but couldn't hear myself. Perhaps because I was only screaming within myself, at the top of my imaginary lungs, "God! Please make them stop! I can't live like this!" I collapsed and moaned for a little while, then got up and began walking with blurred vision, squinting away the hallucinations. My headache was so intense that I began to wonder if a person could die of pain alone. Cause of death: relentless pain. Maybe I would be the first recorded case of this very rare phenomenon. That would be ironic. My whole life completely unimportant and irrelevant to society, my death a new scientific discovery that would change medical science forever. Suddenly they'd give away morphine to save lives. Everyone would be high thanks to me. HA!

When I got to a major street, I quickly located an anonymous, empty café. Like a cat being chased up a tree, I zipped past the hostess while her back was turned and locked myself into the men's bathroom. What I saw in the mirror was a complete horror. Never in my life had I been so filthy! In another era, I would easily have been mistaken for a chimney sweeper. I felt like such a major junkie. Even the whites of my eyes had the lurid, poisoned color of a junkie. Eew, what was wrong with me?

I shuddered and with haste peeled away my clothes down to my briefs and began splashing hot, soapy water on my face and throat, the mud trails dripping down my back and stomach giving me gooseflesh. I stuck most of my head under the faucet and just held it there, wishing I could cry, but being too numb to let the tears come. I was such a loser. If it weren't for the severe headache and other pains, I would have almost been able to laugh at how low and destitute I had become—I always said I wanted glamour!

I used the last piece of paper towel from the dispenser to go over my face one last time, then dropped the ball of paper in the vicinity of the trash can. Crap! The men's room was now in an utter state of nastiness, with puddles of muddy water on every surface and wet paper towels everywhere. I turned in a circle, biting my lip, as I pulled my muddy clothes back on, took a leak, and flushed the toilet on the way out.

"Can I help you?" the perky hostess asked, already holding a menu up to her bosom. She was wearing a heavy black frock with enormous red buttons (tacky).

"Nope, just came in to do my makeup," I declared, making my swift exit.

When I got outside, I ran to the end of the block, race-walked through an alley, and continued at a brisk pace out of the neighborhood. I found a bus stop and a gas station, and, angry with myself, my headache coming on strong again, I did what anyone in my situation would do: I panhandled change for the bus. I found my compact on the bus and looked in the mirror. No wonder everyone buying gas believed me when I said I was homeless! I powdered my face.

By the time I got back to the apartment it was night. My headache had subsided a bit, but I still felt completely tired and strung out. Luckily, Chloe wasn't home. I tossed my muddy clothes into the bathtub. Then I went into the living room naked and lit one of Chloe's cigarettes, only smoking made me cough and I felt like I was choking. I tossed the cigarette into the toilet and stood in front of the mirror.

My own eyes, once so big and brown and beautiful, now looked expressionless. There were still traces of eyeliner left over from before I washed my face, but not enough. I grabbed a tube off the edge of the sink and reapplied. Then I noticed my other features. My nose, sore from snorting chemicals, seemed like it had grown larger and been deformed. My lips, normally the color of a strawberry-flavored Starburst, now looked swollen and purple, as though I had been standing at a bus stop in below-freezing weather and was now on the verge of hypothermia. Even my ears looked like they had grown. Perhaps my features looked bigger because my face and neck were thinner. I could see the outline of each rib in my chest, my sunken collarbone. Even the bones in my arms seemed visible. Suddenly I was scared. Was I hallucinating again or was this the real me? Why had I not noticed how painfully anorexic I looked?

I threw down the eyeliner and ran back to the kitchen. This

was an emergency. I swung open the refrigerator door and saw the water purifier, a Taco Bell bag, half a loaf of bread, and condiments. I grabbed the Taco Bell bag. It was obviously Chloe's, but I knew he wouldn't say anything. Inside were two chicken soft tacos. Chloe never ordered chicken soft tacos. He'd bought them for me because he knew they were my favorite. I gorged myself on them, all the while thinking how Chloe was my only real friend in this world. But then I thought; Why did he buy these? Did he know I was on speed? That I was starving? Was he spying on me? I became paranoid that Chloe had turned against me and was going to call the police and my parents and have me sent away. I knew these thoughts were ludicrous. I knew Chloe loved me, but I was too messed up to see even what was right there in front of me.

In a panic, I tried calling Jake, but I got the wrong number twice in a row, which really stressed me out because I needed more speed. I needed to escape what I was feeling, and taking more speed was the only way. Soon I began talking to myself, rambling. I don't remember everything I said. All I can recall is that I kept hitting myself in the head, saying, "Are you schizophrenic? Are you *fucking* schizophrenic?"

I couldn't sit still. I was unable to organize my thoughts into anything cohesive. I imagined my parents and Father Tom and Sister Mary Jean bursting in at any moment and hauling me off to a mental institution. I pictured myself in one of those padded rooms, wearing a straitjacket, and banging my head on the floor because there was nothing else to do. Groups of AA people would come to look at me through the tiny window on the door so they could see what happens when a person doesn't take care of himself. It would be like one of those *Scared Straight* programs they used to show kids in order to deter them from a life of crime.

Limping to the bathroom to throw up all the Taco Bell I had eaten, I imagined there were video cameras pointed at me, getting real, live footage of a person overdosing on drugs. When I got to the toilet, I couldn't puke. And it wasn't that I was physically unable. I just couldn't bring myself to do it. Maybe it was because I thought I might puke out my soul, and then where would I be? Dead? Or worse: alive with no soul to speak of. It's weird how these thoughts cross your mind when you're kneeling in front of a toilet, staring at clear water.

I remained in that position for a while, waiting for who knows what. Finally I sat back against the wall, a leg on both sides of the toilet. For once I thought seriously about what I was doing to myself. *Why? What is this going to get you, Erick?* I didn't want to be a junkie. I didn't want to turn into Frankentrannie. I was only seventeen years old. According to a McDonald's commercial I remembered from a thousand years ago, I've only lived one-fourth of my life. It wasn't too late to be an artist, a pianist, to blast off in a rocketship to outer space and become a space queen. Realizing this, for perhaps the first time ever, I came to the conclusion: I would sober up for no one else but myself. And after making this resolution, and believing it for the first time ever, I was at peace.

And that weekend was the last time I did speed.

{ twenty-two }

Making a resolution is one thing, but sticking to it is another. My first obstacle was convincing Chloe that I had made this resolution in all seriousness, of my own accord, and that I wasn't lying to him or myself. The problem, he said, was that he wasn't sure if he could trust me because I had made the same promise before. Besides, he said, drug addicts will promise anything out of desperation. I became defensive instantly, telling him that if he cared about me at all he would have faith; that if I wanted to quit, which I did, nothing could stop me. Chloe said I was battling something more powerful than I realized and needed professional help. The reason drug addiction is so evil, he explained, is because it makes you too weak to fight it. You become helpless, so you need to reach out to a higher power.

"What are you," I said, "a spiritual atheist now? Can't you just fuck off and let me be?"

"Fine," Chloe said, "I will let you be. But if I ever come home again and find you passed out by the toilet because you're too fucking strung out to get to bed, you have to move out . . . because I refuse to watch you kill yourself."

I was so horrified and hurt by his words that I completely lost control. "You bitch!" I screamed. "How dare you say this stuff to me? You're not really my friend. You just want to destroy me!"

Suddenly I became so violently angry that I ran into the kitchen and proceeded to send every dish in the cupboard crashing to the floor. I would have gone on to create further mayhem if Chloe had not physically restrained me. Panting, sitting on the floor in a pile of broken dishes, my hands pinned behind my back, we both began crying. Through sobs, Chloe said to me, "Goddamn it, Erick. How is it that you can watch me take drugs every day just to stay alive, while you take drugs every day just to kill yourself?"

"I don't know. It's just so . . . hard."

"What is?"

"Being me."

"Why?"

"Why?" I repeated in exasperation. "Look at my life! It sucks. Every time I try to make it better, I just screw things up. I want to die, but I don't have the nerve to kill myself. I'm fucking stupid, and ugly, and I'm kidding myself whenever I think otherwise."

"You're *not* stupid or ugly."

"Don't say that. You just make it harder when you say things like that because I want to believe you . . . but I can't because you're wrong. You're so, so wrong. Okay? I mean, fuck. My whole life I'm made to feel worthless and then suddenly you come along and act like it's not me that's fucked up, it's just everyone else . . . well, face it, Chloe. I'm a fucking freak! And so are you. You're a fucking drag queen, for God's sake. No one normal respects that. Normal people think guys like you and me are perverts. Normal people think that the reason people like you have AIDS is because God wants it that way!"

Chloe let go of my hands and stood up slowly, saying nothing; he looked as if his mind had been transported to another place. But before I could even look at him or stop him from leaving the apartment, I was overcome by a violent coughing fit that made me feel like my lungs were being ripped to pieces. I don't know how long the fit lasted, because I passed out on the floor.

For the next couple of days, Chloe and I avoided each other. Whenever he was at home he came out of his bedroom only to eat, use the bathroom, or leave. I pretty much just stayed on the futon the entire time, watching TV and occasionally reading. Both of us were just too stubborn to give in. It wasn't like I didn't feel bad about what I had said. I did. But I wanted to prove Chloe wrong before I apologized. I was more determined than ever to quit. And so far, I was feeling good about it. Actually, I was feeling so sick from the hell I had put my body through that this alone seemed like enough to deter me from ever doing speed again. I kept telling myself, "If I can get through this now, I will never have to go through this sickness again."

"How are you feeling?" Chloe broke our silence for the first time in three days.

"Good," I said, even though my entire head felt plugged up with moldy sludge, my nose wouldn't stop running, and my tear ducts were leaking uncontrollably for no emotional reason.

"I'm glad," he said. "I rented a movie. Do you mind if I sit in here and watch it?"

"We don't have a VCR."

"I rented a VCR, too . . . So can I?"

"Of course. You live here, don't you?"

"I was just trying to be polite."

"I know." Suddenly I regretted the wall of attitude I was hiding behind. I looked at Chloe, holding his rented VCR in one hand and a plastic Silver Screen Video bag in the other, and I realized how silly we were for fighting. So I said pitifully, "Sorry I'm a bitch."

"Sorry I'm a bitch, too."

"What movie did you get?"

He walked over to the futon and sat down next to me, pulling a tape out of the bag. *"Desperately Seeking Susan.* It's my favorite."

"Oh my God! Mine, too!"

"Really? That's pretty wild that we both have the same favorite movie."

"I think we both just like Cinderella stories . . . and Madonna."

"I guess it seems pretty obvious when you put it that way."

"Hey, Chloe . . . Sorry I called you a freak and a bitch."

"You better tell me right now that it was just the drugs talking," Chloe said sternly.

"Yeah, probably."

"Probably? You mean you really think I'm a freak and a bitch?"

I started laughing. "No, of course not. I think I was just trying to hurt you because I felt so hurt and I was trying to drag you down with me."

"Did I hurt you?"

"Well, at one point I was in love with you and I thought we would spend the rest of our lives together. Then . . . well, you tell me you have AIDS, and suddenly it's as if that dream of mine was shattered."

"Yeah." He contemplated the gravity of my words. "It was quite a blow when the doctor told me, too . . . Look, sweetie, I'm flattered that you liked me, or whatever, but really, even if I wasn't sick, I still think we make better friends than lovers. If I dated you, I'd feel like I was dating myself."

"It's funny how you can turn rejection into some sort of abstract compliment . . . Of course, it could actually be insulting, considering you're such a big freak."

"Whatever, *bitch."* He grinned. "Let's watch the movie."

"You're on, girl."

And with that, we were friends again. Later we would talk about how silly we had been to ever fight, but that fighting was a turning point in my realization that I needed to quit glass. That fight had motivated me.

But fight or no fight, friendship resolved or not, it wasn't easy quitting. As soon as my body began to recover from its destruction, the cravings came back. And they were severe. I had a constant headache, and no matter how much food I ate or cigarettes I smoked, I had this empty feeling deep in my stomach that I knew only a line of glass would satisfy. Chloe was right about addictions; they are tricky. Mine was constantly trying to convince me that I was completely recuperated and healthy now and that it would be safe and fun to do glass. Sometimes I felt like I had to do at least one more line or I'd die of anxiety. At night I would dream that I was doing lines. Then I would wake up in a panic, as though it had been an intense nightmare, and I would be so relieved that it was only a dream and I hadn't actually done it. Of course, as soon as this feeling subsided, the cravings would hit me again, and they would seem ten times worse than they ever had before. My body would hurt, and I would crawl across the apartment on hands and knees, trying to make it stop.

Then, only one week into my recovery, I faced my biggest temptation. While Chloe was at work one afternoon, Jake showed up at my apartment, unannounced and alone. I reluctantly invited him in for lack of excuse, the inability to slam my door in a friend's face, and plain curiosity, too. As always, the sight of Jake's dark eyes and arresting grin turned me on.

"Do you want to rail?" he asked, dangling a small baggie of glass under my nose.

I hesitated, then turned away, letting the door close behind him. Suddenly I felt nauseous; I couldn't make eye contact. "I can't . . . I quit."

"Oh, you did?" he said. Then I was floored by the biggest

shock of my life. Jake came into the kitchen and wrapped his arms around me from behind. "C'mon, Erick. Don't you want to have fun with the Snake?"

I turned abruptly to face him. "What are you doing?"

His eyes twinkled with amusement at my confusion. He ran his hands firmly down my torso and hooked his fingers around my pant waist. "Don't you want to—."

"But Sam—"

"She doesn't have to know."

I was crushed. I freed myself from his grip and walked around him into the living room. "This isn't how things are supposed to happen."

"So what?"

For a moment, I felt myself fall into his abyss. It was exactly the way I had always fantasized Jake coming on to me. We could have railed on glass and fucked right there on the kitchen floor, and no one would ever have to know about it. But then—all at once—my sobriety overwhelmed me. "I think you should leave now."

"Huh?" He was genuinely perplexed.

"This isn't right. You have to leave . . . I'm sorry."

With a stunned, bewildered expression, he cocked his head to the side, perhaps seeing me differently than he had ever seen me before. I expected him to shout at me and beat me up or something. But surprisingly, without an argument, or apology, or explanation, he meekly walked out the door. Boys! I'll never figure them out.

For the next few days, I dwelled on my friendships with Jake, Zack, Jerome, and, of course, Sam. Even though I missed these guys terribly, I refused to contact them. That was the worst part about quitting speed: ending those friendships. I had to do it, though. It would have been too much of a temptation to be around them and remember all the fun we had had.

Two days after the incident with Jake, Sam called my house.

"You've got some fucking nerve, baby!" She hung up the phone before I could even speak. I spent the next couple days puzzling over what she had meant. Could Jake have told her he made sexual advances toward me? It seemed highly unlikely. Jake was not the kind of person who would willingly admit to anything. I figured Sam was probably just upset that I hadn't called her for so long and, ultimately, I had no choice but to blow the whole thing off.

On the days that my withdrawal wasn't too bad, I watched the movies Chloe brought home on our rented VCR and was reading a novel called *Lost Souls* by Poppy Z. Brite. It was the first novel I'd ever read that wasn't assigned at school. It was about bisexual vampires that road-trip around the country and do lots of acid and heroin. Probably not the best literature to be reading while I was detoxing myself, but it was the only book Chloe owned, and once I began reading it, I couldn't put it down. The story was very erotic.

By my third week of recovery, I was starting to feel pretty confident that I could withstand my cravings—at least enough that I could trust myself not to run out and try to buy crack off the street. I decided that I had kept myself under lockdown long enough. I was bored and Chloe and I were completely poor, so I decided to get a job. I wasn't really sure what kind of job I wanted, however, so I filled out applications everywhere: restaurants, clothing stores, more clothing stores. It took forever and a day. In the end, I was hired to host at Gambino's Italian Restaurant. The job paid about what I made at Silver Scream, which was nothing more than cheap attitude. However, I could be promoted to server eventually and make big bucks in tips.

In the meantime, the job so wasn't worth it. The waitstaff was really rude and impatient whenever I came across something I didn't understand—even on my very first day! As if I'm supposed to enter the position already knowing how to adjust in the tips on credit-card payments or how to seat people according to section so that each waiter had a proportionate number of tables. Also, the uniform they made the hosts wear was borderline obscene: black pants with an oversized maroon button-down shirt (which I was swimming in, of course) and a red tie that completely clashed. It was like putting a straight boy in a dress. I hadn't worn a medium-sized shirt that had to be tucked in since my days at St. John's. Meanwhile, the waiters wore whatever they wanted as long as they had their cute little black apron for notepads and pens and stuff. I so wanted to be a waiter. Some of the waitresses put stickers on their black books, and I was so jealous.

The food there was pretty good. Mostly pastas, but we had all these different homemade sauces to choose from and our self-proclaimed "best garlic bread in the city." All the cooks were Mexican, so Spanish was the dominant language in the kitchen. I never knew what anyone was talking about, so I worked silently. It didn't take long to figure out that the kitchen staff was constantly tormenting the overbearing waitstaff. I witnessed countless screaming fights that the Spanish-speaking and English-speaking managers would have to mediate.

Perhaps since I was the quiet one (although more likely because I was gay), the Mexicans took notice. When the managers weren't around, they'd catcall me whenever I went into the kitchen. They called me *"maricón,"* which Chloe told me meant "faggot." At first I was offended, but I kind of liked the attention, so I started saying things like, "Ooh, it must be hot behind that cramped stove, *amigos,"* in such a way that my meaning couldn't be mistaken. Whenever I passed them, I would wink, and when they were being slammed with orders, I would bring them glasses of water. Soon they were making me free meals, even though you were supposed to pay half price. Eventually all the white snobs realized I was friends with the Mexicans, and they, too, wanted to be friendly to me.

Suddenly I was the most popular guy at work, and it was the first time I'd ever been popular anywhere. I was quickly promoted to waiter, and whenever I walked through the front door at the beginning of my shift, someone would inevitably run up to me to tell me the latest gossip. It was so awesome! For the first time since working at Shades, I actually liked coming into work. Plus, I was now making three times as much money as I had made at Shades, which meant I was able to pay Chloe for all the back rent he had covered. I could also start buying my own groceries as well as some new clothes for my new "mature" phase, which included lots of skintight Banana Republic.

Along with the new mature phase came a new boyfriend. Jason Riggs was a fellow waiter who had shoulder-length dark-brown hair, puppy-dog eyes, and lips that always looked slightly puckered for a kiss. I figured he was eye candy, nothing more. He had a soft yet very masculine voice, and his body language suggested that he was definitely straight. So when he began smiling at me, I had no idea that he already had a crush on me.

One day while I was taking a cigarette break, paging through someone's copy of *Vogue*, he sat down next to me, then set a pack of cigarettes on the table. A pink-triangle gay-pride sticker was inserted in the cellophane. I was instantly nervous and embarrassed but tried to play cool. "Subtle hint," I said, my cigarette trembling between my fingers.

He smiled. "I had to do something. I was starting to think you'd never figure it out." He returned the evidence to his pocket.

"Does anyone else here know?"

"No ... I'm not really open about it at work ... I use my imaginary girlfriend, Sarah, as my alias so all the girls here won't come on to me."

"Does it work?"

"Not all the time," he laughed. "One night Nikki snuck up from behind and felt me up."

"That's major sexual harassment," I laughed.

"Well, when a girl does it to a guy, they usually don't see it like that, unless the guy is gay, I suppose."

"I suppose." I didn't know what to say next. This could turn into something great, I thought, but was scared to let myself be vulnerable again. At this point in my life, love was like falling into an ocean. Even if I waded only up to my knees, I'd probably still find a way to drown.

"I noticed that you take the bus home at night . . . Do you want a ride?" he asked.

"Um, I don't know . . . I wouldn't want to put you out."

"I think I'd really enjoy giving you a ride." He smiled.

"Well . . . I guess since we get off at the same time—"

"I hope that we'll *get off* at the same time."

I laughed self-consciously. "Yeah, that would be cool . . . I mean, the ride."

"Uh-huh." He extinguished his cigarette and swaggered back to the kitchen. I couldn't wipe the smile off my face for the rest of the night. It was embarrassing, actually, because everyone kept telling me I was glowing. I think more than anything I was just nervous. Jason was so cocky! Who says, "I hope we get off at the same time"? It was such a cheesy line. But of course it turned me on nonetheless. I definitely wanted to play it safe, though, so I resolved to do nothing further than share a ride home with him.

On the way home, Jason's advances were more reserved. I wondered if he had changed his mind about hitting on me, or maybe wanted to take things slow. All we talked about was work, how that place was so hetero a year ago but was now turning queer. Not only were we gay, he informed me, but Jen and Carol, both waitresses, were lesbian sisters. I thought he meant that they were dating, like maybe it was some knew gay terminology I wasn't yet familiar with, but he meant sisters genetically. "What?" I said, disbelieving him. He assured me, though, saying that they were each in relationships with different women, even lived in separate suburbs. Carol and her lover were even raising two adopted children. I never would have guessed that was possible. The first thing I thought for some reason was that maybe Tommy had been gay but had died before he even knew it.

When we got to my house, we sat parked, the engine idling. I was nervous—as nervous as I had been with Mike, but in a completely different way. With Mike I was scared to kiss him; with Jason I was scared of not kissing him. I knew he wasn't going to make the first move. He kept massaging his kneecaps, concentrating all the while on his dangling key chain as if it were a Rubik's Cube he was determined to solve.

"I've scared you already?"

"No," he said, still staring at the key chain. Then he looked at me boyishly with those puppy-dog eyes. "I think earlier I was just all talk."

I started laughing. "You mean when you said that thing about us getting *off* at the same time?"

His face turned magenta. "Ahhhh, so, what's your favorite movie?"

"Desperately Seeking Susan . . . What's yours?"

"Total Recall."

"What?"

"Total Recall . . . You know, Arnold Schwarz goes to Mars?"

"Oh my God! I saw that with my fuckin' dad in the theater." I had completely forgotten what it was even called. All I could remember was Arnold kicking ass. *"That's* your favorite movie?" I said accidentally in a superbitchy voice.

"Well, it was just the one I saw most recently. It was pretty good, though . . . I don't really have a favorite, I guess."

"Oh, sorry if I sounded bitchy."

"That's okay . . . I was just—"

Before he could finish, I leaned forward and kissed him on the lips. I pulled away quickly and leaned back against the door.

"—nervous." His lips formed a beautiful new shape.

"Thanks for the ride," I said blissfully.

"You're welcome."

"See ya tomorrow?" I was unable to speak beyond those words.

"Yeah."

"'Kay, 'bye," I stepped out of the car, radiant. I walked up to the front door, turned my key, and looked back. He waved from the driver's seat. I smiled and returned the wave, an entire symphony playing in my head.

I was so glad Chloe was home. Before I'd even crossed the threshold, I began telling him that the cute straight boy at my work was not straight after all. "He gave me a ride home, and I kissed him!" I gushed, adding that I hoped when he got to know me better, he wouldn't freak out. Chloe was happy about the kiss, but scolded me for even thinking that I might have a single personality flaw.

Right at that moment, Sam called. It was the first time she had phoned since that day she told me I had some nerve and hung up. I could tell right away that she was sketched out. Her conversation darted from one subject to the next with frantic urgency. She said that she and Jake and Zack and Jerome were all going to a rave and they wanted me to come; they would share their "go-fast" with me. I pictured the four of them, all dressed up, dancing around the apartment like children hopped up on sugar on Halloween night. I looked at Chloe, wondering if there was even a lie big enough to get me off the hook. But then I thought about everything I had gone through and would go through again if I did speed. I would lose my apartment, my job, and my best friend if I reentered that unpredictable hell. So I said, "Sorry, Sam. I haven't done speed in a month and a half, and I can't do it now."

There was pause on the other end. I could tell she was upset, maybe even trying to stop herself from crying. "So, what the fuck?" she finally retorted. "Are we just . . . not friends anymore?"

"No . . . we're still friends. But if I saw you now, I'd relapse, and I can't jeopardize my life like that anymore . . . I really wish that you wouldn't jeopardize your life, either."

"I'm *not* jeopardizing my life, okay? Maybe you just couldn't handle it . . . You always were a wimp! And, anyways, I think you're being selfish. You're ditching your friends for no good reason . . . Don't call me anymore!" And she hung up on me.

I wanted to remind her, first of all, that she was the one who called me! And secondly, I didn't care if I *was* being selfish. If trying to lead a sane life means you have to be selfish, then of course I was going to be selfish. It's not as though I were heartless. I still cared about my friends—especially Sam. I was so worried about her. She was on a fast downward spiral, and there was nothing I could really do to help if she wasn't prepared to meet me halfway. I began to fear that Sam might never quit. Maybe it was the life she would lead from now on—the life of a junkie. I watched Chloe sitting in his chair and painting his nails. Too bad Sam didn't have a hero like Chloe.

That night I had another nightmare. I was in Jake's car with my speed buddies and we were snorting rail after rail of glass. My entire face was on fire. I felt my brain fizzing like a foul chemistry concoction. It was burning away, fusing into a ball of mush, a plate of scrambled eggs. I wanted to stop, but I had no control. I was a marionette at the hands of a sinister puppeteer. I woke up covered in sweat, in a panic, and clutched my heart. It was thumping like a scared rabbit. For the rest of the night I couldn't sleep. I began to wonder if I could really do this. Maybe I would end up doing speed again anyway. Maybe people like Sam and me were fated to be junkies.

I was completely exhausted the next day at work, as though I had actually done drugs the night before and was now sketched out. I was completely paranoid that everyone at work could tell something was up. I couldn't stop sweating and I would forget the simplest things: soda refills, breadbaskets, dessert menus, even an occasional entree. I tried my best to make it up to the customers with lots of smiles and thank yous and free ice cream sundaes. But there are some people you just can't please.

The most awful customer I had ever served came in halfway through my shift. He accused Gambino's of not serving authentic Italian food because our marinara sauce didn't have grated Parmesan in it. Our customers had to add the Parmesan themselves. I proceeded to bring him linguine instead of penne, and I completely forgot his espresso shot, which he'd ordered to follow the meal. Just as I was taking an order for a party of six, he shouted across the restaurant: "Waiter! You forgot my espresso!" I excused myself from the party of six and ran to the kitchen in a panic. When I brought his espresso, he said that I was the worst waiter he'd ever had. He accused me of microwaving his food— which I hadn't—and said he wouldn't even drink the espresso. He warned me not to charge him full price because the meal and service, he said, were horrible. I was tempted to spill the espresso shot over his bald head, but instead I collected myself, apologized profusely, and asked Tracy to comp his meal.

Though it felt like the shift would never end, closing time finally came, and I was still a Gambino's employee. I was smoking in the break room when Jason joined me for the first time that evening.

"Rough night?" he asked, lighting his own cigarette.

"Yeah."

"I hear ya. Sometimes this job really gets to you. But try not to let it stress you out, you know? It's only money, nothing more than that."

"Alright," I said, even though it would take a lot more than that to cheer me up.

"So can I give you a ride home?"

"Sure."

This time, when he parked in front of my building, I kissed him right away. He pushed me off quickly and said, "Not here. Someone will see us." It was true. All sorts of weirdos could walk by and see us, not that I cared. I wanted too much to tear off his clothes to argue about it being a free country. I could tell he wanted me, too. I could practically see his hard cock pulsating beneath his tight waiter pants. For some reason, though, I couldn't bring myself to invite him up to the apartment because I was embarrassed to have him meet Chloe. First of all, Chloe was *so* queenie and such a bitch about boys I liked. Secondly, I wanted Jason to think I was more masculine and sexy than I really felt I was—not that my butch act could win me an Academy Award or anything.

"Can you have company?" he asked.

"No. My roommate's sick," I said. As soon as I said it I felt terrible, like I had betrayed Chloe for a stranger.

"Is something the matter?"

"No . . ." I trailed off.

"Do you want to come to my place?"

"Perfect!" I exclaimed, then slouched in my seat because I was such a nerd.

"I have to warn you, though, my roommate is kind of a jock . . . He's not homophobic or anything. I mean, he knows I'm gay—not that we sit around and talk about it. But he and his girlfriend, Heather, are as smart as a couple of tree stumps."

So we went over to Jason's place in South Minneapolis. It was an enormous, run-down, two-story house with junkyard-style clutter piled in every room, peeling paint on all the walls, and piles of dirty dishes in the kitchen. His roommate Keith and Heather the girlfriend were on the sofa watching this Zenith nineteen-inch-screen TV circa 1982. The reception was bad, and the actors all had green-colored flesh. After brief introductions, Jason grabbed a couple of bottles of Rolling Rock from the refrigerator and led me upstairs to his bedroom, which, in comparison to the rest of the house, was refreshingly clean. His walls were covered with framed botanical prints. "I'm an avid gardener," he explained, sitting at his desk chair.

"Cool," I said.

We both lit cigarettes, then sipped our beers quickly. He griped about how Keith was a slob and horribly inconsiderate about space and noise and food. Jason couldn't wait until he found a better apartment. I remained elusive about my own living situation. I told him my roommate's name was Chloe (without even specifying gender) and that Chloe worked at the Uptown Mall. We shared details about our picturesque lives as we proceeded to polish off a six-pack. Then he casually joined me on the bed and we began making out.

I loved his mouth. He was more aggressive than Mike (or Sam, for that matter) but didn't suffocate me with his tongue like Troy had. He was playful instead, and receptive to my playfulness as well. I grabbed a handful of hair, which was surprisingly long and thick, and lowered him onto his back, straddling him and kissing his mouth wildly. Something about the situation changed me; I felt manly and in control. I pinned his arms over his head and began kissing his round cheeks and thick, ropy neck. I pressed my hard cock against his stomach, and he began to moan in ecstasy. "Fuck me," he said.

"What?" I stopped and looked at him.

"You heard me," he said, his eyes demanding it.

"Okay . . . Um, roll over." He turned onto his stomach, elevating his ass and sort of rotating it seductively. I was so surprised that I lost my arousal momentarily. He was a bottom? But *I* was the more effeminate one. Not to mention I was a virgin as far as the realms of anal sex are concerned. His butt was starving for it, though. He moved it up and down, as though he was begging for my dick. I was rock hard again as I slid his shirt up over his head and ran my hands down his smooth back. I unbuttoned his pants and pulled them off along with his socks. His naked, round ass was still doing its dance. I put a hand on each cheek, massaging and squeezing them. Then I separated his cheeks and peered down at his puckered pink anus, which looked like the tiny knot in a pink balloon.

"Will you lick it first?"

Eccw, I thought. Lick it? Why would I want to lick someone's butthole? Suddenly it looked like a little baby monster, and I couldn't help but laugh.

He was embarrassed immediately and rolled over onto his back. "What is it?" he asked, a horrified expression on his face. "Is it messy?" He stuck his fingers down there to feel.

I was so mortified that I began to panic. It was the same thing with Troy all over again. I was going to get scared and freak out, and he would hate me and send me home in a cab. "I'm sorry," I said.

But his eyes were filled with compassion, not anger. "It's okay . . . Don't be sorry. You're too fine to be sorry . . . Erick Taylor."

I smiled bashfully when he said my name. "I've never really . . . fucked before. I mean, my ex-boyfriend and I used to sixty-nine and stuff, but that's really all."

"How many guys have you been with?"

"Two . . . but one of them doesn't really count."

"That's it?" He seemed surprised. "How old are you?"

Now I was in for it. "Seventeen," I said with repulsion.

"Really?" He seemed shocked. "You look twenty."

I was startled. The first thing I thought was that the speed had aged me, that not getting enough sleep, losing and gaining weight, had taken their toll. "I've had a rough life, and it shows."

He laughed sympathetically. "Oh, you poor thing," he said, wrapping his arms around my neck and pulling me down on top of his naked body, hugging me tightly. "So far I think you've turned out wonderfully."

"Really?"

"Really."

"And my age doesn't freak you out?"

"Well, sort of. You are a minor."

"Yeah, but I live in an apartment with a twenty-six-year-old man named Chloe . . . Trust me, my parents aren't going to find out about this."

"Chloe's a man?"

"You'd have to meet him to understand . . . How old are you?"

"I just turned twenty-one . . . God, I suddenly feel old."

"Fuck you . . . I'll be eighteen in November."

"So I'm three and a half years older than you."

"Is that a lot?"

"Did high school seem like a long time ago? Oh shit! Are you still in high school?"

"No . . . That's another long story," I said nervously. I felt like my life sounded retarded. "Do you still like me?"

"Of course."

"Do you like to cuddle?"

"I love cuddling . . . It's my favorite thing to do."

"How about I take off my clothes and we cuddle?"

"Sounds perfect," he said.

I undressed quickly and we crawled under the covers, soft flesh intertwined, hard-ons pressed together. Sometime in the middle of the night, I awoke to the amazing sensation of Jason giving me head. At first I didn't stir, but soon I couldn't help moaning, then came in his mouth. He swallowed my cum and slid in next to me, wrapping his arms around my body. It was so soothing. My whole body felt buzzed. Like I had taken a sleeping pill that went straight to my dick. Soon we were asleep again. And that night, for the first time in a while, I suffered no nightmares.

{ twenty-three }

S pending the night at Jason's house became my routine. By summertime I had fallen in love with him. For one, the sex was mind-bending. Since I'd been a virgin, Jason basically had to teach me everything. The first thing we discovered was that I was mainly a bottom—go figure! But I was also versatile, so we did it both ways. Usually we would come home from work and start making out in the shower, then we would get dried off and get into bed and go crazy on each other. Prior to these exploits, I knew that men had booty sex, but I had no idea how erotic the anus is— at least how erotic Jason's was. When we fucked, we took turns. And we always used condoms. At first being a bottom was the most painful experience ever, making me feel like I had to shit and piss and throw up simultaneously. After a while, though, I started to like it. Later I came to crave his dick all day long. Anal sex now made my butt feel warm and fuzzy.

Jason was more than just a fuck-buddy, however. He was my confidant. At night I would tell him everything about my life, including the truth about my family situation, my drug history, and all the gory details about my relationship with Chloe. He agreed that my life had been very tragic, but he assured me that the past didn't matter; if I wanted to be happy, I needed to live for the future. And his idea of my living for the future was me graduating high school. In fact, he even stood over my shoulder as I reluctantly called the Minneapolis Community Alternative Learning Center and enrolled for a one-year high-school diploma program. How it worked was that all my credits from St. John's would transfer over to their school, and I would earn my remaining credits by taking classes and completing packets that were supposedly equivalent to actual high school, only much broader and more generalized in their scope. Ultimately, I would receive a real diploma, not just my GED. Jason was so proud of me for signing up and "taking the first step" that I too began to feel excited about the prospect of going back to school. I would never have thought I could do it, but with my new boyfriend supporting me, everything seemed possible.

I *did* have one major problem, though: Chloe and Jason hated each other. Actually, Jason started it. He felt that Chloe had seduced me into the life of a drugged-out drag-queen wannabe. No matter how many times I tried to explain to him that Chloe was my savior—that if it weren't for him, I would be a junkie—Jason still said that Chloe had led me down the wrong path. Those accusations really upset me and led to a huge fight, which neither of us won because it didn't change anything, except my trust. That was the first time I realized that my new boyfriend was a control freak and that he was envious of my love for Chloe. Soon I told him that if he couldn't accept Chloe as my best friend, I couldn't continue our relationship. That scared him. For the next couple of days, Jason kept telling me that he loved me and he wanted only what was best for me. And then he agreed to meet Chloe.

The meeting took place at my apartment. All Chloe knew about Jason was that he was the one I wanted to spend the rest of my life with. That news made Chloe genuinely happy. He said that I deserved this more than anyone he knew, and we spent that night at our house eating and drinking and smoking bowls while I told him all about my new sex life and how Jason really cared about my future. When it came to meeting Jason, though, Chloe was reluctant and more nervous than I had ever before seen him. For the entire two hours between the time he got home from work and the time Jason was supposed to arrive, he agonized over his outfit and fidgeted in the mirror. Finally he chose fuchsia bell-bottoms and a blue butterfly-collar shirt. His hair was currently bleached, and lately he was using more makeup than ever because his face had become gaunt in spite of all the meds. He'd lost about nine pounds in the last month, which was considerable on his slim frame. He was becoming nearsighted, too, and had started wearing contact lenses. Every morning and night he struggled to get the wet plastic bubbles of vision into and out of his eyes. He refused to wear glasses because they would prohibit him from sporting his array of sunglasses. He was so stubborn about maintaining impeccable style.

I knew that Chloe's dramatic ensemble would freak Jason a little. Though I had told him about the way Chloe and I "sometimes" dressed, he usually only saw me wearing my Gambino's uniform or the sweats we wore when we lounged around his house. He preferred gay men to be discreet and thought that flamboyant attire was in poor taste. This should have been the red flag right there. On the few occasions that I had shown up somewhere dressed fabulous, Jason had been so embarrassed to be seen with me that we fought about it later. I got defensive and told him that this was how people dressed when they were out to the world. Being openly gay and publicly affectionate was another thing we squabbled about constantly.

Just to make Chloe feel more comfortable on the night of their meeting, I wore my maroon cords, Army Girl T-shirt, and spiked belt, even though I knew Jason would be upset. I had decided that throwing a dinner party might make the evening relaxed, so I prepared chicken teriyaki stir-fry, which I had marinated overnight, with onions, carrots, red peppers, green peppers, mushrooms, cashews, and sliced water chestnuts. The dish was garnished with pineapple and served over rice. We ate off of TV trays in the living room. Chloe sat on the green leather chair and Jason and I shared the futon. Everything went smoothly until Jason started in. "I don't mean to offend you," he began with a tactless comment, "but I've never met anyone with AIDS before."

Chloe rolled his zinfandel around in his glass in contemplation. "I'm sure you probably have, but you just don't know it."

"Why would anyone lie about it?"

"Some things are better left unsaid in certain situations."

"I don't know if I agree with that . . . It's sort of misleading." I knew Chloe wasn't going to let that pass.

"I wouldn't imagine it's quite as misleading as telling the people you work with that you have a girlfriend named Sarah," Chloe said nonchalantly.

Jason gave me a dirty look. I laughed of course. What did he expect? No one could mess with Chloe. "Now, now, you two," I said. "Let's play nicely."

"I'm sorry, Erick," Chloe said. "I've forgotten my manners . . . Jason, I'm sure your ambiguity is quite heroic, and I applaud you for your efforts."

"Huh?" Jason grunted.

"I think I need something stronger." Chloe extinguished his cigarette and pulled his pipe out of its hiding place in his new homemade fashion-model-cutout decoupage box. He lit the bowl with his mermaid lighter and offered it to Jason.

"No, thanks . . . I don't smoke pot."

Chloe shrugged and offered it to me. Now I was faced with a serious choice. Saying yes or no to pot would offend one of them. Because I was nervous and figured that getting high would help me cope, I chose to offend Jason. "Okay, but only one hit," I said, taking the bowl.

Jason scowled. "Erick, I thought you weren't doing drugs."

"I'm not doing drugs, this is pot."

"And pot's not a drug?" he asked skeptically.

"More of a therapy," Chloe jumped in.

"Exactly," I added.

Jason rolled his eyes. I could tell he wanted to say more about the subject, but kept his thoughts to himself. Surely his opinion of marijuana differed from ours dramatically. I already knew that he thought Chloe was a bad influence on my life. This was just another example. I passed the bowl back to Chloe, who took another long pull off it, then put it the bowl back in its place. "I'll just save it for later, then," he said.

"So are you guys all fucked up now?" Jason asked begrudgingly.

"Well, I don't reckon I'd say that," Chloe said in a cowgirl accent. "How are you feelin', girl?" he asked me.

"I reckon I'm mighty fine," I answered. And we both started laughing.

"Oh, God . . . Could you two be any queenier?" Jason asked, like he was gagging at the thought of it.

"I just feel comfortable with my sexuality, that's all," Chloe said.

"And I don't?"

"I didn't say that."

"Whatever."

"Don't get all uppity. We're all queer, right?"

Jason snorted derisively, "Well, I wouldn't say that."

"Oh?"

"Clearly you're leading a different lifestyle . . ."

"What do you mean by that?" Chloe wanted to know.

"Nothing."

"Come on, tell me."

"Well, for starters, you're a drag queen."

"And what's wrong with that?"

"Honestly . . . I think it's degrading to the rest of us."

"Oh, really?"

"Yeah. Plus you have AIDS and do drugs, which is irresponsible for someone in your condition, if you ask me—"

"I didn't," Chloe said.

"Look, I'm sorry," Jason said. "I guess drugs and drag queens are just a little extreme for my tastes."

Chloe was clearly flabbergasted by Jason's closely aimed insults. "Fuck you, you little shit . . . I have more class than a snot-nose like you could ever dream of!"

"Oh yeah, you're real sophisticated."

I couldn't believe this was happening. I wanted to slap both of them. Obviously, having my roommate and my best friend meet was the biggest mistake ever.

"I'd like you to leave my house, please," Chloe said.

"Alright." Jason stood up. He shot me a look that said, "Follow me." But I just sat there, stunned. I tried to think of something I could say that would take back everything that went wrong. But I knew that both of them were stubborn, and there was nothing I could do to fix it. Without saying a word, I followed Jason out the door. When we reached the bottom of the staircase, he turned to me and said, "I'm glad you're coming with me."

"I'm *not* coming with you."

"Oh." He was taken aback. "Does this mean . . ."

"It means I'll call you later."

"Look, if I offended him, I'm sorry, b—"

"No buts." I touched his puckered lips with my fingers. "If you and Chloe can't get along, that's fine. But I'm not giving one of you up for the other, okay? So unless you want to end this right now, I'll have to call you later. My place right now is here."

He eyed me skeptically. "Are you stoned?"

I rolled my eyes. "Okay, I'm just going to pretend that that wasn't completely offensive and off the subject."

"Well, what am I supposed to think? You're choosing to stay with that . . . *freak* over me."

"Obviously you're not listening at all to what I've said."

"Do you love me?"

"Yes . . . you know that. But I can't devote my whole life to you." Now he looked completely sad and rejected and I felt like the biggest bitch ever. "I'm sorry."

"Okay, call me later."

"Good-bye," I said, opening the door for him. Before he left, he grabbed me in his arms and laid an enormous kiss on me. I stood there dazed as he drove away. I wasn't sure if that was a see-you-later kiss or a good-bye–forever kiss. Although we'd been dating just two months, the thought of losing Jason was unbearable. Yet I had to make him understand that I was angry with him. He had no right to treat Chloe that way, and I thought hard about our relationship for a couple of minutes. Was it right to stay together when we fought at least once a day? Was real love enough to keep two people from hating each other? Did I even *know* what real love is?

When I came back inside, Chloe sat up in alarm, hastily wiping his eyes. "I . . . I thought you left with him."

"No, I said good-bye."

"Good-bye?"

"I told him I'd talk to him later."

"I see."

Chloe's remorseful expression overcame me with feelings of guilt and sorrow. "I'm so sorry, Chloe."

"For what?" He got up and went to Suz, tapping the bars of her cage to get her attention.

"For everything . . . For what he said. For bringing him over in the first place."

"But you love him?"

"I think so . . . I don't know."

"Does he let you be yourself?"

I pondered the question the deeply. No, I couldn't be Geneva Flowers when I was around Jason. Whoever *she* was. "Being with him . . . has made me discover a new side of myself. Just like being with you did."

Chloe laughed and cried all at once. "Oh Erick, I wish I could have been there for you . . . You know, romantically."

I blushed at his burst of honesty. It had been a long time since I got a sexual charge out of Chloe. Everything was different now, and though his presence never failed to turn me on in an "I have so much fun with you because you make me laugh" sense, physically, he did nothing for my libido anymore.

"Oh, Erick, you little darling, give me a hug." Chloe approached me with extended arms. We embraced tightly. "Sisters?" he whispered in my ear.

"Sisters," I agreed.

After our familial hug, we sat down and finished smoking the bowl we had started while Jason was over. Though I wouldn't have brought up AIDS right then because it seemed like *the* touchy subject, Chloe started talking about his health. He was preparing mentally for the "big phone call" to his mother. He had kept his sero-status a secret from her for six years, and it was time he told her before she got a phone call telling her that her only son was at the morgue. Plus, there was always a chance his health could deteriorate so badly that he'd have to stay with her. He had saved up money, but not nearly enough to pay for a long hospital stay. What I hadn't realized until that night was that each day was more and more of a struggle for Chloe, and his ailments were only partly caused by the ill-effects of his meds. In truth, for some reason the drugs weren't working as well as they'd hoped, and his immune system was weak. In fact, so weak that even a cold could send him to the hospital. He went on to say that I needed to start thinking about myself. I was going back to school? Good. He also said I should have another apartment to fall back on. Luckily, I hadn't signed a lease, so I had no legal obligations for our apartment.

Listening to all of this, I cried out, "Oh, Chloe!" about a dozen times. But in the back of my mind, I was thinking about my family. Suddenly I missed them. Not that I was dreaming of living with them again, but I wanted at least to see them, if only to escape from all the drama in my life: a best friend with AIDS, another best friend addicted to drugs, a controlling, insensitive boyfriend. I wanted to go to my old, messy bedroom, crawl into my twin bed, and take a nap. I wanted to play Monopoly with my parents and Tim and sit around the kitchen table eating dinner. I wondered what they were doing right now. Did they ever think of me? Maybe once they found out I was enrolled in high school again, they would forgive everything and take me back.

Jason followed me around the next day at work, pleading for my forgiveness. He was subtle around our coworkers, of course; lots of whispers, pouty faces, and (when he got frustrated by my callous attitude) harsh glares. I didn't know what to do. Part of me wanted to forgive Jason and take him back—after all, I needed someone by my side now more than ever—another part of me wanted to punish him by making him feel as victimized as he made Chloe feel. Then there was the part of me that longed for the strength to dump him and be single again.

That's when I got an idea. That night, when Jason promised me for the fifteenth time that he would do anything if only I would forgive him, I asked if he was sorry. He said he was. I told him I'd take him back if he wrote a letter of apology to Chloe. He somewhat stubbornly agreed, and I, somewhat stubbornly, took him back.

In his letter, Jason said he had been defensive that night because he felt threatened by the fact that we were doing drugs in front of him. He didn't mean what he said, he added, and was very sorry. Jason wrote that he hoped he and Chloe could be civil with each other because it was important to me and I was important to both of them.

Personally, I thought the letter sucked, but he gave it to Chloe before I could even read it. No matter, though. For whatever reason, Chloe forgave him, and we all moved on—sort of. Jason never came over to my apartment anymore, and whenever he called me, Chloe would say, "It's your *boyfriend*," in a super-bitchy voice. I tried to block it all out and juggled my schedule so I would have time for them both.

Besides all of our differences, there was yet another major problem between Jason and me. Sex. The one thing we had in common was both being bottoms. In the beginning, anal sex was completely new to me, and I was glad to be the top most of the time because it didn't hurt. After a while, though, I began to crave what I was giving him. But when I asked him to do me, he refused. He didn't like ass, he said, just cock. I realized I felt the same way. To help solve the problem, he went on the Internet and found a top to come over and do us both. To me, bringing in a third guy was both alluring and repulsive—I argued only briefly before giving in.

The top was named MPLSTOPP or, in person, Matt. He was Jason's height, which was shorter than mine by two inches, only much skinnier, and he had a shaved head and wore army fatigues. When he came into Jason's bedroom, he immediately tore off his shirt and kicked off his shoes, which revealed a foul odor. Then, in what was perhaps the greatest shock of my life, he spit right on Jason's floor! Seeing foamy saliva glistening on Jason's blue carpeting almost made me throw up. Jason told Matt what he liked, and Matt shoved him onto the bed, tore off all of Jason's clothes and began licking, biting, and pinching Jason's ass. Squealing in pain and trying to fight him off, Jason could not free himself. I left the room in disgust, listening to them for a while only to make sure Jason wasn't getting killed by the freak. I left once I heard Jason moaning with pleasure. He finally got what he really wanted.

"You're kidding!" Chloe exclaimed when I told him what Jason had done. "He spit on the floor? That's just . . . dirty!"

"You're not making me feel better," I groaned.

"Oh, sorry, babe. I just can't even believe it."

"Me either."

"You know something? It's good you got out of there when you did. If a man wants to get his ass bitten by some sleazebag with wretched-smelling feet who spits indoors, then you probably don't want nothing to do with him . . . I bet the crazy sonofabitch is being fisted right now."

"But you don't understand, I can't have 'nothing to do with him.' We work together."

"Just tell him that unless he wants everyone to know he's into getting his ass fucked, he better get lost. That will scare him."

"But do you really think it's ethical for me to use homophobia as a weapon against some closet case?"

"Wow! What a philosophical question for me to ponder," Chloe said with complete sincerity. "It's a good thing you're going back to school with that smart head of yours."

"Oh, for Pete's sake! . . . Hello, big picture?" I extended my arms to mime the hugeness of what we were discussing.

"Oh, yeah, sorry . . . Well, maybe you're right about that whole ethics thing. But I've always stuck to the old standby expression: 'All is fair in love and war.'" Chloe started coughing.

"Are you okay?"

"I'm fine . . . Come on, now. You don't have to go and jump every time I cough. I'm a smoker, for God's sakes. Of course I'm going to cough . . . Now be a dear and pack this bowl." He handed me his sack and pipe and went to the medicine cabinet. Clearly my worries had upset him. I could understand how frustrating it must be to see me always on the lookout for signs, but what was I supposed to think?

"I'm sorry if I offended you," I said.

"That's fine . . . Hey, let's just drop it, okay?" He sounded exasperated.

Now *I* was unhappy. I felt like I was being blamed, as usual, for everything. It wasn't my fault that Chloe was sick of me caring about him. As if he would rather spend the rest of his life alone. Now I was mad—mad at Chloe, mad at Jason, mad at every fucking thing in life. I wanted to escape. I wanted speed. I wanted to see Sam again, my only friend who understood me. It had already been two months since I last heard from her, three and a half months since I quit. I wondered if she was still getting spun. For the rest of the night I thought about calling her, but decided in the end not to. The thought of meeting her somewhere and being offered a line scared me. It was as if all my glass nightmares had at last made me afraid of the drug. I supposed those horrifying little dreams that woke me up in a cold sweat would have to be welcomed if they were what was going to keep me off speed.

I couldn't sleep that night, so I sneaked into Chloe's room and watched him sleep. I sort of wanted to crawl into his bed and hold him, but instead sat on his beanbag chair in the darkened corner. It felt like Chloe was going to die soon. He seemed to get sicker all the time, and lately he was getting even more defensive about his decline than usual. I wondered if he'd called his mom yet.

If Chloe died, I would be completely alone. I couldn't call Sam or my other friends because of drugs, and my family was so ridiculous that they'd only freak out. I couldn't imagine living with my parents and having to keep all the same old secrets plus all the new ones, too. Suddenly I wanted speed severely. Instead, I turned to God.

I prayed: God, please don't let me succumb to the temptation to do speed. I've been doing so good. I can't throw that all away. And don't let Chloe die. If for some reason Chloe dies, though, please help me to be strong. Guide me. Because I don't know if I can do this on my own. I don't think I can handle another death. And I'm scared to be alone. Please God, help my parents to understand me. And help Sam, too . . . She needs your help right now just as much as I do right now. Thank you, God. Sorry I'm so faithless sometimes. I believe in you . . . And be nice to Chloe if you see him up there. He's just angry at the world, not at you. He's the nicest person I've ever met in my life, and I really think he deserves to go to heaven, even though he says he doesn't believe in you. Thank you. I love you and believe in you. I really do. Good night.

Part Three

{ twenty-four }

 I didn't eat any breakfast the morning Chloe was hospitalized, yet I wanted to puke as I sat in the emergency-room waiting room. Meanwhile, every tick of the second hand on the clock that hung on the wall was tapped out in unison with my heartbeat. Together my heart and that clock seemed to be counting down to a future I dared not fathom.

Memories came flooding back. I saw the pen Chloe had given me the first day we met. I saw us in hot-pink spandex pants, platforms, and gay-pride streamers in our hair and around our wrists, dancing to Donna Summer. How I longed for another fashion tip, or drag lesson, or to get back from my mother the pipe he had given me for summer solstice. In fact, I wanted my old life back— the life that ended last night.

The whole thing started with an evening at the movies. It was the only movie Chloe and I had ever gone to together: *Breakfast at Tiffany's*. I had never seen it, much to Chloe's dismay, so when he heard it was playing at the Uptown Theater, he decided to treat me. Although I never go to the movies, I couldn't possibly say no. He was so excited that he had to stop himself about a hundred times from telling me the whole story. I was pretty sure by the time we got to the theater that *Breakfast at Tiffany's* must be the greatest movie ever made. Plus, Chloe caved in finally and did drag with me. We wore black cocktail dresses with black chokers and carried long cigarette holders that we filled with weed. Chloe didn't feel the least bit obligated to stay quiet during the movie; he talked the entire time. Luckily there were only three other people in the entire theater. I'm sure *Breakfast at Tiffany's* was hysterical only because I saw it with Chloe. We did our best impressions of Holly Golightly all the way home.

When we entered our apartment, something wasn't right. Like the feeling that the room had somehow changed while we were out. Then we saw it at the exact same moment: Suz wasn't perched on her swing. We rushed to her cage, to find her laying stiffly on her side. Neither of us knew what to do. We wanted to bury her and have a memorial, but there were no gardens in the ghetto. So, with incredible guilt, we put her in a shoebox and placed her in the Dumpster. We went back up to our apartment and cried. Chloe cried so hard that it scared me—wailing like a child lost in a department store. My tears were more for his loss than my own.

I had been asleep for at least two hours when his big decline began later that night. From the futon, I heard Chloe crying. Not teary crying, though. More like a severe moaning. Getting sick in the middle of the night had been routine for him, so naturally I thought it was his throat again, that the infection was too much to bear and the painkillers simply hadn't kicked in yet. But the moaning turned into sentences of incoherent gibberish. I knocked on the French doors: "Chloe? Are you okay?" But he didn't respond. The noises grew louder and I flung open the doors. It was like turning up the volume on a stereo full-blast until you only hear static from the stressed speakers. There was Chloe, crawling along the floor, feeling the wall with his hands, digging his nails into the plaster. I rushed over to pull him away. He was wearing only boxers; his skin was hot, and drops of sweat hung from his eyelashes, the tip of his nose, and chin.

"Mama," he whispered to me in an almost inaudible rumbling voice. "It hurts so bad."

"Chloe! It's me, Erick. What's happening?!"

"They're everywhere! I can't get rid of them!" he screamed, reaching for the wall.

"What? What's everywhere?"

"The spiders! They're driving me crazy. Please, Mama, call an exterminator."

He was hallucinating, obviously. Perhaps it was his fever. I started to leave to run a cold bath for him, but he pulled me to him, buried his face in my chest, sobbing. "Don't leave me, Mama, please!"

I pulled his face up to my eye level so he could see who I was, but when I looked into his eyes, I saw only panic. He started shivering; then, almost instantly, his sweat became cold and clammy. It was all happening so fast!

"I c-can't stop sh-shaking," he stuttered. I reached onto his bed for the damp, twisted blanket, which I draped around him. Then his hacking came. He sprayed my face with phlegm. I closed my mouth and eyes tightly, scared to leave, yet even more scared to stay. In between the coughing came the most tortured breathing I'd ever heard. It was even louder than the coughing. I realized the snot and saliva I had been showered with was mixed with dark purple blood. It was all over both of us. I threw him off me and ran into the bathroom, rinsing my mouth and splashing water onto my face, trembling so much that I was flooding the bathroom. That's when I called 911.

"911. What's your emergency?" came the rehearsed voice.

"My friend, he needs an ambulance. He's coughing up blood! He has AIDS."

"Did you say blood, ma'am? What color?"

"I don't know. Dark purple."

"How long has this been going on?"

"I don't know! Hurry! He's hallucinating! He called me his mama!"

"Help is already on the way . . . Tell me, ma'am, what's your name?"

"Erick Taylor. I'm a boy. I mean, a guy."

"Sorry, Erick . . . Is your friend with you now? Is he still coughing up blood?"

"Yes! Can't you hear him?" It was all I could hear, and I winced every time he choked out a cough.

"Does he have a fever?"

"Yes! Yes! Hurry, goddamn it! I can't deal with this! I think he's dying!"

"Just stay with him then, and keep me on the line until the ambulance arrives."

I returned to the bedroom, the phone attached to my ear. Meanwhile, Chloe struggled to kill his imaginary spiders. I tried to think of what they looked like. I figured they were his demons. Someone once told me that when you're dying, you face all your demons. Would that be true, though, for an atheist? I wondered if God would be with Chloe when he died. Chloe said "Mama" one last time, then fell to the floor in a snap of the fingers, unconscious.

"Oh my God! He's dead!"

"What?! What do you mean?"

"He just looked at me and dropped dead!"

"Check his pulse!" Now the 911 operator was almost as panicked as I was. I checked for a pulse. I couldn't find it. I put my ear up to his heart. Slight murmur. I put my ear to his mouth and nose. Nothing. "I can't find a pulse and he's not breathing!"

"Erick, stay calm. The ambulance is down the street." I could hear the siren. "Can you go let them in?"

"Yes," I said, running from the apartment. The phone connection turned to static and disconnected by the time I reached the front door. Without thinking, I ran out onto the sidewalk, wearing only boxer shorts, the phone still attached to my ear. I heard the door slam shut behind me. I screamed when I realized what I had just done.

"Where is he?" the paramedic in the front of the stretcher was asking.

"He's in there! And I just locked myself out!" I cried helplessly, my whole world exploding like a car bomb. "We have to hurry! He's not breathing!"

The paramedic rolled his eyes at me. "AIDS patient, right?"

I was sort of stunned by the condescending tone in his voice. "Yeah, that's right. So?"

The paramedic then looked at me: Calvin Klein boxers, hair dyed, nails painted. Suddenly I felt self-conscious. The paramedic smirked disgustedly. For a second it seemed like he wasn't even going to help.

"What the fuck?!" I screamed. "Help him!" I couldn't believe it! I wanted to bash his ugly face in. Finally, he strode up the front steps and began ringing buzzers, trying to get let in. I felt stupid and helpless, thinking I had just sealed Chloe's fate and that he would die alone up there. The other paramedic rushed to the door with an axe, smashing the lock until it broke into pieces and he could open the door. Lights began to flick on in windows all over the building. Curious tenants peered at me from every direction. I wondered if I should go in and get dressed. Before I could act, the two paramedics wheeled Chloe out on a stretcher.

"You coming?" the paramedic with the axe asked.

"Yeah." I jumped into the back of the ambulance, and they wheeled Chloe in after me. "It'll be okay, Chloe," I said to his deaf ears, holding his hand, pretending no one else was around.

"Please don't die, Chloe. I love you so much it scares me. I just don't know what I'd do without you, girl. Please don't die, okay, hon? Just hang on. We're almost to the hospital." I squeezed his hand harder, counting the blessings we'd had and praying for us both. I realized I was still in my boxers with the phone in my hand. It choked me up because I knew that it was something Chloe would have made fun of me about, if he could. Poor Chloe. I couldn't believe it had come to this.

When we got to the hospital, doctors and nurses spoke their foreign language, discussing Chloe's status, pushing him quickly down the hall. I ran behind them, but just as we entered a room, a nurse left the parade, turned around, and stopped me dead in my tracks. "Sorry," she said. "You'll have to wait out here." I must have looked pathetic at that moment because she had a sudden change of heart. "Why don't you come with me and we'll get you something to put on?"

I blushed, futilely trying to hide the fact that I was in my underwear. The nurse swung her arm around me, and led me down the hall to find some scrubs.

Dressed like an expectant father, I was taken to the waiting area and told that as soon as there was any word of Chloe's condition, I would be notified. I waited next to a woman with a nervous-looking face and two towheaded children pulling at her limbs, whining, "Mommy, I'm bored." All she would say to them was, "Just wait, sweeties, Daddy will be back soon." I wondered why "Daddy" was there and so gave the woman an empathetic smile which she returned.

Over an hour later, a doctor came into the waiting room and asked who was there for David Brown. It took a moment for that name to register. I had never before heard anyone call Chloe by his birth name.

"That's me . . . How is he?" I asked.

"Mr. Brown is sleeping right now. His vitals are back up, but he's still in serious condition. He has a severe case of pneumonia. We're doing everything we can to save him."

"Is he going to die?"

"He might pull through."

I squeezed my eyes shut. Weren't doctors supposed to lie better about that stuff to loved ones? I took a slow, deep breath, trying not to fall apart. "Can I see him?"

"Are you a relative?"

"I'm his brother." I had seen enough movies to know that in desperate times they admit only immediate family outside of visiting hours.

The doctor eyed me skeptically, but admitted me anyway, saying that because his condition was fragile, I could stay only five minutes.

I entered Chloe's room cautiously, not wanting to disturb him. The room was dimly lit, and a nurse was monitoring him. He was breathing into a face mask and was hooked up to bunches of tubes. I wondered if he was dreaming. If so, I hoped that he was imagining himself in the mall, or up onstage. Those were definitely his two favorite places. I sat down in the chair next to his bed and started to pray.

I wished Chloe would wake up. I remembered that our apartment was unlocked and the building's front security door had been practically chopped down with an axe. What if we were burglarized? That wasn't out of the question, the way this night was going. "Chloe, why is it that everything in life happens all at once?" I asked out loud. I don't know what I was thinking, but I just kept talking: "Can't you just see me someday dying of a migraine headache while trapped in a burning building during a tornado? . . . I guess you really never know what to expect, huh? . . . Fuck, Chloe. This can't happen. You're supposed to have your own sitcom. You were supposed to become famous." I stared into Chloe's expressionless face. I made sure the nurse wasn't listening in and whispered, "If you die, I'm seriously going to kill myself." As soon as I said that, I regretted it. If I killed myself, Chloe would just feel that his last year had been lived in vain. After all, he was leaving his mark on the world through me. I sank into my chair. "Sorry, I'm such a flop, Chloe. I just wish you'd wake up. I love you. But don't worry, I won't kill myself over you or anything else."

The nurse came back in and told me it was time to leave. I kissed Chloe on the cheek and on his hand. Leaving the room, I hooked my fingers around his toes, daring him to pull me back over to him. But he laid there motionless, so I let go.

Even if I had clothes or money to get home, I wouldn't have left Chloe alone in the hospital that night for anything. I wondered if there was anyone he'd want me to call, now that he was in critical condition. I didn't even know how to contact his mom, or anyone else in his life for that matter. I wanted to call Sam, but I wanted to call Jason even more. I asked a guy sitting nearby if I could borrow a quarter for the pay phone. By the time I finished dialing I was already sobbing. "Jason," I said through tears when he picked up the phone, "it's me, Erick."

"Erick? What's the matter?"

"I'm at the emergency room. Chloe's sick."

For a moment, there was silence on Jason's end. Then he said sweetly, "I'm so sorry, Erick. Really I am. I know how much you care about him."

"I love you," I said before I could stop myself.

"I love you, too . . . My biggest regret right now is that I ever let you go, that I screwed things up. I don't know what my problem is."

"You're just too kinky . . . But that's okay. I'll try to be more kinky."

He laughed. "Oh, Erick. I love you just the way you are . . . Where are you?"

"HCMC."

"Do you want me to come down?"

"But you and Chloe hate each other."

"I'll be good."

"Oh, okay," I said, even though I didn't know why I was agreeing to this. I felt like I was being a traitor to Chloe, that I was being weak by letting myself love Jason after he had hurt me. Now I was ready to take him back like it had been nothing. And though part of me already regretted calling, I felt I needed him badly at that moment. Maybe this time things would work, I told myself hopefully.

Back in the waiting room, a doctor approached me. "Are you with David Brown?"

I nodded. He gestured for me to follow him. Standing in a secluded portion of the hallway, he said, "I'm sorry to have to tell you this, but David has died."

I gasped.

"I'm sorry—we did everything we could to save him."

"Are—you—sure?" I stammered.

The doctor nodded solemnly.

Suddenly my heart started pounding, twisting inside my chest. I gasped for air, but felt I couldn't breathe. I was certain I was dying. My heart was about to pop. *I can't believe we're dying together,* I thought.

I tried to stay on my feet, but it was too difficult. The doctor tried to brace me with his arm. I saw a white light, and then it was over.

{ twenty-five }

When I woke up I was in a hospital bed with a needle in my arm and wires stuck to my chest. The sun was coming up. I looked over my shoulder and saw my mom sitting beside me. Before I could think to ask her where she'd come from, I remembered the pain in my heart—it was gone now, but I clutched my chest nonetheless. "Is he dead?"

Mom seemed momentarily taken aback, as if she had just woken up, too. "The man you came here with? Yes, he died."

My eyes swelled with tears. It couldn't be! God, how could you do this to Chloe?

"I'm sorry, Erick," Mom said.

I eyed her suspiciously. "You don't understand."

She peered at her own clasped hands. "I understand."

I didn't say anything. I just laid back in anguish, listening to my heart monitor beeping. After a moment, I asked, "How did I end up here?"

"You had a panic attack and collapsed. Don't worry, the doctor said it's nothing serious. You can leave as soon as you're dressed."

"Did they call you and Dad?" I wondered how they knew who I was or where to find my parents.

"Yes."

I sucked in my breath.

"I can't tell you what a scare it was to get a call like that."

"Sorry."

"It's not your fault . . . I want you to know, Erick, that you're in my prayers every minute of the day."

"I am?"

Suddenly my mom's composure began to falter. "I can't stand the thought of losing you again . . . I want you to come home. We want you back in the family."

I closed my eyes. Maybe I could move home. Maybe I just didn't care what happened anymore. I stared at the door, imagining Chloe walking through it and embarrassing my mom with a flashy outfit. Please, God, let this all be a dream.

A nurse came in. "Oh, you're awake. Are you feeling better?"

I didn't respond but tried to hold back tears.

"I'm sorry about your friend," she said.

I sniffled wordlessly.

The nurse checked my stats. "I just have to get an okay from the doctor, and you can go," she said, bumping into my dad on her way out. Tim was there, too. Then Jason filled the passage next to them. I figured he'd shown up last night and identified me. For that instant, he was my only hope. I wanted to reach out and embrace him and disappear together to someplace better.

When I realized that no one else would be the first to speak, I found my voice. "Mom, can you and Dad come back in a few minutes? I need to speak to my friend Jason."

She stared at me as if I wasn't in my right mind, then finally rose with a sigh, ushering my dad and Tim out of the room.

Once we were alone, Jason grabbed my hand. "Erick, I'm so sorry—I never would have thought this could happen. I know I was awful to Chloe, even though he was your best friend, and I promise I won't ever judge your friends anymore. I love you and I just want to be there for you if you need me."

I didn't know what I needed. Maybe I needed Jason. He was the only thing I had left. "I love you," I said.

"I love you, too."

We kissed and hugged some more, and I felt briefly that things really would be okay between us. But how could anything ever be the same again? Now that Chloe was gone, I felt like a part of me had died with him.

"I told your parents that I was a friend from work and that you had called me for a ride before . . . well, you passed out. They've been looking at me funny, though."

I moaned.

The nurse returned. "Alright, you're free to leave." She quickly unhooked me from everything.

Dressed in only a hospital gown, I met my family in the waiting room. Talk about an awkward reunion. Tim broke the silence. "Hi, Erick."

"Hey, kid," I said.

"Are you coming home?"

"Um . . . I don't think so."

"We'd love to have you come back home," Dad said.

Although the offering was the first sign of peace between my parents and me in a long time, I felt that if I hopped in their car and went home now, I'd be giving up on my dream of having a fabulous life, as if my friendship with Chloe had never happened. "Jason has invited me to stay with him."

"Erick, it will be different this time. We promise," Mom said.

"Let's wait and see what happens first. Okay?"

"Is this really what you want?" Dad asked, treating me like an adult for the first time ever.

"Yes."

I expected Mom to argue. Instead, she seemed genuinely

concerned. "Are you going to be okay?" I could tell she was talking about my grief.

"He was my best friend," I said.

No one knew what more to say. Finally my mom said, "Just give us a call. We're here for you anytime."

Tim and Dad hugged me good-bye, and with that, they left.

When Jason and I sat in his car, I said, "Can you take me home?"

"What? Why?" he asked.

"Because I want to be alone . . . in my apartment."

Jason petted my thigh. "Baby, I know you miss Chloe, but going back there now will only make things worse."

"Please, Jason. For once, just listen. I want to be alone. I want to get through this my own way. And you just have to respect that. Please."

Jason walked me to the front door. Seeing that splintered wood littered the floor where the paramedics had axed their way in, I wondered who would have to pay for the repairs. Then I wondered for the first time how I would pay rent in two weeks. Maybe I could pick up extra shifts. Once we got to the apartment door, we kissed good-bye. Again I reassured Jason that I'd be better off alone for now, and he left reluctantly.

As I entered the apartment, I braced myself to encounter a bloody scene, but was startled to hear clanging in the kitchen. I poked my chin around the door, and who should I see standing there but Babs Arlington. She was out of drag, but wearing tons of makeup.

"Hello there," Babs said in a sleek voice.

"Babs?"

"In the flesh! And who might you be?"

"I'm Erick. I'm—I mean, I was—I mean, I live here. I'm Chloe's roommate . . . We met at Screwdriver once, remember?"

Babs smiled brilliantly with recognition. "Of course, darling, now I remember you. The cute one that Miss Chloe brought into the dressing room . . . You know, that girl never brought any boy into that room before you."

"Really?"

"Really . . . Say, has anyone ever told you that you would make a *fierce* drag queen?"

"Maybe." I blushed.

"Mmm-hmm . . . I can always spot them." She waved a finger.

I was so entranced by Babs that I almost forgot to ask, "What are you doing here?"

"Well, Chloe was supposed to meet me today, and when he never showed, I just came by to see what was up and found everything unlocked. The place looked like it had been burgled—don't worry, I don't think anything's missing—but I called the police right away and they told me that an ambulance had been sent here. What the hell happened?"

Suddenly the memory of last night threw me into despair again. "Babs, Chloe died this morning," I said.

Babs took a slow moment to respond. "How?"

"AIDS."

"What?"

"I don't know if you even knew he had it, but he did. He didn't think he was dying, though. It just happened suddenly." Now I was seriously in tears.

"Such a terrible thing," Babs said. Now we were both choked up and hastily wiping away tears.

"Oh, I knew it was something terrible when I saw that bathroom," Babs said with a tone of guilt, as if she'd been the one to jinx us with her suspicions. "I hope you don't mind—I was straightening up a little."

I shrugged and went into the living room, falling back on the futon. Babs came in and sat down next to me. "I know how you feel, honey. I've been here before. It's just so fucked up when they're that young. Why, Lord, does a wonderful person get taken so young? I can't hardly stand it sometimes."

"What do you do?" I whispered.

"I just try to be there for people. Just try to do my part, even when I'm up onstage being raunchy, you know. Jesus said, treat people the way you'd expect to be treated. I say, make sure you show a lot of love to those close to you. You know, during the eighties, back when we thought it was the end, when we used to wonder if everyone would be wiped out. I prayed to learn why it is that gay people have always had so much reason to fear love. I still haven't gotten the answer. Why do *you* think it is?"

"I don't know."

"I hate feeling despair . . ."

"Tell me about it," I said.

Babs surprised me with a hug. I returned the gesture, and it felt good. After a while, she said she had to get back home if she wanted to make it to the club on time. Tonight's performance would be in memory of Chloe.

She asked if I'd be okay alone, and I said that I'd be fine, that I was just going to go to sleep soon anyway. Babs wrote down her phone number and handed it to me. "Call me if you ever want to talk," she said.

I promised her I would, and let her out the door.

Chloe didn't have a funeral. Babs had heard that Chloe's mom had been tracked down and had had him cremated. She took his ashes home with her. Our landlady knocked one day and asked me what I wanted to do about the apartment. I told her I wanted to keep it, and she had me sign a six-month lease. Fortunately, I didn't have to cough up a new deposit, and with all my tips, I scraped by.

When I wasn't at Gambino's, I usually sat in my apartment. Most of the time I was depressed, but sometimes, for a moment,

I'd forget Chloe was gone, only to snap out of it and find myself even more depressed.

I thought about Sam often. It was weird to think that she had no idea Chloe had died. I felt I had to call her, but I was afraid. It had been months since I last talked to her. Finally, I picked up the phone, but she wasn't home. I tried Jake's house and, to my surprise, Sam answered. "Hello?"

Suddenly I choked. I didn't even know how to begin.

"Hello?" Sam said again, a little more irritably.

"Hi, Sam. It's Erick." I waited, but she didn't say anything. "You still there?"

"Yeah."

"How's it going?"

"Fine . . . I'm surprised to hear from you . . . I thought you had gotten too good to talk to me."

"C'mon, Sam, don't give me that crap. I wasn't trying to get away from you . . . It was the drugs."

Again she didn't respond.

I took her silence to mean she was still doing glass. "How's Jake?" I asked.

"Same as ever."

"Good. Tell him I said hi . . . Anyways, I was calling because I have bad news . . ." I stopped, unsure if I could go on. Finally I said, "Chloe died."

"What?" Sam gasped.

"He died last week."

"Oh my God, Erick. Are you okay?"

"I'm hanging in there."

"I can't believe it."

"I know . . . I just thought you should know about it. I can let you go if you're busy."

"Well, do you want to hang out sometime?"

"Sure. But I don't do glass."

"I know." She added, "I thought you hated me."

"I could never hate you, I'm just worried about you."

"Why? I mean—you know my life."

"Exactly . . . That's why I'm worried about you."

"It's not like I've completely changed."

"Do you still think about quitting speed?"

"Yeah, I do . . . Sometimes, though, I think that if I do a line and it makes me happy, it's okay. And if I do a line and it kills me, that's okay, too. I guess I'm afraid to quit because, in that case, I don't know if it will be okay. I was thinking that I'm clinically depressed, that speed is my antidepressant, and that I sort of need it to feel okay."

"That sounds like an addiction."

"Did you get depressed when you quit?"

"I think I've been depressed all my life, sweetie," I said.

"Yeah . . ."

"Well . . . call me, I guess."

"Okay," she said in such a way that I wondered if she meant it. "Take care. Sorry again about Chloe."

I hung up the phone with half a mind to call back and say I wanted to get spun. Also, part of me wanted to cry out to Sam things like, "Quit drugs, They're not worth it," and "If I can change my life, so can you." But I could tell that Sam didn't want to hear any of that. Chloe had been so much better at tough love than me. I wished I could save Sam from herself. Hell, I could barely save *me* from myself.

Over the next couple of months, I quit Gambino's and found another job waiting tables. After that I broke my lease for emotional reasons and moved into a new studio apartment in the ghetto, for which my parents cosigned. I kept all of Chloe's furniture and clothes and made them my own. At first I was reluctant to wear any of them because I wanted everything to last forever, but I finally convinced myself that Chloe would have wanted me to work those outfits till they were threadbare—and snap my fingers while doin' it. So every day, just to keep the memories alive, I dressed fierce.

With Babs's help, I was allowed back inside Screwdriver. And this time I was on the bill. My performances in the beginning were only on special occasions, but Babs said I had enough promise to become a featured act in no time. Who knows, maybe someday I really will be a star.

As for my parents, I slowly allowed them back into my life, starting off with phone calls. Babs took everything I told her about them into consideration and finally suggested that it was time I came out to them. She said that with all the lies and secrets floating around in my family, there was no way things would ever mend unless we learned to open up to each other. Finally I gathered up the nerve to call my parents and invite them to my apartment, which they still hadn't seen.

My parents and Tim came over with plans to take me to a restaurant—in other words, neutral ground. Having my entire family standing around in my tiny apartment was very claustrophobic and made my head spin. Even though I had cleaned the place from top to bottom, I was self-conscious of every flaw.

At the dimly lit restaurant, we sat in a booth where I tried to find the right moment to tell them I'm gay. Mom asked how I was coping these days. Tim asked if I liked Batman. Finally, I told them that I had something important to say that had been weighing on my mind for years. They eyed me nervously, probably not ready to hear it but having nowhere to flee. In a single breath I told them that I was gay. For about a thousand years, no one said anything. Then my dad spoke up: "Your mom and I had suspected this for a long time."

"I've been this way all my life."

Mom seemed to be fading. "Please love me," I said, shocking even myself.

No one said a word.

Finally, Mom said, "Are you sure about this? Do you think a talk with Father Tom might—"

"No," I insisted adamantly.

Then Dad jumped in. "No, the time for Father Tom has passed. He's not a child anymore. Erick," he said, "I understand what you're going through. Your mother and I love you no matter who you are."

I believed he loved me, but looked to Mom for confirmation.

She sighed and said, "I know I can't change you—not really. I've always just wanted to do what's right for my son."

"Then love me, and I'll love you, and everything will be all right."

Mom smiled—the first real smile I'd seen from her in years. "Oh, Erick, I *do* love you. I just want you to be happy."

For some reason when she said that, I pictured Chloe. I felt like he was smiling down on me right then. I thought about all the times we'd been happy together and how Babs made me happy now. I felt that somehow, with his magic wand, Chloe had been my fairy godmother, as always, and hadn't really left me alone.

I laughed at the irony of my life. After all these years, all my family cared about was my happiness. And for the first time in my life, I felt that maybe I truly was happy. Maybe from now on, I wouldn't let anything get me down. I would see the future being full of beauty and hope. At last, I was growing up. And my name was Miss Geneva Flowers, diva extraordinare.